G. Richmond del. Engraved by H. W. Smith

Truly Yours
H B Stowe

The
May Flower
and
Miscellaneous Writings
by
Harriet Beecher Stowe.
BOSTON:
Phillips Sampson and Company
1855

THE

MAY FLOWER,

AND

MISCELLANEOUS WRITINGS.

BY

HARRIET BEECHER STOWE,

AUTHOR OF "UNCLE TOM'S CABIN," "SUNNY MEMORIES OF FOREIGN LANDS," ETC.

BOSTON:

PHILLIPS, SAMPSON, AND COMPANY,

13 WINTER STREET

1855.

STEREOTYPED AT THE
BOSTON STEREOTYPE FOUNDRY.

INTRODUCTION.

Mr. G. B. Emerson, in his late report to the legislature of Massachusetts on the trees and shrubs of that state, thus describes

The May Flower.

" Often from beneath the edge of a snow bank are seen rising the fragrant, pearly-white or rose-colored flowers of this earliest harbinger of spring.

" It abounds in the edges of the woods about Plymouth, as elsewhere, and must have been the first flower to salute the storm-beaten crew of the Mayflower on the conclusion of their first terrible winter. Their descendants have thence piously derived the name, although its bloom is often passed before the coming in of May."

No flower could be more appropriately selected as an emblem token by the descendants of the Puritans. Though so fragrant and graceful, it is invariably the product of the hardest and most rocky soils, and seems to draw its ethereal beauty of color and wealth of perfume rather from the air than from the slight hold which its rootlets take of the earth. It may often be found in fullest beauty matting a granite ledge, with scarcely any perceptible soil for its support.

What better emblem of that faith, and hope, and piety, by which our fathers were supported in dreary and barren enterprises, and which drew their life and fragrance from heaven more than earth?

The May Flower was, therefore, many years since selected by the author as the title of a series of New England sketches. That work had comparatively a limited circulation, and is now entirely out of print. Its articles are republished in the present volume, with other miscellaneous writings, which have from time to time appeared in different periodicals. They have been written in all moods, from the gayest to the gravest — they are connected, in many cases, with the memory of friends and scenes most dear.

There are those now scattered through the world who will remember the social literary parties of Cincinnati, for whose genial meetings many of these articles were prepared. With most affectionate remembrances, the author dedicates the book to the yet surviving members of

The Semicolon.

ANDOVER, *April*, 1855.

CONTENTS.

THE MAY FLOWER.

UNCLE LOT.

AND so I am to write a story — but of what, and where? Shall it be radiant with the sky of Italy? or eloquent with the beau ideal of Greece? Shall it breathe odor and languor from the orient, or chivalry from the occident? or gayety from France? or vigor from England? No, no; these are all too old — too romance-like — too obviously picturesque for me. No; let me turn to my own land — my own New England; the land of bright fires and strong hearts; the land of *deeds*, and not of words; the land of fruits, and not of flowers; the land often spoken against, yet always respected; "the latchet of whose shoes the nations of the earth are not worthy to unloose."

Now, from this very heroic apostrophe, you may suppose that I have something very heroic to tell. By no means. It is merely a little introductory breeze of patriotism, such as occasionally brushes over every mind, bearing on its wings the remembrance of all we ever loved or cherished in the land of our early years; and if it should seem to be rodomontade to any people in other parts of the earth, let them only imagine it to be said about "Old Kentuck," old England, or any other corner of the world in which they happened to be born, and they will find it quite rational.

But, as touching our story, it is time to begin. Did you ever see the little village of Newbury, in New England? I dare say you never did; for it was just one of those out of the way places where nobody ever came unless they came on purpose: a green little hollow, wedged like a bird's nest between half a dozen high hills, that kept off the wind and kept out foreigners; so that the little place was as straitly *sui generis* as if there were not another in the world. The inhabitants were all of that respectable old standfast family who make it a point to be born, bred, married, die, and be buried all in the selfsame spot. There were just so many houses, and just so many people lived in them; and nobody ever seemed to be sick, or to die either, at least while I was there. The natives grew old till they could not grow any older, and then they stood still, and *lasted* from generation to generation. There was, too, an unchangeability about all the externals of Newbury. Here was a red house, and there was a brown house, and across the way was a yellow house; and there was a straggling rail fence or a tribe of mullein stalks between. The minister lived here, and 'Squire Moses lived there, and Deacon Hart lived under the hill, and Messrs. Nadab and Abihu Peters lived by the cross road, and the old "widder" Smith lived by the meeting house, and Ebenezer Camp kept a shoemaker's shop on one side, and Patience Mosely kept a milliner's shop in front; and there was old Comfort Scran, who kept store for the whole town, and sold axe heads, brass thimbles, licorice ball, fancy handkerchiefs, and every thing else you can think of. Here, too, was the general post office, where you might see letters marvellously folded, directed wrong side upward, stamped with a thimble, and superscribed to some of the Dollys, or Pollys, or Peters, or Moseses aforenamed or not named.

For the rest, as to manners, morals, arts, and sciences, the people in Newbury always went to their parties at three o'clock in the afternoon, and came home before dark; always stopped all work the minute the sun was down on Saturday night; always went to meeting on Sunday; had a school house with all the ordinary inconveniences; were in neighborly charity with each other; read their Bibles, feared their God, and were content with such things as they had — the best philosophy, after all. Such was the place into which Master James Benton made an irruption in the year eighteen hundred and no matter what. Now, this James is to be our hero, and he is just the hero for a sensation — at least, so you would have thought, if you had been in Newbury the week after his arrival. Master James was one of those whole-hearted, energetic Yankees, who rise in the world as naturally as cork does in water. He possessed a great share of that characteristic national trait so happily denominated "cuteness," which signifies an ability to do every thing without trying, and to know every thing without learning, and to make more use of one's *ignorance* than other people do of their knowledge. This quality in James was mingled with an elasticity of animal spirits, a buoyant cheerfulness of mind, which, though found in the New England character, perhaps, as often as any where else, is not ordinarily regarded as one of its distinguishing traits.

As to the personal appearance of our hero, we have not much to say of it — not half so much as the girls in Newbury found it necessary to remark, the first Sabbath that he shone out in the meeting house. There was a saucy frankness of countenance, a knowing roguery of eye, a joviality and prankishness of demeanor, that was wonderfully captivating, especially to the ladies.

It is true that Master James had an uncommonly comfortable opinion of himself, a full faith that there was nothing in creation that he could not learn and could not do; and this faith was maintained with an abounding and triumphant joyfulness, that fairly carried your sympathies along with him, and made you feel quite as much delighted with his qualifications and prospects as he felt himself. There are two kinds of self-sufficiency; one is amusing, and the other is provoking. His was the amusing kind. It seemed, in truth, to be only the buoyancy and overflow of a vivacious mind, delighted with every thing delightful, in himself or others. He was always ready to magnify his own praise, but quite as ready to exalt his neighbor, if the channel of discourse ran that way: his own perfections being more completely within his knowledge, he rejoiced in them more constantly; but, if those of any one else came within the same range, he was quite as much astonished and edified as if they had been his own.

Master James, at the time of his transit to the town of Newbury, was only eighteen years of age; so that it was difficult to say which predominated in him most, the boy or the man. The belief that he could, and the determination that he would, be something in the world had caused him to abandon his home, and, with all his worldly effects tied in a blue cotton pocket handkerchief, to proceed to seek his fortune in Newbury. And never did stranger in Yankee village rise to promotion with more unparalleled rapidity, or boast a greater plurality of employment. He figured as schoolmaster all the week, and as chorister on Sundays, and taught singing and reading in the evenings, besides studying Latin and Greek with the minister, nobody knew when; thus fitting for college, while he seemed to be doing every thing else in the world besides.

James understood every art and craft of popularity, and made himself mightily at home in all the chimney corners of the region round about; knew the geography of every body's cider barrel and apple bin, helping himself and every one else therefrom with all bountifulness; rejoicing in the good things of this life, devouring the old ladies' doughnuts and pumpkin pies with most flattering appetite, and appearing equally to relish every body and thing that came in his way.

The degree and versatility of his acquirements were truly wonderful. He knew all about arithmetic and history, and all about catching squirrels and planting corn; made poetry and hoe handles with equal celerity; wound yarn and took out grease spots for old ladies, and made nosegays and knick-knacks for young ones; caught trout Saturday afternoons, and discussed doctrines on Sundays, with equal adroitness and effect. In short, Mr. James moved on through the place

"Victorious,
Happy and glorious,"

welcomed and privileged by every body in every place; and when he had told his last ghost story, and fairly flourished himself out of doors at the close of a long winter's evening, you might see the hard face of the good man of the house still phosphorescent with his departing radiance, and hear him exclaim, in a paroxysm of admiration, that "Jemeses talk re'ely did beat all; that he was sartainly most a miraculous cre'tur!"

It was wonderfully contrary to the buoyant activity of Master James's mind to keep a school. He had, moreover, so much of the boy and the rogue in his composition, that he could not be strict with the iniquities of the curly pates under his charge; and when he saw how determinately every little heart was boiling over with mischief and motion, he felt in his soul more disposed to join in and help them to a frolic than to lay justice to the line, as was meet. This would have made a sad case, had it not been that the activity of the master's mind communicated itself to his charge, just as the reaction of one brisk little spring will fill a manufactory with motion; so that there was more of an impulse towards study in the golden, good-natured day of James Benton than in the time of all that went before or came after him.

But when "school was out," James's spirits foamed over as naturally as a tumbler of soda water, and he could jump over benches and burst out of doors with as much rapture as the veriest little elf in his company. Then you might have seen him stepping homeward with a most felicitous expression of countenance, occasionally reaching his hand through the fence for a bunch of currants, or over it after a flower, or bursting into some back yard to help an old lady empty her wash tub, or stopping to pay his *devoirs* to Aunt This or Mistress That, for James well knew the importance of the "powers that be," and always kept the sunny side of the old ladies.

We shall not answer for James's general flirtations, which were sundry and manifold; for he had just the kindly heart that fell in love with every thing in feminine shape that came in his way, and if he had not been blessed with an equal facility in falling out again, we do not know what ever would have become of him. But at length he came into an abiding captivity, and it is quite time that he should; for, having devoted thus much space to the illustration of our hero, it is fit we should do something in behalf of our heroine; and, therefore, we must beg the reader's attention while we draw a diagram or two that will assist him in gaining a right idea of her.

Do you see yonder brown house, with its broad roof sloping almost to the ground on one side, and a great, unsupported, sun bonnet of a piazza shooting out over the front door? You must often have noticed it; you have seen its tall well sweep, relieved against the clear evening sky, or observed the feather beds and bolsters lounging out of its chamber windows on a still summer morning; you recollect its gate, that swung with a chain and a great stone; its pantry window, latticed with little brown slabs, and looking out upon a forest of bean poles. You remember the zephyrs that used to play among its pea brush, and shake the long tassels of its corn patch, and how vainly any zephyr might essay to perform similar flirtations with the considerate cabbages that were solemnly vegetating near by. Then there was the whole neighborhood of purple-leaved beets and feathery parsnips; there were the billows of gooseberry bushes rolled up by the fence, interspersed with rows of quince trees; and far off in one corner was one little patch, penuriously devoted to ornament, which flamed with marigolds, poppies, snappers, and four-o'clocks. Then there was a little box by itself with one rose geranium in it, which seemed to look around the garden as much like a stranger as a French dancing master in a Yankee meeting house.

That is the dwelling of Uncle Lot Griswold. Uncle Lot, as he was commonly called, had a character that a painter would sketch for its lights and contrasts rather than its symmetry. He was a chestnut burr, abounding with briers without and with substantial goodness within. He had the strong-grained practical sense, the calculating worldly wisdom of his class of people in New England; he had, too, a kindly heart; but all the strata of his character were crossed by a vein of surly petulance, that, half way between joke and earnest, colored every thing that he said and did.

If you asked a favor of Uncle Lot, he generally kept you arguing half an hour, to prove that you really needed it, and to tell you that he could not all the while be troubled with helping one body or another, all which time you might observe him regularly making his preparations to grant your request, and see, by an odd glimmer of his eye, that he was preparing to let you hear the "conclusion of the whole matter," which was, "Well, well — I guess — I'll go, on the *hull* — I 'spose I must, at least;" so off he would go and work while the day lasted, and then wind up with a farewell exhortation "not to be a callin' on your neighbors when you could get along without." If any of Uncle Lot's neighbors were in any trouble, he was always at hand to tell them that "they shouldn't a' done so;" that "it was strange they couldn't had more sense;" and then to close his exhortations by laboring more diligently than any to bring them out of their difficulties, groaning in spirit, meanwhile, that folks would make people so much trouble.

"Uncle Lot, father wants to know if you will lend him your hoe to-day," says a little boy, making his way across a cornfield.

"Why don't your father use his own hoe?"

"Ours is broke."

"Broke! How came it broke?"

"I broke it yesterday, trying to hit a squirrel."

"What business had you to be hittin' squirrels with a hoe? say!"

"But father wants to borrow yours."

"Why don't you have that mended? It's a great pester to have every body usin' a body's things."

"Well, I can borrow one some where else, I suppose," says the suppliant. After the boy has stumbled across the ploughed ground, and is fairly over the fence, Uncle Lot calls, —

"Halloo, there, you little rascal! what are you goin' off without the hoe for?"

"I didn't know as you meant to lend it."

"I didn't say I wouldn't, did I? Here, come and take it — stay, I'll bring it; and do tell your father not to be a lettin' you hunt squirrels with his hoes next time."

Uncle Lot's household consisted of Aunt Sally, his wife, and an only son and daughter; the former, at the time our story begins, was at a neighboring literary institution. Aunt Sally was precisely as clever, as easy to be entreated, and kindly in externals, as her helpmate was the reverse. She was one of those respectable, pleasant old ladies whom you might often have met on the way to church on a Sunday, equipped with a great fan and a psalm book, and carrying some dried orange peel or a stalk of fennel, to give to the children if they were sleepy in meeting. She was as cheerful and domestic as the tea kettle that sung by her kitchen fire, and slipped along among Uncle Lot's angles and peculiarities as if there never was any thing the matter in the world; and the same mantle of sunshine seemed to have fallen on Miss Grace, her only daughter.

Pretty in her person and pleasant in her ways, endowed with native self-possession and address, lively and chatty, having a mind and a will of her own, yet good-humored withal, Miss Grace was a universal favorite. It would have puzzled a city lady to understand how Grace, who never was out of Newbury in her life, knew the way to speak, and act, and behave, on all occasions, exactly as if she had been taught how. She was just one of those wild flowers which you may sometimes see waving its little head in the woods, and looking so civilized and garden-like, that you wonder if it really did come up and grow there by nature. She was an adept in all household concerns, and there was something amazingly pretty in her energetic way of bustling about, and "putting things to rights." Like most Yankee damsels, she had a longing after the tree of knowledge, and, having exhausted the literary fountains of a district school, she fell to reading whatsoever came in her way. True, she had but little to read; but what she perused she had her own thoughts upon, so that a person of information, in talking with her, would feel a constant wondering pleasure to find that she had so much more to say of this, that, and the other thing than he expected.

Uncle Lot, like every one else, felt the magical brightness of his daughter, and was delighted with her praises, as might be discerned by his often finding occasion to remark that "he didn't see why the boys need to be all the time a' comin' to see Grace, for she was nothing so extror'nary, after all." About all matters and things at home she generally had her own way, while Uncle Lot would scold and give up with a regular good grace that was quite creditable.

"Father," says Grace, "I want to have a party next week."

"You sha'n't go to havin' your parties, Grace. I always have to eat bits and ends a fortnight after you have one, and I won't have it so." And so Uncle Lot walked out, and Aunt Sally and Miss Grace proceeded to make the cake and pies for the party.

When Uncle Lot came home, he saw a long array of pies and rows of cakes on the kitchen table.

"Grace — Grace — Grace, I say! What is all this here flummery for?"

"Why, it is *to eat*, father," said Grace, with a good-natured look of consciousness.

Uncle Lot tried his best to look sour; but his visage began to wax comical as he looked at his merry daughter; so he said nothing, but quietly sat down to his dinner.

"Father," said Grace, after dinner, "we shall want two more candlesticks next week."

"Why, can't you have your party with what you've got?"

"No, father, we want two more."

"I can't afford it, Grace — there's no sort of use on't — and you sha'n't have any."

"O, father, now do," said Grace.

"I won't, neither," said Uncle Lot, as he sallied out of the house, and took the road to Comfort Scran's store.

In half an hour he returned again; and fumbling in his pocket, and drawing forth a candlestick, levelled it at Grace.

"There's your candlestick."

"But, father, I said I wanted *two*."

"Why, can't you make one do?"

"No, I can't; I must have two."

"Well, then, there's t'other; and here's a fol-de-rol for you to tie round your neck." So saying, he bolted for the door, and took himself off with all speed. It was much after this fashion that matters commonly went on in the brown house.

But having tarried long on the way, we must proceed with the main story.

James thought Miss Grace was a glorious girl; and as to what Miss Grace thought of Master James, perhaps it would not have been developed had she not been called to stand on the defensive for him with Uncle Lot. For, from the time that the whole village of Newbury began to be wholly given unto the praise of Master James, Uncle Lot set his face as a flint against him — from the laudable fear of following the multitude. He therefore made conscience of stoutly gainsaying every thing that was said in his behalf, which, as James was in high favor with Aunt Sally, he had frequent opportunities to do.

So when Miss Grace perceived that Uncle Lot did not like our hero as much as he ought to do, she, of course, was bound to like him well enough to make up for it. Certain it is that they were remarkably happy in finding opportunities of being acquainted; that James waited on her, as a matter of course, from singing school; that he volunteered making a new box for her geranium on an improved plan; and above all, that he was remarkably particular in his attentions to Aunt Sally — a stroke of policy which showed that James had a natural genius for this sort of matters. Even when emerging from the meeting house in full glory, with flute and psalm book under his arm, he would stop to ask her how she did; and if it was cold weather, he would carry her foot stove all the way home from meeting, discoursing upon the sermon, and other serious matters, as Aunt Sally observed, "in the pleasantest, prettiest way that ever ye see." This flute was one of the crying sins of James in the eyes of Uncle Lot. James was particularly fond of it, because he had learned to play on it by intuition; and on the decease of the old pitchpipe, which was slain by a fall from the gallery, he took the liberty to introduce the flute in its place. For this, and other sins, and for the good reasons above named, Uncle Lot's countenance was not towards James, neither could he be moved to him-ward by any manner of means.

To all Aunt Sally's good words and kind speeches, he had only to say that "he didn't like him; that he hated to see him a' manifesting and glorifying there in the front gallery Sundays, and a' acting every where as if he was master of all: he didn't like it, and he wouldn't." But our hero was no whit cast down or discomfited by the malcontent aspect of Uncle Lot. On the contrary, when report was made to him of divers of his hard speeches, he only shrugged his shoulders, with a very satisfied air, and remarked that "he knew a thing or two for all that."

"Why, James," said his companion and chief counsellor, "do you think Grace likes you?"

"I don't know," said our hero, with a comfortable appearance of certainty.

"But you can't get her, James, if Uncle Lot is cross about it."

"Fudge! I can make Uncle Lot like me if I have a mind to try."

"Well then, Jim, you'll have to give up that flute of yours, I tell you now."

"Fa, sol, la — I can make him like me and my flute too."

"Why, how will you do it?"

"O, I'll work it," said our hero.

"Well, Jim, I tell you now, you don't know Uncle Lot if you say so; for he is just the *settest* crittur in his way that ever you saw."

"I *do* know Uncle Lot, though, better than most folks; he is no more cross than I am; and as to his being *set*, you have nothing to do but make him think he is in his own way when he is in yours — that is all."

"Well," said the other, "but you see I don't believe it."

"And I'll bet you a gray squirrel that I'll go there this very evening, and get him to like me and my flute both," said James.

Accordingly the late sunshine of that afternoon shone full on the yellow buttons of James as he proceeded to the place of conflict. It was a bright, beautiful evening. A thunder storm had just cleared away, and the silver clouds lay rolled up in masses around the setting sun; the rain drops were sparkling and winking to each other over the ends of the leaves, and all the bluebirds and robins, breaking forth into song, made the little green valley as merry as a musical box.

James's soul was always overflowing with that kind of poetry which consists in feeling unspeakably happy; and it is not to be wondered at, considering where he was going, that he should feel in a double ecstasy on the present occasion. He stepped gayly along, occasionally springing over a fence to the right to see whether the rain had swollen the trout brook, or to the left to notice the ripening of Mr. Somebody's watermelons — for James always had an eye on all his neighbors' matters as well as his own.

In this way he proceeded till he arrived at the picket fence that marked the commencement of Uncle Lot's ground. Here he stopped to consider. Just then four or five sheep walked up, and began also to consider a loose picket, which was hanging just ready to drop off; and James began to look at the sheep. "Well, mister," said he, as he observed the leader judiciously drawing himself through the gap, "in with you — just what I wanted;" and having waited a moment to ascertain that all the company were likely to follow, he ran with all haste towards the house, and swinging open the gate, pressed all breathless to the door.

"Uncle Lot, there are four or five sheep in your garden!" Uncle Lot dropped his whetstone and scythe.

"I'll drive them out," said our hero; and with that, he ran down the garden alley, and made a furious descent on the enemy; bestirring himself, as Bunyan says, "lustily and with good courage," till every sheep had skipped out much quicker than it skipped in; and then, springing over the fence, he seized a great stone, and nailed on the picket so effectually that no sheep could possibly encourage the hope of getting in again. This was all the work of a minute, and he was back again; but so exceedingly out of breath that it was necessary for him to stop a moment and rest himself. Uncle Lot looked ungraciously satisfied.

"What under the canopy set you to scampering so?" said he; "I could a' driv out them critturs myself."

"If you are at all particular about driving them out *yourself*, I can let them in again," said James.

Uncle Lot looked at him with an odd sort of twinkle in the corner of his eye.

"'Spose I must ask you to walk in," said he.

"Much obliged," said James; "but I am in a great hurry." So saying, he started in very business-like fashion towards the gate.

"You'd better jest stop a minute."

"Can't stay a minute."

"I don't see what possesses you to be all the while in sich a hurry; a body would think you had all creation on your shoulders."

"Just my situation, Uncle Lot," said James, swinging open the gate.

"Well, at any rate, have a drink of cider, can't ye?" said Uncle Lot, who was now quite engaged to have his own way in the case.

James found it convenient to accept this invitation, and Uncle Lot was twice as good-natured as if he had staid in the first of the matter.

Once fairly forced into the premises, James thought fit to forget his long walk and excess of business, especially as about that moment Aunt Sally and Miss Grace returned from an afternoon call. You may be sure that the last thing these respectable ladies looked for was to find Uncle Lot and Master James *tête-à-tête*, over a pitcher of cider; and when, as they entered, our hero looked up with something of a mischievous air, Miss Grace, in particular, was so puzzled that it took her at least a quarter of an hour to untie her bonnet strings. But James staid, and acted the agreeable to perfection. First, he must needs go down into the garden to look at Uncle Lot's wonderful cabbages, and then he promenaded all around the corn patch, stopping every few moments and looking up with an appearance of great gratification, as if he had never seen such corn in his life; and then he examined

Uncle Lot's favorite apple tree with an expression of wonderful interest.

"I never!" he broke forth, having stationed himself against the fence opposite to it; "what kind of an apple tree is that?"

"It's a bellflower, or somethin' another," said Uncle Lot.

"Why, where *did* you get it? I never saw such apples!" said our hero, with his eyes still fixed on the tree.

Uncle Lot pulled up a stalk or two of weeds, and threw them over the fence, just to show that he did not care any thing about the matter; and then he came up and stood by James.

"Nothin' so remarkable, as I know on," said he.

Just then, Grace came to say that supper was ready. Once seated at table, it was astonishing to see the perfect and smiling assurance with which our hero continued his addresses to Uncle Lot. It sometimes goes a great way towards making people like us to take it for granted that they do already; and upon this principle James proceeded. He talked, laughed, told stories, and joked with the most fearless assurance, occasionally seconding his words by looking Uncle Lot in the face, with a countenance so full of good will as would have melted any snowdrift of prejudices in the world.

James also had one natural accomplishment, more courtier-like than all the diplomacy in Europe, and that was the gift of feeling a *real* interest for any body in five minutes; so that, if he began to please in jest, he generally ended in earnest. With great simplicity of mind, he had a natural tact for seeing into others, and watched their motions with the same delight with which a child gazes at the wheels and springs of a watch, to "see what it will do."

The rough exterior and latent kindness of Uncle Lot were quite a spirit-stirring study; and when tea was over, as he and Grace happened to be standing together in the front door, he broke forth, —

"I do really like your father, Grace!"

"Do you?" said Grace.

"Yes, I do. He has something *in him*, and I like him all the better for having to fish it out."

"Well, I hope you will make him like you," said Grace, unconsciously; and then she stopped, and looked a little ashamed.

James was too well bred to see this, or look as if Grace meant any more than she said — a kind of breeding not always attendant on more fashionable polish — so he only answered, —

"I think I shall, Grace, though I doubt whether I can get him to own it."

"He is the kindest man that ever was," said Grace; "and he always acts as if he was ashamed of it."

James turned a little away, and looked at the bright evening sky, which was glowing like a calm, golden sea; and over it was the silver new moon, with one little star to hold the candle for her. He shook some bright drops off from a rosebush near by, and watched to see them shine as they fell, while Grace stood very quietly waiting for him to speak again.

"Grace," said he, at last, "I am going to college this fall."

"So you told me yesterday," said Grace.

James stooped down over Grace's geranium, and began to busy himself with pulling off all the dead leaves, remarking in the mean while, —

"And if I do get *him* to like me, Grace, will you like me too?"

"I like you now very well," said Grace.

"Come, Grace, you know what I mean," said James, looking steadfastly at the top of the apple tree.

"Well, I wish, then, you would understand what *I* mean, without my saying any more about it," said Grace.

"O, to be sure I will!" said our hero, looking up with a very intelligent air; and so, as Aunt Sally would say, the matter was settled, with "no words about it."

Now shall we narrate how our hero, as he saw Uncle Lot approaching the door, had the impudence to take out his flute, and put the parts together, arranging and adjusting the stops with great composure?

"Uncle Lot," said he, looking up, "this is the best flute that ever I saw."

"I hate them tooting critturs," said Uncle Lot, snappishly.

"I declare! I wonder how you can," said James, "for I do think they exceed ——"

So saying, he put the flute to his mouth, and ran up and down a long flourish.

"There! what do you think of that?" said he, looking in Uncle Lot's face with much delight.

Uncle Lot turned and marched into the house, but soon faced to the right-about, and came out again, for James was fingering "Yankee Doodle"—that appropriate national air for the descendants of the Puritans.

Uncle Lot's patriotism began to bestir itself; and now, if it had been any thing, as he said, but "that 'are flute"—as it was, he looked more than once at James's fingers.

"How under the sun *could* you learn to do that?" said he.

"O, it's easy enough," said James, proceeding with another tune; and, having played it through, he stopped a moment to examine the joints of his flute, and in the mean time addressed Uncle Lot: "You can't think how grand this is for pitching tunes — I always pitch the tunes on Sunday with it."

"Yes; but I don't think it's a right and fit instrument for the Lord's house," said Uncle Lot.

"Why not? It is only a kind of a long pitchpipe, you see," said James; "and, seeing the old one is broken, and this will answer, I don't see why it is not better than nothing."

"Why, yes, it may be better than nothing," said Uncle Lot; "but, as I always tell Grace and my wife, it ain't the right kind of instrument, after all; it ain't solemn."

"Solemn!" said James; "that is according as you work it: see here, now."

So saying, he struck up Old Hundred, and proceeded through it with great perseverance.

"There, now!" said he.

"Well, well, I don't know but it is," said Uncle Lot; "but, as I said at first, I don't like the look of it in meetin'."

"But yet you really think it is better than nothing," said James, "for you see I couldn't pitch my tunes without it."

"Maybe 'tis," said Uncle Lot; "but that isn't sayin' much."

This, however, was enough for Master James, who soon after departed, with his flute in his pocket, and Grace's last words in his heart; soliloquizing as he shut the gate, "There, now, I hope Aunt Sally won't go to praising me; for, just so sure as she does, I shall have it all to do over again."

James was right in his apprehension. Uncle Lot could be privately converted, but not brought to open confession; and when, the next morning, Aunt Sally remarked, in the kindness of her heart, —

"Well, I always knew you would come to like James," Uncle Lot only responded, "Who said I did like him?"

"But I'm sure you *seemed* to like him last night."

"Why, I couldn't turn him out o' doors, could I? I don't think nothin' of him but what I always did."

But it was to be remarked that Uncle Lot contented himself at this time with the mere general avowal, without running it into particulars, as was formerly his wont. It was evident that the ice had begun to melt, but it might have been a long time in dissolving, had not collateral incidents assisted.

It so happened that, about this time, George Griswold, the only son before referred to, returned to his native village, after having completed his theological studies at a neighboring institution. It is interesting to mark the gradual development of mind and heart, from the time that the white-headed, bashful boy quits the country village for college, to the period when he returns, a formed and matured man, to notice how gradually the rust of early prejudices begins to cleave from him — how his opinions, like his handwriting, pass from the cramped and limited forms of a country school into that confirmed and characteristic style which is to mark the man for life. In George this change was remarkably striking. He was endowed by nature with uncommon acuteness of feeling and fondness for reflection — qualities as likely as any to render a child backward and uninteresting in early life.

When he left Newbury for college, he was a taciturn and apparently phlegmatic boy, only evincing sensibility by blushing and looking particularly stupefied whenever any body spoke to him. Vacation after vacation passed, and he returned more and more an altered being; and he who once shrunk from the eye of the deacon, and was ready to sink if he met the minister, now moved about among the dignitaries of the place with all the composure of a superior being.

It was only to be regretted that, while the mind improved, the physical energies declined, and that every visit to his home found him paler, thinner, and less prepared in body for the sacred profession to which he had devoted himself. But now he was returned, a minister — a real minister, with a right to stand in the pulpit and preach; and what a joy and glory to Aunt Sally — and to Uncle Lot, if he were not ashamed to own it!

The first Sunday after he came, it was known far and near that George Griswold was to preach; and never was a more ready and expectant audience.

As the time for reading the first psalm approached, you might see the white-headed men turning their faces attentively towards the pulpit; the anxious and expectant old women, with their little black bonnets, bent forward to see him rise. There were the children looking, because every body else looked; there was Uncle Lot in the front pew, his face considerately adjusted; there was Aunt Sally, seeming as pleased as a mother could seem; and Miss Grace, lifting her sweet face to her brother, like a flower to the sun; there was our friend James in the front gallery, his joyous countenance a little touched with sobriety and expectation; in short, a more embarrassingly attentive audience never greeted the first effort of a young minister. Under these circumstances there was something touching in the fervent self-forgetfulness which characterized the first exercises of the morning — something which moved every one in the house.

The devout poetry of his prayer, rich with the Orientalism of Scripture, and eloquent with the expression of strong yet chastened emotion, breathed over his audience like music, hushing every one to silence, and beguiling every one to feeling. In the sermon, there was the strong intellectual nerve, the constant occurrence of argument and statement, which distinguishes a New England discourse; but it was [illegible]uched with life by the intense, yet half-subdued, feeling with which he seemed to utter it. Like the rays of the sun, it enlightened and melted at the same moment.

The strong peculiarities of New England doctrine, involving, as they do, all the hidden machinery of mind, all the mystery of its divine relations and future progression, and all the tremendous uncertainties of its eternal good or ill, seemed to have dwelt in his mind, to have burned in his thoughts, to have wrestled with his powers, and they gave to his manner the fervency almost of another world; while the exceeding paleness of his countenance, and a tremulousness of voice that seemed to spring from bodily weakness, touched the strong workings of his mind with a pathetic interest, as if the being so early absorbed in another world could not be long for this.

When the services were over, the congregation dispersed with the air of people who had *felt* rather than *heard;* and all the criticism that followed was similar to that of old Deacon Hart — an upright, shrewd man — who, as he lingered a moment at the church door, turned and gazed with unwonted feeling at the young preacher.

"He's a blessed cre'tur!" said he, the tears actually making their way to his eyes; "I hain't been so near heaven this many a day. He's a blessed cre'tur of the Lord; that's my mind about him!"

As for our friend James, he was at first sobered, then deeply moved, and at last wholly absorbed by the discourse; and it was only when meeting was over that he began to think where he really was.

With all his versatile activity, James had a greater depth of mental capacity than he was himself aware of, and he began to feel a sort of electric affinity for the mind that had touched him in a way so new; and when he saw the mild minister standing at the foot of the pulpit stairs, he made directly towards him.

"I do want to hear more from you," said he, with a face full of earnestness; "may I walk home with you?"

"It is a long and warm walk," said George, smiling.

"O, I don't care for that, if it does not trouble *you*," said James; and leave being gained, you might have seen them slowly passing along under the trees, James pouring forth all the floods of inquiry which the sudden impulse of his mind had brought out, and supplying his guide with more questions and problems for solution than he could have gone through with in a month.

"I cannot answer all your questions now," said he, as they stopped at Uncle Lot's gate.

"Well, then, when will you?" said James, eagerly. "Let me come home with you to-night?"

The minister smiled assent, and James departed so full of new thoughts, that he passed Grace without even seeing her. From that time a friendship commenced between the two, which was a beautiful illustration of the affinities of opposites. It was like a friendship between morning and evening — all freshness and sunshine on one side, and all gentleness and peace on the other.

The young minister, worn by long-continued ill health, by the fervency of his own feelings, and the gravity of his own reasonings, found pleasure in the healthful buoyancy of a youthful, unexhausted mind, while James felt himself sobered and made better by the moonlight tranquillity of his friend. It is one mark of a superior mind to understand and be influenced by the superiority of others; and this was the case with James. The ascendency which his new friend acquired over him was unlimited, and did more in a month towards consolidating and developing his character than all the four years' course of a college. Our religious habits are likely always to retain the impression of the first seal which stamped them, and in this case it was a peculiarly happy one. The calmness, the settled purpose, the mild devotion of his friend, formed a just alloy to the energetic and reckless buoyancy of James's character, and awakened in him a set of feelings without which the most vigorous mind must be incomplete.

The effect of the ministrations of the young pastor, in awakening attention to the subjects of his calling in the village, was marked, and of a kind which brought pleasure to his own heart. But, like all other excitement, it tends to exhaustion, and it was not long before he sensibly felt the decline of the powers of life. To the best regulated mind there is something bitter in the relinquishment of projects for which we have been long and laboriously preparing, and there is something far more bitter in crossing the long-cherished expectations of friends. All this George felt. He could not bear to look on his mother, hanging on his words and following his steps with eyes of almost childish delight — on his singular father, whose whole earthly ambition was bound up in his success, and think how soon the "candle of their old age" must be put out.

When he returned from a successful effort, it was painful to see the old man, so evidently delighted, and so anxious to conceal his triumph, as he would seat himself in his chair, and begin with, "George, that 'are doctrine is rather of a puzzler; but you seem to think you've got the run on't. I should re'ly like to know what business you have to think you know better than other folks about it;" and, though he would cavil most courageously at all George's explanations, yet you might perceive, through all, that he was inly uplifted to hear how his boy could talk.

If George was engaged in argument with any one else, he would sit by, with his head bowed down, looking out from under his shaggy eyebrows with a shamefaced satisfaction very unusual with him. Expressions of affection from the naturally gentle are not half so touching as those which are forced out from the hard-favored and severe; and George was affected, even to pain, by the evident pride and regard of his father.

"He never said so much to any body before," thought he, "and what will he do if I die?"

In such thoughts as these Grace found her brother engaged one still autumn morning, as he stood leaning against the garden fence.

"What are you solemnizing here for, this bright day, brother George?" said she, as she bounded down the alley.

The young man turned and looked on her happy face with a sort of twilight smile.

"How *happy* you are, Grace!" said he.

"To be sure I am; and you ought to be too, because you are better."

"I am happy, Grace — that is, I hope I shall be."

"You are sick, I know you are," said Grace; "you look

worn out. O, I wish your heart could *spring* once, as mine does."

"I am not well, dear Grace, and I fear I never shall be," said he, turning away, and fixing his eyes on the fading trees opposite.

"O George! dear George, don't, don't say *that;* you'll break all our hearts," said Grace, with tears in her own eyes.

"Yes, but it is *true*, sister: I do not feel it on my own account so much as —— However," he added, "it will all be the same in heaven."

It was but a week after this that a violent cold hastened the progress of debility into a confirmed malady. He sunk very fast. Aunt Sally, with the self-deceit of a fond and cheerful heart, thought every day that "he *would* be better," and Uncle Lot resisted conviction with all the obstinate pertinacity of his character, while the sick man felt that he had not the heart to undeceive them.

James was now at the house every day, exhausting all his energy and invention in the case of his friend; and any one who had seen him in his hours of recklessness and glee, could scarcely recognize him as the being whose step was so careful, whose eye so watchful, whose voice and touch were so gentle, as he moved around the sick bed. But the same quickness which makes a mind buoyant in gladness, often makes it gentlest and most sympathetic in sorrow.

It was now nearly morning in the sick room. George had been restless and feverish all night; but towards day he fell into a slight slumber, and James sat by his side, almost holding his breath lest he should waken him. It was yet dusk, but the sky was brightening with a solemn glow, and the stars were beginning to disappear; all, save the bright and morning one, which, standing alone in the east, looked tenderly through the casement, like the eye of our heavenly Father, watching over us when all earthly friendships are fading.

George awoke with a placid expression of countenance, and fixing his eyes on the brightening sky, murmured faintly, —

> "The sweet, immortal morning sheds
> Its blushes round the spheres."

A moment after, a shade passed over his face; he pressed his fingers over his eyes, and the tears dropped silently on his pillow.

"George! *dear* George!" said James, bending over him.

"It's my friends — it's my father — my mother," said he, faintly.

"Jesus Christ will watch over them," said James, soothingly.

"O, yes, I know he will; for *he* loved his own which were in the world; he loved them unto the end. But I am dying — and before I have done any good."

"O, do not say so," said James; "think, think what you have done, if only for *me.* God bless you for it! God *will* bless you for it; it will follow you to heaven; it will bring me there. Yes, I will do as you have taught me. I will give my life, my soul, my whole strength to it; and then you will not have lived in vain."

George smiled, and looked upward; "his face was as that of an angel;" and James, in his warmth, continued, —

"It is not I alone who can say this; we all bless you; every one in this place blesses you; you will be had in everlasting remembrance by some hearts here, I know."

"Bless God!" said George.

"We do," said James. "I bless him that I ever knew you; we all bless him, and we love you, and shall forever."

The glow that had kindled over the pale face of the invalid again faded as he said, —

"But, James, I must, I ought to tell my father and mother; I ought to, and how can I?"

At that moment the door opened, and Uncle Lot made his appearance. He seemed struck with the paleness of George's face; and coming to the side of the bed, he felt his pulse, and laid his hand anxiously on his forehead, and clearing his voice several times, inquired "if he didn't feel a little better."

"No, father," said George; then taking his hand, he looked anxiously in his face, and seemed to hesitate a moment. "Father," he began, "you know that we ought to submit to God."

There was something in his expression at this moment which flashed the truth into the old man's mind. He dropped his son's hand with an exclamation of agony, and turning quickly, left the room.

"Father! father!" said Grace, trying to rouse him, as he stood with his arms folded by the kitchen window.

"Get away, child!" said he, roughly.

"Father, mother says breakfast is ready."

"I don't want any breakfast," said he, turning short about. "Sally, what are you fixing in that 'ere porringer?"

"O, it's only a little tea for George; 'twill comfort him up, and make him feel better, poor fellow."

"You won't make him feel better — he's gone," said Uncle Lot, hoarsely.

"O, dear heart, no!" said Aunt Sally.

"Be still a' contradicting me; I won't be contradicted all the time by nobody. The short of the case is, that George is goin' to *die* just as we've got him ready to be a minister and all; and I wish to pity I was in my grave myself, and so ——" said Uncle Lot, as he plunged out of the door, and shut it after him.

It is well for man that there is one Being who sees the suffering heart *as it is,* and not as it manifests itself through the repellances of outward infirmity, and who, perhaps, feels more for the stern and wayward than for those whose gentler feelings win for them human sympathy. With all his singularities, there was in the heart of Uncle Lot a depth of religious sincerity; but there are few characters where religion does any thing more than struggle with natural defect, and modify what would else be far worse.

In this hour of trial, all the native obstinacy and pertinacity of the old man's character rose, and while he felt the necessity of submission, it seemed impossible to submit; and thus, reproaching himself, struggling in vain to repress the murmurs of nature, repulsing from him all external sympathy, his mind was "tempest-tossed, and not comforted."

It was on the still afternoon of the following Sabbath that he was sent for, in haste, to the chamber of his son. He entered, and saw that the hour was come. The family were all there. Grace and James, side by side, bent over the dying one, and his mother sat afar off, with her face hid in her apron, "that she might not see the death of the child." The aged minister was there, and the Bible lay open before him. The father walked to the side of the bed. He stood still, and gazed on the face now brightening with "life and immortality." The son lifted up his eyes; he saw his father, smiled, and put out his hand. "I am glad *you* are come," said he. "O George, to the pity, don't! *don't* smile on me so! I know what is coming; I have tried, and tried, and I *can't*, I *can't* have it so;" and his frame shook, and he sobbed audibly. The room was still as death; there was none that seemed able to comfort him. At last the son repeated, in a sweet, but interrupted voice, those words of man's best Friend: "Let not your heart be troubled; in my Father's house are many mansions."

"Yes; but I *can't help* being troubled; I suppose the Lord's will must be done, but it'll *kill* me."

"O father, don't, don't break my heart," said the son, much agitated. "I shall see you again in heaven, and you shall see me again; and then 'your heart shall rejoice, and your joy no man taketh from you.'"

"I never shall get to heaven if I feel as I do now," said the old man. "I *cannot* have it so."

The mild face of the sufferer was overcast. "I wish he saw all that *I* do," said he, in a low voice. Then looking towards the minister, he articulated, "Pray for us."

They knelt in prayer. It was soothing, as *real* prayer always must be; and when they rose, every one seemed more calm. But the sufferer was exhausted; his countenance changed; he looked on his friends; there was a faint whisper, "Peace I leave with you" — and he was in heaven.

We need not dwell on what followed. The seed sown by the righteous often blossoms over their grave; and so was it with this good man. The words of peace which he spoke unto his friends while he was yet with them came into remembrance after he was gone; and though he was laid in the grave with many tears, yet it was with softened and submissive hearts.

"The Lord bless him," said Uncle Lot, as he and James

were standing, last of all, over the grave. "I believe my heart is gone to heaven with him; and I think the Lord really *did* know what was best, after all."

Our friend James seemed now to become the support of the family; and the bereaved old man unconsciously began to transfer to him the affections that had been left vacant.

"James," said he to him one day, "I suppose you know that you are about the same to me as a son."

"I hope so," said James, kindly.

"Well, well, you'll go to college next week, and none o' y'r keepin' school to get along. I've got enough to bring you safe out — that is, if you'll be *car'ful* and *stiddy*."

James knew the heart too well to refuse a favor in which the poor old man's mind was comforting itself. He had the self-command to abstain from any extraordinary expressions of gratitude, but took it kindly, as a matter of course.

"Dear Grace," said he to her, the last evening before he left home, "I am changed; we both are altered since we first knew each other; and now I am going to be gone a long time, but I am sure ——"

He stopped to arrange his thoughts.

"Yes, you may be sure of all those things that you wish to say, and cannot," said Grace.

"Thank you," said James; then, looking thoughtfully, he added, "God help me. I believe I have mind enough to be what I mean to; but whatever I am or have shall be given to God and my fellow-men; and then, Grace, your brother in heaven will rejoice over me."

"I believe he does *now*," said Grace. "God bless you, James; I don't know what would have become of us if you had not been here."

"Yes, you will live to be like him, and to do even more

good," she added, her face brightening as she spoke, till James thought she really must be right.

* * * * *

It was five years after this that James was spoken of as an eloquent and successful minister in the state of C., and was settled in one of its most thriving villages. Late one autumn evening, a tall, bony, hard-favored man was observed making his way into the outskirts of the place.

"Halloa, there!" he called to a man over the other side of a fence; "what town is this 'ere?"

"It's Farmington, sir."

"Well, I want to know if you know any thing of a boy of mine that lives here?"

"A boy of yours? Who?"

"Why, I've got a boy here, that's livin' *on the town*, and I thought I'd jest look him up."

"I don't know any boy that is living on the town. What's his name?"

"Why," said the old man, pushing his hat off from his forehead, "I believe they call him James Benton."

"James Benton! Why, that is our minister's name!"

"O, wal, I believe he *is* the minister, come to think on't. He's a boy o' mine, though. Where does he live?"

"In that white house that you see set back from the road there, with all those trees round it."

At this instant a tall, manly-looking person approached from behind. Have we not seen that face before? It is a touch graver than of old, and its lines have a more thoughtful significance; but all the vivacity of James Benton sparkles in that quick smile as his eye falls on the old man.

"I *thought* you could not keep away from us long," said he, with the prompt cheerfulness of his boyhood, and laying hold of both of Uncle Lot's hard hands.

They approached the gate; a bright face glances past the window, and in a moment Grace is at the door.

"Father! *dear* father!"

"You'd *better* make believe be so glad," said Uncle Lot, his eyes glistening as he spoke.

"Come, come, father, I have authority in these days," said Grace, drawing him towards the house; "so no disrespectful speeches; away with your hat and coat, and sit down in this great chair."

"So, ho! Miss Grace," said Uncle Lot, "you are at your old tricks, ordering round as usual. Well, if I must, I must;" so down he sat.

"Father," said Grace, as he was leaving them, after a few days' stay, "it's Thanksgiving day next month, and you and mother must come and stay with us."

Accordingly, the following month found Aunt Sally and Uncle Lot by the minister's fireside, delighted witnesses of the Thanksgiving presents which a willing people were pouring in; and the next day they had once more the pleasure of seeing a son of theirs in the sacred desk, and hearing a sermon that every body said was "the best that he ever preached;" and it is to be remarked, that this was the standing commentary on all James's discourses, so that it was evident he was going on unto perfection.

"There's a great deal that's worth having in this 'ere life after all," said Uncle Lot, as he sat by the coals of the bright evening fire of that day; "that is, if we'd only take it when the Lord lays it in our way."

"Yes," said James; "and let us only take it as we should, and this life will be cheerfulness, and the next fulness of joy."

LOVE *versus* LAW.

How many kinds of beauty there are! How many even in the human form! There are the bloom and motion of childhood, the freshness and ripe perfection of youth, the dignity of manhood, the softness of woman — all different, yet each in its kind perfect.

But there is none so peculiar, none that bears more the image of the heavenly, than the beauty of *Christian old age.* It is like the loveliness of those calm autumn days, when the heats of summer are past, when the harvest is gathered into the garner, and the sun shines over the placid fields and fading woods, which stand waiting for their last change. It is a beauty more strictly moral, more belonging to the soul, than that of any other period of life. Poetic fiction always paints the old man as a Christian; nor is there any period where the virtues of Christianity seem to find a more harmonious development. The aged man, who has outlived the hurry of passion — who has withstood the urgency of temptation — who has concentrated the religious impulses of youth into habits of obedience and love — who, having served his generation by the will of God, now leans in helplessness on Him whom once he served, is, perhaps, one of the most faultless representations of the beauty of holiness that this world affords.

Thoughts something like these arose in my mind as I slowly turned my footsteps from the graveyard of my native village, where I had been wandering after years of absence. It was a lovely spot — a soft slope of ground close by a little stream, that ran sparkling through the cedars and junipers beyond it, while on the other side arose a green hill, with the white village laid like a necklace of pearls upon its bosom.

There is no feature of the landscape more picturesque and peculiar than that of the graveyard — that "city of the silent," as it is beautifully expressed by the Orientals — standing amid the bloom and rejoicing of nature, its white stones glittering in the sun, a memorial of decay, a link between the living and the dead.

As I moved slowly from mound to mound, and read the inscriptions, which purported that many a money-saving man, and many a busy, anxious housewife, and many a prattling, half-blossomed child, had done with care or mirth, I was struck with a plain slab, bearing the inscription, "*To the memory of Deacon Enos Dudley, who died in his hundredth year.*" My eye was caught by this inscription, for in other years I had well known the person it recorded. At this instant, his mild and venerable form arose before me as erst it used to rise from the deacon's seat, a straight, close slip just below the pulpit. I recollect his quiet and lowly coming into meeting, precisely ten minutes before the time, every Sunday, — his tall form a little stooping, — his best suit of butternut-colored Sunday clothes, with long flaps and wide cuffs, on one of which two pins were always to be seen stuck in with the most reverent precision. When seated, the top of the pew came just to his chin, so that his silvery, placid head rose above it like the moon above the horizon. His head was one that might have been sketched for a St. John — bald at the top, and around the temples adorned with a soft flow of bright fine hair, —

> "That down his shoulders reverently spread,
> As hoary frost with spangles doth attire
> The naked branches of an oak half dead."

He was then of great age, and every line of his patient face seemed to say, "And now, Lord, what wait I for?" Yet still, year after year, was he to be seen in the same place, with the same dutiful punctuality.

The services he offered to his God were all given with the exactness of an ancient Israelite. No words could have persuaded him of the propriety of meditating when the choir was singing, or of sitting down, even through infirmity, before the close of the longest prayer that ever was offered. A mighty contrast was he to his fellow-officer, Deacon Abrams, a tight, little, tripping, well-to-do man, who used to sit beside him with his hair brushed straight up like a little blaze, his coat buttoned up trig and close, his psalm book in hand, and his quick gray eyes turned first on one side of the broad aisle, and then on the other, and then up into the gallery, like a man who came to church on business, and felt responsible for every thing that was going on in the house.

A great hinderance was the business talent of this good little man to the enjoyments of us youngsters, who, perched along in a row on a low seat in front of the pulpit, attempted occasionally to diversify the long hour of sermon by sundry small exercises of our own, such as making our handkerchiefs into rabbits, or exhibiting, in a sly way, the apples and gingerbread we had brought for a Sunday dinner, or pulling the ears of some discreet meeting-going dog, who now and then would soberly pitapat through the broad aisle. But woe be to us during our contraband sports, if we saw Deacon Abrams's sleek head dodging up from behind the top of the deacon's seat. Instantly all the apples, gingerbread, and handkerchiefs vanished, and we all sat with our hands folded, looking as demure as if we understood every word of the sermon, and more too.

There was a great contrast between these two deacons in their services and prayers, when, as was often the case, the absence of the pastor devolved on them the burden of conducting the duties of the sanctuary. That God was great and good, and that we all were sinners, were truths that seemed to have melted into the heart of Deacon Enos, so that his very soul and spirit were bowed down with them. With Deacon Abrams it was an *undisputed fact*, which he had settled long ago, and concerning which he felt that there could be no reasonable doubt, and his bustling way of dealing with the matter seemed to say that he knew *that* and a great many things besides.

Deacon Enos was known far and near as a very proverb for peacefulness of demeanor and unbounded charitableness in covering and excusing the faults of others. As long as there was any doubt in a case of alleged evil doing, Deacon Enos *guessed* "the man did not mean any harm, after all;" and when transgression became too barefaced for this excuse, he always guessed "it wa'n't best to say much about it; nobody could tell what *they* might be left to."

Some incidents in his life will show more clearly these

traits. A certain shrewd landholder, by the name of Jones, who was not well reported of in the matter of honesty, sold to Deacon Enos a valuable lot of land, and received the money for it; but, under various pretences, deferred giving the deed. Soon after, he died; and, to the deacon's amazement, the deed was nowhere to be found, while this very lot of land was left by will to one of his daughters.

The deacon said "it was very extraor'nary: he always knew that Seth Jones was considerably sharp about money, but he did not think he would do such a right up-and-down wicked thing." So the old man repaired to 'Squire Abel to state the case, and see if there was any redress. "I kinder hate to tell of it," said he; "but, 'Squire Abel, you know Mr. Jones was — was — *what he was*, even if he *is* dead and gone!" This was the nearest approach the old gentleman could make to specifying a heavy charge against the dead. On being told that the case admitted of no redress, Deacon Enos comforted himself with half soliloquizing, "Well, at any rate, the land has gone to those two girls, poor lone critters — I hope it will do *them* some good. There is Silence — we won't say much about her; but Sukey is a nice, pretty girl." And so the old man departed, leaving it as his opinion that, since the matter could not be mended, it was just as well not to say any thing about it.

Now, the two girls here mentioned (to wit, Silence and Sukey) were the eldest and the youngest of a numerous family, the offspring of three wives of Seth Jones, of whom these two were the sole survivors. The elder, Silence, was a tall, strong, black-eyed, hard-featured woman, verging upon forty, with a good, loud, resolute voice, and what the Irishman would call "a dacent notion of using it." Why she was called *Silence* was a standing problem to the neighborhood; for she had more faculty and inclination for making a noise than any person in the whole township. Miss Silence was one of those persons who have no disposition to yield any of their own rights. She marched up to all controverted matters, faced down all opposition, held her way lustily and with good courage, making men, women, and children turn out for her, as they would for a mail stage. So evident was her innate determination to be free and independent, that, though she was the daughter of a rich man, and well portioned, only one swain was ever heard of who ventured to solicit her hand in marriage; and he was sent off with the assurance that, if he ever showed his face about the house again, she would set the dogs on him.

But Susan Jones was as different from her sister as the little graceful convolvulus from the great rough stick that supports it. At the time of which we speak she was just eighteen; a modest, slender, blushing girl, as timid and shrinking as her sister was bold and hardy. Indeed, the education of poor Susan had cost Miss Silence much painstaking and trouble, and, after all, she said "the girl would make a fool of herself; she never could teach her to be up and down with people, as she was."

When the report came to Miss Silence's ears that Deacon Enos considered himself as aggrieved by her father's will, she held forth upon the subject with great strength of courage and of lungs. "Deacon Enos might be in better business than in trying to cheat orphans out of their rights — she hoped he would go to law about it, and see what good he would get by it — a pretty church member and deacon, to be sure! getting up such a story about her poor father, dead and gone!

"But, Silence," said Susan, "Deacon Enos is a good man: I do not think he means to injure any one; there must be some mistake about it."

"Susan, you are a little fool, as I have always told you," replied Silence; "you would be cheated out of your eye teeth if you had not me to take care of you."

But subsequent events brought the affairs of these two damsels in closer connection with those of Deacon Enos, as we shall proceed to show.

It happened that the next door neighbor of Deacon Enos was a certain old farmer, whose crabbedness of demeanor had procured for him the name of *Uncle Jaw.* This agreeable surname accorded very well with the general characteristics both of the person and manner of its possessor. He was tall and hard-favored, with an expression of countenance much resembling a north-east rain storm — a drizzling, settled sulkiness, that seemed to defy all prospect of clearing off, and to take comfort in its own disagreeableness. His voice seemed to have taken lessons of his face, in such admirable keeping was its sawing, deliberate growl with the pleasing physiognomy before indicated. By nature he was endowed with one of those active, acute, hair-splitting minds, which can raise forty questions for dispute on any point of the compass; and had he been an educated man, he might have proved as clever a metaphysician as ever threw dust in the eyes of succeeding generations. But being deprived of these advantages, he nevertheless exerted himself to quite as useful a purpose in puzzling and mystifying whomsoever came in his way. But his activity particularly exercised itself in the line of the law, as it was his meat, and drink, and daily meditation, either to find something to go to law about, or to go law about something he had found. There was always some question about an old rail fence that used to run "*a leetle* more to the left hand," or that was built up "*a leetle* more to the right hand," and so cut off a strip of his "*medder land*," or else there was some outrage of Peter Somebody's turkeys getting into his mowing, or Squire Moses's geese were to be shut up in the town pound, or something equally important kept him busy from year's end to year's end. Now, as a matter of private amusement, this might have answered very well; but then Uncle Jaw was not satisfied to fight his own battles, but must needs go from house to house, narrating the whole length and breadth of the case, with all the *says he's* and *says I's*, and the *I tell'd him's* and *he tell'd me's*, which do either accompany or flow therefrom. Moreover, he had such a marvellous facility of finding out matters to quarrel about, and of letting every one else know where they, too, could muster a quarrel, that he generally succeeded in keeping the whole neighborhood by the ears.

And as good Deacon Enos assumed the office of peacemaker for the village, Uncle Jaw's efficiency rendered it no sinecure. The deacon always followed the steps of Uncle Jaw, smoothing, hushing up, and putting matters aright with an assiduity that was truly wonderful.

Uncle Jaw himself had a great respect for the good man, and, in common with all the neighborhood, sought unto him for counsel, though, like other seekers of advice, he appropriated only so much as seemed good in his own eyes.

Still he took a kind of pleasure in dropping in of an evening to Deacon Enos's fire, to recount the various matters which he had taken or was to take in hand; at one time to narrate "how he had been over the milldam, telling old

Granny Clark that she could get the law of Seth Scran about that pasture lot," or else "how he had told Ziah Bacon's widow that she had a right to shut up Bill Scranton's pig every time she caught him in front of her house."

But the grand "matter of matters," and the one that took up the most of Uncle Jaw's spare time, lay in a dispute between him and 'Squire Jones, the father of Susan and Silence; for it so happened that his lands and those of Uncle Jaw were contiguous. Now, the matter of dispute was on this wise: On 'Squire Jones's land there was a mill, which mill Uncle Jaw averred was "always a-flooding his medder land." As Uncle Jaw's "medder land" was by nature half bog and bulrushes, and therefore liable to be found in a wet condition, there was always a happy obscurity as to where the water came from, and whether there was at any time more there than belonged to his share. So, when all other subject matters of dispute failed, Uncle Jaw recreated himself with getting up a lawsuit about his "medder land;" and one of these cases was in pendency when, by the death of the squire, the estate was left to Susan and Silence, his daughters. When, therefore, the report reached him that Deacon Enos had been cheated out of his dues, Uncle Jaw prepared forthwith to go and compare notes. Therefore, one evening, as Deacon Enos was sitting quietly by the fire, musing and reading with his big Bible open before him, he heard the premonitory symptoms of a visitation from Uncle Jaw on his door scraper; and soon the man made his appearance. After seating himself directly in front of the fire, with his elbows on his knees, and his hands spread out over the coals, he looked up in Deacon Enos's mild face with his little inquisitive gray eyes, and remarked, by way of opening the subject, "Well, deacon, old 'Squire Jones is gone at last. I wonder how much good all his land will do him now?"

"Yes," replied Deacon Enos, "it just shows how all these things are not worth striving after. We brought nothing into the world, and it is certain we can carry nothing out."

"Why, yes," replied Uncle Jaw, "that's all very right, deacon; but it was strange how that old 'Squire Jones did hang on to things. Now, that mill of his, that was always soaking off water into these medders of mine — I took and tell'd 'Squire Jones just how it was, pretty nigh twenty times, and yet he would keep it just so; and now he's dead and gone, there is that old gal Silence is full as bad, and makes more noise; and she and Suke have got the land; but, you see, I mean to work it yet."

Here Uncle Jaw paused to see whether he had produced any sympathetic excitement in Deacon Enos; but the old man sat without the least emotion, quietly contemplating the top of the long kitchen shovel. Uncle Jaw fidgeted in his chair, and changed his mode of attack for one more direct. "I heard 'em tell, Deacon Enos, that the squire served you something of an unhandy sort of trick about that 'ere lot of land."

Still Deacon Enos made no reply; but Uncle Jaw's perseverance was not so to be put off, and he recommenced. "'Squire Abel, you see, he tell'd me how the matter was, and he said he did not see as it could be mended; but I took and tell'd him, ''Squire Abel,' says I, 'I'd bet pretty nigh 'most any thing, if Deacon Enos would tell the matter to me, that I could find a hole for him to creep out at; for,' says I, 'I've seen daylight through more twistical cases than that afore now.'"

Still Deacon Enos remained mute; and Uncle Jaw, after waiting a while, recommenced with, "But, railly, deacon, I should like to hear the particulars."

"I have made up my mind not to say any thing more about that business," said Deacon Enos, in a tone which, though mild, was so exceedingly definite, that Uncle Jaw felt that the case was hopeless in that quarter; he therefore betook himself to the statement of his own grievances.

"Why, you see, deacon," he began, at the same time taking the tongs, and picking up all the little brands, and disposing them in the middle of the fire,—"you see, two days arter the funeral, (for I didn't railly like to go any sooner,) I stepped up to hash over the matter with old Silence; for as to Sukey, she ha'n't no more to do with such things than our white kitten. Now, you see, 'Squire Jones, just afore he died, he took away an old rail fence of his'n that lay between his land and mine, and began to build a new stone wall; and when I come to measure, I found he had took and put a'most the whole width of the stone wall on to my land, when there ought not to have been more than half of it come there. Now, you see, I could not say a word to 'Squire Jones, because, jest before I found it out, he took and died; and so I thought I'd speak to old Silence, and see if she meant to do any thing about it, 'cause I knew pretty well she wouldn't; and I tell you, if she didn't put it on to me! We had a regular pitched battle — the old gal, I thought she would 'a screamed herself to death! I don't know but she would, but just then poor Sukey came in, and looked so frightened and scarey — Sukey is a pretty gal, and looks so trembling and delicate, that it's kinder a shame to plague her, and so I took and come away for that time."

Here Uncle Jaw perceived a brightening in the face of the good deacon, and felt exceedingly comforted that at last he was about to interest him in his story.

But all this while the deacon had been in a profound meditation concerning the ways and means of putting a stop to a quarrel that had been his torment from time immemorial, and just at this moment a plan had struck his mind which our story will proceed to unfold.

The mode of settling differences which had occurred to the good man was one which has been considered a specific in reconciling contending sovereigns and states from early antiquity, and the deacon hoped it might have a pacifying influence even in so unpromising a case as that of Miss Silence and Uncle Jaw.

In former days, Deacon Enos had kept the district school for several successive winters, and among his scholars was the gentle Susan Jones, then a plump, rosy little girl, with blue eyes, curly hair, and the sweetest disposition in the world. There was also little Joseph Adams, the only son of Uncle Jaw, a fine, healthy, robust boy, who used to spell the longest words, make the best snowballs and poplar whistles, and read the loudest and fastest in the Columbian Orator of any boy at school.

Little Joe inherited all his father's sharpness, with a double share of good humor; so that, though he was forever effervescing in the way of one funny trick or another, he was a universal favorite, not only with the deacon, but with the whole school.

Master Joseph always took little Susan Jones under his especial protection, drew her to school on his sled, helped her out with all the long sums in her arithmetic, saw to it that nobody pillaged her dinner basket, or knocked down her bonnet, and resolutely whipped or snowballed any other boy who attempted the same gallantries. Years passed on, and Uncle Jaw had sent his son to college. He sent him because, as he said, he had "*a right* to send him; just as good a right as 'Squire Abel or Deacon Abrams to send their boys, and so he *would* send him." It was the remembrance of his old favorite Joseph, and his little pet Susan, that came across the mind of Deacon Enos, and which seemed to open a gleam of light in regard to the future. So, when Uncle Jaw had finished his prelection, the deacon, after some meditation, came out with, "Railly, they say that your son is going to have the valedictory in college."

Though somewhat startled at the abrupt transition, Uncle Jaw found the suggestion too flattering to his pride to be dropped; so, with a countenance grimly expressive of his satisfaction, he replied, "Why, yes — yes — I don't see no reason why a poor man's son ha'n't as much right as any one to be at the top, if he can get there."

"Just so," replied Deacon Enos.

"He was always the boy for larning, and for nothing else," continued Uncle Jaw; "put him to farming, couldn't make nothing of him. If I set him to hoeing corn or hilling potatoes, I'd always find him stopping to chase hop-toads, or off after chip-squirrels. But set him down to a book, and there he was! That boy larnt reading the quickest of any boy that ever I saw: it wasn't a month after he began his *a b, abs*, before he could read in the 'Fox and the Brambles,' and in a month more he could clatter off his chapter in the Testament as fast as any of them; and you see, in college, it's jest so — he has ris right up to be first."

"And he is coming home week after next," said the deacon, meditatively.

The next morning, as Deacon Enos was eating his breakfast, he quietly remarked to his wife, "Sally, I believe it was week after next you were meaning to have your quilting?"

"Why, I never told you so: what alive makes you think that, Deacon Dudley?"

"I thought that was your calculation," said the good man, quietly.

"Why, no; to be sure, I *can* have it, and may be it's the best of any time, if we can get Black Dinah to come and help about the cakes and pies. I guess we will, finally."

"I think it's likely you had better," replied the deacon, "and we will have all the young folks here."

And now let us pass over all the intermediate pounding, and grinding, and chopping, which for the next week foretold approaching festivity in the kitchen of the deacon. Let us forbear to provoke the appetite of a hungry reader by setting in order before him the minced pies, the cranberry tarts, the pumpkin pies, the doughnuts, the cookies, and other sweet cakes of every description, that sprang into being at the magic touch of Black Dinah, the village priestess on all these solemnities. Suffice it to say that the day had arrived, and the auspicious quilt was spread.

The invitation had not failed to include the Misses Silence and Susan Jones — nay, the good deacon had pressed gallantry into the matter so far as to be the bearer of the message himself; for which he was duly rewarded by a broadside from Miss Silence, giving him what she termed a piece of her mind in the matter of the rights of widows and orphans; to all which the good old man listened with great benignity from the beginning to the end, and replied with, —

"Well, well, Miss Silence, I expect you will think better of this before long; there had best not be any hard words about it." So saying, he took up his hat and walked off, while Miss Silence, who felt extremely relieved by having blown off steam, declared that "it was of no more use to hector old Deacon Enos than to fire a gun at a bag of cotton wool. For all that, though, she shouldn't go to the quilting; nor, more, should Susan."

"But, sister, why not?" said the little maiden; "I think I *shall* go." And Susan said this in a tone so mildly positive that Silence was amazed.

"What upon 'arth ails you, Susan?" said she, opening her eyes with astonishment; "haven't you any more spirit than to go to Deacon Enos's when he is doing all he can to ruin us?"

"I like Deacon Enos," replied Susan; "he was always kind to me when I was a little girl, and I am not going to believe that he is a bad man now."

When a young lady states that she is not going to believe a thing, good judges of human nature generally give up the case; but Miss Silence, to whom the language of opposition and argument was entirely new, could scarcely give her ears credit for veracity in the case; she therefore repeated over exactly what she said before, only in a much louder tone of voice, and with much more vehement forms of asseveration — a mode of reasoning which, if not strictly logical, has at least the sanction of very respectable authorities among the enlightened and learned.

"Silence," replied Susan, when the storm had spent itself,

"if it did not look like being angry with Deacon Enos, I would stay away to oblige you; but it would seem to every one to be taking sides in a quarrel, and I never did, and never will, have any part or lot in such things."

"Then you'll just be trod and trampled on all your days, Susan," replied Silence; "but, however, if *you* choose to make a fool of yourself, *I* don't;" and so saying, she flounced out of the room in great wrath. It so happened, however, that Miss Silence was one of those who have so little economy in disposing of a fit of anger, that it was all used up before the time of execution arrived. It followed of consequence, that, having unburdened her mind freely both to Deacon Enos and to Susan, she began to feel very much more comfortable and good-natured; and consequent upon that came divers reflections upon the many gossiping opportunities and comforts of a quilting; and then the intrusive little reflection, "What if she should go, after all; what harm would be done?" and then the inquiry, "Whether it was not her *duty* to go and look after Susan, poor child, who had no mother to watch over her?" In short, before the time of preparation arrived, Miss Silence had fully worked herself up to the magnanimous determination of going to the quilting. Accordingly, the next day, while Susan was standing before her mirror, braiding up her pretty hair, she was startled by the apparition of Miss Silence coming into the room as stiff as a changeable silk and a high horn comb could make her; and "grimly determined was her look."

"Well, Susan," said she, "if you *will* go to the quilting this afternoon, I think it is *my duty* to go and see to you."

What would people do if this convenient shelter of *duty* did not afford them a retreat in cases when they are disposed to change their minds? Susan suppressed the arch smile that, in spite of herself, laughed out at the corners of her eyes, and told her sister that she was much obliged to her for her care. So off they went together.

Silence in the mean time held forth largely on the importance of standing up for one's rights, and not letting one's self be trampled on.

The afternoon passed on, the elderly ladies quilted and talked scandal, and the younger ones discussed the merits of the various beaux who were expected to give vivacity to the evening entertainment. Among these the newly-arrived Joseph Adams, just from college, with all his literary honors thick about him, became a prominent subject of conversation. It was duly canvassed whether the young gentleman might be called handsome, and the affirmative was carried by a large majority, although there were some variations and exceptions; one of the party declaring his whiskers to be in too high a state of cultivation, another maintaining that they were in the exact line of beauty, while a third vigorously disputed the point whether he wore whiskers at all. It was allowed by all, however, that he had been a great beau in the town where he had passed his college days. It was also inquired into whether he were matrimonially engaged; and the negative being understood, they diverted themselves with predicting to one another the capture of such a prize; each prophecy being received with such disclaimers as "Come now!" "Do be still!" "Hush your nonsense!" and the like.

At length the long-wished-for hour arrived, and one by one the lords of the creation began to make their appearance; and one of the last was this much admired youth.

"That is Joe Adams!" "That is he!" was the busy whisper, as a tall, well-looking young man came into the room, with the easy air of one who had seen several things before, and was not to be abashed by the combined blaze of all the village beauties.

In truth, our friend Joseph had made the most of his residence in N., paying his court no less to the Graces than the Muses. His fine person, his frank, manly air, his ready conversation, and his faculty of universal adaptation had made his society much coveted among the *beau monde* of N.; and though the place was small, he had become familiar with much good society.

We hardly know whether we may venture to tell our fair readers the whole truth in regard to our hero. We will merely hint, in the gentlest manner in the world, that Mr. Joseph Adams, being undeniably first in the classics and first in the drawing room, having been gravely commended in his class by his venerable president, and gayly flattered in the drawing room by the elegant Miss This and Miss That, was rather inclining to the opinion that he was an uncommonly fine fellow, and even had the assurance to think that, under present circumstances, he could please without making any great effort — a thing which, however true it were in point of fact, is obviously improper to be thought of by a young man. Be that as it may, he moved about from one to another, shaking hands with all the old ladies, and listening with the greatest affability to the various comments on his growth and personal appearance, his points of resemblance to his father, mother, grandfather, and grandmother, which are always detected by the superior acumen of elderly females.

Among the younger ones, he at once, and with full frankness, recognized old schoolmates, and partners in various whortleberry, chestnut, and strawberry excursions, and thus called out an abundant flow of conversation. Nevertheless, his eye wandered occasionally around the room, as if in search of something not there. What could it be? It kindled, however, with an expression of sudden brightness as he perceived the tall and spare figure of Miss Silence; whether owing to the personal fascinations of that lady, or to other causes, we leave the reader to determine.

Miss Silence had predetermined never to speak a word again to Uncle Jaw or any of his race; but she was taken by surprise at the frank, extended hand and friendly "how d'ye do?" It was not in woman to resist so cordial an address from a handsome young man, and Miss Silence gave her hand, and replied with a graciousness that amazed herself. At this moment, also, certain soft blue eyes peeped forth from a corner, just "to see if he looked as he used to." Yes, there he was! the same dark, mirthful eyes that used to peer on her from behind the corners of the spelling book at the district school; and Susan Jones gave a deep sigh to those times, and then wondered why she happened to think of such nonsense.

"How is your sister, little Miss Susan?" said Joseph.

"Why, she is here — have you not seen her?" said Silence; "there she is, in that corner."

Joseph looked, but could scarcely recognize her. There stood a tall, slender, blooming girl, that might have been selected as a specimen of that union of perfect health with delicate fairness so characteristic of the young New England beauty.

She was engaged in telling some merry story to a knot of young girls, and the rich color that, like a bright spirit, constantly went and came in her cheeks; the dimples, quick and varying as those of a little brook; the clear, mild eye; the clustering curls, and, above all, the happy, rejoicing smile, and the transparent frankness and simplicity of expression which beamed like sunshine about her, all formed a combination of charms that took our hero quite by surprise; and when Silence, who had a remarkable degree of directness in all her dealings, called out, "Here, Susan, is Joe Adams, inquiring after you!" our practised young gentleman felt himself color to the roots of his hair, and for a moment he could scarce recollect that first rudiment of manners, "to make his bow like a good boy." Susan colored also; but, perceiving the confusion of our hero, her countenance assumed an expression of mischievous drollery, which, helped on by the titter of her companions, added not a little to his confusion.

"Deuse take it!" thought he, "what's the matter with me?" and, calling up his courage, he dashed into the formidable circle of fair ones, and began chattering with one and another, calling by name with or without introduction, remembering things that never happened, with a freedom that was perfectly fascinating.

"Really, how handsome he has grown!" thought Susan; and she colored deeply when once or twice the dark eyes of our hero made the same observation with regard to herself, in that quick, intelligible dialect which eyes alone can speak. And when the little party dispersed, as they did very punctually at nine o'clock, our hero requested of Miss Silence the honor of attending her home—an evidence of discriminating taste which materially raised him in the estimation of that lady. It was true, to be sure, that Susan walked on the other side of him, her little white hand just within his arm; and there was something in that light touch that puzzled him unaccountably, as might be inferred from the frequency with which Miss Silence was obliged to bring up the ends of conversation with, "What did you say?" "What were you going to say?" and other persevering forms of inquiry, with which a regular-trained matter-of-fact talker will hunt down a poor fellow-mortal who is in danger of sinking into a comfortable revery.

When they parted at the gate, however, Silence gave our hero a hearty invitation to "come and see them any time," which he mentally regarded as more to the point than any thing else that had been said.

As Joseph soberly retraced his way homeward, his thoughts, by some unaccountable association, began to revert to such topics as the loneliness of man by himself, the need of kindred spirits, the solaces of sympathy, and other like matters.

That night Joseph dreamed of trotting along with his dinner basket to the old brown school house, and vainly endeavoring to overtake Susan Jones, whom he saw with her little pasteboard sun bonnet a few yards in front of him; then he was *teetering* with her on a long board, her bright little face glancing up and down, while every curl around it seemed to be living with delight; and then he was snowballing Tom Williams for knocking down Susan's doll's house, or he sat by her on a bench, helping her out with a long sum in arithmetic; but, with the mischievous fatality of dreams, the more he ciphered and expounded, the longer and more hopeless grew the sum; and he awoke in the morning pshawing at his ill luck, after having done a sum over half a dozen times, while Susan seemed to be looking on with the same air of arch drollery that he saw on her face the evening before.

"Joseph," said Uncle Jaw, the next morning at breakfast, "I s'pose 'Squire Jones's daughters were not at the quilting."

"Yes, sir, they were," said our hero; "they were both there."

"Why, you don't say so!"

"They certainly were," persisted the son.

"Well, I thought the old gal had too much spunk for that: you see there is a quarrel between the deacon and them gals."

"Indeed!" said Joseph. "I thought the deacon never quarrelled with any body."

"But, you see, old Silence there, she will quarrel with *him*: railly, that cretur is a tough one;" and Uncle Jaw leaned back in his chair, and contemplated the quarrelsome propensities of Miss Silence with the satisfaction of a kindred spirit. "But I'll fix her yet," he continued; "I see how to work it."

"Indeed, father, I did not know that you had any thing to do with their affairs."

"Hain't I? I should like to know if I hain't!" replied Uncle Jaw, triumphantly. "Now, see here, Joseph: you see, I mean you shall be a lawyer: I'm pretty considerable of a lawyer myself — that is, for one not college larnt; and I'll tell you how it is" — and thereupon Uncle Jaw launched forth into the case of the *medder* land and the mill, and concluded with, "Now, Joseph, this 'ere is a kinder whetstone for you to hone up your wits on."

In pursuance, therefore, of this plan of sharpening his wits in the manner aforesaid, our hero, after breakfast, went like a dutiful son, directly towards 'Squire Jones's, doubtless for the purpose of taking ocular survey of the meadow land, mill, and stone wall; but, by some unaccountable mistake, lost his way, and found himself standing before the door of 'Squire Jones's house.

The old squire had been among the aristocracy of the

village, and his house had been the ultimate standard of comparison in all matters of style and garniture. Their big front room, instead of being strewn with lumps of sand, duly streaked over twice a week, was resplendent with a carpet of red, yellow, and black stripes, while a towering pair of long-legged brass andirons, scoured to a silvery white, gave an air of magnificence to the chimney, which was materially increased by the tall brass-headed shovel and tongs, which, like a decorous, starched married couple, stood bolt upright in their places on either side. The sanctity of the place was still further maintained by keeping the window shutters always closed, admitting only so much light as could come in by a round hole at the top of the shutter; and it was only on occasions of extraordinary magnificence that the room was thrown open to profane eyes.

Our hero was surprised, therefore, to find both the doors and windows of this apartment open, and symptoms evident of its being in daily occupation. The furniture still retained its massive, clumsy stiffness, but there were various tokens that lighter fingers had been at work there since the notable days of good Dame Jones. There was a vase of flowers on the table, two or three books of poetry, and a little fairy work-basket, from which peeped forth the edges of some worked ruffling; there was a small writing desk, and last, not least, in a lady's collection, an album, with leaves of every color of the rainbow, containing inscriptions, in sundry strong masculine hands, "To Susan," indicating that other people had had their eyes open as well as Mr. Joseph Adams. "So," said he to himself, "this quiet little beauty has had admirers, after all;" and consequent upon this came another question, (which was none of his concern, to be sure,) whether the little lady were or were not engaged; and from these speculations he was aroused by a light footstep, and anon the neat form of Susan made its appearance.

"Good morning, Miss Jones," said he, bowing.

Now, there is something very comical in the feeling, when little boys and girls, who have always known each other as plain Susan or Joseph, first meet as "Mr." or "Miss" So-and-so. Each one feels half disposed, half afraid, to return to the old familiar form, and awkwardly fettered by the recollection that they are no longer children. Both parties had felt this the evening before, when they met in company; but now that they were alone together, the feeling became still stronger; and when Susan had requested Mr. Adams to take a chair, and Mr. Adams had inquired after Miss Susan's health, there ensued a pause, which, the longer it continued, seemed the more difficult to break, and during which Susan's pretty face slowly assumed an expression of the ludicrous, till she was as near laughing as propriety would admit; and Mr. Adams, having looked out at the window, and up at the mantel-piece, and down at the carpet, at last looked at Susan; their eyes met; the effect was electrical; they both smiled, and then laughed outright, after which the whole difficulty of conversation vanished.

"Susan," said Joseph, "do you remember the old school house?"

"I thought that was what you were thinking of," said Susan; "but, really, you have grown and altered so that I could hardly believe my eyes last night."

"Nor I mine," said Joseph, with a glance that gave a very complimentary turn to the expression.

Our readers may imagine that after this the conversation

proceeded to grow increasingly confidential and interesting; that from the account of early life, each proceeded to let the other know something of intervening history, in the course of which each discovered a number of new and admirable traits in the other, such things being matters of very common occurrence. In the course of the conversation Joseph discovered that it was necessary that Susan should have two or three books then in his possession; and as promptitude is a great matter in such cases, he promised to bring them "to-morrow."

For some time our young friends pursued their acquaintance without a distinct consciousness of any thing except that it was a very pleasant thing to be together. During the long, still afternoons, they rambled among the fading woods, now illuminated with the radiance of the dying year, and sentimentalized and quoted poetry; and almost every evening Joseph found some errand to bring him to the house; a book for Miss Susan, or a bundle of roots and herbs for Miss Silence, or some remarkably fine yarn for her to knit — attentions which retained our hero in the good graces of the latter lady, and gained him the credit of being "a young man that knew how to behave himself." As Susan was a leading member in the village choir, our hero was directly attacked with a violent passion for sacred music, which brought him punctually to the singing school, where the young people came together to sing anthems and fuguing tunes, and to eat apples and chestnuts.

It cannot be supposed that all these things passed unnoticed by those wakeful eyes that are ever upon the motions of such "bright, particular stars;" and as is usual in such cases, many things were known to a certainty which were not yet known to the parties themselves. The young belles and beaux whispered and tittered, and passed the original jokes and witticisms common in such cases, while the old ladies soberly took the matter in hand when they went out with their knitting to make afternoon visits, considering how much money Uncle Jaw had, how much his son would have, and what all together would come to, and whether Joseph would be a "smart man," and Susan a good housekeeper, with all the "ifs, ands, and buts" of married life.

But the most fearful wonders and prognostics crowded around the point "what Uncle Jaw would have to say to the matter." His lawsuit with the sisters being well understood, as there was every reason it should be, it was surmised what two such vigorous belligerents as himself and Miss Silence would say to the prospect of a matrimonial conjunction. It was also reported that Deacon Enos Dudley had a claim to the land which constituted the finest part of Susan's portion, the loss of which would render the consent of Uncle Jaw still more doubtful. But all this while Miss Silence knew nothing of the matter, for her habit of considering and treating Susan as a child seemed to gain strength with time. Susan was always to be seen to, and watched, and instructed, and taught; and Miss Silence could not conceive that one who could not even make pickles, without her to oversee, could think of such a matter as setting up housekeeping on her own account. To be sure, she began to observe an extraordinary change in her sister; remarked that "lately Susan seemed to be getting sort o' crazy-headed;" that she seemed not to have any "faculty" for any thing; that she had made gingerbread twice, and forgot the ginger one time, and put in mustard the other; that she shook the saltcellar out in the tablecloth, and let the cat into the pantry half a dozen times; and that when scolded for these sins of omission or commission, she had a fit of crying, and did a little worse than before. Silence was of opinion that Susan was getting to be "weakly and naarvy," and actually concocted an unmerciful pitcher of wormwood and boneset, which she said was to keep off the "shaking weakness" that was coming over her. In vain poor Susan protested that she was well enough; Miss Silence *knew better;* and one evening she entertained Mr. Joseph Adams with a long statement of the case in all its bearings, and ended with demanding his opinion, as a candid listener, whether the wormwood and boneset sentence should not be executed.

Poor Susan had that very afternoon parted from a knot of young friends who had teased her most unmercifully on the score of attentions received, till she began to think the very leaves and stones were so many eyes to pry into her secret feelings; and then to have the whole case set in order before the very person, too, whom she most dreaded. "Certainly he would think she was acting like a fool; perhaps he did not mean any thing more than friendship, *after all;* and she would not for the world have him suppose that she cared a copper more for him than for any other *friend*, or that she was *in love*, of all things." So she sat very busy with her knitting work, scarcely knowing what she was about, till Silence called out,—

"Why, Susan, what a piece of work you are making of that stocking heel! What in the world are you doing to it?"

Susan dropped her knitting, and making some pettish answer, escaped out of the room.

"Now, did you ever?" said Silence, laying down the seam

she had been cross-stitching; "what *is* the matter with her, Mr. Adams?"

"Miss Susan is certainly indisposed," replied our hero gravely. "I must get her to take your advice, Miss Silence."

Our hero followed Susan to the front door, where she stood looking out at the moon, and begged to know what distressed her.

Of course it was "nothing," the young lady's usual complaint when in low spirits; and to show that she was perfectly easy, she began an unsparing attack on a white rosebush near by.

"Susan!" said Joseph, laying his hand on hers, and in a tone that made her start. She shook back her curls, and looked up to him with such an innocent, confiding face!

Ah, my good reader, you may go on with this part of the story for yourself. We are principled against unveiling the "sacred mysteries," the "thoughts that breathe and words that burn," in such little moonlight interviews as these. You may fancy all that followed; and we can only assure all who are doubtful, that, under judicious management, cases of this kind may be disposed of without wormwood or boneset. Our hero and heroine were called to sublunary realities by the voice of Miss Silence, who came into the passage to see what upon earth they were doing. That lady was satisfied by the representations of so friendly and learned a young man as Joseph that nothing immediately alarming was to be apprehended in the case of Susan; and she retired. From that evening Susan stepped about with a heart many pounds lighter than before.

"I'll tell you what, Joseph," said Uncle Jaw, "I'll tell you what, now: I hear 'em tell that you've took and courted that 'ere Susan Jones. Now, I jest want to know if it's true."

There was an explicitness about this mode of inquiry that took our hero quite by surprise, so that he could only reply, —

"Why, sir, supposing I had, would there be any objection to it in your mind?"

"Don't talk to me," said Uncle Jaw. "I jest want to know if it's true."

Our hero put his hands in his pockets, walked to the window, and whistled.

"'Cause if you have," said Uncle Jaw, "you may jest uncourt as fast as you can; for 'Squire Jones's daughter won't get a single cent of my money, I can tell you that."

"Why, father, Susan Jones is not to blame for any thing that her father did; and I'm sure she is a pretty girl enough."

"I don't care if she is pretty. What's that to me? I've got you through college, Joseph; and a hard time I've had of it, a-delvin' and slavin'; and here you come, and the very first thing you do you must take and court that 'ere 'Squire Jones's daughter, who was always putting himself up above me. Besides, I mean to have the law on that estate yet; and Deacon Dudley, he will have the law, too; and it will cut off the best piece of land the girl has; and when you get married, I mean you shall *have* something. It's jest a trick of them gals at me; but I guess I'll come up with 'em yet. I'm just a-goin' down to have a 'regular hash' with old Silence, to let her know she can't come round me that way."

"Silence," said Susan, drawing her head into the window, and looking apprehensive, "there is Mr. Adams coming here."

"What, Joe Adams? Well, and what if he is?"

"No, no, sister, but it is his father — it is Uncle Jaw."

"Well, s'pose 'tis, child — what scares you? S'pose I'm afraid of him? If he wants more than I gave him last time, I'll put it on." So saying, Miss Silence took her knitting work and marched down into the sitting room, and sat herself bolt upright in an attitude of defiance, while poor Susan, feeling her heart beat unaccountably fast, glided out of the room.

"Well, good morning, Miss Silence," said Uncle Jaw, after having scraped his feet on the scraper, and scrubbed them on the mat nearly ten minutes, in silent deliberation.

"Morning, sir," said Silence, abbreviating the "good."

Uncle Jaw helped himself to a chair directly in front of the enemy, dropped his hat on the floor, and surveyed Miss Silence with a dogged air of satisfaction, like one who is sitting down to a regular, comfortable quarrel, and means to make the most of it.

Miss Silence tossed her head disdainfully, but scorned to commence hostilities.

"So, Miss Silence," said Uncle Jaw, deliberately, "you don't think you'll do any thing about that 'ere matter."

"What matter?" said Silence, with an intonation resembling that of a roasted chestnut when it bursts from the fire.

"I really thought, Miss Silence, in that 'ere talk I had with you about 'Squire Jones's cheatin' about that 'ere ——"

"Mr. Adams," said Silence, "I tell you, to begin with, I'm not a going to be sauced in this 'ere way by you. You hain't got common decency, nor common sense, nor common any thing else, to talk so to me about my father; I won't bear it, I tell you."

"Why, Miss Jones," said Uncle Jaw, "how you talk! Well, to be sure, 'Squire Jones is dead and gone, and it's as well not to call it cheatin', as I was tellin' Deacon Enos when he was talking about that 'ere lot — that 'ere lot, you know, that he sold the deacon, and never let him have the deed on't."

"That's a lie," said Silence, starting on her feet; "that's an up and down black lie! I tell you that, now, before you say another word."

"Miss Silence, railly, you seem to be getting touchy," said Uncle Jaw; "well, to be sure, if the deacon can let that pass, other folks can; and maybe the deacon will, because 'Squire Jones was a church member, and the deacon is 'mazin' tender about bringin' out any thing against professors; but railly, now, Miss Silence, I didn't think you and Susan were going to work it so cunning in this here way."

"I don't know what you mean, and, what's more, I don't care," said Silence, resuming her work, and calling back the bolt-upright dignity with which she began.

There was a pause of some moments, during which the features of Silence worked with suppressed rage, which was contemplated by Uncle Jaw with undisguised satisfaction.

"You see, I s'pose, I shouldn't a minded your Susan's setting out to court up my Joe, if it hadn't a been for them things."

"Courting your son! Mr. Adams, I should like to know what you mean by that. I'm sure nobody wants your son, though he's a civil, likely fellow enough; yet with such an old dragon for a father, I'll warrant he won't get any body to court him, nor be courted by him neither."

"Railly, Miss Silence, you ain't hardly civil, now."

"Civil! I should like to know who *could* be civil. You know, now, as well as I do, that you are saying all this out of

7

clear, sheer ugliness; and that's what you keep a doing all round the neighborhood."

"Miss Silence," said Uncle Jaw, "I don't want no hard words with you. It's pretty much known round the neighborhood that your Susan thinks she'll get my Joe, and I s'pose you was thinking that perhaps it would be the best way of settling up matters; but you see, now, I took and tell'd my son I railly didn't see as I could afford it; I took and tell'd him that young folks must have something considerable to start with; and that, if Susan lost that 'ere piece of ground, as is likely she will, it would be cutting off quite too much of a piece; so, you see, I don't want you to take no encouragement about that."

"Well, I think this is pretty well!" exclaimed Silence, provoked beyond measure or endurance; "you old torment! think I don't know what you're at! I and Susan courting your son? I wonder if you ain't ashamed of yourself, now! I should like to know what I or she have done, now, to get that notion into your head?"

"I didn't s'pose you 'spected to get him yourself," said Uncle Jaw, "for I guess by this time you've pretty much gin up trying, hain't ye? But Susan does, I'm pretty sure."

"Here, Susan! Susan! you — come down!" called Miss Silence, in great wrath, throwing open the chamber door. "Mr. Adams wants to speak with you." Susan, fluttering and agitated, slowly descended into the room, where she stopped, and looked hesitatingly, first at Uncle Jaw and then at her sister, who, without ceremony, proposed the subject matter of the interview as follows: —

"Now, Susan, here's this man pretends to say that you've been a courting and snaring to get his son; and I just want you to tell him that you hain't never had no thought of him, and that you won't have, neither."

This considerate way of announcing the subject had the effect of bringing the burning color into Susan's face, as she stood like a convicted culprit, with her eyes bent on the floor.

Uncle Jaw, savage as he was, was always moved by female loveliness, as wild beasts are said to be mysteriously swayed by music, and looked on the beautiful, downcast face with more softening than Miss Silence, who, provoked that Susan did not immediately respond to the question, seized her by the arm, and eagerly reiterated, —

"Susan! why don't you speak, child?"

Gathering desperate courage, Susan shook off the hand of Silence, and straightened herself up with as much dignity as some little flower lifts up its head when it has been bent down by rain drops.

"Silence," she said, "I never would have come down if I had thought it was to hear such things as this. Mr. Adams, all I have to say to you is, that your son has sought me, and not I your son. If you wish to know any more, he can tell you better than I."

"Well, I vow! she is a pretty gal," said Uncle Jaw, as Susan shut the door.

This exclamation was involuntary; then recollecting himself, he picked up his hat, and saying, "Well, I guess I may as well get along hum," he began to depart; but turning round before he shut the door, he said, "Miss Silence, if you should conclude to do any thing about that 'ere fence, just send word over and let me know."

Silence, without deigning any reply, marched up into Susan's little chamber, where our heroine was treating resolution to a good fit of crying.

"Susan, I did not think you had been such a fool," said the lady. "I do want to know, now, if you've railly been thinking of getting married, and to that Joe Adams of all folks!"

Poor Susan! such an interlude in all her pretty, romantic little dreams about kindred feelings and a hundred other delightful ideas, that flutter like singing birds through the fairy land of first love. Such an interlude! to be called on by gruff human voices to give up all the cherished secrets that she had trembled to whisper even to herself. She felt as if love itself had been defiled by the coarse, rough hands that had been meddling with it; so to her sister's soothing address Susan made no answer, only to cry and sob still more bitterly than before.

Miss Silence, if she had a great stout heart, had no less a kind one, and seeing Susan take the matter so bitterly to heart, she began gradually to subside.

"Susan, you poor little fool, you," said she, at the same time giving her a hearty slap, as expressive of earnest sympathy, "I really do feel for you; that good-for-nothing fellow has been a cheatin' you, I do believe."

"O, don't talk any more about it, for mercy's sake," said Susan; "I am sick of the whole of it."

"That's you, Susan! Glad to hear you say so! I'll stand up for you, Susan; if I catch Joe Adams coming here again with his palavering face, I'll let him know!"

"No, no! Don't, for mercy's sake, say any thing to Mr. Adams — don't!"

"Well, child, don't claw hold of a body so! Well, at any rate, I'll just let Joe Adams know that we hain't nothing more to say to him."

"But I don't wish to say that — that is — I don't know — indeed, sister Silence, don't say any thing about it."

"Why not? You ain't such a *natural*, now, as to want to marry him, after all, hey?"

"I don't know what I want, nor what I don't want; only, Silence, do now, if you love me, do promise not to say any thing at all to Mr. Adams — don't."

"Well, then, I won't," said Silence; "but, Susan, if you railly was in love all this while, why hain't you been and told me? Don't you know that I'm as much as a mother to you, and you ought to have told me in the beginning?"

"I don't know, Silence! I couldn't — I don't want to talk about it."

"Well, Susan, you ain't a bit like me," said Silence — a remark evincing great discrimination, certainly, and with which the conversation terminated.

That very evening our friend Joseph walked down towards the dwelling of the sisters, not without some anxiety for the result, for he knew by his father's satisfied appearance that war had been declared. He walked into the family room, and found nobody there but Miss Silence, who was sitting, grim as an Egyptian sphinx, stitching very vigorously on a meal bag, in which interesting employment she thought proper to be so much engaged as not to remark the entrance of our hero. To Joseph's accustomed "Good evening, Miss Silence," she replied merely by looking up with a cold nod, and went on with her sewing. It appeared that she had determined on a literal version of her promise not to say any thing to Mr. Adams.

Our hero, as we have before stated, was familiar with the crooks and turns of the female mind, and mentally resolved to put a bold face on the matter, and give Miss Silence no encouragement in her attempt to make him feel himself unwelcome. It was rather a frosty autumnal evening, and the fire on the hearth was decaying. Mr. Joseph bustled about most energetically, throwing down the tongs, and shovel, and bellows, while he pulled the fire to pieces, raked out ashes and brands, and then, in a twinkling, was at the woodpile, from whence he selected a massive backlog and forestick, with accompaniments, which were soon roaring and crackling in the chimney.

"There, now, that does look something like comfort," said our hero; and drawing forward the big rocking chair, he seated himself in it, and rubbed his hands with an air of great complacency. Miss Silence looked not up, but stitched so much the faster, so that one might distinctly hear the crack of the needle and the whistle of the thread all over the apartment.

"Have you a headache to-night, Miss Silence?"

"No!" was the gruff answer.

"Are you in a hurry about those bags?" said he, glancing at a pile of unmade ones which lay by her side.

No reply. "Hang it all!" said our hero to himself, "I'll make her speak."

Miss Silence's needle book and brown thread lay on a chair beside her. Our friend helped himself to a needle and thread, and taking one of the bags, planted himself bolt upright opposite to Miss Silence, and pinning his work to his knee, commenced stitching at a rate fully equal to her own.

Miss Silence looked up and fidgeted, but went on with her work faster than before; but the faster she worked, the faster and steadier worked our hero, all in "marvellous silence."

There began to be an odd twitching about the muscles of Miss Silence's face; our hero took no notice, having pursed his features into an expression of unexampled gravity, which only grew more intense as he perceived, by certain uneasy movements, that the adversary was beginning to waver.

As they were sitting, stitching away, their needles whizzing at each other like a couple of locomotives engaged in conversation, Susan opened the door.

The poor child had been crying for the greater part of her spare time during the day, and was in no very merry humor; but the moment that her astonished eyes comprehended the scene, she burst into a fit of almost inextinguishable merriment, while Silence laid down her needle, and looked half amused and half angry. Our hero, however, continued his business with inflexible perseverance, unpinning his work and moving the seam along, and going on with increased velocity.

Poor Miss Silence was at length vanquished, and joined in the loud laugh which seemed to convulse her sister. Whereupon our hero unpinned his work, and folding it up, looked up at her with all the assurance of impudence triumphant, and remarked to Susan, —

"Your sister had such a pile of these pillow cases to make, that she was quite discouraged, and engaged me to do half a dozen of them: when I first came in she was so busy she could not even speak to me."

"Well, if you ain't the beater for impudence!" said Miss Silence.

"The beater for *industry* — so I thought," rejoined our hero.

Susan, who had been in a highly tragical state of mind all

day, and who was meditating on nothing less sublime than an eternal separation from her lover, which she had imagined, with all the affecting attendants and consequents, was entirely revolutionized by the unexpected turn thus given to her ideas, while our hero pursued the opportunity he had made for himself, and exerted his powers of entertainment to the utmost, till Miss Silence, declaring that if she had been washing all day she should not have been more tired than she was with laughing, took up her candle, and good-naturedly left our young people to settle matters between themselves. There was a grave pause of some length when she had departed, which was broken by our hero, who, seating himself by Susan, inquired very seriously if his father had made proposals of marriage to Miss Silence that morning.

"No, you provoking creature!" said Susan, at the same time laughing at the absurdity of the idea.

"Well, now, don't draw on your long face again, Susan," said Joseph; "you have been trying to lengthen it down all the evening, if I would have let you. Seriously, now, I know that something painful passed between my father and you this morning, but I shall not inquire what it was. I only tell you, frankly, that he has expressed his disapprobation of our engagement, forbidden me to go on with it, and ——"

"And, consequently, I release you from all engagements and obligations to me, even before you ask it," said Susan.

"You are extremely accommodating," replied Joseph; "but I cannot promise to be as obliging in giving up certain promises made to me, unless, indeed, the feelings that dictated them should have changed."

"O, no — no, indeed," said Susan, earnestly; "you know it is not that; but if your father objects to me ——"

"If my father objects to you, he is welcome not to marry you," said Joseph.

"Now, Joseph, do be serious," said Susan.

"Well, then, seriously, Susan, I know my obligations to my father, and in all that relates to his comfort I will ever be dutiful and submissive, for I have no college boy pride on the subject of submission; but in a matter so individually my own as the choice of a wife, in a matter that will most likely affect my happiness years and years after he has ceased to be, I hold that I have a right to consult my own inclinations, and, by your leave, my dear little lady, I shall take that liberty."

"But, then, if your father is made angry, you know what sort of a man he is; and how could I stand in the way of all your prospects?"

"Why, my dear Susan, do you think I count myself dependent upon my father, like the heir of an English estate, who has nothing to do but sit still and wait for money to come to him? No! I have energy and education to start with, and if I cannot take care of myself, and you too, then cast me off and welcome;" and, as Joseph spoke, his fine face glowed with a conscious power, which unfettered youth never feels so fully as in America. He paused a moment, and resumed: "Nevertheless, Susan, I respect my father; whatever others may say of him, I shall never forget that I owe to his hard earnings the education that enables me to do or be any thing, and I shall not wantonly or rudely cross him. I do not despair of gaining his consent; my father has a great partiality for pretty girls, and if his love of contradiction is not kept awake by open argument, I will trust to time and you to bring him round; but, whatever comes, rest assured, my dearest one, I have chosen for life, and cannot change."

The conversation, after this, took a turn which may readily be imagined by all who have been in the same situation, and will, therefore, need no further illustration.

"Well, deacon, railly I don't know what to think now: there's my Joe, he's took and been a courting that 'ere Susan," said Uncle Jaw.

This was the introduction to one of Uncle Jaw's periodical visits to Deacon Enos, who was sitting with his usual air of mild abstraction, looking into the coals of a bright November fire, while his busy helpmate was industriously rattling her knitting needles by his side.

A close observer might have suspected that this was *no news* to the good deacon, who had given a great deal of good advice, in private, to Master Joseph of late; but he only relaxed his features into a quiet smile, and ejaculated, "I want to know!"

"Yes; and railly, deacon, that 'ere gal is a rail pretty un. I was a tellin' my folks that our new minister's wife was a fool to her."

"And so your son is going to marry her?" said the good lady; "I knew that long ago."

"Well — no — not so fast; ye see there's two to that bargain yet. You see, Joe, he never said a word to me, but took and courted the gal out of his own head; and when I come to know, says I, 'Joe,' says I, 'that 'ere gal won't do for me;' and I took and tell'd him, then, about that 'ere old fence, and all about that old mill, and them *medders* of mine; and I tell'd him, too, about that 'ere lot of Susan's; and I should like to know, now, deacon, how that lot business is a going to turn out."

"Judge Smith and 'Squire Moseley say that my claim to it will stand," said the deacon.

"They do?" said Uncle Jaw, with much satisfaction; "s'pose, then, you'll sue, won't you?"

"I don't know," replied the deacon, meditatively.

Uncle Jaw was thoroughly amazed; that any one should have doubts about entering suit for a fine piece of land, when sure of obtaining it, was a problem quite beyond his powers of solving.

"You say your son has courted the girl," said the deacon, after a long pause; "that strip of land is the best part of Susan's share; I paid down five hundred dollars on the nail for it; I've got papers here that Judge Smith and 'Squire Moseley say will stand good in any court of law."

Uncle Jaw pricked up his ears and was all attention, eying with eager looks the packet; but, to his disappointment, the deacon deliberately laid it into his desk, shut and locked it, and resumed his seat.

"Now, railly," said Uncle Jaw, "I should like to know the particulars."

"Well, well," said the deacon, "the lawyers will be at my house to-morrow evening, and if you have any concern about it, you may as well come along."

Uncle Jaw wondered all the way home at what he could have done to get himself into the confidence of the old deacon, who, he rejoiced to think, was a going to "take" and go to law like other folks.

The next day there was an appearance of some bustle and preparation about the deacon's house; the best room was opened and aired; an ovenful of cake was baked; and our friend Joseph, with a face full of business, was seen passing to and fro, in and out of the house, from various closetings with the deacon. The deacon's lady bustled about the house with an air of wonderful mystery, and even gave her directions about eggs and raisins in a whisper, lest they should possibly let out some eventful secret.

The afternoon of that day Joseph appeared at the house of the sisters, stating that there was to be company at the deacon's that evening, and he was sent to invite them.

"Why, what's got into the deacon's folks lately," said Silence, "to have company so often? Joe Adams, this 'ere is some 'cut up' of yours. Come, what are you up to now?"

"Come, come, dress yourselves and get ready," said Joseph; and, stepping up to Susan, as she was following Silence out of the room, he whispered something into her ear, at which she stopped short and colored violently.

"Why, Joseph, what do you mean?"

"It is so," said he.

"No, no, Joseph; no, I can't, indeed I can't."

"But you *can*, Susan."

"O Joseph, don't."

"O Susan, *do*."

"Why, how strange, Joseph!"

"Come, come, my dear, you keep me waiting. If you have any objections on the score of propriety, we will talk about them *to-morrow;*" and our hero looked so saucy and so resolute that there was no disputing further; so, after a little more lingering and blushing on Susan's part, and a few kisses and persuasions on the part of the suitor, Miss Susan seemed to be brought to a state of resignation.

At a table in the middle of Uncle Enos's north front room were seated the two lawyers, whose legal opinion was that evening to be fully made up. The younger of these, 'Squire Moseley, was a rosy, portly, laughing little bachelor, who boasted that he had offered himself, in rotation, to every pretty girl within twenty miles round, and, among others, to Susan Jones, notwithstanding which he still remained a bachelor, with a fair prospect of being an old one; but none of these things disturbed the boundless flow of good nature and complacency with which he seemed at all times full to overflowing. On the present occasion he appeared to be particularly in his element, as if he had some law business in hand remarkably suited to his turn of mind; for, on finishing the inspection of the papers, he started up, slapped his graver brother on the back, made two or three flourishes round the room, and then seizing the old deacon's hand, shook it violently, exclaiming, —

"All's right, deacon, all's right! Go it! go it! hurrah!"

When Uncle Jaw entered, the deacon, without preface, handed him a chair and the papers, saying, —

"These papers are what you wanted to see. I just wish you would read them over."

Uncle Jaw read them deliberately over. "Didn't I tell ye so, deacon? The case is as clear as a bell: now ye will go to law, won't you?"

"Look here, Mr. Adams; now you have seen these papers, and heard what's to be said, I'll make you an offer. Let your son marry Susan Jones, and I'll burn these papers and say no more about it, and there won't be a girl in the parish with a finer portion."

Uncle Jaw opened his eyes with amazement, and looked at the old man, his mouth gradually expanding wider and wider, as if he hoped, in time, to swallow the idea.

"Well, now, I swan!" at length he ejaculated.

"I mean just as I say," said the deacon.

"Why, that's the same as giving the gal five hundred dollars out of your own pocket, and she ain't no relation neither."

"I know it," said the deacon; "but I have said I will do it."

"What upon 'arth for?" said Uncle Jaw.

"To make peace," said the deacon, "and to let you know that when I say it is better to give up one's rights than to quarrel, I mean so. I am an old man; my children are dead" — his voice faltered — "my treasures are laid up in heaven; if I can make the children happy, why, I will. When I thought I had lost the land, I made up my mind to lose it, and so I can now."

Uncle Jaw looked fixedly on the old deacon, and said, —

"Well, deacon, I believe you. I vow, if you hain't got something ahead in t'other world, I'd like to know who has — that's all; so, if Joe has no objections, and I rather guess he won't have ——"

"The short of the matter is," said the squire, "we'll have a wedding; so come on;" and with that he threw open the parlor door, where stood Susan and Joseph in a recess by the window, while Silence and the Rev. Mr. Bissel were drawn up by the fire, and the deacon's lady was sweeping up the hearth, as she had been doing ever since the party arrived.

Instantly Joseph took the hand of Susan, and led her to the middle of the room; the merry squire seized the hand of Miss Silence, and placed her as bridesmaid, and before any one knew what they were about, the ceremony was in actual progress, and the minister, having been previously instructed, made the two one with extraordinary celerity.

"What! what! what!" said Uncle Jaw. "Joseph! Deacon!"

"Fair bargain, sir," said the squire. "Hand over your papers, deacon."

The deacon handed them, and the squire, having read them aloud, proceeded, with much ceremony, to throw them into the fire; after which, in a mock solemn oration, he gave a statement of the whole affair, and concluded with a grave exhortation to the new couple on the duties of wedlock, which unbent the risibles even of the minister himself.

Uncle Jaw looked at his pretty daughter-in-law, who stood half smiling, half blushing, receiving the congratulations of the party, and then at Miss Silence, who appeared full as much taken by surprise as himself.

"Well, well, Miss Silence, these 'ere young folks have come round us slick enough," said he. "I don't see but we must shake hands upon it." And the warlike powers shook hands accordingly, which was a signal for general merriment.

As the company were dispersing, Miss Silence laid hold of the good deacon, and by main strength dragged him aside. "Deacon," said she, "I take back all that 'ere I said about you, every word on't."

"Don't say any more about it, Miss Silence," said the good man; "it's gone by, and let it go."

"Joseph!" said his father, the next morning, as he was sitting at breakfast with Joseph and Susan, "I calculate I shall feel kinder proud of this 'ere gal! and I'll tell you what, I'll jest give you that nice little delicate Stanton place that I took on Stanton's mortgage: it's a nice little place, with green blinds, and flowers, and all them things, just right for Susan."

And accordingly, many happy years flew over the heads of the young couple in the Stanton place, long after the hoary hairs of their kind benefactor, the deacon, were laid with reverence in the dust. Uncle Jaw was so far wrought upon by the magnanimity of the good old man as to be very materially changed for the better. Instead of quarrelling in real earnest all around the neighborhood, he confined himself merely to battling the opposite side of every question with his son, which, as the latter was somewhat of a logician, afforded a pretty good field for the exercise of his powers; and he was heard to declare at the funeral of the old deacon, that, "after all, a man got as much, and may be more, to go along as the deacon did, than to be all the time fisting and jawing; though I tell you what it is," said he, afterwards, "'tain't every one that has the deacon's *faculty*, any how."

THE TEA ROSE.

THERE it stood, in its little green vase, on a light ebony stand, in the window of the drawing room. The rich satin curtains, with their costly fringes, swept down on either side of it, and around it glittered every rare and fanciful trifle which wealth can offer to luxury; and yet that simple rose was the fairest of them all. So pure it looked, its white leaves just touched with that delicious creamy tint peculiar to its kind; its cup so full, so perfect; its head bending as if it were sinking and melting away in its own richness — O, when did ever man make any thing to equal the living, perfect flower?

But the sunlight that streamed through the window revealed something fairer than the rose. Reclined on an ottoman, in a deep recess, and intently engaged with a book, rested what seemed the counterpart of that so lovely flower. That cheek so pale, that fair forehead so spiritual, that countenance so full of high thought, those long, downcast lashes, and the expression of the beautiful mouth, sorrowful, yet subdued and sweet — it seemed like the picture of a dream.

"Florence! Florence!" echoed a merry and musical voice, in a sweet, impatient tone. Turn your head, reader, and you will see a light and sparkling maiden, the very model of some little wilful elf, born of mischief and motion, with a dancing eye, a foot that scarcely seems to touch the carpet, and a smile so multiplied by dimples that it seems like a thousand smiles at once. "Come, Florence, I say," said the little sprite, "put down that wise, good, and excellent volume, and descend from your cloud, and talk with a poor little mortal."

The fair apparition, thus adjured, obeyed; and, looking up, revealed just such eyes as you expected to see beneath such lids — eyes deep, pathetic, and rich as a strain of sad music.

"I say, cousin," said the "bright ladye," "I have been thinking what you are to do with your pet rose when you go to New York, as, to our consternation, you are determined to do; you know it would be a sad pity to leave it with such a scatterbrain as I am. I do love flowers, that is a fact; that is, I like a regular bouquet, cut off and tied up, to carry to a party; but as to all this tending and fussing, which is needful to keep them growing, I have no gifts in that line."

"Make yourself easy as to that, Kate," said Florence, with a smile; "I have no intention of calling upon your talents; I have an asylum in view for my favorite."

"O, then you know just what I was going to say. Mrs. Marshall, I presume, has been speaking to you; she was here yesterday, and I was quite pathetic upon the subject, telling her the loss your favorite would sustain, and so forth; and she said how delighted she would be to have it in her greenhouse, it is in such a fine state now, so full of buds. I told her I knew you would like to give it to her, you are so fond of Mrs. Marshall, you know."

"Now, Kate, I am sorry, but I have otherwise engaged it."

"Whom can it be to? you have so few intimates here."

"O, it is only one of my odd fancies."

"But do tell me, Florence."

"Well, cousin, you know the little pale girl to whom we give sewing."

"What! little Mary Stephens? How absurd! Florence, this is just another of your motherly, oldmaidish ways — dressing dolls for poor children, making bonnets and knitting socks for all the little dirty babies in the region round about. I do believe you have made more calls in those two vile, ill-smelling alleys back of our house, than ever you have in Chestnut Street, though you know every body is half dying to see you; and now, to crown all, you must give this choice little bijou to a seamstress girl, when one of your most intimate friends, in your own class, would value it so highly. What in the world can people in their circumstances want of flowers?"

"Just the same as I do," replied Florence, calmly. "Have you not noticed that the little girl never comes here without looking wistfully at the opening buds? And don't you remember, the other morning, she asked me so prettily if I would let her mother come and see it, she was so fond of flowers?"

"But, Florence, only think of this rare flower standing on a table with ham, eggs, cheese, and flour, and stifled in that close little room where Mrs. Stephens and her daughter manage to wash, iron, cook, and nobody knows what besides."

"Well, Kate, and if I were obliged to live in one coarse room, and wash, and iron, and cook, as you say, — if I had to spend every moment of my time in toil, with no prospect from my window but a brick wall and dirty lane, — such a flower as this would be untold enjoyment to me."

"Pshaw! Florence — all sentiment: poor people have no

time to be sentimental. Besides, I don't believe it will grow with them; it is a greenhouse flower, and used to delicate living."

"O, as to that, a flower never inquires whether its owner is rich or poor; and Mrs. Stephens, whatever else she has not, has sunshine of as good quality as this that streams through our window. The beautiful things that God makes are his gift to all alike. You will see that my fair rose will be as well and cheerful in Mrs. Stephens's room as in ours."

"Well, after all, how odd! When one gives to poor people, one wants to give them something *useful* — a bushel of potatoes, a ham, and such things."

"Why, certainly, potatoes and ham must be supplied; but, having ministered to the first and most craving wants, why not add any other little pleasures or gratifications we may have it in our power to bestow? I know there are many of the poor who have fine feeling and a keen sense of the beautiful, which rusts out and dies because they are too hard pressed to procure it any gratification. Poor Mrs. Stephens, for example: I know she would enjoy birds, and flowers, and music, as much as I do. I have seen her eye light up as she looked on these things in our drawing room, and yet not one beautiful thing can she command. From necessity, her room, her clothing, all she has, must be coarse and plain. You should have seen the almost rapture she and Mary felt when I offered them my rose."

"Dear me! all this may be true, but I never thought of it before. I never thought that these hard-working people had any ideas of *taste!*"

"Then why do you see the geranium or rose so carefully nursed in the old cracked teapot in the poorest room, or the morning glory planted in a box and twined about the window? Do not these show that the human heart yearns for the beautiful in all ranks of life? You remember, Kate, how our washerwoman sat up a whole night, after a hard day's work, to make her first baby a pretty dress to be baptized in."

"Yes, and I remember how I laughed at you for making such a tasteful little cap for it."

"Well, Katy, I think the look of perfect delight with which the poor mother regarded her baby in its new dress and cap was something quite worth creating: I do believe she could not have felt more grateful if I had sent her a barrel of flour."

"Well, I never thought before of giving any thing to the poor but what they really needed, and I have always been willing to do that when I could without going far out of my way."

"Well, cousin, if our heavenly Father gave to us after this mode, we should have only coarse, shapeless piles of provisions lying about the world, instead of all this beautiful variety of trees, and fruits, and flowers."

"Well, well, cousin, I suppose you are right — but have mercy on my poor head; it is too small to hold so many new ideas all at once — so go on your own way." And the little lady began practising a waltzing step before the glass with great satisfaction.

It was a very small room, lighted by only one window. There was no carpet on the floor; there was a clean, but coarsely-covered bed in one corner; a cupboard, with a few dishes and plates, in the other; a chest of drawers; and before the window stood a small cherry stand, quite new, and, indeed, it was the only article in the room that seemed so.

A pale, sickly-looking woman of about forty was leaning back in her rocking chair, her eyes closed and her lips compressed as if in pain. She rocked backward and forward a few minutes, pressed her hand hard upon her eyes, and then languidly resumed her fine stitching, on which she had been busy since morning. The door opened, and a slender little girl of about twelve years of age entered, her large blue eyes dilated and radiant with delight as she bore in the vase with the rose tree in it.

"O, see, mother, see! Here is one in full bloom, and two more half out, and ever so many more pretty buds peeping out of the green leaves."

The poor woman's face brightened as she looked, first on the rose and then on her sickly child, on whose face she had not seen so bright a color for months.

"God bless her!" she exclaimed, unconsciously.

"Miss Florence — yes, I knew you would feel so, mother. Does it not make your head feel better to see such a beautiful flower? Now, you will not look so longingly at the flowers in the market, for we have a rose that is handsomer than any of them. Why, it seems to me it is worth as much to us as our whole little garden used to be. Only see how many buds there are! Just count them, and only smell the flower! Now, where shall we set it up?" And Mary skipped about, placing her flower first in one position and then in another, and walking off to see the effect, till her mother gently reminded her that the rose tree could not preserve its beauty without sunlight.

"O, yes, truly," said Mary; "well, then, it must stand here

on our new stand. How glad I am that we have such a handsome new stand for it! it will look so much better." And Mrs. Stephens laid down her work, and folded a piece of newspaper, on which the treasure was duly deposited.

"There," said Mary, watching the arrangement eagerly, "that will do — no, for it does not show both the opening buds; a little farther around — a little more; there, that is right;" and then Mary walked around to view the rose in various positions, after which she urged her mother to go with her to the outside, and see how it looked there. "How kind it was in Miss Florence to think of giving this to us!" said Mary; "though she had done so much for us, and given us so many things, yet this seems the best of all, because it seems as if she thought of us, and knew just how we felt; and so few do that, you know, mother."

What a bright afternoon that little gift made in that little room! How much faster Mary's fingers flew the livelong day as she sat sewing by her mother! and Mrs. Stephens, in the happiness of her child, almost forgot that she had a headache, and thought, as she sipped her evening cup of tea, that she felt stronger than she had done for some time.

That rose! its sweet influence died not with the first day. Through all the long, cold winter, the watching, tending, cherishing that flower awakened a thousand pleasant trains of thought, that beguiled the sameness and weariness of their life. Every day the fair, growing thing put forth some fresh beauty — a leaf, a bud, a new shoot, and constantly awakened fresh enjoyment in its possessors. As it stood in the window, the passer by would sometimes stop and gaze, attracted by its beauty, and then proud and happy was Mary; nor did even the serious and care-worn widow notice with indifference this tribute to the beauty of their favorite.

But little did Florence think, when she bestowed the gift, that there twined about it an invisible thread that reached far and brightly into the web of her destiny.

One cold afternoon in early spring, a tall and graceful gentleman called at the lowly room to pay for the making of some linen by the inmates. He was a stranger and wayfarer, recommended through the charity of some of Mrs. Stephens's patrons. As he turned to go, his eye rested admiringly on the rose tree; and he stopped to gaze at it.

"How beautiful!" said he.

"Yes," said little Mary; "and it was given to us by a lady as sweet and beautiful as that is."

"Ah," said the stranger, turning upon her a pair of bright dark eyes, pleased and rather struck by the communication; "and how came she to give it to you, my little girl?"

"O, because we are poor, and mother is sick, and we never can have any thing pretty. We used to have a garden once; and we loved flowers so much, and Miss Florence found it out, and so she gave us this."

"Florence!" echoed the stranger.

"Yes, Miss Florence L'Estrange — a beautiful lady. They say she was from foreign parts; but she speaks English just like other ladies, only sweeter."

"Is she here now? is she in this city?" said the gentleman, eagerly.

"No; she left some months ago," said the widow, noticing the shade of disappointment on his face. "But," said she, "you can find out all about her at her aunt's, Mrs. Carlysle's, No. 10 —— Street."

A short time after Florence received a letter in a handwriting that made her tremble. During the many early years of her life spent in France she had well learned to know that writing — had loved as a woman like her loves only once; but there had been obstacles of parents and friends, long separation, long suspense, till, after anxious years, she had believed the ocean had closed over that hand and heart; and it was this that had touched with such pensive sorrow the lines in her lovely face.

But this letter told that he was living — that he had traced her, even as a hidden streamlet may be traced, by the freshness, the verdure of heart, which her deeds of kindness had left wherever she had passed. Thus much said, our readers need no help in finishing my story for themselves.

TRIALS OF A HOUSEKEEPER.

I HAVE a detail of very homely grievances to present; but such as they are, many a heart will feel them to be heavy — *the trials of a housekeeper.*

"Poh!" says one of the lords of creation, taking his cigar out of his mouth, and twirling it between his two first fingers, "what a fuss these women do make of this simple matter of *managing a family!* I can't see for my life as there is any thing so extraordinary to be done in this matter of housekeeping: only three meals a day to be got and cleared off — and it really seems to take up the whole of their mind from morning till night. *I* could keep house without so much of a flurry, I know."

Now, prithee, good brother, listen to my story, and see how much you know about it. I came to this enlightened West about a year since, and was duly established in a comfortable country residence within a mile and a half of the city, and there commenced the enjoyment of domestic felicity. I had been married about three months, and had been previously *in love* in the most approved romantic way, with all the proprieties of moonlight walks, serenades, sentimental billets doux, and everlasting attachment.

After having been allowed, as I said, about three months to get over this sort of thing, and to prepare for realities, I was located for life as aforesaid. My family consisted of myself and husband, a female friend as a visitor, and two brothers of my good man, who were engaged with him in business.

I pass over the two or three first days, spent in that process of hammering boxes, breaking crockery, knocking things down and picking them up again, which is commonly called getting to housekeeping. As usual, carpets were sewed and stretched, laid down, and taken up to be sewed over; things were formed, and *re*formed, *trans*formed, and *con*formed, till at last a settled order began to appear. But now came up the great point of all. During our confusion we had cooked and eaten our meals in a very miscellaneous and pastoral manner, eating now from the top of a barrel and now from a fireboard laid on two chairs, and drinking, some from teacups, and some from saucers, and some from tumblers, and some from a pitcher big enough to be drowned in, and sleeping, some on sofas, and some on straggling beds and mattresses thrown down here and there wherever there was room. All these pleasant barbarities were now at an end. The house was in order, the dishes put up in their places; three regular meals were to be administered in one day, all in an orderly, civilized form; beds were to be made, rooms swept and dusted, dishes washed, knives scoured, and all the et cetera to be attended to. Now for getting "*help*," as Mrs. Trollope says; and where and how were we to get it? We knew very few persons in the city; and how were we to accomplish the matter? At length the "house of employment" was mentioned; and my husband was despatched thither regularly every day for a week, while I, in the mean time, was very nearly *despatched* by the abundance of work at home. At length, one evening, as I was sitting completely exhausted, thinking of resorting to the last feminine expedient for supporting life, viz., a good fit of crying, my husband made his appearance, with a most triumphant air, at the door. "There, Margaret, I have got you a couple at last — cook and chambermaid." So saying, he flourished open the door, and gave to my view the picture of a little, dry, snuffy-looking old woman, and a great, staring Dutch girl, in a green bonnet with red ribbons, with mouth wide open, and hands and feet that would have made a Greek sculptor open *his* mouth too. I addressed forthwith a few words of encouragement to each of this cultivated-looking couple, and proceeded to ask their names; and forthwith the old woman began to snuffle and to wipe her face with what was left of an old silk pocket handkerchief preparatory to speaking, while the young lady opened her mouth wider, and looked around with a frightened air, as if meditating an escape. After some preliminaries, however, I found out that my old woman was Mrs. Tibbins, and my Hebe's name was *Kotterin;* also, that she knew much more Dutch than English, and not any too much of either. The old lady was the cook. I ventured a few inquiries. "Had she ever cooked?"

"Yes, ma'am, sartain; she had lived at two or three places in the city."

"I suspect, my dear," said my husband confidently, "that she is an experienced cook, and so your troubles are over;" and he went to reading his newspaper. I said no more, but determined to wait till morning. The breakfast, to be sure, did not do much honor to the talents of my official; but it was the first time, and the place was new to her. After breakfast was cleared away I proceeded to give directions for dinner;

it was merely a plain joint of meat, I said, to be roasted in the tin oven. The *experienced cook* looked at me with a stare of entire vacuity. "The tin oven," I repeated, "stands there," pointing to it.

She walked up to it, and touched it with such an appearance of suspicion as if it had been an electrical battery, and then looked round at me with a look of such helpless ignorance that my soul was moved. "I never see one of them things before," said she.

"Never saw a tin oven!" I exclaimed. "I thought you said you had cooked in two or three families."

"They does not have such things as them, though," rejoined my old lady. Nothing was to be done, of course, but to instruct her into the philosophy of the case; and having spitted the joint, and given numberless directions, I walked off to my room to superintend the operations of Kotterin, to whom I had committed the making of my bed and the sweeping of my room, it never having come into my head that there *could be* a wrong way of making a bed; and to this day it is a marvel to me how any one could arrange pillows and quilts to make such a nondescript appearance as mine now presented. One glance showed me that Kotterin also was "*just caught*," and that I had as much to do in her department as in that of my old lady.

Just then the door bell rang. "O, there is the door bell," I exclaimed. "Run, Kotterin, and show them into the parlor."

Kotterin started to run, as directed, and then stopped, and stood looking round on all the doors and on me with a wofully puzzled air. "The street door," said I, pointing towards the entry. Kotterin blundered into the entry, and stood gazing

9 *

with a look of stupid wonder at the bell ringing without hands, while I went to the door and let in the company before she could be fairly made to understand the connection between the ringing and the phenomenon of admission.

As dinner time approached, I sent word into my kitchen to have it set on; but, recollecting the state of the heads of department there, I soon followed my own orders. I found the tin oven standing out in the middle of the kitchen, and my cook seated *à la Turc* in front of it, contemplating the roast meat with full as puzzled an air as in the morning. I once more explained the mystery of taking it off, and assisted her to get it on to the platter, though somewhat cooled by having been so long set out for inspection. I was standing holding the spit in my hands, when Kotterin, who had heard the door bell ring, and was determined this time to be in season, ran into the hall, and soon returning, opened the kitchen door, and politely ushered in three or four fashionable looking ladies, exclaiming, "Here she is." As these were strangers from the city, who had come to make their first call, this introduction was far from proving an eligible one — the look of thunderstruck astonishment with which I greeted their first appearance, as I stood brandishing the spit, and the terrified snuffling and staring of poor Mrs. Tibbins, who again had recourse to her old pocket handkerchief, almost entirely vanquished their gravity, and it was evident that they were on the point of a broad laugh; so, recovering my self-possession, I apologized, and led the way to the parlor.

Let these few incidents be a specimen of the four mortal weeks that I spent with these "*helps*," during which time I did almost as much work, with twice as much anxiety, as when there was nobody there; and yet every thing went wrong besides. The young gentlemen complained of the patches of starch grimed to their collars, and the streaks of black coal ironed into their dickies, while one week every pocket handkerchief in the house was starched so stiff that you might as well have carried an earthen plate in your pocket; the tumblers looked muddy; the plates were never washed clean or wiped dry unless I attended to each one; and as to eating and drinking, we experienced a variety that we had not before considered possible.

At length the old woman vanished from the stage, and was succeeded by a knowing, active, capable damsel, with a temper like a steel-trap, who remained with me just one week, and then went off in a fit of spite. To her succeeded a rosy, good-natured, merry lass, who broke the crockery, burned the dinner, tore the clothes in ironing, and knocked down every thing that stood in her way about the house, without at all discomposing herself about the matter. One night she took the stopper from a barrel of molasses, and came singing off up stairs, while the molasses ran soberly out into the cellar bottom all night, till by morning it was in a state of universal emancipation. Having done this, and also despatched an entire set of tea things by letting the waiter fall, she one day made her disappearance.

Then, for a wonder, there fell to my lot a tidy, efficient-trained English girl; pretty, and genteel, and neat, and knowing how to do every thing, and with the sweetest temper in the world. "Now," said I to myself, "I shall *rest* from my labors." Every thing about the house began to go right, and looked as clean and genteel as Mary's own pretty self. But, alas! this period of repose was interrupted by the vision of a clever, trim-looking young man, who for some weeks could be heard scraping his boots at the kitchen door every Sunday night; and at last Miss Mary, with some smiling and blushing, gave me to understand that she must leave in two weeks.

"Why, Mary," said I, feeling a little mischievous, "don't you like the place?"

"O, yes, ma'am."

"Then why do you look for another?"

"I am not going to another place."

"What, Mary, are you going to learn a trade?"

"No, ma'am."

"Why, then, what do you mean to do?"

"I expect to keep house *myself*, ma'am," said she, laughing and blushing.

"O ho!" said I, "that is it;" and so, in two weeks, I lost the best little girl in the world: peace to her memory.

After this came an interregnum, which put me in mind of the chapter in Chronicles that I used to read with great delight when a child, where Basha, and Elah, and Tibni, and Zimri, and Omri, one after the other, came on to the throne of Israel, all in the compass of half a dozen verses. We had one old woman, who staid a week, and went away with the misery in her tooth; one *young* woman, who ran away and got married; one cook, who came at night and went off before light in the morning; one very clever girl, who staid a month, and then went away because her mother was sick; another, who staid six weeks, and was taken with the fever herself; and during all this time, who can speak the damage and destruction wrought in the domestic paraphernalia by passing through these multiplied hands?

What shall we do? Shall we give up houses, have no furniture to take care of, keep merely a bag of meal, a porridge pot, and a pudding stick, and sit in our tent door in real patriarchal independence? What shall we do?

LITTLE EDWARD.

WERE any of you born in New England, in the good old catechizing, church-going, school-going, orderly times? If so, you may have seen my Uncle Abel; the most perpendicular, rectangular, upright, downright good man that ever labored six days and rested on the seventh.

You remember his hard, weather-beaten countenance, where every line seemed drawn with "a pen of iron and the point of a diamond;" his considerate gray eyes, that moved over objects as if it were not best to be in a hurry about seeing; the circumspect opening and shutting of the mouth; his down-sitting and up-rising, all performed with conviction aforethought — in short, the whole ordering of his life and conversation, which was, according to the tenor of the military order, "to the right about face — forward, march!"

Now, if you supposed, from all this triangularism of exterior, that this good man had nothing kindly within, you were much mistaken. You often find the greenest grass under a snowdrift; and though my uncle's mind was not exactly of the flower garden kind, still there was an abundance of wholesome and kindly vegetation there.

It is true, he seldom laughed, and never joked himself; but

no man had a more serious and weighty conviction of what a good joke was in another; and when some exceeding witticism was dispensed in his presence, you might see Uncle Abel's face slowly relax into an expression of solemn satisfaction, and he would look at the author with a sort of quiet wonder, as if it was past his comprehension how such a thing could ever come into a man's head.

Uncle Abel, too, had some relish for the fine arts; in proof of which, I might adduce the pleasure with which he gazed at the plates in his family Bible, the likeness whereof is neither in heaven, nor on earth, nor under the earth. And he was also such an eminent musician, that he could go through the singing book at one sitting without the least fatigue, beating time like a windmill all the way.

He had, too, a liberal hand, though his liberality was all by the rule of three. He did by his neighbor exactly as he would be done by; he loved some things in this world very sincerely: he loved his God much, but he honored and feared him more; he was exact with others, he was more exact with himself, and he expected his God to be more exact still.

Every thing in Uncle Abel's house was in the same time, place, manner, and form, from year's end to year's end. There was old Master Bose, a dog after my uncle's own heart, who always walked as if he was studying the multiplication table. There was the old clock, forever ticking in the kitchen corner, with a picture on its face of the sun, forever setting behind a perpendicular row of poplar trees. There was the never-failing supply of red peppers and onions hanging over the chimney. There, too, were the yearly hollyhocks and morning-glories blooming about the windows. There was the "best room," with its sanded floor, the cupboard in one corner with its glass doors, the ever green asparagus bushes in the chimney, and there was the stand with the Bible and almanac on it in another corner. There, too, was Aunt Betsey, who never looked any older, because she always looked as old as she could; who always dried her catnip and wormwood the last of September, and began to clean house the first of May. In short, this was the land of continuance. Old Time never took it into his head to practise either addition, or subtraction, or multiplication on its sum total.

This Aunt Betsey aforenamed was the neatest and most efficient piece of human machinery that ever operated in forty places at once. She was always every where, predominating over and seeing to every thing; and though my uncle had been twice married, Aunt Betsey's rule and authority had never been broken. She reigned over his wives when living, and reigned after them when dead, and so seemed likely to reign on to the end of the chapter. But my uncle's latest wife left Aunt Betsey a much less tractable subject than ever before had fallen to her lot. Little Edward was the child of my uncle's old age, and a brighter, merrier little blossom never grew on the verge of an avalanche. He had been committed to the nursing of his grandmamma till he had arrived at the age of *in*discretion, and then my old uncle's heart so yearned for him that he was sent for home.

His introduction into the family excited a terrible sensation. Never was there such a contemner of dignities, such a violator of high places and sanctities, as this very Master Edward. It was all in vain to try to teach him decorum. He was the most outrageously merry elf that ever shook a head of curls; and it was all the same to him whether it was "*Sabba' day*" or any other day. He laughed and frolicked with every body and every thing that came in his way, not even excepting his solemn old father; and when you saw him, with his fair arms around the old man's neck, and his bright blue eyes and blooming cheek peering out beside the bleak face of Uncle Abel, you might fancy you saw spring caressing winter. Uncle Abel's metaphysics were sorely puzzled by this sparkling, dancing compound of spirit and matter; nor could he devise any method of bringing it into any reasonable shape, for he did mischief with an energy and perseverance that was truly astonishing. Once he scoured the floor with Aunt Betsey's very Scotch snuff; once he washed up the hearth with Uncle Abel's most immaculate clothes brush; and once he was found trying to make Bose wear his father's spectacles. In short, there was no use, except the right one, to which he did not put every thing that came in his way.

But Uncle Abel was most of all puzzled to know what to do with him on the Sabbath, for on that day Master Edward seemed to exert himself to be particularly diligent and entertaining.

"Edward! Edward must not play Sunday!" his father would call out; and then Edward would hold up his curly head, and look as grave as the catechism; but in three minutes you would see "pussy" scampering through the "best room," with Edward at her heels, to the entire discomposure of all devotion in Aunt Betsey and all others in authority.

At length my uncle came to the conclusion that "it wasn't in natur' to teach him any better," and that "he could no more keep Sunday than the brook down in the lot." My poor uncle! he did not know what was the matter with his heart, but certain it was, he lost all faculty of scolding when little Edward was in the case, and he would rub his spectacles a quarter of an hour longer than common when Aunt Betsey was detailing his witticisms and clever doings.

In process of time our hero had compassed his third year, and arrived at the dignity of going to school. He went illustriously through the spelling book, and then attacked the catechism; went from "man's chief end" to the "requirin's and forbiddin's" in a fortnight, and at last came home inordinately merry, to tell his father that he had got to "Amen." After this, he made a regular business of saying over the whole every Sunday evening, standing with his hands folded in front and his checked apron folded down, occasionally glancing round to see if pussy gave proper attention. And, being of a practically benevolent turn of mind, he made several commendable efforts to teach Bose the catechism, in which he succeeded as well as might be expected. In short, without further detail, Master Edward bade fair to become a literary wonder.

But alas for poor little Edward! his merry dance was soon over. A day came when he sickened. Aunt Betsey tried her whole herbarium, but in vain: he grew rapidly worse and worse. His father sickened in heart, but said nothing; he only staid by his bedside day and night, trying all means to save, with affecting pertinacity.

"Can't you think of any thing more, doctor?" said he to the physician, when all had been tried in vain.

"Nothing," answered the physician.

A momentary convulsion passed over my uncle's face. "The will of the Lord be done," said he, almost with a groan of anguish.

Just at that moment a ray of the setting sun pierced the checked curtains, and gleamed like an angel's smile across the face of the little sufferer. He woke from troubled sleep.

"O, dear! I am so sick!" he gasped, feebly. His father raised him in his arms; he breathed easier, and looked up with a grateful smile. Just then his old playmate, the cat, crossed the room. "There goes pussy," said he; "O, dear! I shall never play any more."

At that moment a deadly change passed over his face. He looked up in his father's face with an imploring expression, and put out his hand as if for help. There was one moment of agony, and then the sweet features all settled into a smile of peace, and "mortality was swallowed up of life."

My uncle laid him down, and looked one moment at his beautiful face. It was too much for his principles, too much for his consistency, and "he lifted up his voice and wept."

The next morning was the Sabbath — the funeral day — and it rose with "breath all incense and with cheek all bloom." Uncle Abel was as calm and collected as ever; but in his face there was a sorrow-stricken appearance touching to behold. I remember him at family prayers, as he bent over the great Bible and began the psalm, "Lord, thou hast been our dwelling-place in all generations." Apparently he was touched by the melancholy splendor of the poetry, for after reading a few verses he stopped. There was a dead silence, interrupted only by the tick of the clock. He cleared his voice repeatedly, and tried to go on, but in vain. He closed the book, and kneeled down to prayer. The energy of sorrow broke through his usual formal reverence, and his language flowed forth with a deep and sorrowful pathos which I shall never forget. The God so much reverenced, so much feared, seemed to draw near to him as a friend and comforter, his refuge and strength, "a very present help in time of trouble."

My uncle rose, and I saw him walk to the room of the departed one. He uncovered the face. It was set with the seal of death; but O, how surpassingly lovely! The brilliancy of life was gone, but that pure, transparent face was touched with a mysterious, triumphant brightness, which seemed like the dawning of heaven.

My uncle looked long and earnestly. He felt the beauty of what he gazed on; his heart was softened, but he had no words for his feelings. He left the room unconsciously, and stood in the front door. The morning was bright, the bells were ringing for church, the birds were singing merrily, and the pet squirrel of little Edward was frolicking about the door. My uncle watched him as he ran first up one tree, and then down and up another, and then over the fence, whisking his brush and chattering just as if nothing was the matter.

With a deep sigh Uncle Abel broke forth, "How happy that *cretur'* is! Well, the Lord's will be done."

That day the dust was committed to dust, amid the lamentations of all who had known little Edward. Years have passed since then, and all that is mortal of my uncle has long since been gathered to his fathers; but his just and upright spirit has entered the glorious liberty of the sons of God. Yes, the good man may have had opinions which the philosophical scorn, weaknesses at which the thoughtless smile; but death shall change him into all that is enlightened, wise, and refined; for he shall awake in "His" likeness, and "be satisfied."

AUNT MARY.

SINCE sketching character is the mode, I too take up my pencil, not to make you laugh, though peradventure it may be — to get you to sleep.

I am now a tolerably old gentleman — an old bachelor, moreover — and, what is more to the point, an unpretending and sober-minded one. Lest, however, any of the ladies should take exceptions against me in the very outset, I will merely remark, *en passant*, that a man can sometimes become an old bachelor because he has *too much* heart as well as too little.

Years ago — before any of my readers were born — I was a little good-for-nought of a boy, of precisely that unlucky kind who are always in every body's way, and always in mischief. I had, to watch over my uprearing, a father and mother, and a whole army of older brothers and sisters. My relatives bore a very great resemblance to other human beings, neither good angels nor the opposite class, but, as mathematicians say, "in the mean proportion."

As I have before insinuated, I was a sort of family scapegrace among them, and one on whose head all the domestic

10 *

trespasses were regularly visited, either by real, actual desert or by imputation.

For this order of things, there was, I confess, a very solid and serious foundation, in the constitution of my mind. Whether I was born under some cross-eyed planet, or whether I was fairy-smitten in my cradle, certain it is that I was, from the dawn of existence, a sort of "Murad the Unlucky;" an out-of-time, out-of-place, out-of-form sort of a boy, with whom nothing prospered.

Who always left open doors in cold weather? It was Henry. Who was sure to upset his coffee cup at breakfast, or to knock over his tumbler at dinner, or to prostrate saltcellar, pepper box, and mustard pot, if he only happened to move his arm? Why, Henry. Who was plate breaker general for the family? It was Henry. Who tangled mamma's silks and cottons, and tore up the last newspaper for papa, or threw down old Phœbe's clothes horse, with all her clean ironing thereupon? Why, Henry.

Now all this was no "malice prepense" in me, for I solemnly believe that I was the best-natured boy in the world; but something was the matter with the attraction of cohesion, or the attraction of gravitation — with the general dispensation of matter around me — that, let me do what I would, things would fall down, and break, or be torn and damaged, if I only came near them; and my unluckiness in any matter seemed in exact proportion to my carefulness.

If any body in the room with me had a headache, or any kind of nervous irritability, which made it particularly necessary for others to be quiet, and if I was in an especial desire unto the same, I was sure, while stepping around on tiptoe, to fall headlong over a chair, which would give an introductory push to the shovel, which would fall upon the tongs, which would animate the poker, and all together would set in action two or three sticks of wood, and down they would come together, with just that hearty, sociable sort of racket, which showed that they were disposed to make as much of the opportunity as possible.

In the same manner, every thing that came into my hand, or was at all connected with me, was sure to lose by it. If I rejoiced in a clean apron in the morning, I was sure to make a full-length prostration thereupon on my way to school, and come home nothing better, but rather worse. If I was sent on an errand, I was sure either to lose my money in going, or my purchases in returning; and on these occasions my mother would often comfort me with the reflection, that it was well that my ears were fastened to my head, or I should lose them too. Of course, I was a fair mark for the exhortatory powers, not only of my parents, but of all my aunts, uncles, and cousins, to the third and fourth generation, who ceased not to reprove, rebuke, and exhort with all long-suffering and doctrine.

All this would have been very well if nature had not gifted me with a very unnecessary and uncomfortable capacity of *feeling*, which, like a refined ear for music, is undesirable, because, in this world, one meets with discord ninety-nine times where it meets with harmony once. Much, therefore, as I furnished occasion to be scolded at, I never became *used* to scolding, so that I was just as much galled by it the *forty*-first time as the first. There was no such thing as philosophy in me: I had just that unreasonable heart which is not conformed unto the nature of things, neither indeed *can* be. I was timid, and shrinking, and proud; I was nothing to any one around me but an awkward, unlucky boy; nothing to my parents but one of half a dozen children, whose faces were to be washed and stockings mended on Saturday afternoon. If I was very sick, I had medicine and the doctor; if I was a little sick, I was exhorted unto patience; and if I was sick at heart, I was left to prescribe for myself.

Now, all this was very well: what should a child need but meat, and drink, and room to play, and a school to teach him reading and writing, and somebody to take care of him when sick? Certainly, nothing.

But the feelings of grown-up children exist in the mind of little ones oftener than is supposed; and I had, even at this early day, the same keen sense of all that touched the heart wrong; the same longing for something which should touch it aright; the same discontent, with latent, matter-of-course affection, and the same craving for sympathy, which has been the unprofitable fashion of this world in all ages. And no human being possessing such constitutionals has a better chance of being made unhappy by them than the backward, uninteresting, wrong-doing child. We can all sympathize, to some extent, with *men* and *women;* but how few can go back to the sympathies of childhood; can understand the desolate insignificance of not being one of the *grown-up* people; of being sent to bed, to be *out of the way* in the evening, and to school, to be out of the way in the morning; of manifold similar grievances and distresses, which the child has no elocution to set forth, and the grown person no imagination to conceive.

When I was seven years old, I was told one morning, with considerable domestic acclamation, that Aunt Mary was coming to make us a visit; and so, when the carriage that brought her stopped at our door, I pulled off my dirty apron, and ran in among the crowd of brothers and sisters to see what was coming. I shall not describe her first appearance, for, as I think of her, I begin to grow somewhat sentimental, in spite of my spectacles, and might, perhaps, talk a little nonsense.

Perhaps every man, whether married or unmarried, who has lived to the age of fifty or thereabouts, has seen some woman who, in his mind, is *the* woman, in distinction from all others. She may not have been a relative; she may not have been a wife; she may simply have shone on him from afar; she may be remembered in the distance of years as a star that is set, as music that is hushed, as beauty and loveliness faded forever; but *remembered* she is with interest, with fervor, with enthusiasm; with all that heart can feel, and more than words can tell.

To me there has been but one such, and that is she whom I describe. "Was she beautiful?" you ask. I also will ask you one question: "If an angel from heaven should dwell in human form, and animate any human face, would not that face be lovely? It might not be *beautiful*, but would it not be lovely?" She was not beautiful except after this fashion.

How well I remember her, as she used sometimes to sit thinking, with her head resting on her hand, her face mild and placid, with a quiet October sunshine in her blue eyes, and an ever-present smile over her whole countenance. I remember the sudden sweetness of look when any one spoke to her; the prompt attention, the quick comprehension of things before you uttered them, the obliging readiness to leave for you whatever she was doing.

To those who mistake occasional pensiveness for melancholy, it might seem strange to say that my Aunt Mary was always happy. Yet she was so. Her spirits never rose to buoyancy, and never sunk to despondency. I know that it is an article in the sentimental confession of faith that such a character cannot be interesting. For this impression there is some ground. The placidity of a medium commonplace mind is uninteresting, but the placidity of a strong and well-governed one borders on the sublime. Mutability of emotion characterizes inferior orders of being; but He who combines all interest, all excitement, all perfection, is "the same yesterday, to-day, and forever." And if there be any thing sublime in the idea of an almighty mind, in perfect peace itself, and, therefore, at leisure to bestow all its energies on the wants of others, there is at least a reflection of the same sublimity in the character of that human being who has so quieted and governed the world within, that nothing is left to absorb sympathy or distract attention from those around.

Such a woman was my Aunt Mary. Her placidity was not so much the result of temperament as of choice. She had every susceptibility of suffering incident to the noblest and most delicate construction of mind; but they had been so directed, that, instead of concentrating thought on self, they had prepared her to understand and feel for others.

She was, beyond all things else, a sympathetic person, and her character, like the green in a landscape, was less remarkable for what it was in itself than for its perfect and beautiful harmony with all the coloring and shading around it.

Other women have had talents, others have been good; but no woman that ever I knew possessed goodness and talent in union with such an intuitive perception of feelings, and such a faculty of instantaneous adaptation to them. The most troublesome thing in this world is to be condemned to the society of a person who can never understand any thing you say unless you say the whole of it, making your commas and periods as you go along; and the most desirable thing in the world is to live with a person who saves you all the trouble of talking, by knowing just what you mean before you begin to speak.

Something of this kind of talent I began to feel, to my great relief, when Aunt Mary came into the family. I remember the very first evening, as she sat by the hearth, surrounded by all the family, her eye glanced on me with an expression that let me know she *saw* me; and when the clock struck eight, and my mother proclaimed that it was my bedtime, my countenance fell as I moved sorrowfully from the back of her rocking chair, and thought how many beautiful stories Aunt Mary would tell after I was gone to bed. She turned towards me with such a look of real understanding, such an evident insight into the case, that I went into banishment with a lighter heart than ever I did before. How very contrary is the obstinate estimate of the heart to the rational estimate of worldly wisdom! Are there not some who can remember when one word, one look, or even the withholding of a word, has drawn their heart more to a person than all the substantial favors in the world? By ordinary acceptation, substantial kindness respects the necessaries of animal existence; while those wants which are peculiar to mind, and will exist with it forever, by equally correct classification, are designated as sentimental ones, the supply of which, though it will excite more gratitude in fact, ought not to in theory. Before Aunt Mary had lived with us a month, I loved her beyond any body in the world; and a utilitarian would have been amused in ciphering out the amount of favors which produced this result. It was a look — a word — a smile: it was that she seemed pleased with my new kite; that she rejoiced with me when I learned to spin a top; that she alone seemed to estimate my proficiency in playing ball and marbles; that she never looked at all vexed when I upset her workbox upon the floor; that she received all my awkward gallantry and *mal-adroit* helpfulness as if it had been in the best taste in the world; that when she was sick, she insisted on letting me wait on her, though I made my customary havoc among the pitchers and tumblers of her room, and displayed, through my zeal to please, a more than ordinary share of insufficiency for the station. She also was the only person that ever I *conversed* with, and I used to wonder how any body who could talk all about matters and things with grown-up persons could talk so sensibly about marbles, and hoops, and skates, and all sorts of little-boy matters; and I will say, by the by, that the same sort of speculation has often occurred to the minds of older people in connection with her. She knew the value of varied information in making a woman, not a pedant, but a sympathetic, companionable being; and such she was to almost every class of mind.

She had, too, the faculty of drawing others up to her level in conversation, so that I would often find myself going on in most profound style while talking with her, and would wonder, when I was through, whether I was really a little boy still.

When she had enlightened us many months, the time came for her to take leave, and she besought my mother to give me to her for company. All the family wondered what she could find to like in Henry; but if she did like me, it was no matter, and so was the case disposed of.

From that time I *lived* with her — and there are some persons who can make the word *live* signify much more than it commonly does — and she wrought on my character all those miracles which benevolent genius can work. She quieted my heart, directed my feelings, unfolded my mind, and educated me, not harshly or by force, but as the blessed sunshine educates the flower, into full and perfect life; and when all that was mortal of her died to this world, her words and deeds of unutterable love shed a twilight around her memory that will fade only in the brightness of heaven.

FRANKNESS.

THERE is one kind of frankness, which is the result of perfect unsuspiciousness, and which requires a measure of ignorance of the world and of life: this kind appeals to our generosity and tenderness. There is another, which is the frankness of a strong but pure mind, acquainted with life, clear in its discrimination and upright in its intention, yet above disguise or concealment: this kind excites respect. The first seems to proceed simply from impulse, the second from impulse and reflection united; the first proceeds, in a measure, from ignorance, the second from knowledge; the first is born from an undoubting confidence in others, the second from a virtuous and well-grounded reliance on one's self.

Now, if you suppose that this is the beginning of a sermon or of a fourth of July oration, you are very much mistaken, though, I must confess, it hath rather an uncertain sound. I merely prefaced it to a little sketch of character, which you may look at if you please, though I am not sure you will like it.

It was said of Alice H. that she had the mind of a man, the heart of a woman, and the face of an angel — a combination that all my readers will think peculiarly happy.

There never was a woman who was so unlike the mass of society in her modes of thinking and acting, yet so generally popular. But the most remarkable thing about her was her proud superiority to all disguise, in thought, word, and deed. She pleased you; for she spoke out a hundred things that you would conceal, and spoke them with a dignified assurance that made you wonder that you had ever hesitated to say them yourself. Nor did this unreserve appear like the weakness of one who could not conceal, or like a determination to make war on the forms of society. It was rather a calm, well-guided integrity, regulated by a just sense of propriety; knowing when to be silent, but speaking the truth when it spoke at all.

Her extraordinary frankness often beguiled superficial observers into supposing themselves fully acquainted with her long before they were so, as the beautiful transparency of some lakes is said to deceive the eye as to their depth; yet the longer you knew her, the more variety and compass of character appeared through the same transparent medium. But you may just visit Miss Alice for half an hour to-night, and judge for yourselves. You may walk into this little parlor. There sits Miss Alice on that sofa, sewing a pair of lace sleeves into a satin dress, in which peculiarly angelic employment she may persevere till we have finished another sketch.

Do you see that pretty little lady, with sparkling eyes, elastic form, and beautiful hand and foot, sitting opposite to her? She is a belle: the character is written in her face — it sparkles from her eye — it dimples in her smile, and pervades the whole woman.

But there — Alice has risen, and is gone to the mirror, and

is arranging the finest auburn hair in the world in the most tasteful manner. The little lady watches every motion as comically as a kitten watches a pin-ball.

"It is all in vain to deny it, Alice — you are really anxious to *look pretty* this evening," said she.

"I certainly am," said Alice, quietly.

"Ay, and you hope you shall please Mr. A. and Mr. B.," said the little accusing angel.

"Certainly I do," said Alice, as she twisted her fingers in a beautiful curl.

"Well, I would not tell of it, Alice, if I did."

"Then you should not ask me," said Alice.

"I *declare!* Alice!"

"And what do you declare?"

"I never saw such a girl as you are!"

"Very likely," said Alice, stooping to pick up a pin.

"Well, for *my* part," said the little lady, "I never would take any pains to make any body like me —*particularly* a gentleman."

"I would," said Alice, "if they would not like me without."

"Why, Alice! I should not think you were so fond of admiration."

"I like to be admired very much," said Alice, returning to the sofa, "and I suppose every body else does."

"*I* don't care about admiration," said the little lady. "I would be as well satisfied that people shouldn't like me as that they should."

"Then, cousin, I think it's a pity we all like you so well," said Alice, with a good-humored smile. If Miss Alice had penetration, she never made a severe use of it.

"But really, cousin," said the little lady, "I should not

think such a girl as you would think any thing about dress, or admiration, and all that."

"I don't know what sort of a girl you think I am," said Alice, "but, for my own part, *I* only pretend to be a common human being, and am not ashamed of common human feelings. If God has made us so that we love admiration, why should we not honestly say so. *I* love it — *you* love it — every body loves it; and why should not every body say it?"

"Why, yes," said the little lady, "I suppose every body has a — has a — a general love for admiration. I am willing to acknowledge that *I* have; but ——"

"But you have no love for it in particular," said Alice, "I suppose you mean to say; that is just the way the matter is commonly disposed of. Every body is willing to acknowledge a general wish for the good opinion of others, but half the world are ashamed to own it when it comes to a particular case. Now I have made up my mind, that if it is correct in general, it is correct in particular; and I mean to own it both ways."

"But, somehow, it seems mean," said the little lady.

"It is mean to live for it, to be selfishly engrossed in it, but not mean to enjoy it when it comes, or even to seek it, if we neglect no higher interest in doing so. All that God made us to feel is dignified and pure, unless we pervert it."

"But, Alice, I never heard any person speak out so frankly as you do."

"Almost all that is innocent and natural may be spoken out; and as for that which is not innocent and natural, it ought not even to be thought."

"But *can* every thing be spoken that may be thought?" said the lady.

"No; we have an instinct which teaches us to be silent

sometimes: but, if we speak at all, let it be in simplicity and sincerity."

"Now, for instance, Alice," said the lady, "it is very innocent and natural, as you say, to think this, that, and the other nice thing of yourself, especially when every body is telling you of it; now would you speak the truth if any one asked you on this point?"

"If it were a person who had a right to ask, and if it were a proper time and place, I would," said Alice.

"Well, then," said the bright lady, "I ask you, Alice, in this very proper time and place, do you think that you are handsome?"

"Now, I suppose you expect me to make a courtesy to every chair in the room before I answer," said Alice; "but, dispensing with that ceremony, I will tell you fairly, I think I am."

"Do you think that you are good?"

"Not entirely," said Alice.

"Well, but don't you think you are better than most people?"

"As far as I can tell, I think I am better than some people; but really, cousin, I don't trust my own judgment in this matter," said Alice.

"Well, Alice, one more question. Do you think James Martyrs likes you or me best?"

"I do not know," said Alice.

"I did not ask you what you knew, but what you thought," said the lady; "you must have some thought about it."

"Well, then, I think he likes me best," said Alice.

Just then the door opened, and in walked the identical

James Martyrs. Alice blushed, looked a little comical, and went on with her sewing, while the little lady began, —

"Really, Mr. James, I wish you had come a minute sooner, to hear Alice's confessions."

"What has she confessed?" said James.

"Why, that she is handsomer and better than most folks."

"That's nothing to be ashamed of," said James.

"O, that's not all; she wants to look pretty, and loves to be admired, and all ——"

"It sounds very much like her," said James, looking at Alice.

"O, but, besides that," said the lady, "she has been preaching a discourse in justification of vanity and self-love ——"

"And next time you shall take notes when I preach," said Alice, "for I don't think your memory is remarkably happy."

"You see, James," said the lady, "that Alice makes it a point to say exactly the truth when she speaks at all, and I've been puzzling her with questions. I really wish you would ask her some, and see what she will say. But, mercy! there is Uncle C. come to take me to ride. I must run." And off flew the little humming bird, leaving James and Alice *tête-à-tête*.

"There really is one question ——" said James, clearing his voice.

Alice looked up.

"There is one question, Alice, which I wish you *would* answer."

Alice did not inquire what the question was, but began to look very solemn; and just then the door was shut — and so I never knew what the question was — only I observed that James Martyrs seemed in some seventh heaven for a week afterwards, and — and — you can finish for yourself, lady.

THE SABBATH.

SKETCHES FROM A NOTE BOOK OF AN ELDERLY GENTLEMAN.

THE Puritan Sabbath — is there such a thing existing now, or has it gone with the things that were, to be looked at as a curiosity in the museum of the past? Can any one, in memory, take himself back to the unbroken stillness of that day, and recall the sense of religious awe which seemed to brood in the very atmosphere, checking the merry laugh of childhood, and chaining in unwonted stillness the tongue of volatile youth, and imparting even to the sunshine of heaven, and the unconscious notes of animals, a tone of its own gravity and repose? If you cannot remember these things, go back with me to the verge of early boyhood, and live with me one of the Sabbaths that I have spent beneath the roof of my uncle, Phineas Fletcher.

Imagine the long sunny hours of a Saturday afternoon insensibly slipping away, as we youngsters are exploring the length and breadth of a trout stream, or chasing gray squirrels, or building mud milldams in the brook. The sun sinks lower and lower, but we still think it does not want half an hour to sundown. At last, he so evidently is really *going down*, that there is no room for scepticism or latitude of opinion on the subject; and with many a lingering regret, we began to put away our fish-hooks, and hang our hoops over our arm, preparatory to trudging homeward.

"O Henry, don't you wish that Saturday afternoons lasted longer?" said little John to me.

"I do," says Cousin Bill, who was never the boy to mince matters in giving his sentiments; "and I wouldn't care if Sunday didn't come but once a year."

"O Bill, that's wicked, I'm afraid," says little conscientious Susan, who, with her doll in hand, was coming home from a Saturday afternoon visit.

"Can't help it," says Bill, catching Susan's bag, and tossing it in the air; "I never did like to sit still, and that's why I hate Sundays."

"Hate Sundays! O Bill! Why, Aunt Kezzy says heaven is an *eternal* Sabbath — only think of that!"

"Well, I know I must be pretty different from what I am now before I could sit still forever," said Bill, in a lower and somewhat disconcerted tone, as if admitting the force of the consideration.

The rest of us began to look very grave, and to think that we must get to liking Sunday some time or other, or it would be a very bad thing for us. As we drew near the dwelling, the compact and business-like form of Aunt Kezzy was seen emerging from the house to hasten our approach.

"How often have I told you, young ones, not to stay out after sundown on Saturday night? Don't you know it's the same as Sunday, you wicked children, you? Come right into the house, every one of you, and never let me hear of such a thing again."

This was Aunt Kezzy's regular exordium every Saturday night; for we children, being blinded, as she supposed, by natural depravity, always made strange mistakes in reckoning time on Saturday afternoons. After being duly suppered and scrubbed, we were enjoined to go to bed, and remember that to-morrow was Sunday, and that we must not laugh and play in the morning. With many a sorrowful look did Susan deposit her doll in the chest, and give one lingering glance at the patchwork she was piecing for dolly's bed, while William, John, and myself emptied our pockets of all superfluous fish-hooks, bits of twine, popguns, slices of potato, marbles, and all the various items of boy property, which, to keep us from temptation, were taken into Aunt Kezzy's safe keeping over Sunday.

My Uncle Phineas was a man of great exactness, and Sunday was the centre of his whole worldly and religious system. Every thing with regard to his worldly business was so arranged that by Saturday noon it seemed to come to a close of itself. All his accounts were looked over, his workmen paid, all borrowed things returned, and lent things sent after, and every tool and article belonging to the farm was returned to its own place at exactly such an hour every Saturday afternoon, and an hour before sundown every item of preparation, even to the blacking of his Sunday shoes and the brushing of his Sunday coat, was entirely concluded; and at the going down of the sun, the stillness of the Sabbath seemed to settle down over the whole dwelling.

And now it is Sunday morning; and though all without is fragrance, and motion, and beauty, the dewdrops are twinkling, butterflies fluttering, and merry birds carolling and racketing as if they never could sing loud or fast enough, yet within there is such a stillness that the tick of the tall mahogany clock is audible through the whole house, and the buzz of the blue flies, as they whiz along up and down the window panes, is a distinct item of hearing. Look into the best front room, and you may see the upright form of my Uncle Phineas, in his immaculate Sunday clothes, with his Bible spread open on the little stand before him, and even a deeper than usual gravity settling down over his toil-worn features. Alongside, in well-brushed Sunday clothes, with clean faces and smooth hair, sat the whole of us younger people, each drawn up in a chair, with hat and handkerchief, ready for the first stroke of the bell, while Aunt Kezzy, all trimmed, and primmed, and made ready for meeting, sat reading her psalm book, only looking up occasionally to give an additional jerk to some shirt collar, or the fifteenth pull to Susan's frock, or to repress any straggling looks that might be wandering about, "beholding vanity."

A stranger, in glancing at Uncle Phineas as he sat intent on his Sunday reading, might have seen that the Sabbath was *in his heart*—there was no mistake about it. It was plain that he had put by all worldly thoughts when he shut up his account book, and that his mind was as free from every earthly association as his Sunday coat was from dust. The slave of worldliness, who is driven, by perplexing business or adventurous speculation, through the hours of a half-kept Sabbath to the fatigues of another week, might envy the unbroken quiet, the sunny tranquillity, which hallowed the weekly rest of my uncle.

The Sabbath of the Puritan Christian was the golden day,

and all its associations, and all its thoughts, words, and deeds, were so entirely distinct from the ordinary material of life, that it was to him a sort of weekly translation — a quitting of this world to sojourn a day in a better; and year after year, as each Sabbath set its seal on the completed labors of a week, the pilgrim felt that one more stage of his earthly journey was completed, and that he was one week nearer to his eternal rest. And as years, with their changes, came on, and the strong man grew old, and missed, one after another, familiar forms that had risen around his earlier years, the face of the Sabbath became like that of an old and tried friend, carrying him back to the scenes of his youth, and connecting him with scenes long gone by, restoring to him the dew and freshness of brighter and more buoyant days.

Viewed simply as an institution for a Christian and mature mind, nothing could be more perfect than the Puritan Sabbath: if it had any failing, it was in the want of adaptation to children, and to those not interested in its peculiar duties. If you had been in the dwelling of my uncle of a Sabbath morning, you must have found the unbroken stillness delightful; the calm and quiet must have soothed and disposed you for contemplation, and the evident appearance of single-hearted devotion to the duties of the day in the elder part of the family must have been a striking addition to the picture. But, then, if your eye had watched attentively the motions of us juveniles, you might have seen that what was so very invigorating to the disciplined Christian was a weariness to young flesh and bones. Then there was not, as now, the intellectual relaxation afforded by the Sunday school, with its various forms of religious exercise, its thousand modes of interesting and useful information. Our whole stock in this line was the Bible and Primer, and these were our main dependence for whiling away the tedious hours between our early breakfast and the signal for meeting. How often was our invention stretched to find wherewithal to keep up our stock of excitement in a line with the duties of the day! For the first half hour, perhaps, a story in the Bible answered our purpose very well; but, having despatched the history of Joseph, or the story of the ten plagues, we then took to the Primer: and then there was, first, the looking over the system of theological and ethical teaching, commencing, "In Adam's fall we sinned all," and extending through three or four pages of pictorial and poetic embellishment. Next was the death of John Rogers, who was burned at Smithfield; and for a while we could entertain ourselves with counting all his "nine children and one at the breast," as in the picture they stand in a regular row, like a pair of stairs. These being done, came miscellaneous exercises of our own invention, such as counting all the psalms in the psalm book, backward and forward, to and from the Doxology, or numbering the books in the Bible, or some other such device as we deemed within the pale of religious employments. When all these failed, and it still wanted an hour of meeting time, we looked up at the ceiling, and down at the floor, and all around into every corner, to see what we could do next; and happy was he who could spy a pin gleaming in some distant crack, and forthwith muster an occasion for getting down to pick it up. Then there was the infallible recollection that we wanted a drink of water, as an excuse to get out to the well; or else we heard some strange noise among the chickens, and insisted that it was essential that we should see what was the matter; or else pussy would jump on to the table, when all of us would spring to drive her down; while there was a most assiduous watching of the clock to see when the first bell would ring. Happy was it for us, in the interim, if we did not begin to look at each other and make up faces, or slyly slip off and on our shoes, or some other incipient attempts at roguery, which would gradually so undermine our gravity that there would be some sudden explosion of merriment, whereat Uncle Phineas would look up and say, "*Tut, tut,*" and Aunt Kezzy would make a speech about wicked children breaking the Sabbath day. I remember once how my cousin Bill got into deep disgrace one Sunday by a roguish trick. He was just about to close his Bible with all sobriety, when snap came a grasshopper through an open window, and alighted in the middle of the page. Bill instantly kidnapped the intruder, for so important an auxiliary in the way of employment was not to be despised. Presently we children looked towards Bill, and there he sat, very demurely reading his Bible, with the grasshopper hanging by one leg from the corner of his mouth, kicking and sprawling, without in the least disturbing Master William's gravity. We all burst into an uproarious laugh. But it came to be rather a serious affair for Bill, as his good father was in the practice of enforcing truth and duty by certain modes of moral suasion much recommended by Solomon, though fallen into disrepute at the present day.

This morning picture may give a good specimen of the whole livelong Sunday, which presented only an alternation of similar scenes until sunset, when a universal unchaining of tongues and a general scamper proclaimed that the "sun was down."

But, it may be asked, what was the result of all this strictness? Did it not disgust you with the Sabbath and with religion? No, it did not. It did not, because it was the result of *no unkindly feeling*, but of *consistent principle;* and consistency of principle is what even children learn to appreciate and revere. The law of obedience and of reverence for the Sabbath was constraining so equally on the young and the old, that its claims came to be regarded like those immutable laws of nature, which no one thinks of being out of patience with, though they sometimes bear hard on personal convenience. The effect of the system was to ingrain into our character a veneration for the Sabbath which no friction of after life would ever efface. I have lived to wander in many climates and foreign lands, where the Sabbath is an unknown name, or where it is only recognized by noisy mirth; but never has the day returned without bringing with it a breathing of religious awe, and even a yearning for the unbroken stillness, the placid repose, and the simple devotion of the Puritan Sabbath.

ANOTHER SCENE.

"How late we are this morning!" said Mrs. Roberts to her husband, glancing hurriedly at the clock, as they were sitting down to breakfast on a Sabbath morning. "Really, it is a shame to us to be so late Sundays. I wonder John and Henry are not up yet: Hannah, did you speak to them?"

"Yes, ma'am, but I could not make them mind; they said it was Sunday, and that we always have breakfast later Sundays."

"Well, it is a shame to us, I must say," said Mrs. Roberts, sitting down to the table. "I never lie late myself unless something in particular happens. Last night I was out very late, and Sabbath before last I had a bad headache."

"Well, well, my dear," said Mr. Roberts, "it is not worth while to worry yourself about it; Sunday is a day of rest; every body indulges a little of a Sunday morning, it is so very natural, you know; one's work done up, one feels like taking a little rest."

"Well, I must say it was not the way my mother brought me up," said Mrs. Roberts; "and I really can't feel it to be right."

This last part of the discourse had been listened to by two sleepy-looking boys, who had, meanwhile, taken their seats at table with that listless air which is the result of late sleeping.

"O, by the by, my dear, what did you give for those hams Saturday?" said Mr. Roberts.

"Eleven cents a pound, I believe," replied Mrs. Roberts; "but Stephens and Philips have some much nicer, canvas and all, for ten cents. I think we had better get our things at Stephens and Philips's in future, my dear."

"Why? are they much cheaper?"

"O, a great deal; but I forget it is Sunday. We ought to be thinking of other things. Boys, have you looked over your Sunday school lesson?"

"No, ma'am."

"Now, how strange! and here it wants only half an hour of the time, and you are not dressed either. Now, see the bad effects of not being up in time."

The boys looked sullen, and said "they were up as soon as any one else in the house."

"Well, your father and I had some excuse, because we were out late last night; you ought to have been up full three hours ago, and to have been all ready, with your lessons learned. Now, what do you suppose you shall do?"

"O mother, do let us stay at home this one morning; we don't know the lesson, and it won't do any good for us to go."

"No, indeed, I shall not. You must go and get along as well as you can. It is all your own fault. Now, go up stairs and hurry. We shall not find time for prayers this morning."

The boys took themselves up stairs to "hurry," as directed, and soon one of them called from the top of the stairs, "Mother! mother! the buttons are off this vest; so I can't wear it!" and "Mother! here is a long rip in my best coat!" said another.

"Why did you not tell me of it before?" said Mrs. Roberts, coming up stairs.

"I forgot it," said the boy

"Well, well, stand still; I must catch it together somehow, if it is Sunday. There! there is the bell! Stand still a minute!" and Mrs. Roberts plied needle, and thread, and scissors; "there, that will do for to-day. Dear me, how confused every thing is to-day!"

"It is always just so Sundays," said John, flinging up his book and catching it again as he ran down stairs.

"It is always just so Sundays." These words struck rather unpleasantly on Mrs. Roberts's conscience, for something told her that, whatever the reason might be, it *was* just so. On Sunday every thing was later and more irregular than any other day in the week.

"Hannah, you must boil that piece of beef for dinner to-day."

"I thought you told me you did not have cooking done on Sunday."

"No, I do not, generally. I am very sorry Mr. Roberts would get that piece of meat yesterday. We did not need it; but here it is on our hands; the weather is too hot to keep it. It won't do to let it spoil; so I must have it boiled, for aught I see."

Hannah had lived four Sabbaths with Mrs. Roberts, and on two of them she had been required to cook from similar reasoning. "*For once*" is apt, in such cases, to become a phrase of very extensive signification.

"It really worries me to have things go on so as they do on Sundays," said Mrs. Roberts to her husband. "I never do feel as if we kept Sunday as we ought."

"My dear, you have been saying so ever since we were married, and I do not see what you are going to do about it. For my part I do not see why we do not do as well as people in general. We do not visit, nor receive company, nor read improper books. We go to church, and send the children to Sunday school, and so the greater part of the day is spent in a religious way. Then out of church we have the children's Sunday school books, and one or two religious newspapers. I think that is quite enough."

"But, somehow, when I was a child, my mother ——" said Mrs. Roberts, hesitating.

"O my dear, your mother must not be considered an exact pattern for these days. People were too strict in your mother's time; they carried the thing too far, altogether; every body allows it now."

Mrs. Roberts was silenced, but not satisfied. A strict religious education had left just conscience enough on this subject to make her uneasy.

These worthy people had a sort of general idea that Sunday ought to be kept, and they intended to keep it; but they had never taken the trouble to investigate or inquire as to the most proper way, nor was it so much an object of interest that their weekly arrangements were planned with any reference to it. Mr. Roberts would often engage in business at the close of the week, which he knew would so fatigue him that he would be weary and listless on Sunday; and Mrs. Roberts would allow her family cares to accumulate in the same way, so that she was either wearied with efforts to accomplish it before the Sabbath, or perplexed and worried by finding every thing at loose ends on that day. They had the idea that Sunday was to be kept when it was perfectly convenient, and did not demand any sacrifice of time or money. But if stopping to keep the Sabbath in a journey would risk passage money or a seat in the stage, or, in housekeeping, if it would involve any considerable inconvenience or expense, it was deemed a providential intimation that it was "a work of necessity and mercy" to attend to secular matters. To their minds the fourth command read thus: "Remember the Sabbath day to keep it holy when it comes convenient, and costs neither time nor money."

As to the effects of this on the children, there was neither enough of strictness to make them respect the Sabbath, nor of religious interest to make them love it; of course, the little restraint there was proved just enough to lead them to dislike and despise it. Children soon perceive the course of their parents' feelings, and it was evident enough to the children of this family that their father and mother generally found themselves hurried into the Sabbath with hearts and minds full of this world, and their conversation and thoughts were so constantly turning to worldly things, and so awkwardly drawn back by a sense of religious obligation, that the Sabbath appeared more obviously a clog and a fetter than it did under the strictest *régime* of Puritan days.

SKETCH SECOND.

The little quiet village of Camden stands under the brow of a rugged hill in one of the most picturesque parts of New England; and its regular, honest, and industrious villagers were not a little surprised and pleased that Mr. James, a rich man, and pleasant-spoken withal, had concluded to take up his residence among them. He brought with him a pretty, genteel wife, and a group of rosy, romping, but amiable children; and there was so much of good nature and kindness about the manners of every member of the family, that the whole neighborhood were prepossessed in their favor. Mr. James was a man of somewhat visionary and theoretical turn of mind, and very much in the habit of following out his own ideas of right and wrong, without troubling himself particularly as to the appearance his course might make in the eyes of others. He was a supporter of the ordinances of religion, and always ready to give both time and money to promote any benevolent object; and though he had never made any public profession of religion, nor connected himself with any particular set of Christians, still he seemed to possess great reverence for God, and to worship him in spirit and in truth, and he professed to make the Bible the guide of his life. Mr. James had been brought up under a system of injudicious religious restraint. He had determined, in educating his children, to adopt an exactly opposite course, and to make religion and all its institutions sources of enjoyment. His aim, doubtless, was an appropriate one; but his method of carrying it out, to say the least, was one which was not a safe model for general imitation. In regard to the Sabbath, for example, he considered that, although the plan of going to church twice a day, and keeping all the family quiet within doors the rest of the time, was good, other methods would be much better. Accordingly, after the morning service, which he and his whole family regularly attended, he would spend the rest of the day with his children. In bad weather he would instruct them in natural history, show them pictures, and read them various accounts of the works of God, combining all with such religious instruction and influence as a devotional mind might furnish. When the weather permitted, he would range with them through the fields, collecting minerals and plants, or sail with them on the lake, meanwhile directing the thoughts of his young listeners upward to God, by the many beautiful traces of his presence and agency, which superior knowledge and observation enabled him to discover and point out. These Sunday strolls were seasons of most delightful enjoyment to the children. Though it was with some difficulty that their father could restrain them from loud and noisy demonstrations of delight, and he saw with some regret that the mere animal excitement of the stroll seemed to draw the attention too much from religious considerations, and, in particular, to make the exercises of the morning seem like a preparatory penance to the enjoyments of the afternoon, nevertheless, when Mr. James looked back to his own boyhood, and remembered the frigid restraint, the entire want of any kind of mental or bodily excitement, which had made the Sabbath so much a weariness to him, he could not but congratulate himself when he perceived his children looking forward to Sunday as a day of delight, and found himself on that day continually surrounded by a circle of smiling and cheerful faces. His talent of imparting religious instruction in a simple and interesting form was remarkably happy, and it is probable that there was among his children an uncommon degree of real thought and feeling on religious subjects as the result.

The good people of Camden, however, knew not what to think of a course that appeared to them an entire violation of all the requirements of the Sabbath.. The first impulse of human nature is to condemn at once all who vary from what has been commonly regarded as the right way; and, accordingly, Mr. James was unsparingly denounced, by many good people, as a Sabbath breaker, an infidel, and an opposer to religion.

Such was the character heard of him by Mr. Richards, a young clergyman, who, shortly after Mr. James fixed his residence in Camden, accepted the pastoral charge of the village. It happened that Mr. Richards had known Mr. James in college, and, remembering him as a remarkably serious, amiable, and conscientious man, he resolved to ascertain from himself the views which had led him to the course of conduct so offensive to the good people of the neighborhood.

"This is all very well, my good friend," said he, after he had listened to Mr. James's eloquent account of his own system of religious instruction, and its effects upon his family; "I do not doubt that this system does very well for yourself and family; but there are other things to be taken into consideration besides personal and family improvement. Do you not know, Mr. James, that the most worthless and careless part of my congregation quote your example as a respectable precedent for allowing their families to violate the order of the Sabbath? You and your children sail about on the lake, with minds and hearts, I doubt not, elevated and tranquillized by its quiet repose; but Ben Dakes, and his idle, profane army of children, consider themselves as doing very much the same thing when they lie lolling about, sunning themselves on its shore, or skipping stones over its surface the whole of a Sunday afternoon."

"Let every one answer to his own conscience," replied Mr. James. "If I keep the Sabbath conscientiously, I am approved of God; if another transgresses his conscience, 'to his own master he standeth or falleth.' I am not responsible for all the abuses that idle or evil-disposed persons may fall into, in consequence of my doing what is right."

"Let me quote an answer from the same chapter," said Mr. Richards. "'Let no man put a stumbling block, or an occasion to fall, in his brother's way: let not your good be evil spoken of. It is good neither to eat flesh nor drink wine, *nor any thing whereby thy brother stumbleth, or is offended, or made weak.*' Now, my good friend, you happen to be endowed with a certain tone of mind which enables you to carry through your mode of keeping the Sabbath with little comparative evil, and much good, so far as your family is concerned; but how many persons in this neighborhood, do you suppose, would succeed equally well if they were to attempt it? If it were the common custom for families to absent themselves from public worship in the afternoon, and to stroll about the fields, or ride, or sail, how many parents, do you suppose, would have the dexterity and talent to check all that was inconsistent with the duties of the day? Is it not your ready command of language, your uncommon tact in simplifying and illustrating, your knowledge of natural history and of biblical literature, that enable you to accomplish the results that you do? And is there one parent in a hundred that could do the same? Now, just imagine our neighbor, 'Squire Hart, with his ten boys and girls, turned out into the fields on a Sunday afternoon to profit withal: you know he can never finish a sentence without stopping to begin it again half a dozen times. What progress would he make in instructing them? And so of a dozen others I could name along this very street here. Now, you men of cultivated minds must give your countenance to courses which would be best for society at large, or, as the sentiment was expressed by St. Paul, 'We that are strong ought to bear the infirmities of the weak, *and not to please ourselves*, for even Christ *pleased not himself*.' Think, my dear sir, if our Savior had gone only on the principle of avoiding what might be injurious to his own improvement, how unsafe his example might have proved to less elevated minds. Doubtless he might have made a Sabbath day fishing excursion an occasion of much elevated and impressive instruction; but, although he declared himself 'Lord of the Sabbath day,' and at liberty to suspend its obligation at his own discretion, yet he never violated the received method of observing it, except in cases where superstitious tradition trenched directly on those interests which the Sabbath was given to promote. He asserted the right to relieve pressing bodily wants, and to administer to the necessities of others on the Sabbath, but beyond that he allowed himself in no deviation from established custom."

Mr. James looked thoughtful. "I have not reflected on the subject in this view," he replied. "But, my dear sir, considering how little of the public services of the Sabbath is on a level with the capacity of younger children, it seems to me almost a pity to take them to church the whole of the day."

"I have thought of that myself," replied Mr. Richards, "and have sometimes thought that, could persons be found to conduct such a thing, it would be desirable to institute a separate service for children, in which the exercises should be particularly adapted to them."

"I should like to be minister to a congregation of children," said Mr. James, warmly.

"Well," replied Mr. Richards, "give our good people time to get acquainted with you, and do away the prejudices which your extraordinary mode of proceeding has induced, and I think I could easily assemble such a company for you every Sabbath."

After this, much to the surprise of the village, Mr. James and his family were regular attendants at both the services of the Sabbath. Mr. Richards explained to the good people of his congregation the motives which had led their neighbor to the adoption of what, to them, seemed so unchristian a course; and, upon reflection, they came to the perception of the truth, that a man may depart very widely from the received standard of right for other reasons than being an infidel or an opposer of religion. A ready return of cordial feeling was the result; and as Mr. James found himself treated with respect and confidence, he began to feel, notwithstanding his fastidiousness, that there were strong points of congeniality between all real and warm-hearted Christians, however different might be their intellectual culture, and in all simplicity united himself with the little church of Camden. A year from the time of his first residence there, every Sabbath afternoon saw him surrounded by a congregation of young children, for whose benefit he had, at his own expense, provided a room, fitted up with maps, scriptural pictures, and every convenience for the illustration of biblical knowledge; and the parents or guardians who from time to time attended their children during these exercises, often confessed themselves as much interested and benefited as any of their youthful companions.

SKETCH THIRD.

It was near the close of a pleasant Saturday afternoon that I drew up my weary horse in front of a neat little dwelling in the village of N. This, as near as I could gather from description, was the house of my cousin, William Fletcher, the identical rogue of a Bill Fletcher of whom we have aforetime spoken. Bill had always been a thriving, push-ahead sort of a character, and during the course of my rambling life I had improved every occasional opportunity of keeping up our early acquaintance. The last time that I returned to my native country, after some years of absence, I heard of him as married and settled in the village of N., where he was conducting a very prosperous course of business, and shortly after received a pressing invitation to visit him at his own home. Now, as I had gathered from experience the fact that it is of very little use to rap one's knuckles off on the front door of a country house without any knocker, I therefore made the best of my way along a little path, bordered with marigolds and balsams, that led to the back part of the dwelling. The sound of a number of childish voices made me stop, and, looking through the bushes, I saw the very image of my cousin Bill Fletcher, as he used to be twenty years ago; the same bold forehead, the same dark eyes, the same smart, saucy mouth, and the same "who-cares-for-that" toss to his head. "There, now," exclaimed the boy, setting down a pair of shoes that he had been blacking, and arranging them at the head of a long row of all sizes and sorts, from those which might have fitted a two year old foot upward, "there, I've blacked every single one of them, and made them shine too, and done it all in twenty minutes; if any body thinks they can do it quicker than that, I'd just like to have them try; that's all."

"I know they couldn't, though," said a fair-haired little girl, who stood admiring the sight, evidently impressed with the utmost reverence for her brother's ability; "and, Bill, I've been putting up all the playthings in the big chest, and I want you to come and turn the lock — the key hurts my fingers."

"Poh! I can turn it easier than that," said the boy, snapping his fingers; "have you got them all in?"

"Yes, all; only I left out the soft bales, and the string of red beads, and the great rag baby for Fanny to play with — you know mother says babies must have their playthings Sunday."

"O, to be sure," said the brother, very considerately; "babies can't read, you know, as we can, nor hear Bible stories, nor look at pictures." At this moment I stepped forward, for the spell of former times was so powerfully on me, that I was on the very point of springing forward with a "Halloo, there, Bill!" as I used to meet the father in old times; but the look of surprise that greeted my appearance brought me to myself.

"Is your father at home?" said I.

"Father and mother are both gone out; but I guess, sir, they will be home in a few moments: won't you walk in?"

I accepted the invitation, and the little girl showed me into a small and very prettily furnished parlor. There was a piano with music books on one side of the room, some fine pictures hung about the walls, and a little, neat centre table was plentifully strewn with books. Besides this, the two recesses on each side of the fireplace contained each a bookcase with a glass locked door.

The little girl offered me a chair, and then lingered a moment, as if she felt some disposition to entertain me if she could only think of something to say; and at last, looking up in my face, she said, in a confidential tone, "Mother says she left Willie and me to keep house this afternoon while she was gone, and we are putting up all the things for Sunday, so as to get every thing done before she comes home. Willie has gone to put away the playthings, and I'm going to put up the books." So saying, she opened the doors of one of the bookcases, and began busily carrying the books from the centre table to deposit them on the shelves, in which employment she was soon assisted by Willie, who took the matter in hand in a very masterly manner, showing his sister what were and what were not "Sunday books" with the air of a person entirely at home in the business. Robinson Crusoe and the many-volumed Peter Parley were put by without hesitation; there was, however, a short demurring over a North American Review, because Willie said he was sure his father read something one Sunday out of one of them, while Susan averred that he did not commonly read in it, and only read in it then because the piece was something about the Bible; but as nothing could be settled definitively on the point, the review was "laid on the table," like knotty questions in Congress. Then followed a long discussion over an extract book, which, as usual, contained all sorts, both sacred, serious, comic, and profane; and at last Willie, with much gravity, decided to lock it up, on the principle that it was best to be on the *safe side*, in support of which he appealed to me. I was saved from deciding the question by the entrance of the father and mother. My old friend knew me at once, and presented his pretty wife to me with the same look of exultation with which he used to hold up a string of trout or an uncommonly fine perch of his own catching for my admiration, and then looking round on his fine family of children, two more of which he had brought home with him, seemed to say to me, "There! what do you think of that, now?"

And, in truth, a very pretty sight it was — enough to make any one's old bachelor coat sit very uneasily on him. Indeed, there is nothing that gives one such a startling idea of the tricks that old Father Time has been playing on us, as to meet some boyish or girlish companions with half a dozen or so of thriving children about them. My old friend, I found, was in essence just what the boy had been. There was the same upright bearing, the same confident, cheerful tone to his voice, and the same fire in his eye; only that the hand of manhood had slightly touched some of the lines of his face, giving them a staidness of expression becoming the man and the father.

"Very well, my children," said Mrs. Fletcher, as, after tea, William and Susan finished recounting to her the various matters that they had set in order that afternoon; "I believe now we can say that our week's work is finished, and that we have nothing to do but rest and enjoy ourselves."

"O, and papa will show us the pictures in those great books that he brought home for us last Monday, will he not?" said little Robert.

"And, mother, you will tell us some more about Solomon's temple and his palaces, won't you?" said Susan.

"And I should like to know if father has found out the answer to that hard question I gave him last Sunday?" said Willie.

"All will come in good time," said Mrs. Fletcher. "But tell me, my dear children, are you sure that you are quite ready for the Sabbath? You say you have put away the books and the playthings; have you put away, too, all wrong and unkind feelings? Do you feel kindly and pleasantly towards every body?"

"Yes, mother," said Willie, who appeared to have taken a great part of this speech to himself; "I went over to Tom Walter's this very morning to ask him about that chicken of mine, and he said that he did not mean to hit it, and did not know he had till I told him of it; and so we made all up again, and I am glad I went."

"I am inclined to think, Willie," said his father, "that if every body would make it a rule to settle up all their differences *before Sunday*, there would be very few long quarrels and lawsuits. In about half the cases, a quarrel is founded on some misunderstanding that would be got over in five minutes if one would go directly to the person for explanation."

"I suppose I need not ask you," said Mrs. Fletcher, "whether you have fully learned your Sunday school lessons."

"O, to be sure," said William. "You know, mother, that Susan and I were busy about them through Monday and Tuesday, and then this afternoon we looked them over again, and wrote down some questions."

"And I heard Robert say his all through, and showed him all the places on the Bible Atlas," said Susan.

"Well, then," said my friend, "if every thing is done, let us begin Sunday with some music."

Thanks to the recent improvements in the musical instruction of the young, every family can now form a domestic concert, with words and tunes adapted to the capacity and the voices of children; and while these little ones, full of animation, pressed round their mother as she sat at the piano, and accompanied her music with the words of some beautiful hymns, I thought that, though I might have heard finer music, I had never listened to any that answered the purpose of music so well.

It was a custom at my friend's to retire at an early hour on Saturday evening, in order that there might be abundant time for rest, and no excuse for late rising on the Sabbath; and, accordingly, when the children had done singing, after a short season of family devotion, we all betook ourselves to our chambers, and I, for one, fell asleep with the impression of having finished the week most agreeably, and with anticipations of very great pleasure on the morrow.

Early in the morning I was roused from my sleep by the sound of little voices singing with great animation in the room next to mine, and, listening, I caught the following words: —

"Awake! awake! your bed forsake,
To God your praises pay;
The morning sun is clear and bright;
With joy we hail his cheerful light.
In songs of love
Praise God above —
It is the Sabbath day!"

The last words were repeated and prolonged most vehemently by a voice that I knew for Master William's.

"Now, Willie, I like the other one best," said the soft voice of little Susan; and immediately she began, —

"How sweet is the day,
When, leaving our play,
The Saviour we seek!
The fair morning glows
When Jesus arose —
The best in the week."

Master William helped along with great spirit in the singing of this tune, though I heard him observing, at the end of the first verse, that he liked the other one better, because "it seemed to step off so kind o' lively;" and his accommodating sister followed him as he began singing it again with redoubled animation.

It was a beautiful summer morning, and the voices of the children within accorded well with the notes of birds and bleating flocks without — a cheerful, yet Sabbath-like and quieting sound.

"Blessed be children's music!" said I to myself; "how much better this is than the solitary tick, tick, of old Uncle Fletcher's tall mahogany clock!"

The family bell summoned us to the breakfast room just as the children had finished their hymn. The little breakfast parlor had been swept and garnished expressly for the day, and a vase of beautiful flowers, which the children had the day before collected from their gardens, adorned the centre table. The door of one of the bookcases by the fireplace was thrown open, presenting to view a collection of prettily bound books, over the top of which appeared in gilt letters the inscription, "Sabbath Library." The windows were thrown open to let in the invigorating breath of the early morning, and the birds that flitted among the rosebushes without seemed scarcely lighter and more buoyant than did the children as they entered the room. It was legibly written on every face in the house, that the happiest day in the week had arrived, and each one seemed to enter into its duties with a whole soul. It was still early when the breakfast and the season of family devotion were over, and the children eagerly gathered round the table to get a sight of the pictures in the new books which their father had purchased in New York the week before, and which had been reserved as a Sunday's treat. They were a beautiful edition of Calmet's Dictionary, in several large volumes, with very superior engravings.

"It seems to me that this work must be very expensive," I remarked to my friend, as we were turning the leaves.

"Indeed it is so," he replied; "but here is one place where I am less withheld by considerations of expense than in any other. In all that concerns making a show in the world, I am perfectly ready to economize. I can do very well without expensive clothing or fashionable furniture, and am willing that we should be looked on as very plain sort of people in all such matters; but in all that relates to the cultivation of the mind, and the improvement of the hearts of my children, I am willing to go to the extent of my ability. Whatever will give my children a better knowledge of, or deeper interest in, the Bible, or enable them to spend a Sabbath profitably and without weariness, stands first on my list among things to be purchased. I have spent in this way one third as much as the furnishing of my house costs me." On looking over the shelves of the Sabbath library, I perceived that my friend had been at no small pains in the selection. It comprised all the popular standard works for the illustration of the Bible, together with the best of the modern religious publications adapted to the capacity of young children. Two large drawers below were filled with maps and scriptural engravings, some of them of a very superior character.

"We have been collecting these things gradually ever since we have been at housekeeping," said my friend; "the children take an interest in this library, as something more particularly belonging to them, and some of the books are donations from their little earnings."

"Yes," said Willie, "I bought Helon's Pilgrimage with my egg money, and Susan bought the Life of David, and little Robert is going to buy one, too, next new year."

"But," said I, "would not the Sunday school library answer all the purpose of this?"

"The Sabbath school library is an admirable thing," said my friend; "but this does more fully and perfectly what that was intended to do. It makes a sort of central attraction at home on the Sabbath, and makes the acquisition of religious knowledge and the proper observance of the Sabbath a sort of family enterprise. You know," he added, smiling, "that people always feel interested for an object in which they have invested money."

The sound of the first Sabbath school bell put an end to this conversation. The children promptly made themselves ready, and as their father was the superintendent of the school, and their mother one of the teachers, it was quite a family party.

One part of every Sabbath at my friend's was spent by one or both parents with the children, in a sort of review of the week. The attention of the little ones was directed to their own characters, the various defects or improvements of the past week were pointed out, and they were stimulated to be on their guard in the time to come, and the whole was closed by earnest prayer for such heavenly aid as the temptations and faults of each particular one might need. After church in the evening, while the children were thus withdrawn to their mother's apartment, I could not forbear reminding my friend of old times, and of the rather anti-sabbatical turn of his mind in our boyish days.

"Now, William," said I, "do you know that you were the last boy of whom such an enterprise in Sabbath keeping as this was to have been expected? I suppose you remember Sunday at 'the old place'?"

"Nay, now, I think I was the very one," said he, smiling, "for I had sense enough to see, as I grew up, that the day must be kept *thoroughly* or not at all, and I had enough blood and motion in my composition to see that something must be done to enliven and make it interesting; so I set myself about it. It was one of the first of our housekeeping resolutions, that the Sabbath should be made a pleasant day, and yet be as inviolably kept as in the strictest times of our good father; and we have brought things to run in that channel so long, that it seems to be the natural order."

"I have always supposed," said I, "that it required a peculiar talent, and more than common information in a parent, to accomplish this to any extent."

"It requires nothing," replied my friend, "but common sense, and a strong *determination to do it*. Parents who make a definite object of the religious instruction of their children, if they have common sense, can very soon see what is necessary in order to interest them; and, if they find themselves wanting in the requisite information, they can, in these days, very readily acquire it. The sources of religious knowledge are so numerous, and so popular in their form, that all can avail themselves of them. The only difficulty, after all, is, that the keeping of the Sabbath and the imparting of religious instruction are not made enough of a *home* object. Parents pass off the responsibility on to the Sunday school teacher, and suppose, of course, if they send their children to Sunday school, they do the best they can for them. Now, I am satisfied, from my experience as a Sabbath school teacher, that the best religious instruction imparted abroad still stands in need of the coöperation of a systematic plan of religious discipline and instruction at home; for, after all, God gives a power to the efforts of a *parent* that can never be transferred to other hands."

"But do you suppose," said I, "that the *common* class of minds, with ordinary advantages, can do what you have done?"

"I think in most cases they could, *if they begin* right. But when both parents and children have formed *habits*, it is more difficult to change than to begin right at first. However, I think *all* might accomplish a great deal if they would give time, money, and effort towards it. It is because the object is regarded of so little value, compared with other things of a worldly nature, that so little is done."

My friend was here interrupted by the entrance of Mrs. Fletcher with the children. Mrs. Fletcher sat down to the piano, and the Sabbath was closed with the happy songs of the little ones; nor could I notice a single anxious eye turning to the window to see if the sun was not almost down. The tender and softened expression of each countenance bore witness to the subduing power of those instructions which had hallowed the last hour, and their sweet, bird-like voices harmonized well with the beautiful words, —

> "How sweet the light of Sabbath eve!
> How soft the sunbeam lingering there!
> Those holy hours this low earth leave,
> And rise on wings of faith and prayer."

LET EVERY MAN MIND HIS OWN BUSINESS.

"And so you will not sign this paper?" said Alfred Melton to his cousin, a fine-looking young man, who was lounging by the centre table.

"Not I, indeed. What in life have I to do with these decidedly vulgar temperance pledges? Pshaw! they have a relish of whiskey in their very essence!"

"Come, come, Cousin Melton," said a brilliant, dark-eyed girl, who had been lolling on the sofa during the conference, "I beg of you to give over attempting to evangelize Edward. You see, as Falstaff has it, 'he is little better than one of the wicked.' You must not waste such valuable temperance documents on him."

"But, seriously, Melton, my good fellow," resumed Edward, "this signing, and sealing, and pledging is altogether an unnecessary affair for me. My past and present habits, my situation in life, — in short, every thing that can be mentioned with regard to me, — goes against the supposition of my ever becoming the slave of a vice so debasing; and this pledging myself to avoid it is something altogether needless — nay, by implication, it is degrading. As to what you say of my influence, I am inclined to the opinion, that if every man will look to himself, every man will be looked to. This modern notion of tacking the whole responsibility of society on to every individual is one I am not at all inclined to adopt; for, first, I know it is a troublesome doctrine; and, secondly, I doubt if it be a true one. For both which reasons, I shall decline extending to it my patronage."

"Well, positively," exclaimed the lady, "you gentlemen have the gift of continuance in an uncommon degree. You have discussed this matter backward and forward till I am ready to perish. I will take the matter in hand myself, and sign a temperance pledge for Edward, and see that he gets into none of those naughty courses upon which you have been so pathetic."

"I dare say," said Melton, glancing on her brilliant face with evident admiration, "that you will be the best temperance pledge he could have. But every man, cousin, may not be so fortunate."

"But, Melton," said Edward, "seeing my steady habits are so well provided for, you must carry your logic and eloquence to some poor fellow less favored." And thus the conference ended.

"What a good disinterested fellow Melton is!" said Edward, after he had left.

"Yes, good, as the day is long," said Augusta, "but rather prosy, after all. This tiresome temperance business! One never hears the end of it nowadays. Temperance papers — temperance tracts — temperance hotels — temperance this, that, and the other thing, even down to temperance pocket handkerchiefs for little boys! Really, the world is getting intemperately temperate."

"Ah, well! with the security you have offered, Augusta, I shall dread no temptation."

Though there was nothing peculiar in these words, yet there was a certain earnestness of tone that called the color into the face of Augusta, and set her to sewing with uncommon assiduity. And thereupon Edward proceeded with some remark about "guardian angels," together with many other things of the kind, which, though they contain no more that is new than a temperance lecture, always seem to have a peculiar freshness to people in certain circumstances. In fact, before the hour was at an end, Edward and Augusta had forgotten where they began, and had wandered far into that land of anticipations and bright dreams which surrounds the young and loving before they eat of the tree of experience, and gain the fatal knowledge of good and evil.

But here, stopping our sketching pencil, let us throw in a little background and perspective that will enable our readers to perceive more readily the entire picture.

Edward Howard was a young man whose brilliant talents and captivating manners had placed him first in the society in which he moved. Though without property or weight of family connections, he had become a leader in the circles where these appendages are most considered, and there were none of their immunities and privileges that were not freely at his disposal.

Augusta Elmore was conspicuous in all that lies within the sphere of feminine attainment. She was an orphan, and accustomed from a very early age to the free enjoyment and control of an independent property. This circumstance, doubtless, added to the magic of her personal graces in procuring for her that flattering deference which beauty and wealth secure.

Her mental powers were naturally superior, although, from want of motive, they had received no development, except such as would secure success in society. Native good sense, with great strength of feeling and independence of mind, had saved her from becoming heartless and frivolous. She was better fitted to lead and to influence than to be influenced or led. And hence, though not swayed by any habitual sense of moral responsibility, the tone of her character seemed altogether more elevated than the average of fashionable society.

General expectation had united the destiny of two persons who seemed every way fitted for each other, and for once general expectation did not err. A few months after the interview mentioned were witnessed the festivities and congratulations of their brilliant and happy marriage.

Never did two young persons commence life under happier auspices. "What an exact match!" "What a beautiful couple!" said all the gossips. "They seem made for each other," said every one; and so thought the happy lovers themselves.

Love, which with persons of strong character is always an earnest and sobering principle, had made them thoughtful and considerate; and as they looked forward to future life, and talked of the days before them, their plans and ideas were as rational as any plans can be, when formed entirely with reference to this life, without any regard to another.

For a while their absorbing attachment to each other tended to withdraw them from the temptations and allurements of company; and many a long winter evening passed delightfully in the elegant quietude of home, as they read, and sang, and talked of the past, and dreamed of the future in each other's society. But, contradictory as it may appear to the theory of the sentimentalist, it is nevertheless a fact, that two persons cannot always find sufficient excitement in talking to each other merely; and this is especially true of those to whom high excitement has been a necessary of life. After a while, the young couple, though loving each other none the less, began to respond to the many calls which invited them again into society, and the pride they felt in each other added zest to the pleasures of their return.

As the gaze of admiration followed the graceful motions of the beautiful wife, and the whispered tribute went round the circle whenever she entered, Edward felt a pride beyond all that flattery, addressed to himself, had ever excited; and Augusta, when told of the convivial talents and powers of entertainment which distinguished her husband, could not resist the temptation of urging him into society even oftener than his own wishes would have led him.

Alas! neither of them knew the perils of constant excitement, nor supposed that, in thus alienating themselves from the pure and simple pleasures of home, they were risking their whole capital of happiness. It is in indulging the first desire for extra stimulus that the first and deepest danger to domestic peace lies. Let that stimulus be either bodily or mental, its effects are alike to be dreaded.

The man or the woman to whom habitual excitement of any kind has become essential has taken the first step towards ruin. In the case of a woman, it leads to discontent, fretfulness, and dissatisfaction with the quiet duties of domestic life; in the case of a man, it leads almost invariably to animal stimulus, ruinous alike to the powers of body and mind.

Augusta, fondly trusting to the virtue of her husband, saw no danger in the constant round of engagements which were gradually drawing his attention from the graver cares of business, from the pursuit of self-improvement, and from the love of herself. Already there was in her horizon the cloud "as big as a man's hand" — the precursor of future darkness and tempest; but, too confident and buoyant, she saw it not.

It was not until the cares and duties of a mother began to confine her at home, that she first felt, with a startling sensation of fear, that there was an alteration in her husband, though even then the change was so shadowy and indefinite that it could not be defined by words.

It was known by that quick, prophetic sense which reveals to the heart of woman the first variation in the pulse of affection, though it be so slight that no other touch can detect it.

Edward was still fond, affectionate, admiring; and when he tendered her all the little attentions demanded by her situation, or caressed and praised his beautiful son, she felt satisfied and happy. But when she saw that, even without her, the convivial circle had its attractions, and that he could leave her to join it, she sighed, she scarce knew why. "Surely," she said, "I am not so selfish as to wish to rob him of pleasure because I cannot enjoy it with him. But yet, once he told me there was no pleasure where I was not. Alas! is it true, what I have so often heard, that such feelings cannot always last?"

Poor Augusta! she knew not how deep reason she had to fear. She saw not the temptations that surrounded her husband in the circles where to all the stimulus of wit and intellect was often added the zest of *wine*, used far too freely for safety.

Already had Edward become familiar with a degree of physical excitement which touches the very verge of intoxication; yet, strong in self-confidence, and deluded by the customs of society, he dreamed not of danger. The traveller who has passed above the rapids of Niagara may have noticed the spot where the first white sparkling ripple announces the downward tendency of the waters. All here is brilliancy and beauty; and as the waters ripple and dance in the sunbeam, they seem only as if inspired by a spirit of new life, and not as hastening to a dreadful fall. So the first approach to intemperance, that ruins both body and soul, seems only like the buoyancy and exulting freshness of a new life, and the unconscious voyager feels his bark undulating with a thrill of delight, ignorant of the inexorable hurry, the tremendous sweep, with which the laughing waters urge him on beyond the reach of hope or recovery.

It was at this period in the life of Edward that one judicious and manly friend, who would have had the courage to point out to him the danger that every one else perceived, might have saved him. But among the circle of his acquaintances there was none such. "*Let every man mind his own business*" was their universal maxim. True, heads were gravely shaken, and Mr. A. regretted to Mr. B. that so promising a young man seemed about to ruin himself. But one was "*no relation*" of Edward's, and the other "felt a delicacy in speaking on such a subject," and therefore, according to a very ancient precedent, they "passed by on the other side." Yet it was at Mr. A.'s sideboard, always sparkling with the choicest wine, that he had felt the first excitement of extra stimulus; it was at Mr. B.'s house that the convivial club began to hold their meetings, which, after a time, found a more appropriate place in a public hotel. It is thus that the sober, the regular, and the discreet, whose constitution saves them from liabilities to excess, will accompany the ardent and excitable to the very verge of danger, and then wonder at their want of self-control.

It was a cold winter evening, and the wind whistled drearily around the closed shutters of the parlor in which Augusta was sitting. Every thing around her bore the marks of elegance and comfort.

Splendid books and engravings lay about in every direction. Vases of rare and costly flowers exhaled perfume, and magnificent mirrors multiplied every object. All spoke of luxury and repose, save the anxious and sad countenance of its mistress.

It was late, and she had watched anxiously for her husband for many long hours. She drew out her gold and diamond repeater, and looked at it. It was long past midnight. She sighed as she remembered the pleasant evenings they had passed together, as her eye fell on the books they had read together, and on her piano and harp, now silent, and thought of all he had said and looked in those days when each was all to the other.

She was aroused from this melancholy revery by a loud knocking at the street door. She hastened to open it, but started back at the sight it disclosed — her husband borne by four men.

"Dead! is he dead?" she screamed, in agony.

"No, ma'am," said one of the men, "but he might as well be dead as in such a fix as this."

The whole truth, in all its degradation, flashed on the mind of Augusta. Without a question or comment, she motioned to the sofa in the parlor, and her husband was laid there. She locked the street door, and when the last retreating footstep had died away, she turned to the sofa, and stood gazing in fixed and almost stupefied silence on the face of her senseless husband.

At once she realized the whole of her fearful lot. She saw before her the blight of her own affections, the ruin of her helpless children, the disgrace and misery of her husband. She looked around her in helpless despair, for she well knew the power of the vice whose deadly seal was set upon her husband. As one who is struggling and sinking in the waters casts a last dizzy glance at the green sunny banks and distant trees which seem sliding from his view, so did all the scenes of her happy days pass in a moment before her, and she groaned aloud in bitterness of spirit. "Great God! help me, help me," she prayed. "Save him — O, save my husband."

Augusta was a woman of no common energy of spirit, and when the first wild burst of anguish was over, she resolved not to be wanting to her husband and children in a crisis so dreadful.

"When he awakes," she mentally exclaimed, "I will warn and implore; I will pour out my whole soul to save him. My poor husband, you have been misled — betrayed. But you are too good, too generous, too noble to be sacrificed without a struggle."

It was late the next morning before the stupor in which Edward was plunged began to pass off. He slowly opened his eyes, started up wildly, gazed hurriedly around the room, till his eye met the fixed and sorrowful gaze of his wife. The past instantly flashed upon him, and a deep flush passed over his countenance. There was a dead, a solemn silence, until Augusta, yielding to her agony, threw herself into his arms, and wept.

"Then you do not hate me, Augusta?" said he, sorrowfully.

"Hate you — never! But, O Edward, Edward, what has beguiled you?"

"My wife — you once promised to be my guardian in virtue — such you are, and will be. O Augusta! you have looked on what you shall never see again — never — never — so help me God!" said he, looking up with solemn earnestness.

And Augusta, as she gazed on the noble face, the ardent expression of sincerity and remorse, could not doubt that her husband was saved. But Edward's plan of reformation had one grand defect. It was merely modification and retrenchment, and not *entire abandonment.* He could not feel it necessary to cut himself off entirely from the scenes and associations where temptation had met him. He considered not that, when the temperate flow of the blood and the even balance of the nerves have once been destroyed, there is, ever after, a double and fourfold liability, which often makes a man the sport of the first untoward chance.

He still contrived to stimulate sufficiently to prevent the return of a calm and healthy state of the mind and body, and to make constant self-control and watchfulness necessary.

It is a great mistake to call nothing intemperance but that degree of physical excitement which completely overthrows the mental powers. There is a state of nervous excitability, resulting from what is often called moderate stimulation, which often long precedes this, and is, in regard to it, like the premonitory warnings of the fatal cholera — an unsuspected draught on the vital powers, from which, at any moment, they may sink into irremediable collapse.

It is in this state, often, that the spirit of gambling or of wild speculation is induced by the morbid cravings of an over-stimulated system. Unsatisfied with the healthy and regular routine of business, and the laws of gradual and solid prosperity, the excited and unsteady imagination leads its subjects to daring risks, with the alternative of unbounded gain on the one side, or of utter ruin on the other. And when, as is too often the case, that ruin comes, unrestrained and desperate intemperance is the wretched resort to allay the ravings of disappointment and despair.

Such was the case with Edward. He had lost his interest in his regular business, and he embarked the bulk of his property in a brilliant scheme then in vogue; and when he found a crisis coming, threatening ruin and beggary, he had recourse to the fatal stimulus, which, alas! he had never wholly abandoned.

At this time he spent some months in a distant city, separated from his wife and family, while the insidious power of temptation daily increased, as he kept up, by artificial stimulus, the flagging vigor of his mind and nervous system.

It came at last — the blow which shattered alike his brilliant dreams and his real prosperity. The large fortune brought by his wife vanished in a moment, so that scarcely a pittance remained in his hands. From the distant city where he had been to superintend his schemes, he thus wrote to his too confiding wife: —

"Augusta, all is over! expect no more from your husband — believe no more of his promises — for he is lost to you and you to him. Augusta, our property is gone; *your* property, which I have blindly risked, is all swallowed up. But is that the worst? No, no, Augusta; *I* am lost — lost, body and soul, and as irretrievably as the perishing riches I have squandered. Once I had energy — health — nerve — resolution; but all are gone: yes, yes, I have yielded — I do yield daily to what is at once my tormentor and my temporary refuge from intolerable misery. You remember the sad hour you first knew your husband was a drunkard. Your look on that morning of misery — shall I ever forget it? Yet, blind and confiding as you were, how soon did your ill-judged confidence in me return! Vain hopes! I was even then past recovery — even then sealed over to blackness of darkness forever.

"Alas! my wife, my peerless wife, why am I your husband? why the father of such children as you have given me? Is there nothing in your unequalled loveliness — nothing in the innocence of our helpless babes, that is powerful enough to recall me? No, there is not.

"Augusta, you know not the dreadful gnawing, the intolerable agony of this master passion. I walk the floor — I think of my own dear home, my high hopes, my proud expectations, my children, my wife, my own immortal soul. I feel that I am sacrificing all — feel it till I am withered with agony; but the hour comes — the burning hour, and *all is in vain.* I shall return to you no more, Augusta. All the little wreck I have saved I send: you have friends, relatives — above all, you have an energy of mind, a capacity of resolute action, beyond that of ordinary women, and you shall never be bound — the living to the dead. True, you will suffer, thus to burst the bonds that unite us; but be resolute, for you will suffer more to watch from day to day the slow workings of death and ruin in your husband. Would you stay with me, to see every vestige of what you once loved passing away — to endure the caprice, the moroseness, the delirious anger of one no longer master of himself? Would you make your children victims and fellow-sufferers with you? No! dark and dreadful is my path! I will walk it alone: no one shall go with me.

"In some peaceful retirement you may concentrate your strong feelings upon your children, and bring them up to fill a place in your heart which a worthless husband has abandoned. If I leave you now, you will remember me as I have been — you will love me and weep for me when dead; but if you stay with me, your love will be worn out; I shall become the object of disgust and loathing. Therefore farewell, my wife — my first, best love, farewell! with you I part with hope, —

'And with hope, farewell fear,
Farewell remorse: all good to me is lost:
Evil, be thou my good.'

This is a wild strain, but fit for me: do not seek for me, do not write: nothing can save me."

Thus abruptly began and ended the letter that conveyed to Augusta the death doom of her hopes. There are moments of agony when the most worldly heart is pressed upward to God, even as a weight will force upward the reluctant water. Augusta had been a generous, a high-minded, an affectionate woman, but she had lived entirely for this world. Her chief good had been her husband and her children. These had been her pride, her reliance, her dependence. Strong in her own resources, she had never felt the need of looking to a higher power for assistance and happiness. But when this letter fell from her trembling hand, her heart died within her at its wild and reckless bitterness.

In her desperation she looked up to God. "What have I to live for now?" was the first feeling of her heart.

But she repressed this inquiry of selfish agony, and besought almighty assistance to nerve her weakness; and here first began that practical acquaintance with the truths and hopes of religion which changed her whole character.

The possibility of blind, confiding idolatry of any earthly object was swept away by the fall of her husband, and with the full energy of a decided and desolate spirit, she threw herself on the protection of an almighty Helper. She followed her husband to the city whither he had gone, found him, and vainly attempted to save.

There were the usual alternations of short-lived reformations, exciting hopes only to be destroyed. There was the gradual sinking of the body, the decay of moral feeling and principle — the slow but sure approach of disgusting animalism, which marks the progress of the drunkard.

It was some years after that a small and partly ruinous tenement in the outskirts of A. received a new family. The group consisted of four children, whose wan and wistful countenances, and still, unchildlike deportment, testified an early acquaintance with want and sorrow. There was the mother, faded and care-worn, whose dark and melancholy eyes, pale cheeks, and compressed lips told of years of anxiety and endurance. There was the father, with haggard face, unsteady step, and that callous, reckless air, that betrayed long familiarity with degradation and crime. Who, that had seen Edward Howard in the morning and freshness of his days, could have recognized him in this miserable husband and father? or who, in this worn and woe-stricken woman, would have known the eautiful, brilliant, and accomplished Augusta? Yet such changes are not fancy, as many a bitter and broken heart can testify.

Augusta had followed her guilty husband through many a change and many a weary wandering. All hope of reformation had gradually faded away. Her own eyes had seen, her ears had heard, all those disgusting details, too revolting to be portrayed; for in drunkenness there is no royal road — no salvo for greatness of mind, refinement of taste, or tenderness of feeling. All alike are merged in the corruption of a moral death.

The traveller, who met Edward reeling by the roadside, was sometimes startled to hear the fragments of classical lore, or wild bursts of half-remembered poetry, mixing strangely with the imbecile merriment of intoxication. But when he stopped to gaze, there was no further mark on his face or in his eye by which he could be distinguished from the loathsome and lowest drunkard.

Augusta had come with her husband to a city where they were wholly unknown, that she might at least escape the degradation of their lot in the presence of those who had known them in better days. The long and dreadful struggle that annihilated the hopes of this life had raised her feelings to rest upon the next, and the habit of communion with God, induced by sorrows which nothing else could console, had given a tender dignity to her character such as nothing else could bestow.

It is true, she deeply loved her children; but it was with a holy, chastened love, such as inspired the sentiment once breathed by Him "who was made perfect through sufferings." "For their sakes I sanctify myself, that they also may be sanctified."

Poverty, deep poverty, had followed their steps, but yet she had not fainted. Talents which in her happier days had been nourished merely as luxuries, were now stretched to the utmost to furnish a support; while from the resources of her own reading she drew that which laid the foundation for early mental culture in her children.

Augusta had been here but a few weeks before her footsteps were traced by her only brother, who had lately discovered her situation, and urged her to forsake her unworthy husband and find refuge with him.

"Augusta, my sister, I have found you!" he exclaimed, as he suddenly entered one day, while she was busied with the work of her family.

"Henry, my dear brother!" There was a momentary illumination of countenance accompanying these words, which soon faded into a mournful quietness, as she cast her eyes around on the scanty accommodations and mean apartment.

"I see how it is, Augusta; step by step, you are sinking — dragged down by a vain sense of duty to one no longer worthy. I cannot bear it any longer; I have come to take you away."

Augusta turned from him, and looked abstractedly out of the window. Her features settled in thought. Their expression gradually deepened from their usual tone of mild, resigned sorrow to one of keen anguish.

"Henry," said she, turning towards him, "never was mortal woman so blessed in another as I once was in him. How can I forget it? Who knew him in those days that did not admire and love him? They tempted and insnared him; and even I urged him into the path of danger. He fell, and there was none to help. I urged reformation, and he again and again promised, resolved, and began. But again they

15 *

tempted him — even his very best friends; yes, and that, too, when they knew his danger. They led him on as far as it was safe for *them* to go, and when the sweep of his more excitable temperament took him past the point of safety and decency, they stood by, and coolly wondered and lamented. How often was he led on by such heartless friends to humiliating falls, and then driven to desperation by the cold look, averted faces, and cruel sneers of those whose medium temperament and cooler blood saved them from the snares which they saw were enslaving him. What if *I* had forsaken him *then?* What account should I have rendered to God? Every time a friend has been alienated by his comrades, it has seemed to seal him with another seal. I am his wife — and mine will be *the last.* Henry, when I leave him, I *know* his eternal ruin is sealed. I cannot do it now; a little longer — a little longer; the hour, I see, must come. I know my duty to my children forbids me to keep them here; take them — they are my last earthly comforts, Henry — but you must take them away. It may be — O God — perhaps it *must be,* that I shall soon follow; but not till I have tried *once more.* What is this present life to one who has suffered as I have? Nothing. But eternity! O Henry! eternity — how can I abandon him to *everlasting* despair! Under the breaking of my heart I have borne up. I have borne up under *all* that can try a woman; but *this* thought ——" She stopped, and seemed struggling with herself; but at last, borne down by a tide of agony, she leaned her head on her hands; the tears streamed through her fingers, and her whole frame shook with convulsive sobs.

Her brother wept with her; nor dared he again to touch the point so solemnly guarded. The next day Augusta parted from her children, hoping something from feelings that, possibly, might be stirred by their absence in the bosom of their father.

It was about a week after this that Augusta one evening presented herself at the door of a rich Mr. L., whose princely mansion was one of the ornaments of the city of A. It was not till she reached the sumptuous drawing room that she recognized in Mr. L. one whom she and her husband had frequently met in the gay circles of their early life. Altered as she was, Mr. L. did not recognize her, but compassionately handed her a chair, and requested her to wait the return of his lady, who was out; and then turning, he resumed his conversation with another gentleman.

"Now, Dallas," said he, "you are altogether excessive and intemperate in this matter. Society is not to be reformed by every man directing his efforts towards his neighbor, but by every man taking care of himself. It is you and I, my dear sir, who must begin with ourselves, and every other man must do the same; and then society will be effectually reformed. Now this modern way, by which every man considers it his duty to attend to the spiritual matters of his next-door neighbor, is taking the business at the wrong end altogether. It makes a vast deal of appearance, but it does very little good."

"But suppose your neighbor feels no disposition to attend to his own improvement — what then?"

"Why, then it is his own concern, and not mine. What my Maker requires is, that I do *my* duty, and not fret about my neighbor's."

"But, my friend, that is the very question. What is the duty your Maker requires? Does it not include some regard to your neighbor, some care and thought for his interest and improvement?"

"Well, well, I do that by setting a good example. I do not mean by example what you do — that is, that I am to stop drinking wine because it may lead him to drink brandy, any more than that I must stop eating because he may eat too much and become a dyspeptic — but that I am to use my wine, and every thing else, temperately and decently, and thus set him a good example."

The conversation was here interrupted by the return of Mrs. L. It recalled, in all its freshness, to the mind of Augusta the days when both she and her husband had thus spoken and thought.

Ah, how did these sentiments appear to her now — lonely, helpless, forlorn — the wife of a ruined husband, the mother of more than orphan children! How different from what they seemed, when, secure in ease, in wealth, in gratified affections, she thoughtlessly echoed the common phraseology, "Why must people concern themselves so much in their neighbors' affairs? Let every man mind his own business."

Augusta received in silence from Mrs. L. the fine sewing for which she came, and left the room.

"Ellen," said Mr. L. to his wife, "that poor woman must be in trouble of some kind or other. You must go some time, and see if any thing can be done for her."

"How singular!" said Mrs. L.; "she reminds me all the time of Augusta Howard. You remember her, my dear?"

"Yes, poor thing! and her husband too. That was a shocking affair of Edward Howard's. I hear that he became an intemperate, worthless fellow. Who could have thought it!"

"But you recollect, my dear," said Mrs. L., "I predicted it six months before it was talked of. You remember, at the wine party which you gave after Mary's wedding, he was so excited that he was hardly decent. I mentioned then that he was getting into dangerous ways. But he was such an excitable creature, that two or three glasses would put him quite beside himself. And there is George Eldon, who takes off his ten or twelve glasses, and no one suspects it."

"Well, it was a great pity," replied Mr. L.; "Howard was worth a dozen George Eldons."

"Do you suppose," said Dallas, who had listened thus far in silence, "that if he had moved in a circle where it was the universal custom to *banish all stimulating drinks*, he would thus have fallen?"

"I cannot say," said Mr. L.; "perhaps not."

Mr. Dallas was a gentleman of fortune and leisure, and of an ardent and enthusiastic temperament. Whatever engaged him absorbed his whole soul; and of late years, his mind had become deeply engaged in schemes of philanthropy for the improvement of his fellow-men. He had, in his benevolent ministrations, often passed the dwelling of Edward, and was deeply interested in the pale and patient wife and mother. He made acquaintance with her through the aid of her children, and, in one way and another, learned particulars of their history that awakened the deepest interest and concern. None but a mind as sanguine as his would have dreamed of attempting to remedy such hopeless misery by the reformation of him who was its cause. But such a plan had actually occurred to him. The remarks of Mr. and Mrs. L. recalled the idea, and he soon found that his intended *protégé* was the very Edward Howard whose early history was thus disclosed. He learned all the minutiæ from these his early associates without disclosing his aim, and left them still more resolved upon his benevolent plan.

He watched his opportunity when Edward was free from the influence of stimulus, and it was just after the loss of his children had called forth some remains of his better nature. Gradually and kindly he tried to touch the springs of his mind, and awaken some of its buried sensibilities.

"It is in vain, Mr. Dallas, to talk thus to me," said Edward, when, one day, with the strong eloquence of excited feeling, he painted the motives for attempting reformation; "you might as well attempt to reclaim the lost in hell. Do you think," he continued, in a wild, determined manner — "do you think I do not know all you can tell me? I have it all by heart, sir; no one can preach such discourses as I can on this subject: I know all — believe all — as the devils believe and tremble."

"Ay, but," said Dallas, "to you *there is hope;* you *are not* to ruin yourself forever."

"And who the devil are you, to speak to me in this way?" said Edward, looking up from his sullen despair with a gleam of curiosity, if not of hope.

"God's messenger to you, Edward Howard," said Dallas, fixing his keen eye upon him solemnly; "to you, Edward Howard, who have thrown away talents, hope, and health — who have blasted the heart of your wife, and beggared your suffering children. To you I am the messenger of your God — by me he offers health, and hope, and self-respect, and the regard of your fellow-men. You may heal the broken heart of your wife, and give back a father to your helpless children. Think of it, Howard: what if it were possible? Only suppose it. What would it be again to feel yourself a man, beloved and respected as you once were, with a happy home, a cheerful wife, and smiling little ones? Think how you could repay your poor wife for all her tears! What hinders you from gaining all this?"

"Just what hindered the rich man in hell—'*between us there is a great gulf fixed;*' it lies between me and all that is good; my wife, my children, my hope of heaven, are all on the other side."

"Ay, but this gulf can be passed: Howard, what *would you give* to be a temperate man?"

"What would I give?" said Howard. He thought for a moment, and burst into tears.

"Ah, I see how it is," said Dallas; "you need a friend, and God has sent you one."

"What *can* you do for me, Mr. Dallas?" said Edward, in a tone of wonder at the confidence of his assurances.

"I will tell you what I can do: I can take you to my house, and give you a room, and watch over you until the strongest temptations are past—I can give you business again. I can do *all* for you that needs to be done, if you will give yourself to my care."

"O God of mercy!" exclaimed the unhappy man, "is there hope for me? I cannot believe it possible; but take me where you choose—I will follow and obey."

A few hours witnessed the transfer of the lost husband to one of the retired apartments in the elegant mansion of Dallas, where he found his anxious and grateful wife still stationed as his watchful guardian.

Medical treatment, healthful exercise, useful employment, simple food, and pure water were connected with a personal supervision by Dallas, which, while gently and politely sustained, at first amounted to actual imprisonment.

For a time the reaction from the sudden suspension of

habitual stimulus was dreadful, and even with tears did the unhappy man entreat to be permitted to abandon the undertaking. But the resolute steadiness of Dallas and the tender entreaties of his wife prevailed. It is true that he might be said to be saved "so as by fire;" for a fever, and a long and fierce delirium, wasted him almost to the borders of the grave.

But, at length, the struggle between life and death was over, and though it left him stretched on the bed of sickness, emaciated and weak, yet he was restored to his right mind, and was conscious of returning health. Let any one who has laid a friend in the grave, and known what it is to have the heart fail with longing for them day by day, imagine the dreamy and unreal joy of Augusta when she began again to see in Edward the husband so long lost to her. It was as if the grave had given back the dead.

"Augusta!" said he, faintly, as, after a long and quiet sleep, he awoke free from delirium. She bent over him. "Augusta, I am redeemed — I am saved — I feel in myself that I am made whole."

The high heart of Augusta melted at these words. She trembled and wept. Her husband wept also, and after a pause he continued, —

"It is more than being restored to this life — I feel that it is the beginning of eternal life. It is the Savior who sought me out, and I know that he is able to keep me from falling."

But we will draw a veil over a scene which words have little power to paint.

"Pray, Dallas," said Mr. L., one day, "who is that fine-looking young man whom I met in your office this morning? I thought his face seemed familiar."

"It is a Mr. Howard — a young lawyer whom I have lately taken into business with me."

"Strange! Impossible!" said Mr. L. "Surely this cannot be the Howard that I once knew."

"I believe he is," said Mr. Dallas.

"Why, I thought he was gone — dead and done over, long ago, with intemperance."

"He was so; few have ever sunk lower; but he now promises even to outdo all that was hoped of him."

"Strange! Why, Dallas, what did bring about this change?"

"I feel a delicacy in mentioning how it came about to you, Mr. L., as there undoubtedly was a great deal of 'interference with other men's matters' in the business. In short, the young man fell in the way of one of those meddlesome fellows, who go prowling about, distributing tracts, forming temperance societies, and all that sort of stuff."

"Come, come, Dallas," said Mr. L., smiling, "I must hear the story, for all that."

"First call with me at this house," said Dallas, stopping before the door of a neat little mansion. They were soon in the parlor. The first sight that met their eyes was Edward Howard, who, with a cheek glowing with exercise, was tossing aloft a blooming boy, while Augusta was watching his motions, her face radiant with smiles.

"Mr. and Mrs. Howard, this is Mr. L., an old acquaintance, I believe."

There was a moment of mutual embarrassment and surprise, soon dispelled, however, by the frank cordiality of Edward. Mr. L. sat down, but could scarce withdraw his eyes from the countenance of Augusta, in whose eloquent face he recognized a beauty of a higher cast than even in her earlier days.

He glanced about the apartment. It was simply but tastefully furnished, and wore an air of retired, domestic comfort. There were books, engravings, and musical instruments. Above all, there were four happy, healthy-looking children, pursuing studies or sports at the farther end of the room.

After a short call they regained the street.

" Dallas, you are a happy man," said Mr. L.; " that family will be a mine of jewels to you."

He was right. Every soul saved from pollution and ruin is a jewel to him that reclaims it, whose lustre only eternity can disclose; and therefore it is written, " They that be wise shall shine as the brightness of the firmament, and they that turn many to righteousness, as the stars forever and ever."

COUSIN WILLIAM.

In a stately red house, in one of the villages of New England, lived the heroine of our story. She had every advantage of rank and wealth, for her father was a deacon of the church, and owned sheep, and oxen, and exceeding much substance. There was an appearance of respectability and opulence about all the demesnes. The house stood almost concealed amid a forest of apple trees, in spring blushing with blossoms, and in autumn golden with fruit. And near by might be seen the garden, surrounded by a red picket fence, enclosing all sorts of magnificence. There, in autumn, might be seen abundant squash vines, which seemed puzzled for room where to bestow themselves; and bright golden squashes, and full-orbed yellow pumpkins, looking as satisfied as the evening sun when he has just had his face washed in a shower, and is sinking soberly to bed. There were superannuated seed cucumbers, enjoying the pleasures of a contemplative old age; and Indian corn, nicely done up in green silk, with a specimen tassel hanging at the end of each ear. The beams of the summer sun darted through rows of crimson currants, abounding on bushes by the fence, while a sulky black currant bush sat scowling in one corner, a sort of garden curiosity.

But time would fail us were we to enumerate all the wealth of Deacon Israel Taylor. He himself belonged to that necessary class of beings, who, though remarkable for nothing at all, are very useful in filling up the links of society. Far otherwise was his sister-in-law, Mrs. Abigail Evetts, who, on the demise of the deacon's wife, had assumed the reins of government in the household.

This lady was of the same opinion that has animated many illustrious philosophers, namely, that the affairs of this world need a great deal of seeing to in order to have them go on prosperously; and although she did not, like them, engage in the supervision of the universe, she made amends by unremitting diligence in the department under her care. In her mind there was an evident necessity that every one should be up and doing: Monday, because it was washing day; Tuesday, because it was ironing day; Wednesday, because it was baking day; Thursday, because to-morrow was Friday; and so on to the end of the week. Then she had the care of reminding all in the house of every thing each was to do from week's end to week's end; and she was so faithful in this respect, that scarcely an original act of volition took place in the family. The poor deacon was reminded when he went out and when he came in, when he sat down and when he rose up, so that an act of omission could only have been committed through sheer malice prepense.

But the supervision of a whole family of children afforded to a lady of her active turn of mind more abundant matter of exertion. To see that their faces were washed, their clothes mended, and their catechism learned; to see that they did not pick the flowers, nor throw stones at the chickens, nor sophisticate the great house dog, was an accumulation of care that devolved almost entirely on Mrs. Abigail, so that, by her own account, she lived and throve by a perpetual miracle.

The eldest of her charge, at the time this story begins, was a girl just arrived at young ladyhood, and her name was Mary. Now we know that people very seldom have stories written about them who have not sylph-like forms, and glorious eyes, or, at least, "a certain inexpressible charm diffused over their whole person." But stories have of late so much abounded that they actually seem to have used up all the eyes, hair, teeth, lips, and forms necessary for a heroine, so that no one can now pretend to find an original collection wherewith to set one forth. These things considered, I regard it as fortunate that my heroine was not a beauty. She looked neither like a sylph, nor an oread, nor a fairy; she had neither *l'air distingué* nor *l'air magnifique*, but bore a great resemblance to a real mortal girl, such as you might pass a dozen of without any particular comment — one of those appearances, which, though common as water, may, like that, be colored any way by the associations you connect with it. Accordingly, a faultless taste in dress, a perfect ease and gayety of manner, a constant flow of kindly feeling, seemed in her case to produce all the effect of beauty. Her manners had just dignity enough to repel impertinence without destroying the careless freedom and sprightliness in which she commonly indulged. No person had a merrier run of stories, songs, and village traditions, and all those odds and ends of character which form the materials for animated conversation. She had read, too, every thing she could find: Rollin's History, and Scott's Family Bible, that stood in the glass bookcase in the best room, and an odd volume of Shakspeare, and now and then one of Scott's novels, borrowed from a somewhat literary family in the neighborhood. She also kept an album to write her thoughts in, and was in a constant habit of cutting out all the pretty poetry from the corners of the newspapers, besides drying forget-me-nots and rosebuds, in memory of different particular friends, with a number of other little sentimental practices to which young ladies of sixteen and thereabout are addicted. She was also endowed with great constructiveness; so that, in these days of ladies' fairs, there was nothing from bellows-needlebooks down to web-footed pincushions to which she could not turn her hand. Her sewing certainly *was* extraordinary, (we think too little is made of this in the accomplishments of heroines;) her stitching was like rows of pearls, and her cross-stitching was fairy-like; and for sewing over and over, as the village schoolma'am hath it, she had not her equal. And what shall we say of her pies and puddings? They would have converted the most reprobate old bachelor in the world. And then her sweeping and dusting! "Many daughters have done virtuously, but thou excellest them all!"

And now, what do you suppose is coming next? Why, a young gentleman, of course; for about this time comes to settle in the village, and take charge of the academy, a certain William Barton. Now, if you wish to know more particularly who he was, we only wish we could refer you to Mrs. Abigail, who was most accomplished in genealogies and old wifes' fables, and she would have told you that "her gran'ther, Ike Evetts, married a wife who was second cousin to Peter Scranton, who was great uncle to Polly Mosely, whose daughter Mary married William Barton's father, just about the time old 'Squire Peter's house was burned down." And then would follow an account of the domestic history of all branches of the family since they came over from England. Be that as it may, it is certain that Mrs. Abigail denominated him cousin, and that he came to the deacon's to board; and he had not been there more than a week, and made sundry observations on Miss Mary, before he determined to call her cousin too, which he accomplished in the most natural way in the world.

Mary was at first somewhat afraid of him, because she had heard that he had studied through all that was to be studied in Greek, and Latin, and German too; and she saw a library of books in his room, that made her sigh every time she looked at them, to think how much there was to be learned of which she was ignorant. But all this wore away, and presently they were the best friends in the world. He gave her books to read, and he gave her lessons in French, nothing puzzled by that troublesome verb which must be first conjugated, whether in French, Latin, or English. Then he gave her a deal of good advice about the cultivation of her mind and the formation of her character, all of which was very improving, and tended greatly to consolidate their friendship. But, unfortunately for Mary, William made quite as favorable an impression on the female community generally as he did on her, having distinguished himself on certain public occasions, such as delivering lectures on botany, and also, at the earnest request of the fourth of July committee, pronounced an oration which covered him with glory. He had been known, also, to write poetry, and had a retired and romantic air greatly bewitching to those who read Bulwer's novels. In short, it was morally certain, according to all rules of evidence, that if he had chosen to pay any lady of the village a dozen visits a week, she would have considered it as her duty to entertain him.

William did visit; for, like many studious people, he found

a need for the excitement of society; but, whether it was party or singing school, he walked home with Mary, of course, in as steady and domestic a manner as any man who has been married a twelvemonth. His air in conversing with her was inevitably more confidential than with any other one, and this was cause for envy in many a gentle breast, and an interesting diversity of reports with regard to her manner of treating the young gentleman went forth into the village.

"I wonder Mary Taylor will laugh and joke so much with William Barton in company," said one. "Her manners are altogether too free," said another. "It is evident she has designs upon him," remarked a third. "And she cannot even conceal it," pursued a fourth.

Some sayings of this kind at length reached the ears of Mrs. Abigail, who had the best heart in the world, and was so indignant that it might have done your heart good to see her. Still she thought it showed that "the girl needed *advising;*" and "she should *talk* to Mary about the matter."

But she first concluded to advise with William on the subject; and, therefore, after dinner the same day, while he was looking over a treatise on trigonometry or conic sections, she commenced upon him: —

"Our Mary is growing up a fine girl."

William was intent on solving a problem, and only understanding that something had been said, mechanically answered, "Yes."

"A little wild or so," said Mrs. Abigail.

"I know it," said William, fixing his eyes earnestly on E, F, B, C.

"Perhaps you think her a little too talkative and free with you sometimes; you know girls do not always think what they do."

"Certainly," said William, going on with his problem.

"I think you had better speak to her about it," said Mrs. Abigail.

"I think so too," said William, musing over his completed work, till at length he arose, put it in his pocket, and went to school.

O, this unlucky concentrativeness! How many shocking things a man may indorse by the simple habit of saying "Yes" and "No," when he is not hearing what is said to him.

The next morning, when William was gone to the academy, and Mary was washing the breakfast things, Aunt Abigail introduced the subject with great tact and delicacy by remarking, —

"Mary, I guess you had better be rather less free with William than you have been."

"Free!" said Mary, starting, and nearly dropping the cup from her hand; "why, aunt, what *do* you mean?"

"Why, Mary, you must not always be around so free in talking with him, at home, and in company, and every where. It won't do." The color started into Mary's cheek, and mounted even to her forehead, as she answered with a dignified air, —

"I have not been too free; I know what is right and proper; I have not been doing any thing that was improper."

Now, when one is going to give advice, it is very troublesome to have its necessity thus called in question; and Mrs. Abigail, who was fond of her own opinion, felt called upon to defend it.

"Why, yes, you have, Mary; every body in the village notices it."

"I don't care what every body in the village says. I shall always do what I think proper," retorted the young lady; "I know Cousin William does not think so."

"Well, *I* think he does, from some things I have heard him say."

"O aunt! what have you heard him say?" said Mary, nearly upsetting a chair in the eagerness with which she turned to her aunt.

"Mercy on us! you need not knock the house down, Mary. I don't remember exactly about it, only that his way of speaking made me think so."

"O aunt! do tell me what it was, and all about it," said Mary, following her aunt, who went around dusting the furniture.

Mrs. Abigail, like most obstinate people, who feel that they have gone too far, and yet are ashamed to go back, took refuge in an obstinate generalization, and only asserted that she had heard him say things, as if he did not quite like her ways.

This is the most consoling of all methods in which to leave a matter of this kind for a person of active imagination. Of course, in five minutes, Mary had settled in her mind a list of remarks that would have been suited to any of her village companions, as coming from her cousin. All the improbability of the thing vanished in the absorbing consideration of its possibility; and, after a moment's reflection, she pressed her lips together in a very firm way, and remarked that "Mr. Barton would have no occasion to say such things again."

It was very evident, from her heightened color and dignified air, that her state of mind was very heroical. As for poor Aunt Abigail, she felt sorry she had vexed her, and addressed herself most earnestly to her consolation, remarking, "Mary, I don't suppose William meant any thing. He knows you don't mean any thing wrong."

"Don't *mean* any thing wrong!" said Mary, indignantly.

"Why, child, he thinks you don't know much about folks and things, and if you have been a little ——"

"But I have not been. It was he that talked with me first. It was he that did every thing first. He called me cousin — and he *is* my cousin."

"No, child, you are mistaken; for you remember his grandfather was ——"

"I don't care who his grandfather was; he has no right to think of me as he does."

"Now, Mary, don't go to quarrelling with him; he can't help his thoughts, you know."

"I don't care what he thinks," said Mary, flinging out of the room with tears in her eyes.

Now, when a young lady is in such a state of affliction, the first thing to be done is to sit down and cry for two hours or more, which Mary accomplished in the most thorough manner; in the mean while making many reflections on the instability of human friendships, and resolving never to trust any one again as long as she lived, and thinking that this was a cold and hollow-hearted world, together with many other things she had read in books, but never realized so forcibly as at present. But what was to be done? Of course she did not wish to speak a word to William again, and wished he did not board there; and finally she put on her bonnet, and determined to go over to her other aunt's in the neighborhood, and spend the day, so that she might not see him at dinner.

But it so happened that Mr. William, on coming home at

noon, found himself unaccountably lonesome during school recess for dinner, and hearing where Mary was, determined to call after school at night at her aunt's, and attend her home.

Accordingly, in the afternoon, as Mary was sitting in the parlor with two or three cousins, Mr. William entered.

Mary was so anxious to look just as if nothing was the matter, that she turned away her head, and began to look out of the window just as the young gentleman came up to speak to her. So, after he had twice inquired after her health, she drew up very coolly, and said,—

"Did you speak to me, sir?"

William looked a little surprised at first, but seating himself by her, "To be sure," said he; "and I came to know why you ran away without leaving any message for me?"

"It did not occur to me," said Mary, in the dry tone which, in a lady, means, "I will excuse you from any further conversation, if you please." William felt as if there was something different from common in all this, but thought that perhaps he was mistaken, and so continued: —

"What a pity, now, that you should be so careless of me, when I was so thoughtful of you! I have come all this distance to see how you do."

"I am sorry to have given you the trouble," said Mary.

"Cousin, are you unwell to-day?" said William.

"No, sir," said Mary, going on with her sewing.

There was something so marked and decisive in all this, that William could scarcely believe his ears. He turned away, and commenced a conversation with a young lady; and Mary, to show that she could talk if she chose, commenced relating a story to her cousins, and presently they were all in a loud laugh.

"Mary has been full of her knickknacks to-day," said her old uncle, joining them.

William looked at her: she never seemed brighter or in better spirits, and he began to think that even Cousin Mary might puzzle a man sometimes.

He turned away, and began a conversation with old Mr. Zachary Coan on the raising of buckwheat — a subject which evidently required profound thought, for he never looked more grave, not to say melancholy.

Mary glanced that way, and was struck with the sad and almost severe expression with which he was listening to the details of Mr. Zachary, and was convinced that he was no more thinking of buckwheat than she was.

"I never thought of hurting his feelings so much," said she, relenting; "after all, he has been very kind to me. But he might have told me about it, and not somebody else." And hereupon she cast another glance towards him.

William was not talking, but sat with his eyes fixed on the snuffer-tray, with an intense gravity of gaze that quite troubled her, and she could not help again blaming herself.

"To be sure! Aunt was right; he could not help his thoughts. I will try to forget it," thought she.

Now, you must not think Mary was sitting still and gazing during this soliloquy. No, she was talking and laughing, apparently the most unconcerned spectator in the room. So passed the evening till the little company broke up.

"I am ready to attend you home," said William, in a tone of cold and almost haughty deference.

"I am obliged to you," said the young lady, in a similar tone, "but I shall stay all night;" then, suddenly changing her tone, she said, "No, I cannot keep it up any longer. I will go home with you, Cousin William."

"Keep up what?" said William, with surprise.

Mary was gone for her bonnet. She came out, took his arm, and walked on a little way.

"You have advised me always to be frank, cousin," said Mary, "and I must and will be; so I shall tell you all, though I dare say it is not according to rule."

"All what?" said William.

"Cousin," said she, not at all regarding what he said, "I was very much vexed this afternoon."

"So I perceived, Mary."

"Well, it is vexatious," she continued, "though, after all, we cannot expect people to think us perfect; but I did not think it quite fair in you not to tell *me*."

"Tell you what, Mary?"

Here they came to a place where the road turned through a small patch of woods. It was green and shady, and enlivened by a lively chatterbox of a brook. There was a mossy trunk of a tree that had fallen beside it, and made a pretty seat. The moonlight lay in little patches upon it, as it streamed down through the branches of the trees. It was a fairy-looking place, and Mary stopped and sat down, as if to collect her thoughts. After picking up a stick, and playing a moment in the water, she began: —

"After all, cousin, it was very natural in you to say so, if you thought so; though I should not have supposed you would think so."

"Well, I should be glad if I could know what it is," said William, in a tone of patient resignation.

"O, I forgot that I had not told you," said she, pushing back her hat, and speaking like one determined to go through with the thing. "Why, cousin, I have been told that you spoke of my manners towards yourself as being freer — more — obtrusive than they should be. And now," said she, her eyes flashing, "you see it was not a very easy thing to tell you, but I began with being frank, and I will be so, for the sake of satisfying *myself*."

To this William simply replied, "Who told you this, Mary?"

"My aunt."

"Did she say I said it to her?"

"Yes; and I do not so much object to your saying it as to your *thinking* it, for you know I did not force myself on your notice; it was you who sought my acquaintance and won my confidence; and that you, above all others, should think of me in this way!"

"I never did think so, Mary," said William, quietly.

"Nor ever *said* so?"

"Never. I should think you might have *known* it, Mary."

"But ——" said Mary.

"But," said William, firmly, "Aunt Abigail is certainly mistaken."

"Well, I am glad of it," said Mary, looking relieved, and gazing in the brook. Then looking up with warmth, "and, cousin, you never must think so. I am ardent, and I express myself freely; but I never meant, I am sure I never *should* mean, any thing more than a sister might say."

"And are you sure you never could, if all my happiness depended on it, Mary?"

She turned and looked up in his face, and saw a look that brought conviction. She rose to go on, and her hand was taken and drawn into the arm of her cousin, and that was the end of the first and the last difficulty that ever arose between them.

THE MINISTRATION OF OUR DEPARTED FRIENDS.

A NEW YEAR'S REVERY.

" It is a beautiful belief,
That ever round our head
Are hovering on viewless wings
The spirits of the dead."

WHILE every year is taking one and another from the ranks of life and usefulness, or the charmed circle of friendship and love, it is soothing to remember that the spiritual world is gaining in riches through the poverty of this.

In early life, with our friends all around us, — hearing their voices, cheered by their smiles, — death and the spiritual world are to us remote, misty, and half-fabulous; but as we advance in our journey, and voice after voice is hushed, and form after form vanishes from our side, and our shadow falls almost solitary on the hillside of life, the soul, by a necessity of its being, tends to the unseen and spiritual, and pursues in another life those it seeks in vain in this.

For with every friend that dies, dies also some especial form of social enjoyment, whose being depended on the peculiar character of that friend; till, late in the afternoon of life, the pilgrim seems to himself to have passed over to the unseen world in successive portions half his own spirit; and poor indeed is he who has not familiarized himself with that unknown, whither, despite himself, his soul is earnestly tending.

One of the deepest and most imperative cravings of the human heart, as it follows its beloved ones beyond the veil, is for some assurance that they still love and care for us. Could we firmly believe this, bereavement would lose half its bitterness. As a German writer beautifully expresses it, "Our friend is not wholly gone from us; we see across the river of death, in the blue distance, the smoke of his cottage;" hence the heart, always creating what it desires, has ever made the guardianship and ministration of departed spirits a favorite theme of poetic fiction.

But is it, then, fiction? Does revelation, which gives so many hopes which nature had not, give none here? Is there no sober certainty to correspond to the inborn and passionate craving of the soul? Do departed spirits in verity retain any knowledge of what transpires in this world, and take any part in its scenes? All that revelation says of a spiritual state is more intimation than assertion; it has no distinct treatise, and teaches nothing apparently of set purpose; but gives vague, glorious images, while now and then some accidental ray of intelligence looks out, —

"——— like eyes of cherubs shining
From out the veil that hid the ark."

But out of all the different hints and assertions of the Bible we think a better inferential argument might be constructed to prove the ministration of departed spirits than for many a doctrine which has passed in its day for the height of orthodoxy.

First, then, the Bible distinctly says that there is a class of invisible spirits who minister to the children of men: "Are they not all ministering spirits, sent forth to minister to those who shall be heirs of salvation?" It is said of little children, that "their angels do always behold the face of our Father which is in heaven." This last passage, from the words of our Savior, taken in connection with the well-known tradition of his time, fully recognizes the idea of individual guardian spirits; for God's government over mind is, it seems, throughout, one of intermediate agencies, and these not chosen at random, but with the nicest reference to their adaptation to the purpose intended. Not even the All-seeing, All-knowing One was deemed perfectly adapted to become a human Savior without a human experience. Knowledge intuitive, gained from above, of human wants and woes was not enough — to it must be added the home-born certainty of consciousness and memory; the Head of all mediation must become human. Is it likely, then, that, in selecting subordinate agencies, this so necessary a requisite of a human life and experience is overlooked? While around the throne of God stand spirits, now sainted and glorified, yet thrillingly conscious of a past experience of sin and sorrow, and trembling in sympathy with temptations and struggles like their own, is it likely that he would pass by these souls, thus burning for the work, and commit it to those bright abstract beings whose knowledge and experience are comparatively so distant and so cold?

It is strongly in confirmation of this idea, that in the transfiguration scene — which seems to have been intended purposely to give the disciples a glimpse of the glorified state of their Master — we find him attended by two spirits of earth, Moses and Elias, "which appeared with him in glory, and spake of his death which he should accomplish at Jerusalem." It appears that these so long departed ones were still mingling in deep sympathy with the tide of human affairs — not only aware of the present, but also informed as to the future. In coincidence with this idea are all those passages which speak of the redeemed of earth as being closely and indissolubly identified with Christ, members of his body, of his flesh and his bones. It is not to be supposed that those united to Jesus above all others by so vivid a sympathy and community of interests are left out as instruments in that great work of human regeneration which so engrosses him; and when we hear Christians spoken of as kings and priests unto God, as those who shall judge angels, we see it more than intimated that they are to be the partners and actors in that great work of spiritual regeneration of which Jesus is the head.

What then? May we look among the band of ministering spirits for our own departed ones? Whom would God be more likely to send us? Have we in heaven a friend who knew us to the heart's core? a friend to whom we have unfolded our soul in its most secret recesses? to whom we have confessed our weaknesses and deplored our griefs? If we are to have a ministering spirit, who better adapted? Have we not memories which correspond to such a belief? When our soul has been cast down, has never an invisible voice whispered, "There is lifting up"? Have not gales and breezes of sweet and healing thought been wafted over us, as if an angel had shaken from his wings the odors of paradise?

Many a one, we are confident, can remember such things — and whence come they? Why do the children of the pious mother, whose grave has grown green and smooth with years, seem often to walk through perils and dangers fearful and imminent as the crossing Mohammed's fiery gulf on the edge of a drawn sword, yet walk unhurt? Ah! could we see that attendant form, that face where the angel conceals not the mother, our question would be answered.

It may be possible that a friend is sometimes taken because the Divine One sees that his ministry can act more powerfully from the unseen world than amid the infirmities of mortal intercourse. Here the soul, distracted and hemmed in by human events and by bodily infirmities, often scarce knows itself, and makes no impression on others correspondent to its desires. The mother would fain electrify the heart of her child; she yearns and burns in vain to make her soul effective on its soul, and to inspire it with a spiritual and holy life; but all her own weaknesses, faults, and mortal cares cramp and confine her, till death breaks all fetters; and then, first truly alive, risen, purified, and at rest, she may do calmly, sweetly, and certainly, what, amid the tempests and tossings of life, she labored for painfully and fitfully. So, also, to generous souls, who burn for the good of man, who deplore the shortness of life, and the little that is permitted to any individual agency on earth, does this belief open a heavenly field. Think not, father or brother, long laboring for man, till thy sun stands on the western mountains, — think not that thy day in this world is over. Perhaps, like Jesus, thou hast lived a human life, and gained a human experience, to become, under and like him, a savior of thousands; thou hast been through the preparation, but thy real work of good, thy full power of doing, is yet to begin.

But again: there are some spirits (and those of earth's choicest) to whom, so far as enjoyment to themselves or others is concerned, this life seems to have been a total failure. A hard hand from the first, and all the way through life, seems to have been laid upon them; they seem to live only to be chastened and crushed, and we lay them in the grave at last in mournful silence. To such, what a vision is opened by this belief! This hard discipline has been the school and task-work by which their soul has been fitted for their invisible labors in a future life; and when they pass the gates of the grave, their course of benevolent acting first begins, and they find themselves delighted possessors of what through many years they have sighed for — the power of doing good. The year just past, like all other years, has taken from a thousand circles the sainted, the just, and the beloved; there are spots in a thousand graveyards which have become this year dearer than all the living world; but in the loneliness of sorrow how cheering to think that our lost ones are not wholly gone from us! They still may move about in our homes, shedding around an atmosphere of purity and peace, promptings of good, and reproofs of evil. We are compassed about by a cloud of witnesses, whose hearts throb in sympathy with every effort and struggle, and who thrill with joy at every success. How should this thought check and rebuke every worldly feeling and unworthy purpose, and enshrine us, in the midst of a forgetful and unspiritual world, with an atmosphere of heavenly peace! They have overcome — have risen — are crowned, glorified;

but still they remain to us, our assistants, our comforters, and in every hour of darkness their voice speaks to us: "So we grieved, so we struggled, so we fainted, so we doubted; but we have overcome, we have obtained, we have seen, we have found — and in our victory behold the certainty of thy own."

MRS. A. AND MRS. B.;

OR, WHAT SHE THINKS ABOUT IT.

Mrs. A. and Mrs. B. were next-door neighbors and intimate friends — that is to say, they took tea with each other very often, and, in confidential strains, discoursed of stockings and pocket handkerchiefs, of puddings and carpets, of cookery and domestic economy, through all its branches.

"I think, on the whole," said Mrs. A., with an air of profound reflection, "that gingerbread is the cheapest and healthiest cake one can make. I make a good deal of it, and let my children have as much as they want of it."

"I used to do so," said Mrs. B., "but I haven't had any made these two months."

"Ah! Why not?" said Mrs. A.

"Why, it is some trouble; and then, though it is cheap, it is cheaper not to have any; and, on the whole, the children are quite as well contented without it, and so we are fallen into the way of not having any."

"But one must keep some kind of cake in the house," said Mrs. A.

"So I have always heard, and thought, and practised," said Mrs. B.; "but really of late I have questioned the need of it."

The conversation gradually digressed from this point into various intricate speculations on domestic economy, and at last each lady went home to put her children to bed.

A fortnight after, the two ladies were again in conclave at Mrs. B.'s tea table, which was graced by some unusually nice gingerbread.

"I thought you had given up making gingerbread," said Mrs. A.; "you told me so a fortnight ago at my house."

"So I had," said Mrs. A.; "but since that conversation I have been making it again."

"Why so?"

"O, I thought that since you thought it economical enough, certainly I might; and that if you thought it necessary to keep some sort of cake in the closet, perhaps it was best I should."

Mrs. A. laughed.

"Well, now," said she, "I have *not* made any gingerbread, or cake of any kind, since that same conversation."

"Indeed?"

"No. I said to myself, If Mrs. B. thinks it will do to go without cake in the house, I suppose I might, as she says it *is* some additional expense and trouble; and so I gave it up."

Both ladies laughed, and you laugh, too, my dear lady reader; but have you never done the same thing? Have you never altered your dress, or your arrangements, or your housekeeping because somebody else was of a different way of thinking or managing — and may not that very somebody at the same time have been moved to make some change through a similar observation on you?

18

A large party is to be given by the young lads of N. to the young lassies of the same place; they are to drive out together to a picnic in the woods, and to come home by moonlight; the weather is damp and uncertain, the ground chill, and young people, as in all ages before the flood and since, not famous for the grace of prudence; for all which reasons, almost every mamma hesitates about her daughters' going — thinks it a very great pity the thing has been started.

"I really don't like this thing," says Mrs. G.; "it's not a kind of thing that I approve of, and if Mrs. X. was not going to let her daughters go, I should set myself against it. How Mrs. X., who is so very nice in her notions, can sanction such a thing, I cannot see. I am really surprised at Mrs. X."

All this time, poor unconscious Mrs. X. is in a similar tribulation.

"This is a very disagreeable affair to me," she says. "I really have almost a mind to say that my girls shall not go; but Mrs. G.'s daughters are going, and Mrs. C.'s, and Mrs. W.'s, and of course it would be idle for me to oppose it. I should not like to cast any reflections on a course sanctioned by ladies of such prudence and discretion."

In the same manner Mrs. A., B., and C., and the good matrons through the alphabet generally, with doleful lamentations, each one consents to the thing that she allows not, and the affair proceeds swimmingly to the great satisfaction of the juveniles.

Now and then, it is true, some individual sort of body, who might be designated by the angular and decided letters K or L, says to her son or daughter, "No. I don't approve of the thing," and is deaf to the oft-urged, "Mrs. A., B., and C. do so."

"I have nothing to do with Mrs. A., B., and C.'s arrangements," says this impracticable Mrs. K. or L. "I only know what is best for my children, and they shall not go."

Again: Mrs. G. is going to give a party; and, now, shall she give wine, or not? Mrs. G. has heard an abundance of temperance speeches and appeals, heard the duties of ladies in the matter of sanctioning temperance movements aptly set forth, but "none of these things move her half so much as another consideration." She has heard that Mrs. D. introduced wine into her last *soirée.* Mrs. D's husband has been a leading orator of the temperance society, and Mrs. D. is no less a leading member in the circles of fashion. Now, Mrs. G.'s soul is in great perplexity. If she only could be sure that the report about Mrs. D. is authentic, why, then, of course the thing is settled; regret it as much as she may, she cannot get through her party without the wine; and so at last come the party and the wine. Mrs. D., who was incorrectly stated to have had the article at her last *soirée*, has it at her next one, and quotes discreet Mrs. G. as her precedent. Mrs. P. is greatly scandalized at this, because Mrs. G. is a member of the church, and Mr. D. a leading temperance orator; but since *they will do it,* it is not for her to be nice, and so she follows the fashion.

Mrs. N. comes home from church on Sunday, rolling up her eyes with various appearances of horror and surprise.

"Well! I am going to give up trying to restrain my girls from dressing extravagantly; it's of no use trying! — no use in the world."

"Why, mother, what's the matter?" exclaimed the girls aforesaid, delighted to hear such encouraging declarations.

"Why, didn't you see Mrs. K.'s daughters sitting in the

pew before us with *feathers* in their bonnets? If Mrs. K. is coming out in this way, *I* shall give up. I shan't try any longer. I am going to get just what I want, and dress as much as I've a mind to. Girls, you may get those visites that you were looking at at Mr. B.'s store last week!"

The next Sunday, Mrs. K.'s girls in turn begin: —

"There, mamma, you are always lecturing us about economy, and all that, and wanting us to wear our old mantillas another winter, and there are Mrs. N.'s girls shining out in new visites."

Mamma looks sensible and judicious, and tells the girls they ought not to see what people are wearing in church on Sundays; but it becomes evident, before the week is through, that she has not forgotten the observation. She is anxiously pricing visites, and looking thoughtful as one on the eve of an important determination; and the next Sunday the girls appear in full splendor, with new visites, to the increasing horror of Mrs. N.

So goes the shuttlecock back and forward, kept up on both sides by most judicious hands.

In like manner, at a modern party, a circle of matrons sit in edifying conclave, and lament the degeneracy of the age.

"These parties that begin at nine o'clock and end at two or three in the morning are shameful things," says fat Mrs. Q., complacently fanning herself. (N. B. Mrs. Q. is plotting to have one the very next week, and has come just to see the fashions.)

"O, dreadful, dreadful!" exclaim, in one chorus, meek Mrs. M., and tall Mrs. F., and stiff Mrs. J.

"They are very unhealthy," says Mrs. F.

"They disturb all family order, says Mrs. J.

"They make one so sleepy the next day," says Mrs. M.

"They are very laborious to get up, and entirely useless," says Mrs. Q.; at the same time counting across the room the people that she shall invite next week.

Mrs. M. and Mrs. F. diverge into a most edifying strain of moral reflections on the improvement of time, the necessity of sobriety and moderation, the evils of conformity to the world, till one is tempted to feel that the tract society ought to have their remarks for general circulation, were one not damped by the certain knowledge that before the winter is out each of these ladies will give exactly such another party.

And, now, are all these respectable ladies hypocritical or insincere? By no means — they believe every word they say; but a sort of necessity is laid upon them — a spell; and before the breath of the multitude their individual resolution melts away as the frosty tracery melts from the window panes of a crowded room.

A great many do this habitually, resignedly, as a matter of course. Ask them what they think to be right and proper, and they will tell you sensibly, coherently, and quite to the point in one direction; ask them what they are going to do. Ah! that is quite another matter.

They are going to do what is generally done — what Mrs. A., B., and C. do. They have long since made over their conscience to the keeping of the public, — that is to say, of good society, — and are thus rid of a troublesome burden of responsibility.

Again, there are others who mean in general to have an opinion and will of their own; but, imperceptibly, as one and another take a course opposed to their own sense of right and propriety, their resolution quietly melts, and melts, till every individual outline of it is gone, and they do as others do.

Yet is this influence of one human being over another — in some sense, God-appointed — a necessary result of the human constitution. There is scarcely a human being that is not varied and swerved by it, as the trembling needle is swerved by the approaching magnet. Oppose conflict with it, as one may at a distance, yet when it breathes on us through the breath, and shines on us through the eye of an associate, it possesses an invisible magnetic power. He who is not at all conscious of such impressibility can scarce be amiable or human. Nevertheless, one of the most important habits for the acquisition of a generous and noble character, is to learn to act *individually*, unswerved by the feelings and opinions of others. It may help us to do this, to reflect that the very person whose opinion we fear may be in equal dread of ours, and that the person to whom we are looking for a precedent may, at that very time, be looking to us.

In short, Mrs. A., if you think that you could spend your money more like a Christian than in laying it out on a fashionable party, go forward and do it, and twenty others, whose supposed opinion you fear, will be glad of your example for a precedent. And, Mrs. B., if you do think it would be better for your children to observe early hours, and form simple habits, than to dress and dance, and give and go to juvenile balls, carry out your opinion in practice, and many an anxious mother, who is of the same opinion, will quote your example as her shield and defence.

And for you, young ladies, let us pray you to reflect — *individuality of character*, maintained with womanly sweetness, is an irresistible grace and adornment. Have some principles of taste for yourself, and do not adopt every fashion of dress that is in vogue, whether it suits you or not — whether it is becoming or not — but, without a startling variation from general form, let your dress show something of your own taste and opinions. Have some principles of right and wrong for yourself, and do not do every thing that every one else does, *because* every one else does it.

Nothing is more tedious than a circle of young ladies who have got by rote a certain set of phrases and opinions — all admiring in the same terms the same things, and detesting in like terms certain others — with anxious solicitude each dressing, thinking, and acting, one as much like another as is possible. A genuine original opinion, even though it were so heretical as to assert that Jenny Lind is a little lower than the angels, or that Shakspeare is rather dull reading, would be better than such a universal Dead Sea of acquiescence.

These remarks have borne reference to the female sex principally, because they are the dependent, the acquiescent sex — from nature, and habit, and position, most exposed to be swayed by opinion — and yet, too, in a certain very wide department they are the lawgivers and custom-makers of society. If, amid the multiplied schools, whose advertisements now throng our papers, purporting to teach girls every thing, both ancient and modern, high and low, from playing on the harp and working pin-cushions, up to civil engineering, surveying, and navigation, there were any which could teach them to be women — to have thoughts, opinions, and modes of action of their own — such a school would be worth having. If one half of the good purposes which are in the hearts of the ladies of our nation were only acted out without fear of any body's opinion, we should certainly be a step nearer the millennium.

CHRISTMAS; OR, THE GOOD FAIRY.

"O, DEAR! Christmas is coming in a fortnight, and I have got to think up presents for every body!" said young Ellen Stuart, as she leaned languidly back in her chair. "Dear me, it's so tedious! Every body has got every thing that can be thought of."

"O, no," said her confidential adviser, Miss Lester, in a soothing tone. "You have means of buying every thing you can fancy; and when every shop and store is glittering with all manner of splendors, you cannot surely be at a loss."

"Well, now, just listen. To begin with, there's mamma. What can I get for her? I have thought of ever so many things. She has three card cases, four gold thimbles, two or three gold chains, two writing desks of different patterns; and then as to rings, brooches, boxes, and all other things, I should think she might be sick of the sight of them. I am sure I am," said she, languidly gazing on her white and jewelled fingers.

This view of the case seemed rather puzzling to the adviser, and there was silence for a few moments, when Ellen, yawning, resumed: —

"And then there's Cousins Jane and Mary; I suppose they

will be coming down on me with a whole load of presents; and Mrs. B. will send me something — she did last year; and then there's Cousins William and Tom — I must get them something; and I would like to do it well enough, if I only knew what to get."

"Well," said Eleanor's aunt, who had been sitting quietly rattling her knitting needles during this speech, "it's a pity that you had not such a subject to practise on as I was when I was a girl. Presents did not fly about in those days as they do now. I remember, when I was ten years, old my father gave me a most marvellously ugly sugar dog for a Christmas gift, and I was perfectly delighted with it, the very idea of a present was so new to us."

"Dear aunt, how delighted I should be if I had any such fresh, unsophisticated body to get presents for! But to get and get for people that have more than they know what to do with now; to add pictures, books, and gilding when the centre tables are loaded with them now, and rings and jewels when they are a perfect drug! I wish myself that I were not sick, and sated, and tired with having every thing in the world given me."

"Well, Eleanor," said her aunt, "if you really do want unsophisticated subjects to practise on, I can put you in the way of it. I can show you more than one family to whom you might seem to be a very good fairy, and where such gifts as you could give with all ease would seem like a magic dream."

"Why, that would really be worth while, aunt."

"Look over in that back alley," said her aunt. "You see those buildings?"

"That miserable row of shanties? Yes."

"Well, I have several acquaintances there who have never

been tired of Christmas gifts, or gifts of any other kind. I assure you, you could make quite a sensation over there."

"Well, who is there? Let us know."

"Do you remember Owen, that used to make your shoes?"

"Yes, I remember something about him."

"Well, he has fallen into a consumption, and cannot work any more; and he, and his wife, and three little children live in one of the rooms."

"How do they get along?"

"His wife takes in sewing sometimes, and sometimes goes out washing. Poor Owen! I was over there yesterday; he looks thin and wasted, and his wife was saying that he was parched with constant fever, and had very little appetite. She had, with great self-denial, and by restricting herself almost of necessary food, got him two or three oranges; and the poor fellow seemed so eager after them!"

"Poor fellow!" said Eleanor, involuntarily.

"Now," said her aunt, "suppose Owen's wife should get up on Christmas morning and find at the door a couple of dozen of oranges, and some of those nice white grapes, such as you had at your party last week; don't you think it would make a sensation?"

"Why, yes, I think very likely it might; but who else, aunt? You spoke of a great many."

"Well, on the lower floor there is a neat little room, that is always kept perfectly trim and tidy; it belongs to a young couple who have nothing beyond the husband's day wages to live on. They are, nevertheless, as cheerful and chipper as a couple of wrens; and she is up and down half a dozen times a day, to help poor Mrs. Owen. She has a baby of her own, about five months old, and of course does all the cooking, washing, and ironing for herself and husband; and yet, when Mrs. Owen goes out to wash, she takes her baby, and keeps it whole days for her."

"I'm sure she deserves that the good fairies should smile on her," said Eleanor; "one baby exhausts my stock of virtues very rapidly."

"But you ought to see her baby," said Aunt E.; "so plump, so rosy, and good-natured, and always clean as a lily. This baby is a sort of household shrine; nothing is too sacred or too good for it; and I believe the little thrifty woman feels only one temptation to be extravagant, and that is to get some ornaments to adorn this little divinity."

"Why, did she ever tell you so?"

"No; but one day, when I was coming down stairs, the door of their room was partly open, and I saw a pedler there with open box. John, the husband, was standing with a little purple cap on his hand, which he was regarding with mystified, admiring air, as if he didn't quite comprehend it, and trim little Mary gazing at it with longing eyes.

"'I think we might get it,' said John.

"'O, no,' said she, regretfully; 'yet I wish we could, it's *so pretty!*'"

"Say no more, aunt. I see the good fairy must pop a cap into the window on Christmas morning. Indeed, it shall be done. How they will wonder where it came from, and talk about it for months to come!"

"Well, then," continued her aunt, "in the next street to ours there is a miserable building, that looks as if it were just going to topple over; and away up in the third story, in a little room just under the eaves, live two poor, lonely old women. They are both nearly on to ninety. I was in there day before yesterday. One of them is constantly confined to her bed with rheumatism; the other, weak and feeble, with failing sight and trembling hands, totters about, her only helper; and they are entirely dependent on charity."

"Can't they do any thing? Can't they knit?" said Eleanor.

"You are young and strong, Eleanor, and have quick eyes and nimble fingers; how long would it take you to knit a pair of stockings?"

"I?" said Eleanor. "What an idea! I never tried, but I think I could get a pair done in a week, perhaps."

"And if somebody gave you twenty-five cents for them, and out of this you had to get food, and pay room rent, and buy coal for your fire, and oil for your lamp ——"

"Stop, aunt, for pity's sake!"

"Well, I will stop; but they can't: they must pay so much every month for that miserable shell they live in, or be turned into the street. The meal and flour that some kind person sends goes off for them just as it does for others, and they must get more or starve; and coal is now scarce and high priced."

"O aunt, I'm quite convinced, I'm sure; don't run me down and annihilate me with all these terrible realities. What shall I do to play good fairy to these poor old women?"

"If you will give me full power, Eleanor, I will put up a basket to be sent to them that will give them something to remember all winter."

"O, certainly I will. Let me see if I can't think of something myself."

"Well, Eleanor, suppose, then, some fifty or sixty years hence, *if* you were old, and your father, and mother, and aunts, and uncles, now so thick around you, lay cold and silent in so many graves — you have somehow got away off to a strange city, where you were never known — you live in a miserable garret, where snow blows at night through the cracks, and the fire is very apt to go out in the old cracked stove — you sit crouching over the dying embers the evening before Christmas — nobody to speak to you, nobody to care for you, except another poor old soul who lies moaning in the bed. Now, what would you like to have sent you?"

"O aunt, what a dismal picture!"

"And yet, Ella, all poor, forsaken old women are made of young girls, who expected it in their youth as little as you do, perhaps."

"Say no more, aunt. I'll buy — let me see — a comfortable warm shawl for each of these poor women; and I'll send them — let me see — O, some tea — nothing goes down with old women like tea; and I'll make John wheel some coal over to them; and, aunt, it would not be a very bad thought to send them a new stove. I remember, the other day, when mamma was pricing stoves, I saw some such nice ones for two or three dollars."

"For a new hand, Ella, you work up the idea very well," said her aunt.

"But how much ought I to give, for any one case, to these women, say?"

"How much did you give last year for any single Christmas present?"

"Why, six or seven dollars for some; those elegant souvenirs were seven dollars; that ring I gave Mrs. B. was twenty."

"And do you suppose Mrs. B. was any happier for it?"

"No, really, I don't think she cared much about it; but I

had to give her something, because she had sent me something the year before, and I did not want to send a paltry present to one in her circumstances."

"Then, Ella, give the same to any poor, distressed, suffering creature who really needs it, and see in how many forms of good such a sum will appear. That one hard, cold, glittering ring, that now cheers nobody, and means nothing, that you give because you must, and she takes because she must, might, if broken up into smaller sums, send real warm and heartfelt gladness through many a cold and cheerless dwelling, through many an aching heart."

"You are getting to be an orator, aunt; but don't you approve of Christmas presents, among friends and equals?"

"Yes, indeed," said her aunt, fondly stroking her head. "I have had some Christmas presents that did me a world of good — a little book mark, for instance, that a certain niece of mine worked for me, with wonderful secrecy, three years ago, when she was not a young lady with a purse full of money — that book mark was a true Christmas present; and my young couple across the way are plotting a profound surprise to each other on Christmas morning. John has contrived, by an hour of extra work every night, to lay by enough to get Mary a new calico dress; and she, poor soul, has bargained away the only thing in the jewelry line she ever possessed, to be laid out on a new hat for him.

"I know, too, a washerwoman who has a poor, lame boy — a patient, gentle little fellow — who has lain quietly for weeks and months in his little crib, and his mother is going to give him a splendid Christmas present."

"What is it, pray?"

"A whole orange! Don't laugh. She will pay ten whole

cents for it; for it shall be none of your common oranges, but a picked one of the very best going! She has put by the money, a cent at a time, for a whole month; and nobody knows which will be happiest in it, Willie or his mother. These are such Christmas presents as I like to think of — gifts coming from love, and tending to produce love; these are the appropriate gifts of the day."

"But don't you think that it's right for those who *have* money to give expensive presents, supposing always, as you say, they are given from real affection?"

"Sometimes, undoubtedly. The Savior did not condemn her who broke an alabaster box of ointment — *very precious* — simply as a proof of love, even although the suggestion was made, 'This might have been sold for three hundred pence, and given to the poor.' I have thought he would regard with sympathy the fond efforts which human love sometimes makes to express itself by gifts, the rarest and most costly. How I rejoiced with all my heart, when Charles Elton gave his poor mother that splendid Chinese shawl and gold watch! because I knew they came from the very fulness of his heart to a mother that he could not do too much for — a mother that has done and suffered every thing for him. In some such cases, when resources are ample, a costly gift seems to have a graceful appropriateness; but I cannot approve of it if it exhausts all the means of doing for the poor; it is better, then, to give a simple offering, and to do something for those who really need it."

Eleanor looked thoughtful; her aunt laid down her knitting, and said, in a tone of gentle seriousness, "Whose birth does Christmas commemorate, Ella?"

"Our Savior's, certainly, aunt."

"Yes," said her aunt. "And when and how was he born? In a stable! laid in a manger; thus born, that in all ages he might be known as the brother and friend of the poor. And surely, it seems but appropriate to commemorate his birthday by an especial remembrance of the lowly, the poor, the outcast, and distressed; and if Christ should come back to our city on a Christmas day, where should we think it most appropriate to his character to find him? Would he be carrying splendid gifts to splendid dwellings, or would he be gliding about in the cheerless haunts of the desolate, the poor, the forsaken, and the sorrowful?"

And here the conversation ended.

* * * * *

"What sort of Christmas presents is Ella buying?" said Cousin Tom, as the waiter handed in a portentous-looking package, which had been just rung in at the door.

"Let's open it," said saucy Will. "Upon my word, two great gray blanket shawls! These must be for you and me, Tom! And what's this? A great bolt of cotton flannel and gray yarn stockings!"

The door bell rang again, and the waiter brought in another bulky parcel, and deposited it on the marble-topped centre table.

"What's here?" said Will, cutting the cord. "Whew! a perfect nest of packages! oolong tea! oranges! grapes! white sugar! Bless me, Ella must be going to housekeeping!"

"Or going crazy!" said Tom; "and on my word," said he, looking out of the window, "there's a drayman ringing at our door, with a stove, with a teakettle set in the top of it!"

"Ella's cook stove, of course," said Will; and just at this

moment the young lady entered, with her purse hanging gracefully over her hand.

" Now, boys, you are too bad ! " she exclaimed, as each of the mischievous youngsters were gravely marching up and down, attired in a gray shawl.

" Didn't you get them for us ? We thought you did," said both.

" Ella, I want some of that cotton flannel, to make me a pair of pantaloons," said Tom.

" I say, Ella," said Will, " when are you going to housekeeping ? Your cooking stove is standing down in the street ; 'pon my word, John is loading some coal on the dray with it."

" Ella, isn't that going to be sent to my office ? " said Tom ; do you know I do so languish for a new stove with a teakettle in the top, to heat a fellow's shaving water ! "

Just then, another ring at the door, and the grinning waiter handed in a small brown paper parcel for Miss Ella. Tom made a dive at it, and staving off the brown paper, developed a janty little purple velvet cap, with silver tassels.

" My smoking cap, as I live ! " said he ; " only I shall have to wear it on my thumb, instead of my head — too small entirely," said he, shaking his head gravely.

" Come, you saucy boys," said Aunt E., entering briskly, " what are you teasing Ella for ? "

" Why, do see this lot of things, aunt ! What in the world is Ella going to do with them ? "

" O, I know ! "

" You know ! Then I can guess, aunt, it is some of your charitable works. You are going to make a juvenile Lady Bountiful of El, eh ? "

Ella, who had colored to the roots of her hair at the *exposé* of her very unfashionable Christmas preparations, now took heart, and bestowed a very gentle and salutary little cuff on the saucy head that still wore the purple cap, and then hastened to gather up her various purchases.

" Laugh away," said she, gayly; " and a good many others will laugh, too, over these things. I got them to make people laugh — people that are not in the habit of laughing!"

" Well, well, I see into it," said Will; " and I tell you I think right well of the idea, too. There are worlds of money wasted, at this time of the year, in getting things that nobody wants, and nobody cares for after they are got; and I am glad, for my part, that you are going to get up a variety in this line; in fact, I should like to give you one of these stray leaves to help on," said he, dropping a ten dollar note into her paper. I like to encourage girls to think of something besides breastpins and sugar candy."

But our story spins on too long. If any body wants to see the results of Ella's first attempts at *good fairyism*, they can call at the doors of two or three old buildings on Christmas morning, and they shall hear all about it.

EARTHLY CARE A HEAVENLY DISCIPLINE.

"Why should these cares my heart divide,
If Thou, indeed, hast set me free?
Why am I thus, if Thou hast died —
If Thou hast died to ransom me?"

Nothing is more frequently felt and spoken of, as a hinderance to the inward life of devotion, than the "cares of life;" and even upon the showing of our Lord himself, the cares of the world are the *thorns* that choke the word, and it becometh unfruitful.

And yet, if this is a necessary and inevitable result of worldly care, why does the providence of God so order things that it forms so large and unavoidable a part of every human experience? Why is the physical system of man arranged with such daily, oft-recurring wants? Why does his nature, in its full development, tend to that state of society in which wants multiply, and the business of supply becomes more complicated, and requiring constantly more thought and attention, and bringing the outward and seen into a state of constant friction and pressure on the inner and spiritual?

Has God arranged an outward system to be a constant

diversion from the inward — a weight on its wheels — a burden on its wings — and then commanded a strict and rigid inwardness and spirituality? Why placed us where the things that are seen and temporal must unavoidably have so much of our thoughts, and time, and care, yet said to us, "Set your affections on things above, and not on things on the earth. Love not the world, neither the things of the world"? And why does one of our brightest examples of Christian experience, as it should be, say, "While we look not on the things which are seen, but on the things which are not seen; for the things which are seen are temporal, but the things that are not seen are eternal"?

The Bible tells us that our whole existence here is a disciplinary one; that this whole physical system, by which our spirit is enclosed with all the joys and sorrows, hopes and fears, and wants which form a part of it, are designed as an education to fit the soul for its immortality; and as worldly care forms the greater part of the staple of every human life, there must be some mode of viewing and meeting it, which converts it from an enemy of spirituality into a means of grace and spiritual advancement.

Why, then, do we so often hear the lamentation, "It seems to me as if I could advance to the higher stages of Christian life, if it were not for the pressure of my business and the multitude of my worldly cares"? Is it not God, O Christian, who, in ordering thy lot, has laid these cares upon thee, and who still holds them about thee, and permits no escape from them? And as his great, undivided object is thy spiritual improvement, is there not some misapprehension or wrong use of these cares, if they do not tend to advance it? Is it not even as if a scholar should say, I could advance in science were it not for all the time and care which lessons, and books, and lectures require?

How, then, shall earthly care become heavenly discipline? How shall the disposition of the weight be altered so as to press the spirit upward towards God, instead of downward and away? How shall the pillar of cloud which rises between us and him become one of fire, to reflect upon us constantly the light of his countenance, and to guide us over the sands of life's desert?

It appears to us that the great radical difficulty is an intellectual one, and lies in a wrong belief. There is not a genuine and real belief of the presence and agency of God in the minor events and details of life, which is necessary to change them from secular cares into spiritual blessings.

It is true there is much loose talk about an overruling Providence; and yet, if fairly stated, the belief of a great many Christians might be thus expressed: God has organized and set in operation certain general laws of matter and mind, which work out the particular results of life, and over these laws he exercises a general supervision and care, so that all the great affairs of the world are carried on after the counsel of his own will; and in a certain general sense, all things are working together for good to those that love God. But when some simple-minded, childlike Christian really proceeds to refer all the smaller events of life to God's immediate care and agency, there is a smile of incredulity, and it is thought that the good brother displays more Christian feeling than sound philosophy.

But as life for every individual is made up of fractions and minute atoms — as those things which go to affect habits and character are small and hourly recurring, it comes to pass that a belief in Providence so very wide and general, is altogether inefficient for consecrating and rendering sacred the great body of what comes in contact with the mind in the experience of life. Only once in years does the Christian with this kind of belief hear the voice of the Lord God speaking to him. When the hand of death is laid on his child, or the bolt strikes down the brother by his side, *then*, indeed, he feels that God is drawing near; he listens humbly for the inward voice that shall explain the meaning and need of this discipline. When by some unforeseen occurrence the whole of his earthly property is swept away, — he becomes a poor man, — this event, in his eyes, assumes sufficient magnitude to have come from God, and to have a design and meaning; but when smaller comforts are removed, smaller losses are encountered, and the petty, every-day vexations and annoyances of life press about him, he recognizes no God, and hears no voice, and sees no design. Hence John Newton says, "Many Christians, who bear the loss of a child, or the destruction of all their property, with the most heroic Christian fortitude, are entirely vanquished and overcome by the breaking of a dish, or the blunders of a servant, and show so unchristian a spirit, that we cannot but wonder at them."

So when the breath of slander, or the pressure of human injustice, comes so heavily on a man as really to threaten loss of character, and destruction of his temporal interests, he seems forced to recognize the hand and voice of God, through the veil of human agencies, and in time-honored words to say, —

"When men of spite against me join,
They are the *sword;* the hand is thine."

But the smaller injustice and fault-finding which meet every one more or less in the daily intercourse of life, the overheard remark, the implied censure, too petty, perhaps, to be even spoken of, these daily recurring sources of disquietude and unhappiness are not referred to God's providence, nor considered as a part of his probation and discipline. Those thousand vexations which come upon us through the unreasonableness, the carelessness, the various constitutional failings, or ill-adaptedness of others to our peculiarities of character, form a very large item of the disquietudes of life; and yet how very few look beyond the human agent, and feel these are trials coming from God! Yet it is true, in many cases, that these so called minor vexations form the greater part, and in many cases the only discipline of *life;* and to those that do not view them as ordered individually by God, and coming upon them by specified design, "their affliction 'really' cometh of the dust, and their trouble springs out of the ground;" it is sanctified and relieved by no divine presence and aid, but borne alone and in a mere human spirit, and by mere human reliances, it acts on the mind as a constant diversion and hinderance, instead of a moral discipline.

Hence, too, come a coldness, and generality, and wandering of mind in prayer: the things that are on the heart, that are distracting the mind, that have filled the soul so full that there is no room for any thing else, are all considered too small and undignified to come within the pale of a prayer, and so, with a wandering mind and a distracted heart, the Christian offers up his prayer for things which he thinks he *ought* to want, and makes no mention of those which he *does.* He prays that God would pour out his spirit on the heathen, and convert the world, and build up his kingdom every where, when perhaps a whole set of little anxieties, and wants, and vexations are so distracting his thoughts, that he hardly knows what he has been saying: a faithless servant is wasting his property; a careless or blundering workman has spoiled a lot of goods; a child is vexatious or unruly; a friend has made promises and failed to keep them; an acquaintance has made unjust or satirical remarks; some new furniture has been damaged or ruined by carelessness in the household; but all this trouble forms no subject matter for prayer, though there it is, all the while lying like lead on the heart, and keeping it down, so that it has no power to expand and take in any thing else. But were God known and regarded as the soul's familiar friend, were every trouble of the heart as it rises, breathed into his bosom; were it felt that there is not one of the smallest of life's troubles that has not been permitted by him, and permitted for specific good purpose to the soul, how much more would these be in prayer! how constant, how daily might it become! how it might settle and clear the atmosphere of the soul! how it might so dispose and lay away many anxieties which now take up their place there, that there might be *room* for the higher themes and considerations of religion!

Many sensitive and fastidious natures are worn away by the constant friction of what are called *little troubles*. Without any great affliction, they feel that all the flower and sweetness of their life have faded; their eye grows dim, their cheek care-worn, and their spirit loses hope and elasticity, and becomes bowed with premature age; and in the midst of tangible and physical comfort, they are restless and unhappy. The constant under-current of little cares and vexations, which is slowly wearing on the finer springs of life, is seen by no one; scarce ever do they speak of these things to their nearest friends. Yet were there a friend of a spirit so discerning as to feel and sympathize in all these things, how much of this repressed electric restlessness would pass off through such a sympathizing mind.

Yet among human friends this is all but impossible, for minds are so diverse that what is a trial and a care to one is a matter of sport and amusement to another; and all the inner world breathed into a human ear only excites a surprised or contemptuous pity. Whom, then, shall the soul turn to? Who will feel *that* to be affliction which each spirit feels to be so? If the soul shut itself within itself, it becomes morbid; the fine chords of the mind and nerves by constant wear become jarring and discordant; hence fretfulness, discontent, and habitual irritability steal over the sincere Christian.

But to the Christian that really believes in the agency of God in the smallest events of life, that confides in his love, and makes his sympathy his refuge, the thousand minute cares and perplexities of life become each one a fine affiliating bond between the soul and its God. God is known, not by abstract definition, and by high-raised conceptions of the soul's aspiring hours, but known as a man knoweth his friend; he is known by the hourly wants he supplies; known by every care with which he momentarily sympathizes, every apprehension which he relieves, every temptation which he enables us to surmount. We learn to know God as the infant child learns to know its mother and its father, by all the helplessness and all the dependence which are incident to this commencement of our moral existence; and as we go on thus year by year, and find in every changing situation, in every reverse, in every trouble, from the lightest sorrow to those which wring our soul from its depths, that he is equally present, and that his gracious aid is equally adequate, our faith seems gradually almost to change to sight; and God's existence, his love and care, seem to us more real than any other source of reliance, and multiplied cares and trials are only new avenues of acquaintance between us and heaven.

Suppose, in some bright vision unfolding to our view, in tranquil evening or solemn midnight, the glorified form of some departed friend should appear to us with the announcement, "This year is to be to you one of especial probation and discipline, with reference to perfecting you for a heavenly state. Weigh well and consider every incident of your daily life, for not one shall fall out by accident, but each one is to be a finished and indispensable link in a bright chain that is to draw you upward to the skies!"

With what new eyes should we now look on our daily lot! and if we found in it not a single change, — the same old cares, the same perplexities, the same uninteresting drudgeries still, — with what new meaning would every incident be invested! and with what other and sublimer spirit could we meet them? Yet, if announced by one rising from the dead with the visible glory of a spiritual world, this truth could be asserted no more clearly and distinctly than Jesus Christ has stated it already. Not a sparrow falleth to the ground without our Father. Not one of them is forgotten by him; and we are of more value than many sparrows; yea, even the hairs of our head are all numbered. Not till belief in these declarations, in their most literal sense, becomes the calm and settled habit of the soul, is life ever redeemed from drudgery and dreary emptiness, and made full of interest, meaning, and divine significance. Not till then do its grovelling wants, its wearing cares, its stinging vexations, become to us ministering spirits, each one, by a silent but certain agency, fitting us for a higher and perfect sphere.

CONVERSATION ON CONVERSATION.

"For every idle word that men shall speak, they shall give account thereof in the day of judgment."

"A VERY solemn sermon," said Miss B., shaking her head impressively, as she sat down to table on Sunday noon; then giving a deep sigh, she added, "I am afraid that if an account is to be rendered for all our idle words, some people will have a great deal to answer for."

"Why, Cousin Anna," replied a sprightly young lady opposite, "what do you mean by *idle words?*"

"All words that have not a strictly useful tendency, Helen," replied Miss B.

"I don't know what is to become of me, then," answered Helen, "for I never can think of any thing useful to say. I sit and try sometimes, but it always stops my talking. I don't think any thing in the world is so doleful as a set of persons sitting round, all trying to say something useful, like a parcel of old clocks ticking at each other. I think one might as well take the vow of entire silence, like the monks of La Trappe."

"It is probable," said Miss B., "that a greater part of our ordinary conversation had better be dispensed with. 'In the multitude of words there wanteth not sin.' For my own part, my conscience often reproaches me with the sins of my tongue."

"I'm sure you don't sin much that way, I must say," said Helen; "but, cousin, I really think it is a freezing business sitting still and reflecting all the time when friends are together; and after all I can't bring myself to feel as if it were wrong to talk and chatter away a good part of the time, just for the sake of talking. For instance, if a friend comes in of a morning to make a call, I talk about the weather, my roses, my Canary birds, or any thing that comes uppermost."

"And about lace, and bonnet patterns, and the last fashions," added Miss B., sarcastically.

"Well, supposing we do; where's the harm?"

"Where's the good?" said Miss B.

"The good! why, it passes time agreeably, and makes us feel kindly towards each other."

"I think, Helen," said Miss B., "if you had a higher view of Christian responsibility, you would not be satisfied with merely passing time agreeably, or exciting agreeable feelings in others. Does not the very text we are speaking of show that we have an account to give in the day of judgment for all this trifling, useless conversation?"

"I don't know what that text does mean," replied Helen, looking seriously; "but if it means as you say, I think it is a very hard, strait rule."

"Well," replied Miss B., "is not duty always hard and strait? 'Strait is the gate, and narrow is the way,' you know."

Helen sighed.

"What do you think of this, Uncle C.?" she said, after some

pause. The uncle of the two young ladies had been listening thus far in silence.

"I think," he replied, "that before people begin to discuss, they should be quite sure as to what they are talking about; and I am not exactly clear in this case. You say, Anna," said he, turning to Miss B., "that all conversation is idle which has not a directly useful tendency. Now, what do you mean by that? Are we never to say any thing that has not for its direct and specific object to benefit others or ourselves?"

"Yes," replied Miss B., "I suppose not."

"Well, then, when I say, 'Good morning, sir; 'tis a pleasant day,' I have no such object. Are these, then, idle words?"

"Why, no, not exactly," replied Miss B.; "in some cases it is necessary to say something, so as not to appear rude."

"Very well," replied her uncle. "You admit, then, that some things, which are not instructive in themselves considered, are to be said to keep up the intercourse of society."

"Certainly; some things," said Miss B.

"Well, now, in the case mentioned by Helen, when two or three people with whom you are in different degrees of intimacy call upon you, I think she is perfectly right, as she said, in talking of roses, and Canary birds, and even of bonnet patterns, and lace, or any thing of the kind, for the sake of making conversation. It amounts to the same thing as 'good morning,' and 'good evening,' and the other courtesies of society. This sort of small talk has nothing instructive in it, and yet it may be *useful* in its place. It makes people comfortable and easy, promotes kind and social feelings; and making people comfortable by any innocent means is certainly not a thing to be despised."

"But is there not great danger of becoming light and trifling if one allows this?" said Miss B., doubtfully.

"To be sure; there is always danger of running every innocent thing to excess. One might eat to excess, or drink to excess; yet eating and drinking are both useful in their way. Now, our lively young friend Helen, here, might perhaps be in some temptation of this sort; but as for you, Anna, I think you in more danger of another extreme."

"And what is that?"

"Of overstraining your mind by endeavoring to keep up a constant, fixed state of seriousness and solemnity, and not allowing yourself the relaxation necessary to preserve its healthy tone. In order to be healthy, every mind must have variety and amusement; and if you would sit down at least one hour a day, and join your friends in some amusing conversation, and indulge in a good laugh, I think, my dear, that you would not only be a happier person, but a better Christian."

"My dear uncle," said Miss B., "this is the very thing that I have been most on my guard against; I can never tell stories, or laugh and joke, without feeling condemned for it afterwards."

"But, my dear, you must do the thing in the testimony of a good conscience before you can do it to any purpose. You must make up your mind that cheerful and entertaining conversation — conversation whose first object is to amuse — is *useful conversation* in its place, and then your conscience will not be injured by joining in it."

"But what good does it do, uncle?"

"Do you not often complain of coldness and deadness in your religious feelings? of lifelessness and want of interest?"

"Yes, uncle."

"Well, this coldness and lifelessness is the result of forcing your mind to one set of thoughts and feelings. You become worn out — your feelings exhausted — deadness and depression ensues. Now, turn your mind off from these subjects — divert it by a cheerful and animated conversation, and you will find, after a while, that it will return to them with new life and energy."

"But are not foolish talking and jesting expressly forbidden?"

"That text, if you will look at the connections, does not forbid jesting in the abstract; but jesting on immodest subjects — which are often designated in the New Testament by the phraseology there employed. I should give the sense of it — neither filthiness, nor foolish talking, nor indelicate jests. The kind of sprightly and amusing conversation to which I referred, I should not denominate foolish, by any means, at proper times and places."

"Yet people often speak of gayety as inconsistent in Christians — even worldly people," said Miss B.

"Yes, because, in the first place, they often have wrong ideas as to what Christianity requires in this respect, and suppose Christians to be violating their own principles in indulging in it. In the second place, there are some, especially among young people, who never talk in any other way — with whom this kind of conversation is not an amusement, but a habit — giving the impression that they never think seriously at all. But I think, that if persons are really possessed by the tender, affectionate, benevolent spirit of Christianity — if they regulate their temper and their tongue by it, and in all their actions show an evident effort to conform to its precepts, they will not do harm by occasionally indulging in sprightly and amusing conversation — they will not make the impression that they are not sincerely Christians."

"Besides," said Helen, "are not people sometimes repelled from religion by a want of cheerfulness in its professors?"

"Certainly," replied her uncle, "and the difference is just this: if a person is habitually trifling and thoughtless, it is thought that they have *no* religion; if they are ascetic and gloomy, it is attributed *to* their religion; and you know what Miss E. Smith says — that 'to be good and disagreeable is high treason against virtue.' The more sincerely and earnestly religious a person is, the more important it is that they should be agreeable."

"But, uncle," said Helen, "what does that text mean that we began with? What are idle words?"

"My dear, if you will turn to the place where the passage is (Matt. xii.) and read the whole page, you will see the meaning of it. Christ was not reproving any body for trifling conversation at the time; but for a very serious slander. The Pharisees, in their bitterness, accused him of being in league with evil spirits. It seems, by what follows, that this was a charge which involved an unpardonable sin. They were not, indeed, conscious of its full guilt — they said it merely from the impulse of excited and envious feeling — but he warns them that in the day of judgment, God will hold them accountable for the full consequences of all such language, however little they may have thought of it at the time of uttering it. The sense of the passage I take to be, 'God will hold you responsible in the day of judgment for the consequences of all you have said in your most idle and thoughtless moments.'"

"For example," said Helen, "if one makes unguarded and

unfounded assertions about the Bible, which excite doubt and prejudice."

"There are many instances," said her uncle, "that are quite in point. Suppose in conversation, either under the influence of envy or ill will, or merely from love of talking, you make remarks and statements about another person which may be true or may not, — you do not stop to inquire, — your unguarded words set reports in motion, and unhappiness, and hard feeling, and loss of character are the result. You spoke idly, it is true, but nevertheless you are held responsible by God for all the consequences of your words. So professors of religion often make unguarded remarks about each other, which lead observers to doubt the truth of all religion; and they are responsible for every such doubt they excite. Parents and guardians often allow themselves to speak of the faults and weaknesses of their ministers in the presence of children and younger people — they do it thoughtlessly — but in so doing they destroy an influence which might otherwise have saved the souls of their children; they are responsible for it. People of cultivated minds and fastidious taste often allow themselves to come home from church, and criticize a sermon, and unfold all its weak points in the presence of others on whom it may have made a very serious impression. While the critic is holding up the bad arrangement, and setting in a ludicrous point of view the lame figures, perhaps the servant behind his chair, who was almost persuaded to be a Christian by that very discourse, gives up his purposes, in losing his respect for the sermon; this was thoughtless — but the evil is done, and the man who did it is responsible for it."

"I think," said Helen, "that a great deal of evil is done to children in this way, by our not thinking of what we are saying."

"It seems to me," said Miss B., "that this view of the subject will reduce us to silence almost as much as the other. How is one ever to estimate the consequences of their words, people are affected in so many different ways by the same thing?"

"I suppose," said her uncle, "we are only responsible for such results as by carefulness and reflection we might have foreseen. It is not for *ill-judged* words, but for idle words, that we are to be judged — words uttered without any consideration at all, and producing bad results. If a person really anxious to do right misjudges as to the probable effect of what he is about to say on others, it is quite another thing."

"But, uncle, will not such carefulness destroy all freedom in conversation?" said Helen.

"If you are talking with a beloved friend, Helen, do you not use an *instinctive* care to avoid all that might pain that friend?"

"Certainly."

"And do you find this effort a restraint on your enjoyment?"

"Certainly not."

"And you, from your own feelings, avoid what is indelicate and impure in conversation, and yet feel it no restraint?"

"Certainly."

"Well, I suppose the object of Christian effort should be so to realize the character of our Savior, and conform our tastes and sympathies to his, that we shall *instinctively* avoid all in our conversation that would be displeasing to him. A person habitually indulging jealous, angry, or revengeful feeling — a person habitually worldly in his spirit — a person allowing himself in sceptical and unsettled habits of thought, *cannot* talk without doing harm. This is our Savior's account of the matter in the verses immediately before the passage we were speaking of — 'How *can* ye, being evil, speak good things? for out of the abundance of the heart the mouth speaketh. A good man out of the good treasure of his heart bringeth forth good things, and an evil man out of the evil treasure of his heart bringeth forth evil things.' The highest flow of animal spirits would never hurry a pure-minded person to say any thing indelicate or gross; and in the same manner, if a person is habitually Christian in all his habits of thought and feeling, he will be able without irksome watchfulness to avoid what may be injurious even in the most unrestrained conversation."

HOW DO WE KNOW?

It was a splendid room. Rich curtains swept down to the floor in graceful folds, half excluding the light, and shedding it in soft hues over the fine old paintings on the walls, and over the broad mirrors that reflect all that taste can accomplish by the hand of wealth. Books, the rarest and most costly, were around, in every form of gorgeous binding and gilding, and among them, glittering in ornament, lay a magnificent Bible — a Bible too beautiful in its appointments, too showy, too ornamental, ever to have been meant to be read — a Bible which every visitor should take up and exclaim, "What a beautiful edition! what superb bindings!" and then lay it down again.

And the master of the house was lounging on a sofa, looking over a late review — for he was a man of leisure, taste, and reading — but, then, as to reading the Bible! — *that* forms, we suppose, no part of the pretensions of a man of letters. The Bible — certainly he considered it a very *respectable* book — a fine specimen of ancient literature — an admirable book of moral precepts; but, then, as to its divine origin, he had not exactly made up his mind: some parts appeared strange and inconsistent to his reason — others were revolting to his taste: true, he had never studied it very attentively, yet such was his *general impression* about it; but, on the whole, he thought it well enough to keep an elegant copy of it on his drawing room table.

So much for one picture. Now for another.

Come with us into this little dark alley, and up a flight of ruinous stairs. It is a bitter night, and the wind and snow might drive through the crevices of the poor room, were it not that careful hands have stopped them with paper or cloth. But for all this carefulness, the room is bitter cold — cold even with those few decaying brands on the hearth, which that sorrowful woman is trying to kindle with her breath. Do you see that pale, little, thin girl, with large, bright eyes, who is crouching so near her mother? — hark! — how she coughs! Now listen.

"Mary, my dear child," says the mother, "do keep that shawl close about you; you are cold, I know," and the woman shivers as she speaks.

"No, mother, not *very*," replies the child, again relapsing into that hollow, ominous cough. "I wish you wouldn't make me always wear your shawl when it is cold, mother."

"Dear child, you need it most. How you cough to-night!" replies the mother; "it really don't seem right for me to send you up that long, cold street; now your shoes have grown so poor, too; I must go myself after this."

"O mother, you must stay with the baby — what if he should have one of those dreadful fits while you are gone! No, I can go very well; I have got used to the cold now."

"But, mother, I'm cold," says a little voice from the scanty bed in the corner; "mayn't I get up and come to the fire?"

"Dear child, it would not warm you; it is very cold here, and I can't make any more fire to-night."

"Why can't you, mother? There are four whole sticks of wood in the box; do put one on, and let's get warm once."

"No, my dear little Henry," says the mother, soothingly, "that is all the wood mother has, and I haven't any money to get more."

And now wakens the sick baby in the cradle, and mother and daughter are both for some time busy in attempting to supply its little wants, and lulling it again to sleep.

And now look you well at that mother. Six months ago she had a husband, whose earnings procured for her both the necessaries and comforts of life; her children were clothed, fed, and schooled, without thoughts of hers. But husbandless, friendless, and alone in the heart of a great, busy city, with feeble health, and only the precarious resource of her needle, she has gone down from comfort to extreme poverty. Look at her now, as she is to-night. She knows full well that the pale, bright-eyed girl, whose hollow cough constantly rings in her ears, is far from well. She knows that cold, and hunger, and exposure of every kind, are daily and surely wearing away her life. And yet what can she do? Poor soul! how many times has she calculated all her little resources, to see if she could pay a doctor and get medicine for Mary — yet all in vain. She knows that timely medicine, ease, fresh air, and warmth might save her; but she knows that all these things are out of the question for her. She feels, too, as a mother would feel, when she sees her once rosy, happy little boy becoming pale, and anxious, and fretful; and even when he teases her most, she only stops her work a moment, and strokes his little thin cheeks, and thinks what a laughing, happy little fellow he once was, till she has not a heart to reprove him. And all this day she has toiled with a sick and fretful baby in her lap, and her little shivering, hungry boy at her side, whom Mary's patient artifices cannot always keep quiet; she has toiled over the last piece of work which she can procure from the shop, for the man has told her that after this he can furnish no more; and the little money that is to come from this is already portioned out in her own mind, and after that she has no human prospect of support.

But yet that woman's face is patient, quiet, firm. Nay, you may even see in her suffering eye something like peace. And whence comes it? I will tell you.

There is a Bible in that room, as well as in the rich man's apartment. Not splendidly bound, to be sure, but faithfully read — a plain, homely, much-worn book.

Hearken now while she says to her children, "Listen to me, dear children, and I will read you something out of this book. 'Let not your heart be troubled; in my Father's house are many mansions.' So you see, my children, we shall not always live in this little, cold, dark room. Jesus Christ has promised to take us to a better home."

"Shall we be warm there all day?" says the little boy, earnestly; "and shall we have enough to eat?"

"Yes, dear child," says the mother; "listen to what the Bible says: 'They shall hunger no more, neither thirst any more; for the Lamb which is in the midst of the throne shall feed them; and God shall wipe away all tears from their eyes.'"

"I am glad of that," said little Mary, "for, mother, I never can bear to see you cry."

"But, mother," says little Henry, "won't God send us something to eat to-morrow?"

"See," says the mother, "what the Bible says: 'Seek ye not what ye shall eat, nor what ye shall drink, neither be of anxious mind. For your Father knoweth that ye have need of these things.'"

"But, mother," says little Mary, "if God is our Father, and loves us, what does he let us be so poor for?"

"Nay," says the mother, "our dear Lord Jesus Christ was as poor as we are, and God certainly loved him."

"Was he, mother?"

"Yes, children; you remember how he said, 'The Son of man hath not where to lay his head.' And it tells us more than once that Jesus was hungry when there was none to give him food."

"O mother, what should we do without the Bible?" says Mary.

Now, if the rich man, who had not yet made up his mind what to think of the Bible, should visit this poor woman, and ask her on what she grounded her belief of its truth, what could she answer? Could she give the arguments from miracles and prophecy? Could she account for all the changes which might have taken place in it through translators and copyists, and prove that we have a genuine and uncorrupted version? Not she! But how, then, does she know that it is true? How, say you? How does she know that she has warm life blood in her heart? How does she know that there is such a thing as air and sunshine? She does not *believe* these things — she *knows* them; and in like manner, with a deep heart consciousness, she is certain that the words of her Bible are truth and life. Is it by reasoning that the frightened child, bewildered in the dark, knows its mother's voice? No! Nor is it only by reasoning that the forlorn and distressed human heart knows the voice of its Savior, and is still.

WHICH IS THE LIBERAL MAN?

It was a beaming and beautiful summer morning, and the little town of V. was alive with all the hurry and motion of a college commencement. Rows of carriages lined the rural streets, and groups of well-dressed auditors were thronging to the hall of exhibition. All was gayety and animation.

And among them all what heart beat higher with hope and gratified ambition than that of James Stanton? Young, buoyant, prepossessing in person and manners, he was this day, in the presence of all the world, to carry off the highest palm of scholarship in his institution, and to receive, on the threshold of the great world, the utmost that youthful ambition can ask before it enters the arena of actual life. Did not his pulse flutter, and his heart beat thick, when he heard himself announced in the crowded house as the valedictorian of the day? when he saw aged men, and fair, youthful faces, ruddy childhood, and sober, calculating manhood alike bending in hushed and eager curiosity, to listen to his words? Nay, did not his heart rise in his throat as he caught the gleam of his father's eye, while, bending forward on his staff, with white, reverend locks falling about his face, he listened to the voice of his pride — his first born? And did he not see the glistening tears in his mother's eye, as with rapt ear she hung upon his every word? Ah, the young man's first triumph! When, full of confidence and hope, he enters the field of life, all his white glistening as yet unsoiled by the dust of the combat, the unproved world turning towards him with flatteries and promises in both hands, what other triumph does life give so fresh, so full, so replete with hope and joy? So felt James Stanton this day, when he heard his father congratulated on having a son of such promise; when old men, revered for talents and worth, shook hands with him, and bade him warmly God speed in the course of life; when bright eyes cast glances of favor, and from among the fairest were overheard whispers of admiration.

"Your son is designed for the bar, I trust," said the venerable Judge L. to the father of James, at the commencement dinner. "I have seldom seen a turn of mind better fitted for success in the legal profession. And then his voice! his manner! let him go to the bar, sir, and I prophesy that he will yet outdo us all."

And this was said in James's hearing, and by one whose commendation was not often so warmly called forth. It was not in any young heart not to beat quicker at such prospects. Honor, station, wealth, political ambition, all seemed to offer themselves to his grasp; but long ere this, in the solitude of retirement, in the stillness of prayer and self-examination, the young graduate had vowed himself to a different destiny; and if we may listen to a conversation, a few evenings after commencement, with a classmate, we shall learn more of the secret workings of his mind.

"And so, Stanton," said George Lennox to him, as they sat by their evening fireside, "you have not yet decided whether to accept Judge L.'s offer or not."

"I have decided that matter long ago," said James.

"So, then, you choose the ministry."

"Yes."

"Well, for my part," replied George Lennox, "I choose the law. There must be Christians, you know, in every vocation; the law seems to suit my turn of mind. I trust it will be my effort to live as becomes a Christian, whatever be my calling."

"I trust so," replied James.

"But really, Stanton," added the other, after some thought, "it seems a pity to cast away such prospects as open before you. You know your tuition is offered gratis; and then the patronage of Judge L., and such influences as he can command to secure your success — pray, do not these things seem to you like a providential indication that the law is to be your profession? Besides, here in these New England States, the ministry is overflowed already — ministers enough, and too many, if one may judge by the number of applicants for every unoccupied place."

"Nay," replied James, "my place is not here. I know, if all accounts are true, that my profession is not overflowed in our Western States, and there I mean to go."

"And is it possible that you can contemplate such an entire sacrifice of your talents, your manners, your literary and scientific tastes, your capabilities for refined society, as to bury yourself in a log cabin in one of our new states? You will never be appreciated there; your privations and sacrifices will be entirely disregarded, and you placed on a level with the coarsest and most uneducated sectaries. I really do not think you are called to this."

"Who, then, is called?" replied James.

"Why, men with much less of all these good things — men with real coarse, substantial, backwoods furniture in their minds, who will not appreciate, and of course not feel, the want of all the refinements and comforts which you must sacrifice."

"And are there enough such men ready to meet the emergencies in our western world, so that no others need be called upon?" replied James. "Men of the class you speak of may do better than I; but, if after all their efforts I still am needed, and can work well, ought I not to go? Must those only be drafted for religious enterprises to whom they involve no sacrifice?"

"Well, for my part," replied the other, "I trust I am willing to do any thing that is my duty; yet I never could feel it to be my duty to bury myself in a new state, among stumps and log cabins. My mind would rust itself out; and, missing the stimulus of such society as I have been accustomed to, I should run down completely, and be useless in body and in mind."

"If you feel so, it would be so," replied James. "If the work there to be done would not be stimulus and excitement enough to compensate for the absence of all other stimulus, — if the business of the ministry, the *saving of human souls*, is not the one all-absorbing purpose, and desire, and impulse of the whole being, — then woe to the man who goes to preach the gospel where there is nothing but human souls to be gained by it."

"Well, Stanton," replied the other, after a pause of some seriousness, "I cannot say that I have attained to this yet. I don't know but I might be brought to it; but at present I must confess it is not so. We ought not to rush into a state and employment which we have not the moral fortitude to sustain well. In short, for myself, I may make a respectable, and, I trust, not useless man in the law, when I could do nothing in the circumstances which you choose. However, I respect your feelings, and heartily wish that I could share them myself."

A few days after this conversation the young friends parted for their several destinations — the one to a law school, the other to a theological seminary.

It was many years after this that a middle-aged man, of somewhat threadbare appearance and restricted travelling conveniences, was seen carefully tying his horse at the outer enclosure of an elegant mansion in the town of ——, in one of our Western States; which being done, he eyed the house rather inquisitively, as people sometimes do when they are doubtful as to the question of entering or not entering. The house belonged to George Lennox, Esq., a lawyer reputed to be doing a more extensive business than any other in the state, and the threadbare gentleman who plies the knocker at the front door is the Reverend Mr. Stanton, a name widely spread in the ecclesiastical circles of the land. The door opens, and the old college acquaintances meet with a cordial grasp of the hand, and Mr. Stanton soon finds himself pressed to the most comfortable accommodations in the warm parlor of his friend; and even the slight uneasiness which the wisest are not always exempt from, when conscious of a little shabbiness in exterior, was entirely dissipated by the evident cordiality of his reception. Since the conversation we have alluded to, the two friends pursued their separate courses with but few opportunities of personal intercourse. In the true zeal of the missionary, James Stanton had thrown himself into the field, where it seemed hardest and darkest, and where labor seemed most needed. In neighborhoods without churches, without school houses, without settled roads, among a population of disorganized and heterogeneous material, he had exhorted from house to house, labored individually with one after another, till he had, in place after place, brought together the elements of a Christian church. Far from all ordinances, means of grace, or Christian brotherhood, or coöperation, he had seemed to himself to be merely the lonely, solitary "*voice* of one crying in the wilderness," as unassisted, and, to human view, as powerless. With poverty, and cold, and physical fatigue he had daily been familiar; and where no vehicle could penetrate the miry depths of the forest, where it was impracticable even to guide a horse, he had walked miles and miles, through mud and rain, to preach. With a wife in delicate health, and a young and growing family, he had more than once seen the year when fifty dollars was the whole amount of money that had passed through his hands; and the whole of the rest of his support had come in disconnected contributions from one and another of his people. He had lived without books, without newspapers, except as he had found them by chance snatches here and there,* and felt, as one so circumstanced only can feel, the difficulty of maintaining intellectual vigor and energy in default of all those stimulants to which cultivated minds in more favorable circumstances are so much indebted. At the time that he is now introduced to the reader, he had been recently made pastor in one of the most important settlements

* These particulars the writer heard stated personally as a part of the experience of one of the most devoted ministers of Ohio.

in the state, and among those who, so far as worldly circumstances were concerned, were able to afford him a competent support. But among communities like those at the west, settled for expressly money-making purposes, and by those who have for years been taught the lesson to save, and have scarcely begun to feel the duty to give, a minister, however laborious, however eloquent and successful, may often feel the most serious embarrassments of poverty. Too often is his salary regarded as a charity which may be given or retrenched to suit every emergency of the times, and his family expenditures watched with a jealous and censorious eye.

On the other hand, George Lennox, the lawyer, had by his talents and efficiency placed himself at the head of his profession, and was realizing an income which brought all the comforts and elegances of life within his reach. He was a member of the Christian church in the place where he lived, irreproachable in life and conduct. From natural generosity of disposition, seconded by principle, he was a liberal contributor to all religious and benevolent enterprises, and was often quoted and referred to as an example in good works. Surrounded by an affectionate and growing family, with ample means for providing in the best manner both for their physical and mental development, he justly regarded himself as a happy man, and was well satisfied with the world he lived in.

Now, there is nothing more trying to the Christianity or the philosophy which teaches the vanity of riches than a few hours' domestication in a family where wealth is employed, not for purposes of ostentation, but for the perfecting of home comfort and the gratification of refined intellectual tastes; and as Mr. Stanton leaned back, slippered and gowned, in one of the easiest of chairs, and began to look over periodicals and valuable new books from which he had long been excluded, he might be forgiven for giving a half sigh to the reflection that he could never be a rich man. "Have you read this review?" said his companion, handing him one of the leading periodicals of the day across the table.

"I seldom see reviews," said Mr. Stanton, taking it.

"You lose a great deal," replied the other, "if you have not seen those by this author — altogether the ablest series of literary efforts in our time. You clerical gentlemen ought not to sacrifice your literary tastes entirely to your professional cares. A moderate attention to current literature liberalizes the mind, and gives influence that you could not otherwise acquire."

"Literary taste is an expensive thing to a minister," said Mr. Stanton, smiling: "for the mind, as well as the body, we must forego all luxuries, and confine ourselves simply to necessaries."

"I would always indulge myself with books and periodicals, even if I had to scrimp elsewhere," said Mr. Lennox; and he spoke of scrimping with all the serious good faith with which people of two or three thousand a year usually speak of these matters.

Mr. Stanton smiled, and waived the subject, wondering mentally where his friend would find an elsewhere to scrimp, if he had the management of *his* concerns. The conversation gradually flowed back to college days and scenes, and the friends amused themselves with tracing the history of their various classmates.

"And so Alsop is in the Senate," said Mr. Stanton.

"Strange! We did not at all expect it of him. But do you know any thing of George Bush?"

"O, yes," replied the other; "he went into mercantile life, and the last I heard he had turned a speculation worth thirty thousand — a shrewd fellow. I always knew he would make his way in the world."

"But what has become of Langdon?"

"O, he is doing well; he is professor of languages in —— College, and I hear he has lately issued a Latin Grammar that promises to have quite a run."

"And Smithson?"

"Smithson has an office at Washington, and was there living in great style the last time I saw him."

It may be questioned whether the minister sank to sleep that night, amid the many comfortable provisions of his friend's guest chamber, without rebuking in his heart a certain rising of regret that he had turned his back on all the honors, and distinctions, and comforts which lay around the path of others, who had not, in the opening of the race, half the advantages of himself. "See," said the insidious voice — "what have you gained? See your early friends surrounded by riches and comfort, while you are pinched and harassed by poverty. Have they not, many of them, as good a hope of heaven as you have, and all this besides? Could you not have lived easier, and been a good man after all?" The reflection was only silenced by remembering that the only Being who ever had the perfect power of choosing his worldly condition, chose, of his own accord, a poverty deeper than that of any of his servants. Had Christ consented to be rich, what check could there have been to the desire of it among his followers? But he chose to stoop so low that none could be lower; and that in extremest want none could ever say, "I am poorer than was my Savior and God."

The friends at parting the next morning shook hands warmly, and promised a frequent renewal of their resumed intercourse. Nor was the bill for twenty dollars, which the minister found in his hand, at all an unacceptable addition to the pleasures of his visit; and though the November wind whistled keenly through a dull, comfortless sky, he turned his horse's head homeward with a lightened heart.

"Mother's sick, and *I'm* a-keeping house!" said a little flaxen-headed girl, in all the importance of seven years, as her father entered the dwelling.

"Your mother sick! what's the matter?" inquired Mr. Stanton.

"She caught cold washing, yesterday, while you were gone;" and when the minister stood by the bedside of his sick wife, saw her flushed face, and felt her feverish pulse, he felt seriously alarmed. She had scarcely recovered from a dangerous fever when he left home, and with reason he dreaded a relapse.

"My dear, why have you done so?" was the first expostulation; "why did you not send for old Agnes to do your washing, as I told you."

"I felt so well, I thought I was quite able," was the reply; "and you know it will take all the money we have now in hand to get the children's shoes before cold weather comes, and nobody knows when we shall have any more."

"Well, Mary, comfort your heart as to that. I have had

a present to-day of twenty dollars — that will last us some time. God always provides when need is greatest." And so, after administering a little to the comfort of his wife, the minister addressed himself to the business of cooking something for dinner for himself and his little hungry flock.

"There is no bread in the house," he exclaimed, after a survey of the ways and means at his disposal.

"I must try and sit up long enough to make some," said his wife faintly.

"You must try to be quiet," replied the husband. "We can do very well on potatoes. But yet," he added, "I think if I bring the things to your bedside, and you show me how to mix them, I could make some bread."

A burst of laughter from the young fry chorused his proposal; nevertheless, as Mr. Stanton was a man of decided genius, by help of much showing, and of strong arms and good will, the feat was at length accomplished in no unworkmanlike manner; and while the bread was put down to the fire to rise, and the potatoes were baking in the oven, Mr. Stanton having enjoined silence on his noisy troop, sat down, pencil in hand, by his wife's bed, to prepare a sermon.

We would that those ministers who feel that they cannot compose without a study, and that the airiest and pleasantest room in the house, where the floor is guarded by the thick carpet, the light carefully relieved by curtains, where papers are filed and arranged neatly in conveniences purposely adjusted, with books of reference standing invitingly around, could once figure to themselves the process of composing a sermon in circumstances such as we have painted. Mr. Stanton had written his text, and jotted down something of an introduction, when a circumstance occurred which is almost inevitable in situations where a person has any thing else to attend to — *the baby woke.* The little interloper was to be tied into a chair, while the flaxen-headed young housekeeper was now installed into the office of waiter in ordinary to her majesty, and by shaking a newspaper before her face, plying a rattle, or other arts known only to the initiate, to prevent her from indulging in any unpleasant demonstrations, while Mr. Stanton proceeded with his train of thought.

"Papa, papa! the teakettle! only look!" cried all the younger ones, just as he was again beginning to abstract his mind.

Mr. Stanton rose, and adapting part of his sermon paper to the handle of the teakettle, poured the boiling water on some herb drink for his wife, and then recommenced.

"I sha'n't have much of a sermon!" he soliloquized, as his youngest but one, with the ingenuity common to children of her standing, had contrived to tip herself over in her chair, and cut her under lip, which for the time being threw the whole settlement into commotion; and this conviction was strengthened by finding that it was now time to give the children their dinner.

"I fear Mrs. Stanton is imprudent in exerting herself," said the medical man to the husband, as he examined her symptoms.

"I know she is," replied her husband, "but I cannot keep her from it."

"It is absolutely indispensable that she should rest and keep her mind easy," said the doctor.

"Rest and keep easy" — how easily the words are said! yet how they fall on the ear of a mother, who knows that her whole flock have not yet a garment prepared for winter, that hiring assistance is out of the question, and that the work must all be done by herself — who sees that while she is sick her husband is perplexed, and kept from his appropriate duties, and her children, despite his well-meant efforts, suffering for the want of those attentions that only a mother can give. Will not any mother, so tried, rise from her sick bed before she feels able, to be again prostrated by over-exertion, until the vigor of the constitution year by year declines, and she sinks into an early grave? Yet this is the true history of many a wife and mother, who, in consenting to share the privations of a western minister, has as truly sacrificed her life as did ever martyr on heathen shores. The graves of Harriet Newell and Mrs. Judson are hallowed as the shrines of saints, and their memory made as a watchword among Christians; yet the western valley is full of green and nameless graves, where patient, long-enduring wives and mothers have lain down, worn out by the privations of as severe a missionary field, and "no man knoweth the place of their sepulchre."

The crisp air of a November evening was enlivened by the fire that blazed merrily in the bar room of the tavern in L., while a more than usual number crowded about the hearth, owing to the session of the county court in that place.

"Mr. Lennox is a pretty smart lawyer," began an old gentleman, who sat in one of the corners, in the half interrogative tone which indicated a wish to start conversation."

"Yes, sir, no mistake about that," was the reply; "does the largest business in the state — very smart man, sir, and honest — a church member too, and one of the tallest kinds of Christians they say — gives more money for building meeting houses, and all sorts of religious concerns, than any man around."

"Well, he can afford it," said a man with a thin, care-taking visage, and a nervous, anxious twitch of the hand, as if it were his constant effort to hold on to something — "he can afford it, for he makes money hand over hand. It is not every body can afford to do as he does."

A sly look of intelligence pervaded the company; for the speaker, one of the most substantial householders in the settlement, was always taken with distressing symptoms of poverty and destitution when any allusion to public or religious charity was made.

"Mr. C. is thinking about parish matters," said a wicked wag of the company; "you see, sir, our minister urged pretty hard last Sunday to have his salary paid up. He has had sickness in his family, and nothing on hand for winter expenses."

"I don't think Mr. Stanton is judicious in making such public statements," said the former speaker, nervously; "he ought to consult his friends privately, and not bring temporalities into the pulpit."

"That is to say, starve decently, and make no fuss," replied the other.

"Nonsense! Who talks of starving, when provision is as plenty as blackberries? I tell you I understand this matter, and know how little a man can get along with. I've tried it myself. When I first set out in life, my wife and I had not a pair of andirons or a shovel and tongs for two or three years, and we never thought of complaining. The times are hard. We are all losing, and must get along as we can; and Mr. Stanton must bear some rubs as well as the rest of us."

"It appears to me, Mr. C.," said the waggish gentleman aforesaid, "that if you'd put Mr. Stanton into your good brick house, and give him your furniture and income, he would be well satisfied to rub along as you do."

"Mr. Stanton isn't so careful in his expenses as he might be," said Mr. C., petulantly, disregarding the idea started by his neighbor; "he buys things *I* should not think of buying. Now, I was in his house the other day, and he had just given three dollars for a single book."

"Perhaps it was a book he needed in his studies," suggested the old gentleman who began the conversation.

"What's the use of book larnin' to a minister, if he's got the real spirit in him?" chimed in a rough-looking man in the farthest corner; "only wish you could have heard Elder North give it off — *there* was a real genuine preacher for you, couldn't even read his text in the Bible; yet, sir, he would get up and reel it off as smooth and fast as the best of them, that come out of the colleges. My notion is, it's the *spirit* that's the thing, after all."

Several of the auditors seemed inclined to express their approbation of this doctrine, though some remarked that Mr. Stanton was a smarter preacher than Elder North, for all his book larnin'.

Some of the more intelligent of the circle here exchanged smiles, but declined entering the lists in favor of "larnin'."

"O, for my part," resumed Mr. C., "I am for having a minister study, and have books and all that, if he can afford it; but in hard times like these, books are neither meat, drink, nor fire; and I know I can't afford them. Now, I'm as willing to contribute my part to the minister's salary, and every other charity, as any body, when I can get money to do it; but in these times I *can't* get it."

The elderly gentleman here interrupted the conversation by

saying, abruptly, "I am a townsman of Mr. Stanton's, and it is *my* opinion that *he* has impoverished himself by giving in religious charity."

"Giving in charity!" exclaimed several voices; "where did he ever get any thing to give?"

"Yet I think I speak within bounds," said the old gentleman, "when I say that he has given more than the amount of two thousand dollars yearly to the support of the gospel in this state; and I think I can show it to be so."

The eyes of the auditors were now enlarged to their utmost limits, while the old gentleman, after the fashion of shrewd old gentlemen generally, screwed up his mouth in a very dry twist, and looked in the fire without saying a word.

"Come now, pray tell us how this is," said several of the company.

"Well, sir," said the old man, "addressing himself to Mr. C., "you are a man of business, and will perhaps understand the case as I view it. You were speaking this evening of lawyer Lennox. He and your minister were both from my native place, and both there and in college your minister was always reckoned the smartest of the two, and went ahead in every thing they undertook. Now, you see Mr. Lennox, out of his talents and education, makes say three thousand a year. Mr. Stanton had more talent, and more education, and might have made even more; but by devoting himself to the work of the ministry in your state, he gains, we will say, about four hundred dollars. Does he not, therefore, in fact, give all the difference between four hundred and three thousand to the cause of religion in this state? If, during the business season of the year, you, Mr. C., should devote your whole time to some benevolent enterprise, would you not feel that you had virtually given to that enterprise all the money you would otherwise have made? Instead, therefore, of calling it a charity for you to subscribe to your minister's support, you ought to consider it a very expensive charity for him to devote his existence in preaching to you. To bring the gospel to your state, he has given up a reasonable prospect of an income of two or three thousand, and contents himself with the least sum which will keep soul and body together, without the possibility of laying up a cent for his family in case of his sickness and death. This, sir, is what *I* call giving in charity."

THE ELDER'S FEAST.

A TRADITION OF LAODICEA.

At a certain time in the earlier ages there lived in the city of Laodicea a Christian elder of some repute, named Onesiphorus. The world had smiled on him, and though a Christian, he was rich and full of honors. All men, even the heathen, spoke well of him, for he was a man courteous of speech and mild of manner.

His wife, a fair Ionian lady but half reclaimed from idolatry, though baptized and accredited as a member of the Christian church, still lingered lovingly on the confines of old heathenism, and if she did not believe, still cherished with pleasure the poetic legends of Apollo and Venus, of Jove and Diana.

A large and fair family of sons and daughters had risen around these parents; but their education had been much after the rudiments of this world, and not after Christ. Though, according to the customs of the church, they were brought to the font of baptism, and sealed in the name of the Father, and the Son, and Holy Ghost, and although daily, instead of libations to the Penates, or flower offerings to Diana and Juno, the name of Jesus was invoked, yet the *spirit* of Jesus was wanting. The chosen associates of all these children, as they grew older, were among the heathen; and daily they urged their parents, by their entreaties, to conform, in one thing after another, to heathen usage. "Why should we be singular, mother?" said the dark-eyed Myrrah, as she bound her hair and arranged her dress after the fashion of the girls in the temple of Venus. "Why may we not wear the golden ornaments and images which have been consecrated to heathen goddesses?" said the sprightly Thalia; "surely none others are to be bought, and are we to do altogether without?" "And why may we not be at feasts where libations are made to Apollo or Jupiter?" said the sons; "so long as we do not consent to it or believe in it, will our faith be shaken thereby?" "How are we ever to reclaim the heathen, if we do not mingle among them?" said another son; "did not our Master eat with publicans and sinners?"

It was, however, to be remarked, that no conversions of the heathen to Christianity ever took place through the means of these complying sons and daughters, or any of the number who followed their example. Instead of withdrawing any from the confines of heathenism, they themselves were drawn so nearly over, that in certain situations and circumstances they would undoubtedly have been ranked among them by any but a most scrutinizing observer. If any in the city of Laodicea were ever led to unite themselves with Jesus, it was by means of a few who observed the full simplicity of the ancient faith, and who, though honest, tender, and courteous in all their dealings with the heathen, still went not a step with them in conformity to any of their customs.

In time, though the family we speak of never broke off

from the Christian church, yet if you had been in it, you might have heard much warm and earnest conversation about things that took place at the baths, or in feasts to various divinities; but if any one spoke of Jesus, there was immediately a cold silence, a decorous, chilling, respectful pause, after which the conversation, with a bound, flew back into the old channel again.

It was now night; and the house of Onesiphorus the Elder was blazing with torches, alive with music, and all the hurry and stir of a sumptuous banquet. All the wealth and fashion of Laodicea were there, Christian and heathen; and all that the classic voluptuousness of Oriental Greece could give to shed enchantment over the scene was there. In ancient times the festivals of Christians in Laodicea had been regulated in the spirit of the command of Jesus, as recorded by Luke, whose classical Greek had made his the established version in Asia Minor. "And thou, when thou makest a feast, call not thy friends and thy kinsmen, nor thy rich neighbors, lest they also bid thee, and a recompense be made thee. But when thou makest a feast, call the poor, and the maimed, and the lame, and the blind, and thou shalt be blessed; for they cannot recompense thee, but thou shalt be recompensed at the resurrection of the just."

That very day, before the entertainment, had this passage been quoted in the ears of the family by Cleon, the youngest son, who, different from all his family, had cherished in his bosom the simplicity of the old belief.

"How ridiculous! how absurd!" had been the reply of the more thoughtless members of the family, when Cleon cited the above passage as in point to the evening's entertainment.

The dark-eyed mother looked reproof on the levity of the younger children, and decorously applauded the passage, which she said had no application to the matter in hand.

"But, mother, even if the passage be not literally taken, it must mean *something*. What did the Lord Jesus intend by it? If we Christians may make entertainments with all the parade and expense of our heathen neighbors, and thus spend the money that might be devoted to charity, what does this passage mean?"

"Your father gives in charity as handsomely as any Christian in Laodicea," said his mother warmly.

"Nay, mother, that may be; but I bethink me now of two or three times when means have been wanting for the relieving of the poor, and the ransoming of captives, and the support of apostles, when we have said that we could give no more."

"My son," said his mother, "you do not understand the ways of the world."

"Nay, how should he?" said Thalia, "shut up day and night with that old papyrus of St. Luke and Paul's Epistles. One may have too much of a good thing."

"But does not the holy Paul say, 'Be not conformed to this world'?"

"Certainly," said the elder; "that means that we should be baptized, and not worship in the heathen temples."

"My dear son," said his mother, "you intend well, doubtless; but you have not sufficient knowledge of life to estimate our relations to society. Entertainments of this sort are absolutely necessary to sustain our position in the world. If we accept, we must return them."

But not to dwell on this conversation, let us suppose ourselves in the rooms now glittering with lights, and gay with every costly luxury of wealth and taste. Here were statues to Diana and Apollo, and to the household Juno — not meant for worship — of course not — but simply to conform to the general usages of good society; and so far had this complaisance been carried, that the shrine of a peerless Venus was adorned with garlands and votive offerings, and an exquisitely wrought silver censer diffused its perfume on the marble altar in front. This complaisance on the part of some of the younger members of the family drew from the elder a gentle remonstrance, as having an unseemly appearance for those bearing the Christian name; but they readily answered, "Has not Paul said, 'We know that an idol is nothing'? Where is the harm of an elegant statue, considered merely as a consummate work of art? As for the flowers, are they not simply the most appropriate ornament? And where is the harm of burning exquisite perfume? And is it worse to burn it in one place than another?"

"Upon my sword," said one of the heathen guests, as he wandered through the gay scene, "how liberal and accommodating these Christians are becoming! Except in a few small matters in the temple, they seem to be with us entirely."

"Ah," said another, "it was not so years back. Nothing was heard among them, then, but prayers, and alms, and visits to the poor and sick; and when they met together in their feasts, there was so much of their talk of Christ, and such singing of hymns and prayer, that one of us found himself quite out of place."

"Yes," said an old man present, "in those days I quite bethought me of being some day a Christian; but look you, they are grown so near like us now, it is scarce worth one's while to change. A little matter of ceremony in the temple, and offering incense to Jesus, instead of Jupiter, when all else is the same, can make small odds in a man."

But now, the ancient legend goes on to say, that in the midst of that gay and brilliant evening, a stranger of remarkable appearance and manners was noticed among the throng. None knew him, or whence he came. He mingled not in the mirth, and seemed to recognize no one present, though he regarded all that was passing with a peculiar air of still and earnest attention; and wherever he moved, his calm, penetrating gaze seemed to diffuse a singular uneasiness about him. Now his eye was fixed with a quiet scrutiny on the idolatrous statues, with their votive adornments — now it followed earnestly the young forms that were wreathing in the graceful waves of the dance; and then he turned towards the tables, loaded with every luxury and sparkling with wines, where the devotion to Bacchus became more than poetic fiction; and as he gazed, a high, indignant sorrow seemed to overshadow the calmness of his majestic face. When, in thoughtless merriment, some of the gay company sought to address him, they found themselves shrinking involuntarily from the soft, piercing eye, and trembling at the low, sweet tones in which he replied. What he spoke was brief; but there was a gravity and tender wisdom in it that strangely contrasted with the frivolous scene, and awakened unwonted ideas of heavenly purity even in thoughtless and dissipated minds.

The only one of the company who seemed to seek his society was the youngest, the fair little child Isa. She seemed as strangely attracted towards him as others were repelled; and when, unsolicited, in the frank confidence of childhood she pressed to his side, and placed her little hand in his, the look of radiant compassion and tenderness which beamed down from those eyes was indeed glorious to behold. Yet here and there, as he glided among the crowd, he spoke in the ear of some Christian words which, though soft and low, seemed to have a mysterious and startling power; for one after another, pensive, abashed, and confounded, they drew aside from the gay scene, and seemed lost in thought. That stranger — who was he? Who? The inquiry passed from mouth to mouth, and one and another, who had listened to his low, earnest tones, looked on each other with a troubled air. Ere long he had glided hither and thither in the crowd; he had spoken in the ear of every Christian — and suddenly again he was gone, and they saw him no more. Each had felt the heart thrill within — each spirit had vibrated as if the finger of its Creator had touched it, and shrunk conscious as if an omniscient eye were upon it. Each heart was stirred from its depths. Vain sophistries, worldly maxims, making the false look true, all appeared to rise and clear away like a mist; and at once each one seemed to see, as God sees, the true state of the inner world, the true motive and reason of action, and in the instinctive pause that passed through the company, the banquet was broken up and deserted.

"And what if their God were present?" said one of the heathen members of the company, next day. "Why did they all look so blank? A most favorable omen, we should call it, to have one's patron divinity at a feast."

"Besides," said another, "these Christians hold that their God is always every where present; so, at most, they have but had their eyes opened to see Him who is always there!"

What is practically the meaning of the precept, "Be not conformed to the world?" In its every-day results, it presents many problems difficult of solution. There are so many shades and blendings of situation and circumstances, so many things, innocent and graceful in themselves, which, like flowers and incense on a heathen altar, become unchristian only through position and circumstances, that the most honest and well-intentioned are often perplexed.

That we must conform in some things, is conceded; yet the whole tenor of the New Testament shows that this conformity must have its limits — that Christians are to be *transformed*, so as to exhibit to the world a higher and more complete style of life, and thus "*prove* what is the good, and acceptable, and perfect will of God."

But in many particulars as to style of living and modes of social intercourse, there can be no definite rules laid down, and no Christian can venture to judge another by his standard.

One Christian condemns dress adornment, and the whole application of taste to the usages of life, as a sinful waste of time and money. Another, perceiving in every work of God a love and appreciation of the beautiful, believes that there is a sphere in which he is pleased to see the same trait in his children, if the indulgence do not become excessive, and thus interfere with higher duties.

One condemns all time and expense laid out in social visiting as so much waste. Another remembers that Jesus, when just entering on the most vast and absorbing work, turned aside to attend a wedding feast, and wrought his first miracle to enhance its social enjoyment. Again, there are others who, because *some* indulgence of taste and some exercise for the social powers are admissible, go all lengths in extravagance, and in company, dress, and the externals of life.

In the same manner, with regard to style of life and social

entertainment — most of the items which go to constitute what is called style of living, or the style of particular parties, may be in themselves innocent, and yet they may be so interwoven and combined with evils, that the whole effect shall be felt to be decidedly unchristian, both by Christians and the world. How, then, shall the well-disposed person know where to stop, and how to strike the just medium?

We know of but one safe rule: read the life of Jesus with attention — *study* it — inquire earnestly with yourself, "What sort of a person, in thought, in feeling, in action, was my Savior?" — live in constant sympathy and communion with him — and there will be within a kind of instinctive rule by which to try all things. A young man, who was to be exposed to the temptations of one of the most dissipated European capitals, carried with him his father's picture, and hung it in his apartment. Before going out to any of the numerous resorts of the city, he was accustomed to contemplate this picture, and say to himself, "Would my father wish to see me in the place to which I am going?" and thus was he saved from many a temptation. In like manner the Christian, who has always by his side the beautiful ideal of his Savior, finds it a holy charm, by which he is gently restrained from all that is unsuitable to his profession. He has but to inquire of any scene or employment, "Should I be well pleased to meet my Savior there? Would the trains of thought I should there fall into, the state of mind that would there be induced, be such as would harmonize with an interview with him?" Thus protected and defended, social enjoyment might be like that of Mary and John, and the disciples, when, under the mild, approving eye of the Son of God, they shared the festivities of Cana.

LITTLE FRED, THE CANAL BOY.

PART I.

IN the outskirts of the little town of Toledo, in Ohio, might be seen a small, one-story cottage, whose external architecture no way distinguished it from dozens of other residences of the poor, by which it was surrounded. But over this dwelling, a presiding air of sanctity and neatness, of quiet and repose, marked it out as different from every other.

The little patch before the door, instead of being a loafing ground for swine, and a receptacle of litter and filth, was trimly set with flowers, weeded, watered, and fenced with dainty care. The scarlet bignonia clambered over the mouldering logs of the sides, shrouding their roughness in its gorgeous mantle of green and crimson, and the good old-fashioned morning glory, laced across the window, unfolded, every day, tints whose beauty, though cheap and common, the finest French milliner might in vain seek to rival.

When, in travelling the western country, you meet such a dwelling, do you not instinctively know what you shall see inside of it? Do you not seem to see the trimly-sanded floor, the well-kept furniture, the snowy muslin curtain? Are you not sure that on a neat stand you shall see, as on an altar, the dear old family Bible, brought, like the ancient ark of the covenant, into the far wilderness, and ever overshadowed, as a bright cloud, with remembered prayers and counsels of father and mother, in a far off New England home?

And in this cottage there was such a Bible, brought from the wild hills of New Hampshire, and its middle page recorded the marriage of James Sandford to Mary Irving; and alas! after it another record, traced in a trembling hand — the death of James Sandford, at Toledo. And this fair, thin woman, in the black dress, with soft brown hair parted over a pale forehead, with calm, patient blue eyes, and fading cheek, is the once energetic, buoyant, light-hearted New Hampshire girl, who has brought with her the strongest religious faith, the active practical knowledge, the skilful, well-trained hand and clear head, with which cold New England portions her daughters. She had left all, and come to the western wilds with no other capital than her husband's manly heart and active brain — he young, strong, full of hope, prompt, energetic, and skilled to acquire — she careful, prudent, steady, no less skilled to save; and between the two no better firm for acquisition and prospective success could be desired. Every body prophesied that James Sandford would succeed, and Mary heard these praises with a quiet exultation. But alas! that whole capital of hers — that one strong, young heart, that ready, helpful hand — two weeks of the country's fever sufficed to lay them cold and low forever.

And Mary yet lived, with her babe in her arms, and one bright little boy by her side; and this boy is our little brown-eyed Fred — the hero of our story. But few years had rolled over his curly head, when he first looked, weeping and wondering, on the face of death. Ah, one look on that awful face adds years at once to the age of the heart; and little Fred felt manly thoughts aroused in him by the cold stillness of his father, and the deep, calm anguish of his mother.

"O mamma, don't cry so, don't," said the little fellow. "I am alive, and I can take care of you. Dear mamma, I pray for you every day." And Mary was comforted even in her tears and thought, as she looked into those clear, loving brown eyes, that her little intercessor would not plead in vain; for saith Jesus, "Their angels do always behold the face of my Father which is in heaven."

In a few days she learned to look her sorrows calmly in the face, like a brave, true woman, as she was. She was a widow, and out of the sudden wreck of her husband's plans but a pittance remained to her, and she cast about, with busy hand and head, for some means to eke it out. She took in sewing —she took in washing and ironing; and happy did the young exquisite deem himself, whose shirts came with such faultless plaits, such snowy freshness, from the slender hands of Mary. With that matchless gift which old Yankee housewives call faculty, Mary kept together all the ends of her ravelled skein of life, and began to make them wind smoothly. Her baby was the neatest of all babies, as it was assuredly the prettiest, and her little Fred the handiest and most universal genius of all boys. It was Fred that could wring out all the stockings, and hang out all the small clothes, that tended the baby by night and by day, that made her a wagon out of an old soap box, in which he drew her in triumph; and at their meals he stood reverently in his father's place, and with folded hands repeated, "Bless the Lord, O my soul, and forget not all his mercies;" and his mother's heart responded amen to the simple prayer. Then he learned, with manifold puffing and much haggling, to saw wood quite decently, and to swing an axe almost as big as himself in wood splitting; and he ran of errands, and did business with an air of bustling importance that was edifying to see; he knew the prices of lard, butter, and dried apples, as well as any man about, and, as the store-keeper approvingly told him, was a smart chap at a bargain. Fred grew three inches higher the moment he heard it.

In the evenings after the baby was asleep, Fred sat by his mother with slate and book, deep in the mysteries of reading, writing, and ciphering; and then the mother and son talked over their little plans, and hallowed their nightly rest by prayer; and when, before retiring, his mother knelt with him by his little bed and prayed, the child often sobbed with a strange emotion, for which he could give no reason. Something there is in the voice of real prayer that thrills a child's heart, even before he understands it; the holy tones are a kind of heavenly music, and far off in distant years, the callous and worldly man, often thrills to his heart's core, when some turn of life recalls to him his mother's prayer.

So passed the first years of the life of Fred. Meanwhile his little sister had come to toddle about the cottage floor, full of insatiable and immeasurable schemes of mischief. It was she that upset the clothes basket, and pulled over the molasses pitcher on to her own astonished head, and with incredible labor upset every pail of water that by momentary thoughtlessness was put within reach. It was she that was found stuffing poor, solemn old pussy head first into the water jar, that wiped up the floor with her mother's freshly-ironed clothes, and jabbered meanwhile, in most unexampled Babylonish dialect, her own vindications and explanations of these misdemeanors. Every day her mother declared that she must begin to get that child into some kind of order; but still the merry little curly pate contemned law and order, and laughed at all ideas of retributive justice, and Fred and his mother laughed and deplored, in the same invariable succession, the various direful results of her activity and enterprise.

But still, as Mary toiled on, heavy cares weighed down her heart. Her boy grew larger and larger, and her own health grew feebler in proportion as it needed to be stronger. Sometimes a whole week at a time found her scarce able to crawl from her bed, shaking with ague, or burning with fever; and when there is little or nothing with which to replace them, how fast food seems to be consumed, and clothing to be worn out! And so at length it came to pass that, notwithstanding the labors of the most tireless of needles, and the cutting, clipping, and contriving of the most ingenious of hands, the poor mother was forced to own to herself that her darlings looked really shabby, and kind neighbors one by one hinted and said that she must do something with her boy — that he was old enough to earn his own living; and the same idea occurred to the spirited little fellow himself.

He had often been along by the side of the canal, and admired the horses; for between a horse and Fred there was a perfect magnetic sympathy, and no lot in life looked to him so bright and desirable as to be able to sit on a horse and drive all day long; and when Captain W., pleased with the boy's bright face and prompt motions, sought to enlist him as one of his drivers, he found a delighted listener. "If he could only persuade mother, there was nothing like it." For many nights after the matter was proposed, Mary only cried; and all Fred's eloquence, and his brave promises of never doing any thing wrong, and being the best of all supposable boys, were insufficient to console her.

Every time she looked at the neat, pure little bed, beside her own, that bed hallowed by so many prayers, and saw her boy, with his glowing cheeks and long and dark lashes, sleeping so innocently and trustfully, her heart died within her, as she thought of a dirty berth on the canal boat, and rough boatmen, swearing, chewing tobacco, and drinking; and should she take her darling from her bosom and throw him out among these? Ah, happy mother! look at your little son of ten years, and ask yourself, if you were obliged to do this, should you not tremble! Give God thanks, therefore, you can hold your child to your heart till he is old enough to breast the dark wave of life. The poor must throw them in, to sink or swim, as happens. Not for ease — not for freedom from care — not for commodious house and fine furniture, and all that competence gives, should you thank God so much as for this, that you are able to shelter, guide, restrain, and educate the helpless years of your children.

Mary yielded at last to that master who can subdue all wills — necessity. Sorrowfully, yet with hope in God, she made up the little package for her boy, and communicated to him with renewed minuteness her parting counsels and instructions. Fred was bright and full of hope. He was sure of the great point about which his mother's anxiety clustered — he should be a good boy, he knew he should; he never should swear; he never should touch a drop of spirits, no matter who asked him — that he was sure of. Then he liked horses so much: he should ride all day and never get tired, and he would come back and bring her some money; and so the boy and his mother parted.

Physical want or hardship is not the great thing which a mother need dread for her child in our country. There is scarce any situation in America where a child would not receive, as a matter of course, good food and shelter; nor is he often overworked. In these respects a general spirit of good nature is perceptible among employers, so that our Fred meets none of the harrowing adventures of an Oliver Twist in his new situation.

To be sure he soon found it was not as good fun to ride a horse hour after hour, and day after day, as it was to prance and caper about for the first few minutes. At first his back ached, and his little hands grew stiff, and he wished his turn were out, hours before the time; but time mended all this. He grew healthy and strong, and though occasionally kicked and tumbled about rather unceremoniously by the rough men among whom he had been cast, yet, as they said, "he was a chap that always came down on his feet, throw him which way you would;" and for this reason he was rather a favorite among them. The fat, black cook, who piqued himself particularly on making corn cake and singing Methodist hymns in a style of unsurpassed excellence, took Fred into particular favor, and being equally at home in kitchen and camp meeting lore, not only put by for him various dainty scraps and fragments, but also undertook to further his moral education by occasional luminous exhortations and expositions of Scripture, which somewhat puzzled poor Fred, and greatly amused the deck hands.

Often, after driving all day, Fred sat on deck beside his fat friend, while the boat glided on through miles and miles of solemn, unbroken old woods, and heard him sing about "de New Jerusalem," about "good old Moses, and Paul, and Silas," with a kind of dreamy, wild pleasure. To be sure it was not like his mother's singing; but then it had a sort of good sound, although he never could very precisely make out the meaning.

As to being a good boy, Fred, to do him justice, certainly tried to very considerable purpose. He did not swear as yet, although he heard so much of it daily that it seemed the most natural thing in the world; and although one and another of the hands often offered him tempting portions of their potations, as they said, "to make a man of him," yet Fred faithfully kept his little temperance pledge to his mother. Many a weary hour, as he rode, and rode, and rode through hundreds of miles of unvarying forest, he strengthened his good resolutions by thoughts of home and its scenes.

There sat his mother; there stood his own little bed; there his baby sister, toddling about in her night gown; and he repeated the prayers and sung the hymns his mother taught him, and thus the good seed still grew within him. In fact, with no very distinguished adventures, Fred achieved the journey to Cincinnati and back, and proud of his laurels, and with his wages in his pocket, found himself again at the familiar door.

Poor Fred! a sad surprise awaited him. The elfin shadow that was once ever flitting about the dwelling was gone; the little pattering footsteps, the tireless, busy fingers, all gone! and his mother, paler, sicker, sadder than before, clasped him to her bosom, and called him her only comfort. Fred had brought a pocket full of sugar plums, and the brightest of yellow oranges to his little pet; alas! how mournfully he regarded them now!

How little do we realize, when we hear that such and such

a poor woman has lost her baby, how much is implied to her in the loss! She is poor; she must work hard; the child was a great addition to her cares; and even pitying neighbors say, "It was better for her, poor thing! and for the child too." But perhaps this very child was the only flower of a life else wholly barren and desolate. There is often, even in the humblest and most uncultured nature, an undefined longing and pining for the beautiful. It expresses itself sometimes in the love of birds and of flowers, and one sees the rosebush or the canary bird in a dwelling from which is banished every trace of luxury. But the little child, with its sweet, spiritual eyes, its thousand bird-like tones, its prattling, endearing ways, its guileless, loving heart, is a full and perfect answer to the most ardent craving of the soul. It is a whole little Eden of itself; and the poor woman whose whole life else is one dreary waste of toil, clasps her babe to her bosom, and feels proud, and rich, and happy. Truly said the Son of God, "Of such are the kingdom of heaven."

Poor Mary! how glad she was to see her boy again — most of all, that they could talk together of their lost one! How they discoursed for hours about her! How they cried together over the little faded bonnet, that once could scarce be kept for a moment on the busy, curly head! How they treasured, as relics, the small finger marks on the doors, and consecrated with sacred care even the traces of her merry mischief about the cottage, and never tired of telling over to each other, with smiles and tears, the record of the past gleesome pranks!

But the fact was, that Mary herself was fast wearing away. She had borne up bravely against life; but she had but a gentle nature, and gradually she sank from day to day. Fred

24*

was her patient, unwearied nurse, and neighbors — never wanting in such kindnesses as they can understand — supplied her few wants. The child never wanted for food, and the mantle shelf was filled with infallible specifics, each one of which was able, according to the showing, to insure perfect recovery in every case whatever; and yet, strange to tell, she still declined. At last, one still autumn morning, Fred awoke, and started at the icy coldness of the hand clasped in his own. He looked in his mother's face; it was sweet and calm as that of a sleeping infant, but he knew in his heart that she was dead.

PART II.

Months afterwards, a cold December day found Fred turned loose in the streets of Cincinnati. Since his mother's death he had driven on the canal boat; but now the boat was to lie by for winter, and the hands of course turned loose to find employment till spring. Fred was told that he must look up a place; every body was busy about their own affairs, and he must shift for himself; and so with half his wages in his pocket, and promises for the rest, he started to seek his fortune.

It was a cold, cheerless, gray-eyed day, with an air that pinched fingers and toes, and seemed to penetrate one's clothes like snow water — such a day as it needs the brightest fire and the happiest heart to get along at all with; and, unluckily, Fred had neither. Christmas was approaching, and all the shops had put on their holiday dresses; the confectioners' windows were glittering with sparkling pyramids of candy, with frosted cake, and unfading fruits and flowers of the very best of sugar. There, too, was Santa Claus, large as life, with queer, wrinkled visage, and back bowed with the weight of all desirable knickknacks, going down chimney, in sight of all the children of Cincinnati, who gathered around the shop with constantly-renewed acclamations. On all sides might be seen the little people, thronging, gazing, chattering, while anxious papas and mammas in the shops were gravely discussing tin trumpets, dolls, spades, wheelbarrows, and toy wagons.

Fred never had heard of the man who said, "How sad a thing it is to look into happiness through another man's eyes!" but he felt something very like it as he moved through the gay and bustling streets, where every body seemed to be finding what they wanted but himself.

He had determined to keep up a stout heart; but in spite of himself, all this bustling show and merriment made him feel sadder and sadder, and lonelier and lonelier. He knocked and rang at door after door, but nobody wanted a boy: nobody ever does want a boy when a boy is wanting a place. He got tired of ringing door bells, and tried some of the shops. No, they didn't want him. One said if he was bigger he might do; another wanted to know if he could keep accounts; one thought that the man around the corner wanted a boy, and when Fred got there he had just engaged one. Weary, disappointed, and discouraged, he sat down by the iron railing that fenced a showy house, and thought what he should do. It was almost five in the afternoon: cold, dismal, leaden-gray was the sky — the darkness already coming on. Fred sat listlessly watching the great snow feathers, as they slowly sailed down from the sky. Now he heard gay laughs, as groups of merry children passed; and then he started, as he saw some woman in a black bonnet, and thought she looked like his mother. But all passed, and nobody looked at him, nobody wanted him, nobody noticed him.

Just then a patter of little feet was heard behind him on the flagstones, and a soft, baby voice said, "How do 'oo do?" Fred turned in amazement; and there stood a plump, rosy little creature of about two years, with dimpled cheek, ruby lips, and long, fair hair curling about her sweet face. She was dressed in a blue pelisse, trimmed with swan's down, and her complexion was so exquisitely fair, her eyes so clear and sweet, that Fred felt almost as if it were an angel. The little thing toddled up to him, and holding up before him a new wax doll, all splendid in silk and lace, seemed quite disposed te make his acquaintance. Fred thought of his lost sister, and his eyes filled up with tears. The little one put up one dimpled hand to wipe them away, while with the other holding up before him the wax doll, she said, coaxingly, "No no ky."

Just then the house door opened, and a lady, richly dressed, darted out, exclaiming, "Why, Mary, you little rogue, how came you out here?" Then stopping short, and looking narrowly on Fred, she said, somewhat sharply, "Whose boy are you? and how came you here?"

"I'm nobody's boy," said Fred, getting up, with a bitter choking in his throat; "my mother's dead; I only sat down here to rest me for a while."

"Well, run away from here," said the lady; but the little girl pressed before her mother, and jabbering very earnestly in unimaginable English, seemed determined to give Fred her wax doll, in which, she evidently thought, resided every possible consolation.

The lady felt in her pocket and found a quarter, which she threw towards Fred. "There, my boy, that will get you lodging and supper, and to-morrow you can find some place to work, I dare say;" and she hurried in with the little girl, and shut the door.

It was not money that Fred wanted just then, and he picked up the quarter with a heavy heart. The sky looked darker, and the street drearier, and the cold wind froze the tear on his cheeks as he walked listlessly down the street in the dismal twilight.

"I can go back to the canal boat, and find the cook," he thought to himself. "He told me I might sleep with him to-night if I couldn't find a place;" and he quickened his steps with this determination. Just as he was passing a brightly-lighted coffee house, familiar voices hailed him, and Fred stopped; he would be glad even to see a dog he had ever met before, and of course he was glad when two boys, old canal boat acquaintances, hailed him, and invited him into the coffee house. The blazing fire was a brave light on that dismal night, and the faces of the two boys were full of glee, and they began rallying Fred on his doleful appearance, and insisting on it that he should take something warm with them.

Fred hesitated a moment; but he was tired and desperate, and the steaming, well-sweetened beverage was too tempting. "Who cares for me?" thought he, "and why should I care?" and down went the first spirituous liquor the boy had ever tasted; and in a few moments, he felt a wonderful change. He was no longer a timid, cold, disheartened, heart-sick boy, but felt somehow so brave, so full of hope and courage, that he began to swagger, to laugh very loud, and to boast in such high terms of the money in his pocket, and of his future intentions and prospects, that the two boys winked significantly at each other. They proposed, after sitting a while, to walk out and see the shop windows. All three of the boys had taken enough to put them to extra merriment; but Fred, who was entirely unused to the stimulant, was quite beside himself. If they sung, he shouted; if they laughed, he screamed; and he thought within himself he never had heard and thought so many witty things as on that very evening. At last they fell in with quite a press of boys, who were crowding round a confectionery window, and, as usual in such cases, there began an elbowing and scuffling contest for places, in which Fred was quite conspicuous. At last a big boy presumed on his superior size to edge in front of our hero, and cut off his prospect; and Fred, without more ado, sent him smashing through the shop window. There was a general scrabble, every one ran for himself, and Fred, never having been used to the business, was not very skilful in escaping, and of course was caught, and committed to an officer, who, with small ceremony, carried him off and locked him up in the watch house, from which he was the next morning taken before the mayor, and after examination sent to jail.

This sobered Fred. He came to himself as out of a dream, and he was overwhelmed with an agony of shame and self-reproach. He had broken his promise to his dead mother — he had been drinking! and his heart failed him when he thought of the horrors that his mother had always associated with that word. And then he was in jail — that place that his mother had always represented as an almost impossible horror, the climax of shame and disgrace. The next night the poor boy stretched himself on his hard, lonely bed, and laid under his head his little bundle, containing his few clothes and his mother's Bible, and then sobbed himself to sleep.

Cold and gray dawned the following morning on little Fred,

as he slowly and heavily awoke, and with a bitter chill of despair recalled the events of the last two nights, and looked up at the iron-grated window, and round on the cheerless walls; and, as if in bitter contrast, arose before him an image of his lost home — the neat, quiet room, the white curtains and snowy floor, his mother's bed, with his own little cot beside it, and his mother's mild blue eyes, as they looked upon him only six months ago. Mechanically he untied the check handkerchief which contained his few clothes, and worldly possessions, and relics of home.

There was the small, clean-printed Bible his mother had given him with so many tears on their first parting; there was a lock of her soft brown hair; there, too, were a pair of little worn shoes and stockings, a baby's rattle, and a curl of golden hair, which he had laid up in memory of his lost little pet. Fred laid his head down over all these, his forlorn treasures, and sobbed as if his heart would break.

After a while the jailer came in, and really seemed affected by the distress of the child, and said what he could to console him; and in the course of the day, as the boy "seemed to be so lonesome like," he introduced another boy into the room as company for him. This was a cruel mercy; for while the child was alone with himself and the memories of the past, he was, if sad, at least safe, and in a few hours after this new introduction he was neither. His new companion was a tall boy of fourteen, with small, cunning, gray eyes, to which a slight cast gave an additional expression of shrewdness and drollery. He was a young gentleman of great natural talent, — in a certain line, — with very precocious attainments in all that kind of information which a boy gains by running at large for several years in a city's streets without any thing particular to do, or any body in particular to obey — any conscience, any principle, any fear either of God or man. We should not say that he had never seen the inside of a church, for he had been, for various purposes, into every one of the city, and to every camp meeting for miles around; and so much had he profited by these exercises, that he could mimic to perfection every minister who had any perceptible peculiarity, could caricature every species of psalm-singing, and give ludicrous imitations of every form of worship. Then he was *au fait* in all coffee house lore, and knew the names and qualities of every kind of beverage therein compounded; and as to smoking and chewing, the first elements of which he mastered when he was about six years old, he was now a *connoisseur* in the higher branches. He had been in jail dozens of times — rather liked the fun; had served one term on the chain-gang — not so bad either — shouldn't mind another — learned a good many prime things there.

At first Fred seemed inclined to shrink from his new associate. An instinctive feeling, like the warning of an invisible angel, seemed to whisper, "Beware!" But he was alone, with a heart full of bitter thoughts, and the sight of a fellow-face was some comfort. Then his companion was so dashing, so funny, so free and easy, and seemed to make such a comfortable matter of being in jail, that Fred's heart, naturally buoyant, began to come up again in his breast. Dick Jones soon drew out of him his simple history as to how he came there, and finding that he was a raw hand, seemed to feel bound to patronize and take him under his wing. He laughed quite heartily at Fred's story, and soon succeeded in getting him to laugh at it too.

How strange! — the very scenes that in the morning he

looked at only with bitter anguish and remorse, this noon he was laughing at as good jokes — so much for the influence of good society! An instinctive feeling, soon after Dick Jones came in, led Fred to push his little bundle into the farthest corner, under the bed, far out of sight or inquiry; and the same reason led him to suppress all mention of his mother, and all the sacred part of his former life. He did this more studiously, because, having once accidentally remarked how his mother used to forbid him certain things, the well-educated Dick broke out, —

"Well, for my part, I could whip my mother when I wa'n't higher than *that!*" with a significant gesture.

"Whip your mother!" exclaimed Fred, with a face full of horror.

"To be sure, greenie! Why not? Precious fun it was in those times. I used to slip in and steal the old woman's whiskey and sugar when she was just too far over to walk a crack — she'd throw the tongs at me, and I'd throw the shovel at her, and so it went square and square."

Goethe says somewhere, "Miserable is that man whose *mother* has not made all other mothers venerable." Our new acquaintance bade fair to come under this category.

Fred's education, under this talented instructor, made progress. He sat hours and hours laughing at his stories — sometimes obscene, sometimes profane, but always so full of life, drollery, and mimicry that a more steady head than Fred's was needed to withstand the contagion. Dick had been to the theatre — knew it all like a book, and would take Fred there as soon as they got out; then he had a first-rate pack of cards, and he could teach Fred to play; and the gay tempters were soon spread out on their bed, and Fred and his instructor sat hour after hour absorbed in what to him was a new world of interest. He soon learned, could play for small stakes, and felt in himself the first glimmering of that fire which, when fully kindled, many waters cannot quench, nor floods drown!

Dick was, as we said, precocious. He had the cool eye and steady hand of an experienced gamester, and in a few days he won, of course, all Fred's little earnings. But then he was quite liberal and free with his money. He added to their prison fare such various improvements as his abundance of money enabled him to buy. He had brought with him the foundation of good cheer in a capacious bottle which emerged the first night from his pocket, for he said he never went to jail without his provision; then hot water, and sugar, and lemons, and peppermint drops were all forthcoming for money, and Fred learned once and again, and again, the fatal secret of hushing conscience, and memory, and bitter despair in delirious happiness, and as Dick said, was "getting to be a right jolly 'un that would make something yet."

And was it all gone, all washed away by this sudden wave of evil? — every trace of prayer, and hope, and sacred memory in this poor child's heart? No, not all; for many a night, when his tempter slept by his side, the child lived over the past; again he kneeled in prayer, and felt his mother's guardian hand on his head, and he wept tears of bitter remorse, and wondered at the dread change that had come over him. Then he dreamed, and he saw his mother and sister walking in white, fair as angels, and would go to them; but between him and them was a great gulf fixed, which widened and widened, and grew darker and darker, till he could see them no more, and he awoke in utter misery and despair.

Again and again he resolved, in the darkness of the night,

that to-morrow he would not drink, and he would not speak a wicked word, and he would not play cards, nor laugh at Dick's bad stories. Ah, how many such midnight resolves have evil angels sneered at and good ones sighed over! for with daylight back comes the old temptation, and with it the old mind; and with daylight came back the inexorable prison walls which held Fred and his successful tempter together.

At last he gave himself up. No, he could not be good with Dick — there was no use in trying! — and he made no more midnight resolves, and drank more freely of the dreadful remedy for unquiet thoughts.

And now is Fred growing in truth a wicked boy. In a little while more and he shall be such a one as you will on no account take under your roof, lest he corrupt your own children; and yet, father, mother, look at your son of twelve years, your bright, darling boy, and think of him shut up for a month with such a companion, in such a cell, and ask yourselves if he would be any better.

And was there no eye, heavenly or earthly, to look after this lost one? Was there no eye which could see through all the traces of sin, the yet lingering drops of that baptism and early prayer and watchfulness which consecrated it? Yes; He whose mercy extends to the third and fourth generations of those who love him, sent a friend to our poor boy in his last distress.

It is one of the most refined and characteristic modifications of Christianity, that those who are themselves sheltered, guarded, fenced by good education, knowledge, and competence, appoint and sustain a pastor and guardian in our large cities to be the shepherd of the wandering and lost, and of them who, in the Scripture phrase, "have none to help." Justly is he called the " City Missionary," for what is more truly missionary ground? In the hospital, among the old, the sick, the friendless, the forlorn — in the prison, among the hardened, the blaspheming — among the discouraged and despairing, still holding with unsteady hand on to some forlorn fragment of virtue and self-respect, goes this missionary to stir the dying embers of good, to warn, entreat, implore, to adjure by sacred recollections of father, mother, and home, the fallen wanderers to return. He finds friends, and places, and employment for some, and by timely aid and encouragement saves many a one from destruction.

In this friendly shape appeared a man of prayer to visit the cell in which Fred was confined. Dick listened to his instructions with cool complacency, rolling his tobacco from side to side in his mouth, and meditating on him as a subject for some future histrionic exercise of his talent.

But his voice was as welcome to poor Fred as daylight in a dungeon. All the smothered remorse and despair of his heart burst forth in bitter confessions, as, with many tears, he poured forth his story to the friendly man. It needs not to prolong our story, for now the day has dawned and the hour of release is come.

It is not needful to carry our readers through all the steps by which Fred was transferred, first to the fireside of the friendly missionary, and afterwards to the guardian care of a good old couple who resided on a thriving farm not far from Cincinnati. Set free from evil influences, the first carefully planted and watered seeds of good began to grow again, and he became as a son to the kind family who had adopted him.

THE CANAL BOAT.

Of all the ways of travelling which obtain among our locomotive nation, this said vehicle, the canal boat, is the most absolutely prosaic and inglorious. There is something picturesque, nay, almost sublime, in the lordly march of your well-built, high-bred steamboat. Go, take your stand on some overhanging bluff, where the blue Ohio winds its thread of silver, or the sturdy Mississippi tears its path through unbroken forests, and it will do your heart good to see the gallant boat walking the waters with unbroken and powerful tread; and, like some fabled monster of the wave, breathing fire, and making the shores resound with its deep respirations. Then there is something mysterious, even awful, in the power of steam. See it curling up against a blue sky, some rosy morning — graceful, floating, intangible, and to all appearance the softest and gentlest of all spiritual things; and then think that it is this fairy spirit that keeps all the world alive and hot with motion; think how excellent a servant it is, doing all sorts of gigantic works, like the genii of old; and yet, if you let slip the talisman only for a moment, what terrible advantage it will take of you! and you will confess that steam has some claims both to the beautiful and the terrible. For our own part, when we are down among the machinery of a steamboat in full play, we conduct ourself very reverently, for we consider it as a very serious neighborhood; and every time the steam whizzes with such red-hot determination from the escape valve, we start as if some of the spirits were after us. But in a canal boat there is no power, no mystery, no danger; one cannot blow up, one cannot be drowned, unless by some special effort: one sees clearly all there is in the case — a horse, a rope, and a muddy strip of water — and that is all.

Did you ever try it, reader? If not, take an imaginary trip with us, just for experiment. "There's the boat!" exclaims a passenger in the omnibus, as we are rolling down from the Pittsburg Mansion House to the canal. "Where?" exclaim a dozen of voices, and forthwith a dozen heads go out of the window. "Why, down there, under that bridge; don't you see those lights?" "What! that little thing?" exclaims an inexperienced traveller; "dear me! we can't half of us get into it!" "We! indeed," says some old hand in the business; "I think you'll find it will hold us and a dozen more loads like us." "Impossible!" say some. "You'll see," say the initiated; and, as soon as you get out, you *do* see, and hear too, what seems like a general breaking loose from the Tower of Babel, amid a perfect hail storm of trunks, boxes, valises, carpet bags, and every describable and indescribable form of what a westerner calls "plunder."

"That's my trunk!" barks out a big, round man. "That's my bandbox!" screams a heart-stricken old lady, in terror for her immaculate Sunday caps. "Where's my little red box? I had two carpet bags and a — My trunk had a scarle — Halloo! where are you going with that portmanteau?

Husband! husband! do see after the large basket and the little hair trunk — O, and the baby's little chair!" "Go below — go below, for mercy's sake, my dear; I'll see to the baggage." At last, the feminine part of creation, perceiving that, in this particular instance, they gain nothing by public speaking, are content to be led quietly under hatches; and amusing is the look of dismay which each new comer gives to the confined quarters that present themselves. Those who were so ignorant of the power of compression as to suppose the boat scarce large enough to contain them and theirs, find, with dismay, a respectable colony of old ladies, babies, mothers, big baskets, and carpet bags already established. "Mercy on us!" says one, after surveying the little room, about ten feet long and six high, "where are we all to sleep to-night?" "O me! what a sight of children!" says a young lady, in a despairing tone. "Poh!" says an initiated traveller; "children! scarce any here; let's see: one; the woman in the corner, two; that child with the bread and butter, three; and then there's that other woman with two. Really, it's quite moderate for a canal boat. However, we can't tell till they have all come."

"All! for mercy's sake, you don't say there are any more coming!" exclaim two or three in a breath; "they *can't* come; *there is not room!*"

Notwithstanding the impressive utterance of this sentence, the contrary is immediately demonstrated by the appearance of a very corpulent, elderly lady, with three well-grown daughters, who come down looking about them most complacently, entirely regardless of the unchristian looks of the company. What a mercy it is that fat people are always good natured!

After this follows an indiscriminate raining down of all

shapes, sizes, sexes, and ages — men, women, children, babies, and nurses. The state of feeling becomes perfectly desperate. Darkness gathers on all faces. "We shall be smothered! we shall be crowded to death! we *can't stay* here!" are heard faintly from one and another; and yet, though the boat grows no wider, the walls no higher, they do live, and do stay there, in spite of repeated protestations to the contrary. Truly, as Sam Slick says, "there's a *sight of wear* in human natur'."

But, mean while, the children grow sleepy, and divers interesting little duets and trios arise from one part or another of the cabin.

"Hush, Johnny! be a good boy," says a pale, nursing mamma, to a great, bristling, white-headed phenomenon, who is kicking very much at large in her lap.

"I won't be a good boy, neither," responds Johnny, with interesting explicitness; "I want to go to bed, and so-o-o-o!" and Johnny makes up a mouth as big as a teacup, and roars with good courage, and his mamma asks him "if he ever saw pa do so," and tells him that "he is mamma's dear, good little boy, and must not make a noise," with various observations of the kind, which are so strikingly efficacious in such cases. Meanwhile, the domestic concert in other quarters proceeds with vigor. "Mamma, I'm tired!" bawls a child. "Where's the baby's night gown?" calls a nurse. "Do take Peter up in your lap, and keep him still." "Pray get out some biscuits to stop their mouths." Meanwhile, sundry babies strike in "con spirito," as the music books have it, and execute various flourishes; the disconsolate mothers sigh, and look as if all was over with them; and the young ladies appear extremely disgusted, and wonder "what business women have to be travelling round with babies."

To these troubles succeeds the turning-out scene, when the whole caravan is ejected into the gentlemen's cabin, that the beds may be made. The red curtains are put down, and in solemn silence all, the last mysterious preparations begin. At length it is announced that all is ready. Forthwith the whole company rush back, and find the walls embellished by a series of little shelves, about a foot wide, each furnished with a mattress and bedding, and hooked to the ceiling by a very suspiciously slender cord. Direful are the ruminations and exclamations of inexperienced travellers, particularly young ones, as they eye these very equivocal accommodations. "What, sleep up there! *I* won't sleep on one of those top shelves, *I* know. The cords will certainly break." The chambermaid here takes up the conversation, and solemnly assures them that such an accident is not to be thought of at all; that it is a natural impossibility — a thing that could not happen without an actual miracle; and since it becomes increasingly evident that thirty ladies cannot all sleep on the lowest shelf, there is some effort made to exercise faith in this doctrine; nevertheless, all look on their neighbors with fear and trembling; and when the stout lady talks of taking a shelf, she is most urgently pressed to change places with her alarmed neighbor below. Points of location being after a while adjusted, comes the last struggle. Every body wants to take off a bonnet, or look for a shawl, to find a cloak, or get a carpet bag, and all set about it with such zeal that nothing can be done. "Ma'am, you're on my foot!" says one. "Will you please to move, ma'am?" says somebody, who is gasping and struggling behind you. "Move!" you echo. "Indeed, I should be very glad to, but I don't see much prospect of it." "Chambermaid!" calls a lady, who is struggling among a heap of carpet bags and children at one end of the cabin. "Ma'am!" echoes the poor chambermaid, who is wedged fast, in a similar situation, at the other. "Where's my cloak, chambermaid?" "I'd find it, ma'am, if I could move." "Chambermaid, my basket!" "Chambermaid, my parasol!" "Chambermaid, my carpet bag!" "Mamma, they push me so!" "Hush, child; crawl under there, and lie still till I can undress you." At last, however, the various distresses are over, the babies sink to sleep, and even that much-enduring being, the chambermaid, seeks out some corner for repose. Tired and drowsy, you are just sinking into a doze, when bang! goes the boat against the sides of a lock; ropes scrape, men run and shout, and up fly the heads of all the top shelfites, who are generally the more juvenile and airy part of the company.

"What's that! what's that!" flies from mouth to mouth; and forthwith they proceed to awaken their respective relations. "Mother! Aunt Hannah! do wake up; what is this awful noise?" "O, only a lock!" "Pray be still," groan out the sleepy members from below.

"A lock!" exclaim the vivacious creatures, ever on the alert for information; "and what *is* a lock, pray?"

"Don't you know what a lock is, you silly creatures? Do lie down and go to sleep."

"But say, there ain't any *danger* in a lock, is there?" respond the querists. "Danger!" exclaims a deaf old lady, poking up her head; "what's the matter? There hain't nothin' burst, has there?" "No, no, no!" exclaim the provoked and despairing opposition party, who find that there is no such thing as going to sleep till they have made the old lady below and the young ladies above understand exactly the philosophy of a lock. After a while the conversation again subsides; again all is still; you hear only the trampling of horses and the rippling of the rope in the water, and sleep again is stealing over you. You doze, you dream, and all of a sudden you are started by a cry, "Chambermaid! wake up the lady that wants to be set ashore." Up jumps chambermaid, and up jump the lady and two children, and forthwith form a committee of inquiry as to ways and means. "Where's my bonnet?" says the lady, half awake, and fumbling among the various articles of that name. "I thought I hung it up behind the door." "Can't you find it?" says poor chambermaid, yawning and rubbing her eyes. "O, yes, here it is," says the lady; and then the cloak, the shawl, the gloves, the shoes, receive each a separate discussion. At last all seems ready, and they begin to move off, when, lo! Peter's cap is missing. "Now, where can it be?" soliloquizes the lady. "I put it right here by the table leg; maybe it got into some of the berths." At this suggestion, the chambermaid takes the candle, and goes round deliberately to every berth, poking the light directly in the face of every sleeper. "Here it is," she exclaims, pulling at something black under one pillow. "No, indeed, those are my shoes," says the vexed sleeper. "Maybe it's here," she resumes, darting upon something dark in another berth. "No, that's my bag," responds the occupant. The chambermaid then proceeds to turn over all the children on the floor, to see if it is not under them. In the course of which process they are most agreeably waked up and enlivened; and when every body is broad awake, and most uncharitably wishing the cap, and Peter too, at the bottom of the canal, the good lady exclaims, "Well, if this isn't lucky; here I had it safe in my basket all the time!"

And she departs amid the — what shall I say? — execrations? — of the whole company, ladies though they be.

Well, after this follows a hushing up and wiping up among the juvenile population, and a series of remarks commences from the various shelves, of a very edifying and instructive tendency. One says that the woman did not seem to know where any thing was; another says that she has waked them all up; a third adds that she has waked up all the children, too; and the elderly ladies make moral reflections on the importance of putting your things where you can find them — being always ready; which observations, being delivered in an exceedingly doleful and drowsy tone, form a sort of sub-bass to the lively chattering of the upper shelfites, who declare that they feel quite wide awake, — that they don't think they shall go to sleep again to-night, — and discourse over every thing in creation, until you heartily wish you were enough related to them to give them a scolding.

At last, however, voice after voice drops off; you fall into a most refreshing slumber; it seems to you that you sleep about a quarter of an hour, when the chambermaid pulls you by the sleeve. "Will you please to get up, ma'am? We want to make the beds." You start and stare. Sure enough, the night is gone. So much for sleeping on board canal boats.

Let us not enumerate the manifold perplexities of the morning toilet in a place where every lady realizes most forcibly the condition of the old woman who lived under a broom: "All she wanted was elbow room." Let us not tell how one glass is made to answer for thirty fair faces, one ewer and vase for thirty lavations; and — tell it not in Gath! — one towel for a company! Let us not intimate how ladies' shoes have, in a night, clandestinely slid into the gentlemen's cabin, and gentlemen's boots elbowed, or, rather, *toed* their way among ladies' gear, nor recite the exclamations after runaway property that are heard. "I can't find nothin' of Johnny's shoe!" "Here's a shoe in the water pitcher — is this it?" "My side combs are gone!" exclaims a nymph with dishevelled curls. "Massy! do look at my bonnet!" exclaims an old lady, elevating an article crushed into as many angles as there are pieces in a minced pie. "I never did sleep *so much together* in my life," echoes a poor little French lady, whom despair has driven into talking English.

But our shortening paper warns us not to prolong our catalogue of distresses beyond reasonable bounds, and therefore we will close with advising all our friends, who intend to try this way of travelling for *pleasure*, to take a good stock both of patience and clean towels with them, for we think that they will find abundant need for both.

FEELING.

THERE is one way of studying human nature, which surveys mankind only as a set of instruments for the accomplishment of personal plans. There is another, which regards them simply as a gallery of pictures, to be admired or laughed at as the caricature or the *beau ideal* predominates. A third way regards them as human beings, having hearts that can suffer and enjoy, that can be improved or be ruined; as those who are linked to us by mysterious reciprocal influences, by the common dangers of a present existence, and the uncertainties of a future one; as presenting, wherever we meet them, claims on our sympathy and assistance.

Those who adopt the last method are interested in human beings, not so much by *present* attractions as by their capabilities as intelligent, immortal beings; by a high belief of what every mind may attain in an immortal existence; by anxieties for its temptations and dangers, and often by the perception of errors and faults which threaten its ruin. The first two modes are adopted by the great mass of society; the last is the office of those few scattered stars in the sky of life, who look down on its dark selfishness to remind us that there is a world of light and love.

To this class did *He* belong, whose rising and setting on earth were for " the healing of the nations ; " and to this class has belonged many a pure and devoted spirit, like him shining to cheer, like him fading away into the heavens. To this class many a one *wishes* to belong, who has an eye to distinguish the divinity of virtue, without the resolution to attain it; who, while they sweep along with the selfish current of society, still regret that society is not different — that they themselves are not different. If this train of thought has no very particular application to what follows, it was nevertheless suggested by it, and of its relevancy others must judge.

Look into this school room. It is a warm, sleepy afternoon in July ; there is scarcely air enough to stir the leaves of the tall buttonwood tree before the door, or to lift the loose leaves of the copy book in the window; the sun has been diligently shining into those curtainless west windows ever since three o'clock, upon those blotted and mangled desks, and those decrepit and tottering benches, and that great arm chair, the high place of authority.

You can faintly hear, about the door, the " craw, craw," of some neighboring chickens, which have stepped around to consider the dinner baskets, and pick up the crumbs of the noon's repast. For a marvel, the busy school is still, because, in truth, it is too warm to stir. You will find nothing to disturb your meditation on character, for you cannot hear the beat of those little hearts, nor the bustle of all those busy thoughts.

Now look around. Who of these is the most interesting? Is it that tall, slender, hazel-eyed boy, with a glance like a falcon, whose elbows rest on his book as he gazes out on the great buttonwood tree, and is calculating how he shall fix his squirrel trap when school is out? Or is it that curly-headed little rogue, who is shaking with repressed laughter at seeing a chicken roll over in a dinner basket? Or is it that arch boy with black eyelashes, and deep, mischievous dimple in his cheeks, who is slyly fixing a fish hook to the skirts of the master's coat, yet looking as abstracted as Archimedes whenever the good man turns his head that way? No; these are intelligent, bright, beautiful, but it is not these.

Perhaps, then, it is that sleepy little girl, with golden curls, and a mouth like a half-blown rosebud. See, the small brass thimble has fallen to the floor, her patchwork drops from her lap, her blue eyes close like two sleepy violets, her little head is nodding, and she sinks on her sister's shoulder: surely it is she. No, it is not.

But look in that corner. Do you see that boy with such a gloomy countenance — so vacant, yet so ill natured? He is doing nothing, and he very seldom does any thing. He is surly and gloomy in his looks and actions. He never showed any more aptitude for saying or doing a pretty thing than his straight white hair does for curling. He is regularly blamed and punished every day, and the more he is blamed and punished, the worse he grows. None of the boys and girls in school will play with him; or, if they do, they will be sorry for it. And every day the master assures him that "he does not know what to do with him," and that he "makes him more trouble than any boy in school," with similar judicious information, that has a striking tendency to promote improvement. That is the boy to whom I apply the title of "the most interesting one."

He is interesting because he is *not* pleasing; because he has bad habits; because he does wrong; because, under present influences, he is always likely to do wrong. He is interesting because he has become what he is now by means of the very temperament which often makes the noblest virtue. It is feeling, acuteness of feeling, which has given that countenance its expression, that character its moroseness.

He has no father, and that long-suffering friend, his mother, is gone too. Yet he has relations, and kind ones too; and, in the compassionate language of worldly charity, it may be said of him, "He would have nothing of which to complain, if he would only behave himself."

His little sister is always bright, always pleasant and cheerful; and his friends say, "Why should not he be so too? He is in exactly the same circumstances." No, he is not. In one circumstance they differ. He has a mind to feel and remember every thing that can pain; she can feel and remember but little. If you blame him, he is exasperated, gloomy, and cannot forget it. If you blame her, she can say she has done wrong in a moment, and all is forgotten. Her mind can no more be wounded than the little brook where she loves to play. The bright waters close again, and smile and prattle as merry as before.

Which is the most desirable temperament? It would be hard to say. The power of feeling is necessary for all that is noble in man, and yet it involves the greatest risks. They who catch at happiness on the bright surface of things, secure a portion, such as it is, with more certainty; those who dive for it in the waters of deeper feeling, if they succeed, will bring up pearls and diamonds, but if they sink they are lost forever!

But now comes Saturday, and school is just out. Can any one of my readers remember the rapturous prospect of a long, bright Saturday afternoon? "Where are you going?" "Will you come and see me?" "We are going a fishing!" "Let us go a strawberrying!" may be heard rising from the happy group. But no one comes near the ill-humored James, and the little party going to visit his sister "wish James was out of the way." He sees every motion, hears every whisper, knows, suspects, feels it all, and turns to go home more sullen and ill tempered than common. The world looks dark — nobody loves him — and he is told that it is "all his own fault," and that makes the matter still worse.

When the little party arrive, he is suspicious and irritable, and, of course, soon excommunicated. Then, as he stands in disconsolate anger, looking over the garden fence at the gay group making dandelion chains, and playing baby house under the trees, he wonders why he is not like other children. He wishes he were different, and yet he does not know what to do. He looks around, and every thing is blooming and bright. His little bed of flowers is even brighter and sweeter than ever before, and a new rose is just opening on his rosebush.

There goes pussy, too, racing and scampering, with little Ellen after her, in among the alleys and flowers; and the birds are singing in the trees; and the soft winds brush the blossoms of the sweet pea against his cheek; and yet, though all nature looks on him so kindly, he is wretched.

Let us now change the scene. Why is that crowded assembly so attentive — so silent? Who is speaking? It is our old friend, the little disconsolate schoolboy. But his eyes are flashing with intellect, his face fervent with emotion, his voice breathes like music, and every mind is enchained.

Again, it is a splendid sunset, and yonder enthusiast meets it face to face, as a friend. He is silent — rapt — happy. He feels the poetry which God has written; he is touched by it, as God meant that the feeling spirit should be touched.

Again, he is watching by the bed of sickness, and it is

blessed to have such a watcher! anticipating every want; relieving, not in a cold, uninterested way, but with the quick perceptions, the tenderness, the gentleness of an angel.

Follow him into the circle of friendship, and why is he so loved and trusted? Why can you so easily tell to him what you can say to no one else besides? Why is it that all around him feel that he can understand, appreciate, be touched by all that touches them?

And when heaven uncloses its doors of light, when all its knowledge, its purity, its bliss, rises on the eye and passes into the soul, who then will be looked on as the one who might be envied — he who *can*, or he who *cannot feel?*

THE SEAMSTRESS.

"Few, save the poor, feel for the poor;
The rich know not how hard
It is to be of needful food
And needful rest debarred.

Their paths are paths of plenteousness;
They sleep on silk and down;
They never think how wearily
The weary head lies down.

They never by the window sit,
And see the gay pass by,
Yet take their weary work again,
And with a mournful eye."

L. E. L.

However fine and elevated, in a sentimental point of view, may have been the poetry of this gifted writer, we think we have never seen any thing from this source that *ought* to give a better opinion of her than the little ballad from which the above verses are taken.

They show that the accomplished authoress possessed, not merely a knowledge of the dreamy ideal wants of human beings, but the more pressing and homely ones, which the fastidious and poetical are often the last to appreciate. The sufferings of poverty are not confined to those of the common, squalid, every day inured to hardships, and ready, with open hand, to receive charity, let it come to them as it will. There is another class on whom it presses with still heavier power — the generous, the decent, the self-respecting, who have struggled with their lot in silence, "bearing all things, hoping all things," and willing to endure all things, rather than breathe a word of complaint, or to acknowledge, even to themselves, that their own efforts will not be sufficient for their own necessities.

Pause with me a while at the door of yonder room, whose small window overlooks a little court below. It is inhabited by a widow and her daughter, dependent entirely on the labors of the needle, and those other slight and precarious resources, which are all that remain to woman when left to struggle her way through the world alone. It contains all their small earthly store, and there is scarce an article of its little stock of furniture that has not been thought of, and toiled for, and its price calculated over and over again, before every thing could be made right for its purchase. Every article is arranged with the utmost neatness and care; nor is the most costly furniture of a fashionable parlor more sedulously guarded from a scratch or a rub, than is that brightly-varnished bureau, and that neat cherry tea table and bedstead. The floor, too, boasted once a carpet; but old Time has been busy with it, picking a hole here, and making a thin place there; and though the old fellow has been followed up by the most indefatigable zeal in darning, the marks of his mischievous fingers are too plain to be mistaken. It is true, a kindly neighbor has given a bit of faded baize, which has been neatly clipped and bound, and spread down over an entirely unmanageable hole in front of the fireplace; and other places have been repaired with pieces of different colors; and yet, after all, it is evident that the poor carpet is not long for this world.

But the best face is put upon every thing. The little cupboard in the corner, that contains a few china cups, and one or two antiquated silver spoons, relics of better days, is arranged with jealous neatness, and the white muslin window curtain, albeit the muslin be old, has been carefully whitened and starched, and smoothly ironed, and put up with exact precision; and on the bureau, covered by a snowy cloth, are arranged a few books and other memorials of former times, and a faded miniature, which, though it have little about it to interest a stranger, is more precious to the poor widow than every thing besides.

Mrs. Ames is seated in her rocking chair, supported by a pillow, and busy cutting out work, while her daughter, a slender, sickly-looking girl, is sitting by the window, intent on some fine stitching.

Mrs. Ames, in former days, was the wife of a respectable merchant, and the mother of an affectionate family. But evil fortune had followed her with a steadiness that seemed like the stern decree of some adverse fate rather than the ordinary dealings of a merciful Providence. First came a heavy run of losses in business; then long and expensive sickness in the family, and the death of children. Then there was the selling of the large house and elegant furniture, to retire to a humbler style of living; and finally, the sale of all the property, with the view of quitting the shores of a native land, and commencing life again in a new one. But scarcely had the exiled family found themselves in the port of a foreign land, when the father was suddenly smitten down by the hand of death, and his lonely grave made in a land of strangers. The widow, broken-hearted and discouraged, had still a wearisome journey before her ere she could reach any whom she could consider as her friends. With her two daughters, entirely unattended, and with her finances impoverished by detention and sickness, she performed the tedious journey.

Arrived at the place of her destination, she found herself not only without immediate resources, but considerably in debt to one who had advanced money for her travelling expenses. With silent endurance she met the necessities of her situation. Her daughters, delicately reared, and hitherto carefully educated, were placed out to service, and Mrs. Ames sought for employment as a nurse. The younger child fell sick, and the hard earnings of the mother were all exhausted in the care of her; and though she recovered in part, she was declared by her physician to be the victim of a disease which would never leave her till it terminated her life.

As soon, however, as her daughter was so far restored as not to need her immediate care, Mrs. Ames resumed her laborious employment. Scarcely had she been able, in this way, to discharge the debts for her journey and to furnish the small room we have described, when the hand of disease was laid heavily on herself. Too resolute and persevering to give way to the first attacks of pain and weakness, she still continued her fatiguing employment till her system was entirely prostrated. Thus all possibility of pursuing her business was cut off, and nothing remained but what could be accomplished by her own and her daughter's dexterity at the needle. It is at this time we ask you to look in upon the mother and daughter.

Mrs. Ames is sitting up, the first time for a week, and even to-day she is scarcely fit to do so; but she remembers that the month is coming round, and her rent will soon be due; and in her feebleness she will stretch every nerve to meet her engagements with punctilious exactness.

Wearied at length with cutting out, and measuring, and drawing threads, she leans back in her chair, and her eye rests on the pale face of her daughter, who has been sitting for two hours intent on her stitching.

"Ellen, my child, your head aches; don't work so steadily."

"O, no, it don't ache *much*," said she, too conscious of looking very much tired. Poor girl! had she remained in the situation in which she was born, she would now have been skipping about, and enjoying life as other young girls of fifteen do; but now there is no choice of employments for her — no youthful companions — no visiting — no pleasant walks in the fresh air. Evening and morning, it is all the same; headache or sideache, it is all one. She must hold on the same unvarying task — a wearisome thing for a girl of fifteen.

But see! the door opens, and Mrs. Ames's face brightens as her other daughter enters. Mary has become a domestic in a neighboring family, where her faithfulness and kindness of heart have caused her to be regarded more as a daughter and a sister than as a servant. "Here, mother, is your rent money," she exclaimed; "so do put up your work and rest a while. I can get enough to pay it next time before the month comes around again."

"Dear child, I do wish you would ever think to get any thing for yourself," said Mrs. Ames. "I cannot consent to use up all your earnings, as I have done lately, and all Ellen's too; you must have a new dress this spring, and that bonnet of yours is not decent any longer."

"O, no, mother! I have made over my blue calico, and you would be surprised to see how well it looks; and my best frock, when it is washed and darned, will answer some time longer. And then Mrs. Grant has given me a ribbon, and when my bonnet is whitened and trimmed it will look very well. And so," she added, "I brought you some wine this afternoon; you know the doctor says you need wine."

"Dear child, I want to see you take some comfort of your money yourself."

"Well, I do take comfort of it, mother. It is more comfort to be able to help you than to wear all the finest dresses in the world."

Two months from this dialogue found our little family still more straitened and perplexed. Mrs. Ames had been confined all the time with sickness, and the greater part of Ellen's time and strength was occupied with attending to her.

Very little sewing could the poor girl now do, in the broken intervals that remained to her; and the wages of Mary were not only used as fast as earned, but she anticipated two months in advance.

Mrs. Ames had been better for a day or two, and had been sitting up, exerting all her strength to finish a set of shirts which had been sent in to make. "The money for them will just pay our rent," sighed she; "and if we can do a little more this week —— "

"Dear mother, you are so tired," said Ellen; "do lie down, and not worry any more till I come back."

Ellen went out, and passed on till she came to the door of

an elegant house, whose damask and muslin window curtains indicated a fashionable residence.

Mrs. Elmore was sitting in her splendidly-furnished parlor, and around her lay various fancy articles which two young girls were busily unrolling. "What a lovely pink scarf!" said one, throwing it over her shoulders and skipping before a mirror; while the other exclaimed, "Do look at these pocket handkerchiefs, mother! what elegant lace!"

"Well, girls," said Mrs. Elmore, "these handkerchiefs are a shameful piece of extravagance. I wonder you will insist on having such things."

"La, mamma, every body has such now; Laura Seymour has half a dozen that cost more than these, and her father is no richer than ours."

"Well," said Mrs. Elmore, "rich or not rich, it seems to make very little odds; we do not seem to have half as much money to spare as we did when we lived in the little house in Spring Street. What with new furnishing the house, and getting every thing you boys and girls say you must have, we are poorer, if any thing, than we were then."

"Ma'am, here is Mrs. Ames's girl come with some sewing," said the servant.

"Show her in," said Mrs. Elmore.

Ellen entered timidly, and handed her bundle of work to Mrs. Elmore, who forthwith proceeded to a minute scrutiny of the articles; for she prided herself on being very particular as to her sewing. But, though the work had been executed by feeble hands and aching eyes, even Mrs. Elmore could detect no fault in it.

"Well, it is very prettily done," said she. "What does your mother charge?"

Ellen handed a neatly-folded bill which she had drawn for her mother. "I must say, I think your mother's prices are very high," said Mrs. Elmore, examining her nearly empty purse; "every thing is getting so dear that one hardly knows how to live." Ellen looked at the fancy articles, and glanced around the room with an air of innocent astonishment. "Ah," said Mrs. Elmore, "I dare say it seems to you as if persons in our situation had no need of economy; but, for my part, I feel the need of it more and more every day." As she spoke she handed Ellen the three dollars, which, though it was not a quarter the price of one of the handkerchiefs, was all that she and her sick mother could claim in the world. "There," said she; "tell your mother I like her work very much, but I do not think I can afford to employ her, if I can find any one to work cheaper."

Now, Mrs. Elmore was not a hard-hearted woman, and if Ellen had come as a beggar to solicit help for her sick mother, Mrs. Elmore would have fitted out a basket of provisions, and sent a bottle of wine, and a bundle of old clothes, and all the *et cetera* of such occasions; but the sight of *a bill* always aroused all the instinctive sharpness of her business-like education. She never had the dawning of an idea that it was her duty to pay any body any more than she could possibly help; nay, she had an indistinct notion that it was her *duty* as an economist to make every body take as little as possible. When she and her daughters lived in Spring Street, to which she had alluded, they used to spend the greater part of their time at home, and the family sewing was commonly done among themselves. But since they had moved into a large house, and set up a carriage, and addressed themselves to being genteel, the girls found that they had altogether too much to do to attend to their own sewing, much less to perform any for their father and brothers. And their mother found her hands abundantly full in overlooking her large house, in taking care of expensive furniture, and in superintending her increased train of servants. The sewing, therefore, was put out; and Mrs. Elmore *felt it a duty* to get it done the cheapest way she could. Nevertheless, Mrs. Elmore was too notable a lady, and her sons and daughters were altogether too fastidious as to the make and quality of their clothing, to admit the idea of its being done in any but the most complete and perfect manner.

Mrs. Elmore never accused herself of want of charity for the poor; but she had never considered that the best class of the poor are those who never ask charity. She did not consider that, by paying liberally those who were honestly and independently struggling for themselves, she was really doing a greater charity than by giving indiscriminately to a dozen applicants.

"Don't you think, mother, she says we charge too high for this work!" said Ellen, when she returned. "I am sure she did not know how much work we put in those shirts. She says she cannot give us any more work; she must look out for somebody that will do it cheaper. I do not see how it is that people who live in such houses, and have so many beautiful things, can feel that they cannot afford to pay for what costs us so much."

"Well, child, they are more apt to feel so than people who live plainer."

"Well, I am sure," said Ellen, "we cannot afford to spend so much time as we have over these shirts for less money."

"Never mind, my dear," said the mother, soothingly; "here is a bundle of work that another lady has sent in, and if we get it done, we shall have enough for our rent, and something over to buy bread with."

It is needless to carry our readers over all the process of cutting, and fitting, and gathering, and stitching, necessary in making up six fine shirts. Suffice it to say that on Saturday evening all but one were finished, and Ellen proceeded to carry them home, promising to bring the remaining one on Tuesday morning. The lady examined the work, and gave Ellen the money; but on Tuesday, when the child came with the remaining work, she found her in great ill humor. Upon reëxamining the shirts, she had discovered that in some important respects they differed from directions she meant to have given, and supposed she had given; and, accordingly, she vented her displeasure on Ellen.

"Why didn't you make these shirts as I told you?" said she, sharply.

"We did," said Ellen, mildly; "mother measured by the pattern every part, and cut them herself."

"Your mother must be a fool, then, to make such a piece of work. I wish you would just take them back and alter them over;" and the lady proceeded with the directions, of which neither Ellen nor her mother till then had had any intimation. Unused to such language, the frightened Ellen took up her work and slowly walked homeward.

"O, dear, how my head does ache!" thought she to herself; "and poor mother! she said this morning she was afraid another of her sick turns was coming on, and we have all this work to pull out and do over."

"See here, mother," said she, with a disconsolate air, as she entered the room; "Mrs. Rudd says, take out all the bosoms, and rip off all the collars, and fix them quite another way. She says they are not like the pattern she sent; but she must have forgotten, for here it is. Look, mother; it is exactly as we made them."

"Well, my child, carry back the pattern, and show her that it is so."

"Indeed, mother, she spoke so cross to me, and looked at me so, that I do not feel as if I could go back."

"I will go for you, then," said the kind Maria Stephens, who had been sitting with Mrs. Ames while Ellen was out. "I will take the pattern and shirts, and tell her the exact truth about it. I am not afraid of her." Maria Stephens was a tailoress, who rented a room on the same floor with Mrs. Ames, a cheerful, resolute, go-forward little body, and ready always to give a helping hand to a neighbor in trouble. So she took the pattern and shirts, and set out on her mission.

But poor Mrs. Ames, though she professed to take a right view of the matter, and was very earnest in showing Ellen why she ought not to distress herself about it, still felt a shivering sense of the hardness and unkindness of the world coming over her. The bitter tears would spring to her eyes, in spite of every effort to suppress them, as she sat mournfully gazing on the little faded miniature before mentioned. "When *he* was alive, I never knew what poverty or trouble was," was the thought that often passed through her mind. And how many a poor forlorn one has thought the same!

Poor Mrs. Ames was confined to her bed for most of that week. The doctor gave absolute directions that she should do nothing, and keep entirely quiet — a direction very sensible indeed in the chamber of ease and competence, but hard to be observed in poverty and want.

What pains the kind and dutiful Ellen took that week to make her mother feel easy! How often she replied to her anxious questions, "that she was quite well," or "that her head did not ache *much!*" and by various other evasive expedients the child tried to persuade herself that she was speaking the truth. And during the times her mother slept, in the day or evening, she accomplished one or two pieces of plain work, with the price of which she expected to surprise her mother.

It was towards evening when Ellen took her finished work to the elegant dwelling of Mrs. Page. "I shall get a dollar for this," said she; "enough to pay for mother's wine and medicine."

"This work is done very neatly," said Mrs. Page, "and here is some more I should like to have finished in the same way."

Ellen looked up wistfully, hoping Mrs. Page was going to pay her for the last work. But Mrs. Page was only searching a drawer for a pattern, which she put into Ellen's hands, and after explaining how she wanted her work done, dismissed her without saying a word about the expected dollar.

Poor Ellen tried two or three times, as she was going out, to turn round and ask for it; but before she could decide what to say, she found herself in the street.

Mrs. Page was an amiable, kind-hearted woman, but one who was so used to large sums of money that she did not realize how great an affair a single dollar might seem to other persons. For this reason, when Ellen had worked incessantly at the new work put into her hands, that she might get the money for all together, she again disappointed her in the payment.

"I'll send the money round to-morrow," said she, when Ellen at last found courage to ask for it. But to-morrow came, and Ellen was forgotten; and it was not till after one or two applications more that the small sum was paid.

But these sketches are already long enough, and let us hasten to close them. Mrs. Ames found liberal friends, who could appreciate and honor her integrity of principle and loveliness of character, and by their assistance she was raised to see more prosperous days; and she, and the delicate Ellen, and warm-hearted Mary were enabled to have a home and fireside of their own, and to enjoy something like the return of their former prosperity.

We have given these sketches, drawn from real life, because we think there is in general too little consideration on the part of those who give employment to those in situations like the widow here described. The giving of employment is a very important branch of charity, inasmuch as it assists that class of the poor who are the most deserving. It should be looked on in this light, and the arrangements of a family be so made that a suitable compensation can be given, and prompt and cheerful payment be made, without the dread of transgressing the rules of economy.

It is better to teach our daughters to do without expensive ornaments or fashionable elegances; better even to deny ourselves the pleasure of large donations or direct subscriptions to public charities, rather than to curtail the small stipend of her whose "candle goeth not out by night," and who labors with her needle for herself and the helpless dear ones dependent on her exertions.

OLD FATHER MORRIS.

A SKETCH FROM NATURE.

Of all the marvels that astonished my childhood, there is none I remember to this day with so much interest as the old man whose name forms my caption. When I knew him, he was an aged clergyman, settled over an obscure village in New England. He had enjoyed the advantages of a liberal education, had a strong, original power of thought, an omnipotent imagination, and much general information; but so early and so deeply had the habits and associations of the plough, the farm, and country life wrought themselves into his mind, that his after acquirements could only mingle with them, forming an unexampled amalgam like unto nothing but itself.

He was an ingrain New Englander, and whatever might have been the source of his information, it came out in Yankee form, with the strong provinciality of Yankee dialect.

It is in vain to attempt to give a full picture of such a genuine *unique;* but some slight and imperfect dashes may help the imagination to a faint idea of what none can fully conceive but those who have seen and heard old Father Morris.

Suppose yourself one of half a dozen children, and you hear

the cry, "Father Morris is coming!" You run to the window or door, and you see a tall, bulky old man, with a pair of saddle bags on one arm, hitching his old horse with a fumbling carefulness, and then deliberately stumping towards the house. You notice his tranquil, florid, full-moon face, enlightened by a pair of great round blue eyes, that roll with dreamy inattentiveness on all the objects around; and as he takes off his hat, you see the white curling wig that sets off his round head. He comes towards you, and as you stand staring, with all the children around, he deliberately puts his great hand on your head, and, with deep, rumbling voice, inquires, —

"How d'ye do, my darter? is your daddy at home?" "My darter" usually makes off as fast as possible, in an unconquerable giggle. Father Morris goes into the house, and we watch him at every turn, as, with the most liberal simplicity, he makes himself at home, takes off his wig, wipes down his great face with a checked pocket handkerchief, helps himself hither and thither to whatever he wants, and asks for such things as he cannot lay his hands on, with all the comfortable easiness of childhood.

I remember to this day how we used to peep through the crack of the door, or hold it half ajar and peer in, to watch his motions; and how mightily diverted we were with his deep, slow manner of speaking, his heavy, cumbrous walk, but, above all, with the wonderful faculty of "*hemming*" which he possessed.

His deep, thundering, protracted "A-hem-em" was like nothing else that ever I heard; and when once, as he was in the midst of one of these performances, the parlor door suddenly happened to swing open, I heard one of my roguish brothers calling, in a suppressed tone, "Charles! Charles!

Father Morris has *hemmed* the door open!" — and then followed the signs of a long and desperate titter, in which I sincerely sympathized.

But the morrow is Sunday. The old man rises in the pulpit. He is not now in his own humble little parish, preaching simply to the hoers of corn and planters of potatoes, but there sits Governor D., and there is Judge R., and Counsellor P., and Judge G. In short, he is before a refined and literary audience. But Father Morris rises; he thinks nothing of this; he cares nothing; he knows nothing, as he himself would say, but "Jesus Christ, and him crucified." He takes a passage of Scripture to explain; perhaps it is the walk to Emmaus, and the conversation of Jesus with his disciples. Immediately the whole start out before you, living and picturesque: the road to Emmaus is a New England turnpike; you can see its mile stones, its mullein stalks, its toll gates. Next the disciples rise, and you have before you all their anguish, and hesitation, and dismay talked out to you in the language of your own fireside. You smile; you are amused; yet you are touched, and the illusion grows every moment. You see the approaching stranger, and the mysterious conversation grows more and more interesting. Emmaus rises in the distance, in the likeness of a New England village, with a white meeting house and spire. You follow the travellers; you enter the house with them; nor do you wake from your trance until, with streaming eyes, the preacher tells you that "they saw it was the Lord Jesus — and *what a pity* it was they could not have known it before!"

It was after a sermon on this very chapter of Scripture history that Governor Griswold, in passing out of the house, laid hold on the sleeve of his first acquaintance: "Pray tell me," said he, "who is this minister?"

"Why, it is old Father Morris."

"Well, he is an oddity — and a genius too, I declare!" he continued. "I have been wondering all the morning how I could have read the Bible to so little purpose as not to see all these particulars he has presented."

I once heard him narrate in this picturesque way the story of Lazarus. The great bustling city of Jerusalem first rises to view, and you are told, with great simplicity, how the Lord Jesus "used to get tired of the noise;" and how he was "tired of preaching, again and again, to people who would not mind a word he said;" and how, "when it came evening, he used to go out and see his friends in Bethany." Then he told about the house of Martha and Mary: "a little white house among the trees," he said; "you could just see it from Jerusalem." And there the Lord Jesus and his disciples used to go and sit in the evenings, with Martha, and Mary, and Lazarus.

Then the narrator went on to tell how Lazarus died, describing, with tears and a choking voice, the distress they were in, and how they sent a message to the Lord Jesus, and he did not come, and how they wondered and wondered; and thus on he went, winding up the interest by the graphic *minutiæ* of an eye witness, till he woke you from the dream by his triumphant joy at the resurrection scene.

On another occasion, as he was sitting at a tea table, unusually supplied with cakes and sweetmeats, he found an opportunity to make a practical allusion to the same family story. He said that Mary was quiet and humble, sitting at her Savior's feet to hear his words; but Martha thought more of what was to be got for tea. Martha could not find time to listen to Christ. No; she was "'cumbered with much serving'—around the house, frying fritters and making gingerbread."

Among his own simple people, his style of Scripture painting was listened to with breathless interest. But it was particularly in those rustic circles, called "conference meetings," that his whole warm soul unfolded, and the Bible in his hands became a gallery of New England paintings.

He particularly loved the evangelists, following the footsteps of Jesus Christ, dwelling upon his words, repeating over and over again the stories of what he did, with all the fond veneration of an old and favored servant.

Sometimes, too, he would give the narration an exceedingly practical turn, as one example will illustrate.

He had noticed a falling off in his little circle that met for social prayer, and took occasion, the first time he collected a tolerable audience, to tell concerning "the conference meeting that the disciples attended" after the resurrection.

"But Thomas was not with them." "Thomas not with them!" said the old man, in a sorrowful voice. "Why, what could keep Thomas away? Perhaps," said he, glancing at some of his backward auditors, "Thomas had got cold-hearted, and was afraid they would ask him to make the first prayer; or perhaps," said he, looking at some of the farmers, "Thomas was afraid the roads were bad; or perhaps," he added, after a pause, "Thomas had got proud, and thought he could not come in his old clothes." Thus he went on, significantly summing up the common excuses of his people; and then, with great simplicity and emotion, he added, "But only think what Thomas lost! for in the middle of the meeting, the Lord Jesus came and stood among them! How sorry Thomas must have been!" This representation served to fill the vacant seats for some time to come.

At another time Father Morris gave the details of the anointing of David to be king. He told them how Samuel went to Bethlehem, to Jesse's house, and went in with a "How d'ye do, Jesse?" and how, when Jesse asked him to take a chair, he said he could not stay a minute; that the Lord had sent him to anoint one of his sons for a king; and how, when Jesse called in the tallest and handsomest, Samuel said "he would not do;" and how all the rest passed the same test; and at last, how Samuel says, "Why, have not you any more sons, Jesse?" and Jesse says, "Why, yes, there is little David down in the lot;" and how, as soon as ever Samuel saw David, "he slashed the oil right on to him;" and how Jesse said "he never was so beat in all his life."

Father Morris sometimes used his illustrative talent to very good purpose in the way of rebuke. He had on his farm a fine orchard of peaches, from which some of the ten and twelve-year-old gentlemen helped themselves more liberally than even the old man's kindness thought expedient.

Accordingly, he took occasion to introduce into his sermon one Sunday, in his little parish, an account of a journey he took; and how he was "very warm and very dry;" and how he saw a fine orchard of peaches that made his mouth water to look at them. "So," says he, "I came up to the fence and looked all around, for I would not have touched one of them *without leave* for all the world. At last I spied a man, and says I, 'Mister, won't you give me some of your peaches?' So the man came and gave me nigh about a hat full. And while I stood there eating, I said, 'Mister, how do you manage to keep your peaches?' 'Keep them!' said he, and he stared at me; 'what do you mean?' 'Yes, sir,' said I; 'don't the boys steal them?' 'Boys steal them!' said he. 'No, indeed!' 'Why, sir,' said I, 'I have a whole lot full of peaches, and I cannot get half of them'" — here the old man's voice grew tremulous — "'because the boys in my parish steal them so.' 'Why, sir,' said he, 'don't their parents teach them not to steal?' And I grew all over in a cold sweat, and I told him 'I was afeard they didn't.' 'Why, how you talk!' says the man; 'do tell me where you live?' Then," said Father Morris, the tears running over, "I was obliged to tell him I lived in the town of G." After this Father Morris kept his peaches.

Our old friend was not less original in the logical than in the illustrative portions of his discourses. His logic was of that familiar, colloquial kind which shakes hands with common sense like an old friend. Sometimes, too, his great mind and great heart would be poured out on the vast themes of religion, in language which, though homely, produced all the effects of the sublime. He once preached a discourse on the text, "the High and Holy One that inhabiteth eternity;" and from the beginning to the end it was a train of lofty and solemn thought. With his usual simple earnestness, and his great, rolling voice, he told about "the Great God — the Great Jehovah — and how the people in this world were flustering and worrying, and afraid they should not get time to do this, and that, and t'other. But," he added, with full-hearted satisfaction, "the Lord is never in a hurry; he has it all to do, but he has time enough, for he inhabiteth eternity." And the grand idea of infinite leisure and almighty resources was carried through the sermon with equal strength and simplicity.

Although the old man never seemed to be sensible of any thing tending to the ludicrous in his own mode of expressing himself, yet he had considerable relish for humor, and some shrewdness of repartee. One time, as he was walking through a neighboring parish, famous for its profanity, he was stopped by a whole flock of the youthful reprobates of the place: —

"Father Morris, Father Morris! the devil's dead!"

"Is he?" said the old man, benignly laying his hand on the head of the nearest urchin; "you poor fatherless children!"

But the sayings and doings of this good old man, as reported in the legends of the neighborhood, are more than can be gathered or reported. He lived far beyond the common age of man, and continued, when age had impaired his powers, to tell over and over again the same Bible stories that he had told so often before.

I recollect hearing of the joy that almost broke the old man's heart, when, after many years' diligent watching and nurture of the good seed in his parish, it began to spring into vegetation, sudden and beautiful as that which answers the patient watching of the husbandman. Many a hard, worldly-hearted man — many a sleepy, inattentive hearer — many a listless, idle young person, began to give ear to words that had long fallen unheeded. A neighboring minister, who had been sent for to see and rejoice in these results, describes the scene, when, on entering the little church, he found an anxious, crowded auditory assembled around their venerable teacher, waiting for direction and instruction. The old man was sitting in his pulpit, almost choking with fulness of emotion as he gazed around. "Father," said the youthful minister, "I suppose you are ready to say with old Simeon, 'Now, Lord, lettest thou thy servant depart in peace, for my eyes have seen thy salvation.'" "*Sartin, sartin,*" said the old man, while the tears streamed down his cheeks, and his whole frame shook with emotion.

It was not many years after that this simple and loving servant of Christ was gathered in peace unto Him whom he loved. His name is fast passing from remembrance, and in a few years, his memory, like his humble grave, will be entirely grown over and forgotten among men, though it will be had in everlasting remembrance by Him who "forgetteth not his servants," and in whose sight the death of his saints is precious.

THE TWO ALTARS,

OR TWO PICTURES IN ONE.

I. THE ALTAR OF LIBERTY, OR 1776.

THE wellsweep of the old house on the hill was relieved, dark and clear, against the reddening sky, as the early winter sun was going down in the west. It was a brisk, clear, metallic evening; the long drifts of snow blushed crimson red on their tops, and lay in shades of purple and lilac in the hollows; and the old wintry wind brushed shrewdly along the plain, tingling people's noses, blowing open their cloaks, puffing in the back of their necks, and showing other unmistakable indications that he was getting up steam for a real roistering night.

"Hurrah! How it blows!" said little Dick Ward, from the top of the mossy wood pile.

Now Dick had been sent to said wood pile, in company with his little sister Grace, to pick up chips, which, every body knows, was in the olden time considered a wholesome and gracious employment, and the peculiar duty of the rising generation. But said Dick, being a boy, had mounted the wood pile, and erected there a flagstaff, on which he was busily tying a little red pocket handkerchief, occasionally exhorting Grace "to be sure and pick up fast."

"O, yes, I will," said Grace; "but you see the chips have got ice on 'em, and make my hands so cold!"

"O, don't stop to suck your thumbs! Who cares for ice? Pick away, I say, while I set up the flag of liberty."

So Grace picked away as fast as she could, nothing doubting but that her cold thumbs were in some mysterious sense an offering on the shrine of liberty; while soon the red handkerchief, duly secured, fluttered and snapped in the brisk evening wind.

"Now you must hurrah, Gracie, and throw up your bonnet," said Dick, as he descended from the pile.

"But won't it lodge down in some place in the wood pile?" suggested Grace, thoughtfully.

"O, never fear; give it to me, and just holler now, Gracie, 'Hurrah for liberty;' and we'll throw up your bonnet and my cap; and we'll play, you know, that we are a whole army, and I'm General Washington."

So Grace gave up her little red hood, and Dick swung his cap, and up they both went into the air; and the children shouted, and the flag snapped and fluttered, and altogether they had a merry time of it. But then the wind — good for nothing, roguish fellow! — made an ungenerous plunge at poor Grace's little hood, and snipped it up in a twinkling, and whisked it off, off, off, — fluttering and bobbing up and down, quite across a wide, waste, snowy field, and finally lodged it on the top of a tall, strutting rail, that was leaning, very independently, quite another way from all the other rails of the fence.

"Now see, do see!" said Grace; "there goes my bonnet! What will Aunt Hitty say?" and Grace began to cry.

"Don't you cry, Gracie; you offered it up to liberty, you know: it's glorious to give up every thing for liberty."

"O, but Aunt Hitty won't think so."

"Well, don't cry, Gracie, you foolish girl! Do you think I can't get it? Now, only play that that great rail is a fort, and your bonnet is a prisoner in it, and see how quick I'll take the fort and get it!" and Dick shouldered a stick and started off.

"What upon *airth* keeps those children so long? I should think they were *making* chips!" said Aunt Mehetabel; "the fire's just a going out under the tea kettle."

By this time Grace had lugged her heavy basket to the door, and was stamping the snow off her little feet, which were so numb that she needed to stamp, to be quite sure they were yet there. Aunt Mehetabel's shrewd face was the first that greeted her as the door opened.

"Gracie — what upon *airth!* — wipe your nose, child; your hands are frozen. Where alive is Dick? — and what's kept you out all this time? — and where's your bonnet?"

Poor Grace, stunned by this cataract of questions, neither wiped her nose nor gave any answer, but sidled up into the warm corner, where grandmamma was knitting, and began quietly rubbing and blowing her fingers, while the tears silently rolled down her cheeks, as the fire made the former ache intolerably.

"Poor little dear!" said grandmamma, taking her hands in hers; "Hitty shan't scold you. Grandma knows you've been a good girl — the wind blew poor Gracie's bonnet away;"

and grandmamma wiped both eyes and nose, and gave her, moreover, a stalk of dried fennel out of her pocket; whereat Grace took heart once more.

"Mother always makes fools of Roxy's children," said Mehetabel, puffing zealously under the tea kettle. "There's a little maple sugar in that saucer up there, mother, if you will keep giving it to her," she said, still vigorously puffing. "And now, Gracie," she said, when, after a while, the fire seemed in tolerable order, "will you answer my question? Where is Dick?"

"Gone over in the lot, to get my bonnet."

"How came your bonnet off?" said Aunt Mehetabel. "I tied it on firm enough."

"Dick wanted me to take it off for him, to throw up for liberty," said Grace.

"Throw up for fiddlestick! Just one of Dick's cut-ups; and you was silly enough to mind him!"

"Why, he put up a flagstaff on the wood pile, and a flag to liberty, you know, that papa's fighting for," said Grace, more confidently, as she saw her quiet, blue-eyed mother, who had silently walked into the room during the conversation.

Grace's mother smiled and said, encouragingly, "And what then?"

"Why, he wanted me to throw up my bonnet and he his cap, and shout for liberty; and then the wind took it and carried it off, and he said I ought not to be sorry if I did lose it — it was an offering to liberty."

"And so I did," said Dick, who was standing as straight as a poplar behind the group; "and I heard it in one of father's letters to mother, that we ought to offer up every thing on the altar of liberty — and so I made an altar of the wood pile."

"Good boy!" said his mother; "always remember every thing your father writes. He has offered up every thing on the altar of liberty, true enough; and I hope you, son, will live to do the same."

"Only, if I have the hoods and caps to make," said Aunt Hitty, "I hope he won't offer them up every week — that's all!"

"O! well, Aunt Hitty, I've got the hood; let me alone for that. It blew clear over into the Daddy Ward pasture lot, and there stuck on the top of the great rail; and I played that the rail was a fort, and besieged it, and took it."

"O, yes! you're always up to taking forts, and any thing else that nobody wants done. I'll warrant, now, you left Gracie to pick up every blessed one of them chips."

"Picking up chips is girl's work," said Dick; "and taking forts and defending the country is men's work."

"And pray, Mister Pomp, how long have you been a man?" said Aunt Hitty.

"If I ain't a man, I soon shall be; my head is 'most up to my mother's shoulder, and I can fire off a gun, too. I tried, the other day, when I was up to the store. Mother, I wish you'd let me clean and load the old gun, so that, if the British should come ——"

"Well, if you are so big and grand, just lift me out that table, sir," said Aunt Hitty; "for it's past supper time."

Dick sprang, and had the table out in a trice, with an abundant clatter, and put up the leaves with quite an air. His mother, with the silent and gliding motion characteristic of her, quietly took out the table cloth and spread it, and began to set the cups and saucers in order, and to put on the plates and knives, while Aunt Hitty bustled about the tea.

"I'll be glad when the war's over, for one reason," said she. "I'm pretty much tired of drinking sage tea, for one, I know."

"Well, Aunt Hitty, how you scolded that pedler last week, that brought along that real tea!"

"To be sure I did. S'pose I'd be taking any of his old tea, bought of the British? — fling every teacup in his face first."

"Well, mother," said Dick, "I never exactly understood what it was about the tea, and why the Boston folks threw it all overboard."

"Because there was an unlawful tax laid upon it, that the government had no right to lay. It wasn't much in itself; but it was a part of a whole system of oppressive meanness, designed to take away our rights, and make us slaves of a foreign power."

"Slaves!" said Dick, straightening himself proudly. "Father a slave!"

"But they would not be slaves! They saw clearly where it would all end, and they would not begin to submit to it in ever so little," said the mother.

"I wouldn't, if I was they," said Dick.

"Besides," said his mother, drawing him towards her, "it wasn't for themselves alone they did it. This is a great country, and it will be greater and greater; and it's very important that it should have free and equal laws, because it will by and by be so great. This country, if it is a free one, will be a light of the world — a city set on a hill, that cannot be hid; and all the oppressed and distressed from other countries shall come here to enjoy equal rights and freedom. This, dear boy, is why your father and uncles have gone to fight, and why they do stay and fight, though God knows what they suffer, and ——" and the large blue eyes of the mother were full of tears; yet a strong, bright beam of pride and exultation shone through those tears.

"Well, well, Roxy, you can always talk, every body knows," said Aunt Hitty, who had been not the least attentive listener of this little patriotic harangue; "but, you see, the tea is getting cold, and yonder I see the sleigh is at the door, and John's come; so let's set up our chairs for supper."

The chairs were soon set up, when John, the eldest son, a lad of about fifteen, entered with a letter. There was one general exclamation, and stretching out of hands towards it. John threw it into his mother's lap; the tea table was forgotten, and the tea kettle sang unnoticed by the fire, as all hands crowded about mother's chair to hear the news. It was from Captain Ward, then in the American army, at Valley Forge. Mrs. Ward ran it over hastily, and then read it aloud. A few words we may extract.

"There is still," it said, "much suffering. I have given away every pair of stockings you sent me, reserving to myself only one; for I will not be one whit better off than the poorest soldier that fights for his country. Poor fellows! it makes my heart ache sometimes to go round among them, and see them with their worn clothes and torn shoes, and often bleeding feet, yet cheerful and hopeful, and every one willing to do his very best. Often the spirit of discouragement comes over them, particularly at night, when, weary, cold, and hungry, they turn into their comfortless huts, on the snowy ground. Then sometimes there is a thought of home, and warm fires, and some speak of giving up; but next morning out come Washington's general orders — little short note, but it's wonderful the good it does! and then they all resolve to hold on, come what may. There are commissioners going all through the country to pick up supplies. If they come to you, I need not tell you what to do. I know all that will be in your hearts."

"There, children, see what your father suffers," said the mother, "and what it costs these poor soldiers to gain our liberty."

"Ephraim Scranton told me that the commissioners had come as far as the Three Mile Tavern, and that he rather 'spected they'd be along here to-night," said John, as he was helping round the baked beans to the silent company at the tea table.

"To-night? — do tell, now!" said Aunt Hitty. "Then it's time we were awake and stirring. Let's see what can be got."

"I'll send my new overcoat, for one," said John. "That old one isn't cut up yet, is it, Aunt Hitty?"

"No," said Aunt Hitty; "I was laying out to cut it over next Wednesday, when Desire Smith could be here to do the tailoring.

"There's the south room," said Aunt Hitty, musing; "that bed has the two old Aunt Ward blankets on it, and the great blue quilt, and two comforters. Then mother's and my room, two pair — four comforters — two quilts — the best chamber has got ——"

"O Aunt Hitty, send all that's in the best chamber! If any company comes, we can make it up off from our beds," said John. "I can send a blanket or two off from my bed, I know; — can't but just turn over in it, so many clothes on, now."

"Aunt Hitty, take a blanket off from our bed," said Grace and Dick at once.

"Well, well, we'll see," said Aunt Hitty, bustling up.

Up rose grandmamma, with great earnestness, now, and going into the next room, and opening a large cedar wood chest, returned, bearing in her arms two large snow white blankets, which she deposited flat on the table, just as Aunt Hitty was whisking off the table cloth.

"Mortal! mother, what are you going to do?" said Aunt Hitty.

"There," she said; "I spun those, every thread of 'em, when my name was Mary Evans. Those were my wedding blankets, made of real nice wool, and worked with roses in all the corners. I've got *them* to give!" and grandmamma stroked and smoothed the blankets, and patted them down, with great pride and tenderness. It was evident she was giving something that lay very near her heart; but she never faltered.

"La! mother, there's no need of that," said Aunt Hitty. "Use them on your own bed, and send the blankets off from that; they are just as good for the soldiers."

"No, I shan't!" said the old lady, waxing warm; "'tisn't a bit too good for 'em. I'll send the very best I've got, before they shall suffer. Send 'em the *best!*" and the old lady gestured oratorically.

They were interrupted by a rap at the door, and two men entered, and announced themselves as commissioned by Congress to search out supplies for the army. Now the plot thickens. Aunt Hitty flew in every direction, — through entry passage, meal room, milk room, down cellar, up chamber, — her cap border on end with patriotic zeal; and followed by John, Dick, and Grace, who eagerly bore to the kitchen the supplies that she turned out, while Mrs. Ward busied herself in quietly sorting and arranging, in the best possible travelling order, the various contributions that were precipitately launched on the kitchen floor.

Aunt Hitty soon appeared in the kitchen with an armful of stockings, which, kneeling on the floor, she began counting and laying out.

"There," she said, laying down a large bundle on some blankets, "that leaves just two pair apiece all round."

"La!" said John, "what's the use of saving two pair for me? I can do with one pair, as well as father."

"Sure enough," said his mother; "besides, I can knit you another pair in a day."

"And I can do with one pair," said Dick.

"Yours will be too small, young master, I guess," said one of the commissioners.

"No," said Dick; "I've got a pretty good foot of my own, and Aunt Hitty will always knit my stockings an inch too long, 'cause she says I grow so. See here — these will do;" and the boy shook his, triumphantly.

"And mine, too," said Grace, nothing doubting, having been busy all the time in pulling off her little stockings.

"Here," she said to the man who was packing the things into a wide-mouthed sack; "here's mine," and her large blue eyes looked earnestly through her tears.

Aunt Hitty flew at her. "Good land! the child's crazy. Don't think the men could wear your stockings — take 'em away!"

Grace looked around with an air of utter desolation, and began to cry. "I wanted to give them something," said she. "I'd rather go barefoot on the snow all day than not send 'em any thing."

"Give me the stockings, my child," said the old soldier, tenderly. "There, I'll take 'em, and show 'em to the soldiers, and tell them what the little girl said that sent them. And it will do them as much good as if they could wear them. They've got little girls at home, too." Grace fell on her mother's bosom completely happy, and Aunt Hitty only muttered, —

"Every body does spile that child; and no wonder, neither!"

Soon the old sleigh drove off from the brown house, tightly packed and heavily loaded. And Grace and Dick were creeping up to their little beds.

"There's been something put on the altar of Liberty tonight, hasn't there, Dick?"

"Yes, indeed," said Dick; and, looking up to his mother, he said, "But, mother, what did you give?"

"I?" said the mother, musingly.

"Yes, you, mother; what have you given to the country?"

"All that I have, dears," said she, laying her hands gently on their heads — "my husband and my children!"

II. THE ALTAR OF ——, OR 1850.

The setting sun of chill December lighted up the solitary front window of a small tenement on —— Street, in Boston, which we now have occasion to visit. As we push gently aside the open door, we gain sight of a small room, clean as busy hands can make it, where a neat, cheerful young mulatto woman is busy at an ironing table. A basket full of glossy-bosomed shirts, and faultless collars and wristbands, is beside her, into which she is placing the last few items with evident pride and satisfaction. A bright black-eyed boy, just come in from school, with his satchel of books over his shoulder, stands, cap in hand, relating to his mother how he has been at the head of his class, and showing his school tickets, which his mother, with untiring admiration, deposits in the little real china tea pot — which, as being their most reliable article of gentility, is made the deposit of all the money and most especial valuables of the family.

"Now, Henry," says the mother, "look out and see if father is coming along the street;" and she begins filling the little black tea kettle, which is soon set singing on the stove.

From the inner room now daughter Mary, a well-grown girl of thirteen, brings the baby, just roused from a nap, and very impatient to renew his acquaintance with his mamma.

"Bless his bright eyes! — mother will take him," ejaculates the busy little woman, whose hands are by this time in a very floury condition, in the incipient stages of wetting up biscuit, — "in a minute;" and she quickly frees herself from the flour and paste, and, deputing Mary to roll out her biscuit, proceeds to the consolation and succor of young master.

"Now, Henry," says the mother, "you'll have time, before supper, to take that basket of clothes up to Mr. Sheldin's; put in that nice bill, that you made out last night. I shall give you a cent for every bill you write out for me. What a comfort it is, now, for one's children to be gettin' learnin' so!"

Henry shouldered the basket, and passed out the door, just as a neatly-dressed colored man walked up, with his pail and whitewash brushes.

"O, you've come, father, have you? Mary, are the biscuits in? You may as well set the table, now. Well, George, what's the news?"

"Nothing, only a pretty smart day's work. I've brought home five dollars, and shall have as much as I can do, these two weeks;" and the man, having washed his hands, proceeded to count out his change on the ironing table.

"Well, it takes you to bring in the money," said the delighted wife; "nobody but you could turn off that much in a day."

"Well, they do say — those that's had me once — that they never want any other hand to take hold in their rooms. I s'pose its a kinder practice I've got, and kinder natural!"

"Tell ye what," said the little woman, taking down the family strong box, — to wit, the china tea pot, aforenamed, — and pouring the contents on the table, "we're getting mighty rich, now! We can afford to get Henry his new Sunday cap, and Mary her mousseline-de-laine dress — take care, baby, you rogue!" she hastily interposed, as young master made a dive at a dollar bill, for his share in the proceeds.

"He wants something, too, I suppose," said the father; "let him get his hand in while he's young."

The baby gazed, with round, astonished eyes, while mother, with some difficulty, rescued the bill from his grasp; but, before any one could at all anticipate his purpose, he dashed in among the small change with such zeal as to send it flying all over the table.

"Hurrah! Bob's a smasher!" said the father, delighted; "he'll make it fly, he thinks;" and, taking the baby on his knee, he laughed merrily, as Mary and her mother pursued the rolling coin all over the room.

"He knows now, as well as can be, that he's been doing mischief," said the delighted mother, as the baby kicked and crowed uproariously: "he's such a forward child, now, to be only six months old! O, you've no idea, father, how mischievous he grows;" and therewith the little woman began to roll and tumble the little mischief maker about, uttering divers frightful threats, which appeared to contribute, in no small degree, to the general hilarity.

"Come, come, Mary," said the mother, at last, with a sudden burst of recollection; "you mustn't be always on your knees fooling with this child! Look in the oven at them biscuits."

"They're done exactly, mother—just the brown!" and, with the word, the mother dumped baby on to his father's knee, where he sat contentedly munching a very ancient crust of bread, occasionally improving the flavor thereof by rubbing it on his father's coat sleeve.

"What have you got in that blue dish, there?" said George, when the whole little circle were seated around the table.

"Well, now, what *do* you suppose?" said the little woman, delighted: "a quart of nice oysters—just for a treat, you know. I wouldn't tell you till this minute," said she, raising the cover.

"Well," said George, "we both work hard for our money, and we don't owe any body a cent; and why shouldn't we have our treats, now and then, as well as rich folks?"

And gayly passed the supper hour; the tea kettle sung, the baby crowed, and all chatted and laughed abundantly.

"I'll tell you," said George, wiping his mouth; "wife, these times are quite another thing from what it used to be down in Georgia. I remember then old mas'r used to hire me out by the year; and one time, I remember, I came and paid him in two hundred dollars—every cent I'd taken. He just looked it over, counted it, and put it in his pocket book, and said, 'You are a good boy, George' — and he gave me *half a dollar!*"

"I want to know, now!" said his wife.

"Yes, he did, and that was every cent I ever got of it; and, I tell you, I was mighty bad off for clothes, them times."

"Well, well, the Lord be praised, they're over, and you are in a free country now!" said the wife, as she rose thoughtfully from the table, and brought her husband the great Bible. The little circle were ranged around the stove for evening prayers.

"Henry, my boy, you must read — you are a better reader than your father — thank God, that let you learn early!"

The boy, with a cheerful readiness, read, "The Lord is my Shepherd," and the mother gently stilled the noisy baby, to listen to the holy words. Then all kneeled, while the father, with simple earnestness, poured out his soul to God.

They had but just risen — the words of Christian hope and trust scarce died on their lips — when, lo! the door was burst open, and two men entered; and one of them, advancing, laid his hand on the father's shoulder. "This is the fellow," said he.

"You are arrested in the name of the United States!" said the other.

"Gentlemen, what is this?" said the poor man, trembling.

"Are you not the property of *Mr. B.*, of Georgia?" said the officer.

"Gentlemen, I've been a free, hard-working man these ten years."

"Yes; but you are arrested, on suit of Mr. B., as his slave."

Shall we describe the leave taking — the sorrowing wife, the dismayed children, the tears, the anguish, that simple, honest, kindly home, in a moment so desolated? Ah, ye who defend this because it is law, think, for one hour, what if this that happens to your poor brother should happen to you!

It was a crowded court room, and the man stood there to be tried — for life? — no; but for the life of life — for liberty!

Lawyers hurried to and fro, buzzing, consulting, bringing authorities, — all anxious, zealous, engaged, — for what? To save a fellow-man from bondage? No; anxious and zealous lest he might escape; full of zeal to deliver him over to slavery. The poor man's anxious eyes follow vainly the busy course of affairs, from which he dimly learns that he is to be sacrificed — on the altar of the Union; and that his heart-break and anguish, and the tears of his wife, and the desolation of his children are, in the eyes of these well-informed men, only the bleat of a sacrifice, bound to the horns of the glorious American altar!

Again it is a bright day, and business walks brisk in this market. Senator and statesman, the learned and patriotic, are out, this day, to give their countenance to an edifying, and impressive, and truly American spectacle — the sale of a man! All the preliminaries of the scene are there; dusky-browed mothers, looking with sad eyes while speculators are turning round their children, looking at their teeth, and feeling of their arms; a poor, old, trembling woman, helpless, half blind, whose last child is to be sold, holds on to her bright boy with trembling hands. Husbands and wives, sisters and friends, all soon to be scattered like the chaff of the threshing floor, look sadly on each other with poor nature's last tears; and among them walk briskly, glib, oily politicians, and thriving men of law, letters, and religion, exceedingly sprightly, and in good spirits — for why? — it isn't *they* that are going to be sold; it's only somebody else. And so they are very comfortable, and look on the whole thing as quite a matter-of-course affair, and, as it is to be conducted to-day, a decidedly valuable and judicious exhibition.

And now, after so many hearts and souls have been knocked and thumped this way and that way by the auctioneer's hammer, comes the *instructive* part of the whole; and the husband and father, whom we saw in his simple home, reading and praying with his children, and rejoicing in the joy of his poor ignorant heart that he lived in a free country, is now set up to be admonished of his mistake.

Now there is great excitement, and pressing to see, and exultation and approbation; for it is important and interesting to see a man put down that has tried to be a *free man.*

"That's he, is it? Couldn't come it, could he?" says one.

"No; and he will never come it, that's more," says another, triumphantly.

"I don't generally take much interest in scenes of this nature," says a grave representative; "but I came here to-day for the sake of the *principle!*"

"Gentlemen," says the auctioneer, "we've got a specimen here that some of your northern abolitionists would give any price for; but they shan't have him! no! we've looked out for that. The man that buys him must give bonds never to sell him to go north again!"

"Go it!" shout the crowd; "good! good! hurrah!" "An impressive idea!" says a senator; "a noble maintaining of principle!" and the man is bid off, and the hammer falls with a last crash on his heart, his hopes, his manhood, and he lies a bleeding wreck on the altar of Liberty!

Such was the altar in 1776; such is the altar in 1850!

A SCHOLAR'S ADVENTURES IN THE COUNTRY.

"If we could only live in the country," said my wife, "how much easier it would be to live!"

"And how much cheaper!" said I.

"To have a little place of our own, and raise our own things!" said my wife. "Dear me! I am heart sick when I think of the old place at home, and father's great garden. What peaches and melons we used to have! what green peas and corn! Now one has to buy every cent's worth of these things — and how they taste! Such wilted, miserable corn! Such peas! Then, if we lived in the country, we should have our own cow, and milk and cream in abundance; our own hens and chickens. We could have custard and ice cream every day."

"To say nothing of the trees and flowers, and all that," said I.

The result of this little domestic duet was, that my wife and I began to ride about the city of ——— to look up some pretty, interesting cottage, where our visions of rural bliss might be realized. Country residences, near the city, we found to bear rather a high price; so that it was no easy matter to find a situation suitable to the length of our purse; till, at last, a judicious friend suggested a happy expedient.

"Borrow a few hundred," he said, "and give your note; you can save enough, very soon, to make the difference. When you raise every thing you eat, you know it will make your salary go a wonderful deal further."

"Certainly it will," said I. "And what can be more beautiful than to buy places by the simple process of giving one's note?—'tis so neat, and handy, and convenient!"

"Why," pursued my friend, "there is Mr. B., my next door neighbor—'tis enough to make one sick of life in the city to spend a week out on his farm. Such princely living as one gets! And he assures me that it costs him very little—scarce any thing, perceptible, in fact."

"Indeed!" said I; "few people can say that."

"Why," said my friend, "he has a couple of peach trees for every month, from June till frost, that furnish as many peaches as he, and his wife, and ten children can dispose of. And then he has grapes, apricots, &c.; and last year his wife sold fifty dollars' worth from her strawberry patch, and had an abundance for the table besides. Out of the milk of only one cow they had butter enough to sell three or four pounds a week, besides abundance of milk and cream; and madam has the butter for her pocket money. This is the way country people manage."

"Glorious!" thought I. And my wife and I could scarce sleep, all night, for the brilliancy of our anticipations!

To be sure our delight was somewhat damped the next day by the coldness with which my good old uncle, Jeremiah Standfast, who happened along at precisely this crisis, listened to our visions.

"You'll find it *pleasant*, children, in the summer time," said the hard-fisted old man, twirling his blue-checked pocket handkerchief; "but I'm sorry you've gone in debt for the land."

"O, but we shall soon save that — it's so much cheaper living in the country!" said both of us together.

"Well, as to that, I don't think it is to city-bred folks."

Here I broke in with a flood of accounts of Mr. B.'s peach trees, and Mrs. B.'s strawberries, butter, apricots, &c., &c.; to which the old gentleman listened with such a long, leathery, unmoved quietude of visage as quite provoked me, and gave me the worst possible opinion of his judgment. I was disappointed too; for, as he was reckoned one of the best practical farmers in the county, I had counted on an enthusiastic sympathy with all my agricultural designs.

"I tell you what, children," he said, "a body can live in the country, as you say, amazin' cheap; but then a body must *know how*" — and my uncle spread his pocket handkerchief thoughtfully out upon his knees, and shook his head gravely.

I thought him a terribly slow, stupid old body, and wondered how I had always entertained so high an opinion of his sense.

"He is evidently getting old," said I to my wife; "his judgment is not what it used to be."

At all events, our place was bought, and we moved out, well pleased, the first morning in April, not at all remembering the ill savor of that day for matters of wisdom. Our place was a pretty cottage, about two miles from the city, with grounds that had been tastefully laid out. There was no lack of winding paths, arbors, flower borders, and rosebushes, with which my wife was especially pleased. There was a little green lot, strolling off down to a brook, with a thick grove of trees at the end, where our cow was to be pastured.

The first week or two went on happily enough in getting our little new pet of a house into trimness and good order; for, as it had been long for sale, of course there was any amount of little repairs that had been left to amuse the leisure hours of the purchaser. Here a door step had given away, and needed replacing; there a shutter hung loose, and wanted a hinge; abundance of glass needed setting; and as to painting and papering, there was no end to that. Then my wife wanted a door cut here, to make our bed room more convenient, and a china closet knocked up there, where no china closet before had been. We even ventured on throwing out a bay window from our sitting room, because we had luckily lighted on a workman who was so cheap that it was an actual saving of money to employ him. And to be sure our darling little cottage did lift up its head wonderfully for all this garnishing and furbishing. I got up early every morning, and nailed up the rosebushes, and my wife got up and watered geraniums, and both flattered ourselves and each other on our early hours and thrifty habits. But soon, like Adam and Eve in Paradise, we found our little domain to ask more hands than ours to get it into shape. So says I to my wife, "I will bring out a gardener when I come next time, and he shall lay the garden out, and get it into order; and after that, I can easily keep it by the work of my leisure hours."

Our gardener was a very sublime sort of man, — an Englishman, and, of course, used to laying out noblemen's places, — and we became as grasshoppers in our own eyes when he talked of lord this and that's estate, and began to question us about our carriage drive and conservatory; and we could with difficulty bring the gentleman down to any understanding of the humble limits of our expectations: merely to dress out the walks, and lay out a kitchen garden, and plant potatoes, turnips, beets, and carrots, was quite a descent for him. In fact, so strong were his æsthetic preferences, that he persuaded my wife to let him dig all the turf off from a green square opposite the bay window, and to lay it out into divers little triangles, resembling small pieces of pie, together with circles, mounds, and various other geometrical ornaments, the planning and planting of which soon engrossed my wife's whole soul. The planting of the potatoes, beets, carrots, &c., was intrusted to a raw Irishman; for, as to me, to confess the truth, I began to fear that digging did not agree with me. It is true that I was exceedingly vigorous at first, and actually planted with my own hands two or three long rows of potatoes; after which I got a turn of rheumatism in my shoulder, which lasted me a week. Stooping down to plant beets and radishes gave me a vertigo, so that I was obliged to content myself with a general superintendence of the garden; that is to say, I charged my Englishman to see that my Irishman did his duty properly, and then got on to my horse and rode to the city. But about one part of the matter, I must say, I was not remiss; and that is, in the purchase of seed and garden utensils. Not a day passed that I did not come home with my pockets stuffed with choice seeds, roots, &c.; and the variety of my garden utensils was unequalled. There was not a pruning hook, of any pattern, not a hoe, rake, or spade, great or small, that I did not have specimens of; and flower seeds and bulbs were also forthcoming in liberal proportions. In fact, I had opened an account at a thriving seed store; for, when a man is driving business on a large scale, it is not always convenient to hand out the change for every little matter, and buying things on account is as neat and agreeable a mode of acquisition as paying bills with one's notes.

"You know we must have a cow," said my wife, the morning of our second week. Our friend the gardener, who had now worked with us at the rate of two dollars a day for two weeks, was at hand in a moment in our emergency. We wanted to buy a cow, and he had one to sell — a wonderful cow, of a real English breed. He would not sell her for any money, except to oblige particular friends; but as we had patronized him, we should have her for forty dollars. How much we were obliged to him! The forty dollars were speedily forthcoming, and so also was the cow.

"What makes her shake her head in that way?" said my wife, apprehensively, as she observed the interesting beast making sundry demonstrations with her horns. "I hope she's gentle."

The gardener fluently demonstrated that the animal was a pattern of all the softer graces, and that this head-shaking was merely a little nervous affection consequent on the embarrassment of a new position. We had faith to believe almost any thing at this time, and therefore came from the barn yard to the house as much satisfied with our purchase as Job with his three thousand camels and five hundred yoke of oxen. Her quondam master milked her for us the first evening, out of a delicate regard to her feelings as a stranger, and we fancied that we discerned forty dollars' worth of excellence in the very quality of the milk.

But alas! the next morning our Irish girl came in with a most rueful face. "And is it milking that baste you'd have me be after?" she said; "sure, and she won't let me come near her?"

"Nonsense, Biddy!" said I; "you frightened her, perhaps; the cow is perfectly gentle;" and with the pail on my arm, I sallied forth. The moment madam saw me entering the cow yard, she greeted me with a very expressive flourish of her horns.

"This won't do," said I, and I stopped. The lady evidently was serious in her intentions of resisting any personal approaches. I cut a cudgel, and putting on a bold face, marched towards her, while Biddy followed with her milking stool. Apparently, the beast saw the necessity of temporizing, for she assumed a demure expression, and Biddy sat down to milk. I stood sentry, and if the lady shook her head, I shook my stick; and thus the milking operation proceeded with tolerable serenity and success.

"There!" said I, with dignity, when the frothing pail was full to the brim. "That will do, Biddy," and I dropped my stick. Dump! came madam's heel on the side of the pail, and it flew like a rocket into the air, while the milky flood showered plentifully over me, and a new broadcloth riding-coat that I had assumed for the first time that morning. "Whew!" said I, as soon as I could get my breath from this extraordinary shower bath; "what's all this?" My wife came running towards the cow yard, as I stood with the milk streaming from my hair, filling my eyes, and dropping from the tip of my nose; and she and Biddy performed a recitative lamentation over me in alternate strophes, like the chorus in a Greek tragedy. Such was our first morning's experience; but as we had announced our bargain with some considerable flourish of trumpets among our neighbors and friends, we concluded to hush the matter up as much as possible.

"These very superior cows are apt to be cross," said I; "we must bear with it as we do with the eccentricities of genius; besides, when she gets accustomed to us, it will be better."

Madam was therefore installed into her pretty pasture lot, and my wife contemplated with pleasure the picturesque effect of her appearance, reclining on the green slope of the pasture lot, or standing ankle deep in the gurgling brook, or reclining under the deep shadows of the trees. She was, in fact, a handsome cow, which may account, in part, for some of her sins; and this consideration inspired me with some degree of indulgence towards her foibles.

But when I found that Biddy could never succeed in getting near her in the pasture, and that any kind of success in the milking operations required my vigorous personal exertions morning and evening, the matter wore a more serious aspect, and I began to feel quite pensive and apprehensive. It is very well to talk of the pleasures of the milkmaid going out in the balmy freshness of the purple dawn; but imagine a poor fellow pulled out of bed on a drizzly, rainy morning, and equipping himself for a scamper through a wet pasture lot, rope in hand, at the heels of such a termagant as mine! In fact, madam established a regular series of exercises, which had all to be gone through before she would suffer herself to be captured; as, first, she would station herself plump in the middle of a marsh, which lay at the lower part of the lot, and look very innocent and absent-minded, as if reflecting on some sentimental subject. "Suke! Suke! Suke!" I ejaculate, cautiously tottering along the edge of the marsh, and holding out an ear of corn. The lady looks gracious, and comes forward, almost within reach of my hand. I make a plunge to throw the rope over her horns, and away she goes, kicking up mud and water into my face in her flight, while I, losing my balance, tumble forward into the marsh. I pick myself up, and, full of wrath, behold her placidly chewing her cud on the other side, with the meekest air imaginable, as who should say, "I hope you are not hurt, sir." I dash through swamp and bog furiously, resolving to carry all by a *coup de main.* Then follows a miscellaneous season of dodging, scampering, and bopeeping, among the trees of the grove, interspersed with sundry occasional races across the bog aforesaid. I always wondered how I caught her every day; and when I had tied her head to one post and her heels to another, I wiped the sweat from my brow, and thought I was paying dear for the eccentricities of genius. A genius she certainly was, for besides her surprising agility, she had other talents equally extraordinary. There was no fence that she could not take down; nowhere that she could not go. She took the pickets off the garden fence at her pleasure, using her horns as handily as I could use a claw hammer. Whatever she had a mind to, whether it were a bite in the cabbage garden, or a run in the corn patch, or a foraging expedition into the flower borders, she made herself equally welcome and at home. Such a scampering and driving, such cries of "Suke here" and "Suke there," as constantly greeted our ears, kept our little establishment in a constant commotion. At last, when she one morning made a plunge at the skirts of my new broadcloth frock coat, and carried off one flap on her horns, my patience gave out, and I determined to sell her.

As, however, I had made a good story of my misfortunes

among my friends and neighbors, and amused them with sundry whimsical accounts of my various adventures in the cow-catching line, I found, when I came to speak of selling, that there was a general coolness on the subject, and nobody seemed disposed to be the recipient of my responsibilities. In short, I was glad, at last, to get fifteen dollars for her, and comforted myself with thinking that I had at least gained twenty-five dollars worth of experience in the transaction, to say nothing of the fine exercise.

I comforted my soul, however, the day after, by purchasing and bringing home to my wife a fine swarm of bees.

"Your bee, now," says I, "is a really classical insect, and breathes of Virgil and the Augustan age — and then she is a domestic, tranquil, placid creature. How beautiful the murmuring of a hive near our honeysuckle of a calm, summer evening! Then they are tranquilly and peacefully amassing for us their stores of sweetness, while they lull us with their murmurs. What a beautiful image of disinterested benevolence!"

My wife declared that I was quite a poet, and the beehive was duly installed near the flower plots, that the delicate creatures might have the full benefit of the honeysuckle and mignonette. My spirits began to rise. I bought three different treatises on the rearing of bees, and also one or two new patterns of hives, and proposed to rear my bees on the most approved model. I charged all the establishment to let me know when there was any indication of an emigrating spirit, that I might be ready to receive the new swarm into my patent mansion.

Accordingly, one afternoon, when I was deep in an article that I was preparing for the North American Review, intelligence was brought me that a swarm had risen. I was on the alert at once, and discovered, on going out, that the provoking creatures had chosen the top of a tree about thirty feet high to settle on. Now my books had carefully instructed me just how to approach the swarm and cover them with a new hive; but I had never contemplated the possibility of the swarm being, like Haman's gallows, forty cubits high. I looked despairingly upon the smooth-bark tree, which rose, like a column, full twenty feet, without branch or twig. "What is to be done?" said I, appealing to two or three neighbors. At last, at the recommendation of one of them, a ladder was raised against the tree, and, equipped with a shirt outside of my clothes, a green veil over my head, and a pair of leather gloves on my hands, I went up with a saw at my girdle to saw off the branch on which they had settled, and lower it by a rope to a neighbor, similarly equipped, who stood below with the hive.

As a result of this manœuvre the fastidious little insects were at length fairly installed at housekeeping in my new patent hive, and, rejoicing in my success, I again sat down to my article.

That evening my wife and I took tea in our honeysuckle arbor, with our little ones and a friend or two, to whom I showed my treasures, and expatiated at large on the comforts and conveniences of the new patent hive.

But alas for the hopes of man! The little ungrateful wretches — what must they do but take advantage of my oversleeping myself, the next morning, to clear out for new quarters without so much as leaving me a P. P. C.! Such was the fact; at eight o'clock I found the new patent hive as good as ever; but the bees I have never seen from that day to this!

"The rascally little conservatives!" said I; "I believe they have never had a new idea from the days of Virgil down, and are entirely unprepared to appreciate improvements."

Meanwhile the seeds began to germinate in our garden, when we found, to our chagrin, that, between John Bull and Paddy, there had occurred sundry confusions in the several departments. Radishes had been planted broadcast, carrots and beets arranged in hills, and here and there a whole paper of seed appeared to have been planted bodily. My good old uncle, who, somewhat to my confusion, made me a call at this time, was greatly distressed and scandalized by the appearance of our garden. But, by a deal of fussing, transplanting, and replanting, it was got into some shape and order. My uncle was rather troublesome, as careful old people are apt to be — annoying us by perpetual inquiries of what we gave for this, and that, and running up provoking calculations on the final cost of matters; and we began to wish that his visits might be as short as would be convenient.

But when, on taking leave, he promised to send us a fine young cow of his own raising, our hearts rather smote us for our impatience.

"'Tain't any of your new breeds, nephew," said the old man, "yet I can say that she's a gentle, likely young crittur, and better worth forty dollars than many a one that's cried up for Ayrshire or Durham; and you shall be quite welcome to her."

We thanked him, as in duty bound, and thought that if he was full of old-fashioned notions, he was no less full of kindness and good will.

And now, with a new cow, with our garden beginning to thrive under the gentle showers of May, with our flower borders blooming, my wife and I began to think ourselves in Paradise. But alas! the same sun and rain that warmed our fruit and flowers brought up from the earth, like sulky gnomes, a vast array of purple-leaved weeds, that almost in a night seemed to cover the whole surface of the garden beds. Our gardeners both being gone, the weeding was expected to be done by me — one of the anticipated relaxations of my leisure hours.

"Well," said I, in reply to a gentle intimation from my wife, "when my article is finished, I'll take a day and weed all up clean."

Thus days slipped by, till at length the article was despatched, and I proceeded to my garden. Amazement! Who could have possibly foreseen that any thing earthly could grow so fast in a few days! There were no bounds, no alleys, no beds, no distinction of beet and carrot, nothing but a flourishing congregation of weeds nodding and bobbing in the morning breeze, as if to say, "We hope you are well, sir — we've got the ground, you see!" I began to explore, and to hoe, and to weed. Ah! did any body ever try to clean a neglected carrot or beet bed, or bend his back in a hot sun over rows of weedy onions! He is the man to feel for my despair! How I weeded, and sweat, and sighed! till, when high noon came on, as the result of all my toils, only three beds were cleaned! And how disconsolate looked the good seed, thus unexpectedly delivered from its sheltering tares, and laid open to a broiling July sun! Every juvenile beet and carrot lay flat down, wilted and drooping, as if, like me, they had been weeding, instead of being weeded.

"This weeding is quite a serious matter," said I to my wife; "the fact is, I must have help about it!"

"Just what I was myself thinking," said my wife. "My flower borders are all in confusion, and my petunia mounds so completely overgrown, that nobody would dream what they were meant for!"

In short, it was agreed between us that we could not afford the expense of a full-grown man to keep our place; yet we must reënforce ourselves by the addition of a boy, and a brisk youngster from the vicinity was pitched upon as the happy addition. This youth was a fellow of decidedly quick parts, and in one forenoon made such a clearing in our garden that I was delighted. Bed after bed appeared to view, all cleared and dressed out with such celerity that I was quite ashamed of my own slowness, until, on examination, I discovered that he had, with great impartiality, pulled up both weeds and vegetables.

This hopeful beginning was followed up by a succession of proceedings which should be recorded for the instruction of all who seek for help from the race of boys. Such a loser of all tools, great and small; such an invariable leaver-open of all gates, and letter-down of bars; such a personification of all manner of anarchy and ill luck, had never before been seen on the estate. His time, while I was gone to the city, was agreeably diversified with roosting on the fence, swinging on the gates, making poplar whistles for the children, hunting eggs, and eating whatever fruit happened to be in season, in which latter accomplishment he was certainly quite distinguished. After about three weeks of this kind of joint gardening, we concluded to dismiss Master Tom from the firm, and employ a man.

"Things must be taken care of," said I, "and I cannot do it. 'Tis out of the question." And so the man was secured.

But I am making a long story, and may chance to outrun the sympathies of my readers. Time would fail me to tell of the distresses manifold that fell upon me — of cows dried up by poor milkers; of hens that wouldn't set at all, and hens that, despite all law and reason, would set on one egg; of hens that, having hatched families, straightway led them into all manner of high grass and weeds, by which means numerous young chicks caught premature colds and perished; and how, when I, with manifold toil, had driven one of these inconsiderate gadders into a coop, to teach her domestic habits, the rats came down upon her and slew every chick in one night; how my pigs were always practising gymnastic exercises over the fence of the sty, and marauding in the garden. I wonder that Fourier never conceived the idea of having his garden land ploughed by pigs; for certainly they manifest quite a decided elective attraction for turning up the earth.

When autumn came, I went soberly to market, in the neighboring city, and bought my potatoes and turnips like any other man; for, between all the various systems of gardening pursued, I was obliged to confess that my first horticultural effort was a decided failure. But though all my rural visions had proved illusive, there were some very substantial realities. My bill at the seed store, for seeds, roots, and tools, for example, had run up to an amount that was perfectly unaccountable; then there were various smaller items, such as horse shoeing, carriage mending — for he who lives in the country and does business in the city must keep his vehicle and appurtenances. I had always prided myself on being an exact man, and settling every account, great and small, with the going out of the old year; but this season I found myself sorely put to it. In fact, had not I received a timely lift from my good old uncle, I should have made a complete break down. The old gentleman's troublesome habit of ciphering and calculating, it seems, had led him beforehand to foresee that I was not exactly in the money-making line, nor likely to possess much surplus revenue to meet the note which I had given for my place; and, therefore, he quietly paid it himself, as I discovered, when, after much anxiety and some sleepless nights, I went to the holder to ask for an extension of credit.

"He was right, after all," said I to my wife; "'to live cheap in the country, a body must know how.'"

"WOMAN, BEHOLD THY SON!"

THE golden rays of a summer afternoon were streaming through the windows of a quiet apartment, where every thing was the picture of orderly repose. Gently and noiselessly they glide, gilding the glossy old chairs, polished by years of care; fluttering with flickering gleam on the bookcases, by the fire, and the antique China vases on the mantel, and even coqueting with sparkles of fanciful gayety over the face of the perpendicular, sombre old clock, which, though at times apparently coaxed almost to the verge of a smile, still continued its inevitable tick, as for a century before.

On the hearth rug lay outstretched a great, lazy-looking, Maltese cat, evidently enjoying the golden beam that fell upon his sober sides, and sleepily opening and shutting his great green eyes, as if lost in luxurious contemplation.

But the most characteristic figure in the whole picture was that of an aged woman, who sat quietly rocking to and fro in a great chair by the side of a large round table covered with books. There was a quiet beauty in that placid face — that silvery hair brushed neatly under the snowy border of the cap. Every line in that furrowed face told some tale of sorrow long assuaged, and passions hushed to rest, as on the calm ocean shore the golden-furrowed sand shows traces of storms and fluctuations long past.

On the round, green-covered table beside her lay the quiet companion of her age, the large Bible, whose pages, like the gates of the celestial city, were not shut at all by day, a few old standard books, and the pleasant, rippling knitting, whose dreamy, irresponsible monotony is the best music of age.

A fair, girlish form was seated by the table; the dress bonnet had fallen back on her shoulders, the soft cheeks were suffused and earnest, the long lashes and the veiled eyes were eloquent of subdued feeling, as she read aloud from the letter in her hand. It was from "our Harry," a name to both of them comprising all that was dear and valued on earth, for he was "the only son of his mother, and she a widow;" yet had he not been always an only one; flower after flower on the tree of her life had bloomed and died, and gradually, as waters cut off from many channels, the streams of love had centred deeper in this last and only one.

And, in truth, Harry Sargeant was all that a mother might desire or be proud of. Generous, high-minded, witty, and talented, and with a strong and noble physical development, he seemed born to command the love of women. The only trouble with him was, in common parlance, that he was too clever a fellow; he was too social, too impressible, too versatile, too attractive, and too much in demand for his own good. He always drew company about him, as honey draws flies, and was indispensable every where and to every body; and it needs a steady head and firm nerves for such a one to escape ruin.

Harry's course in college, though brilliant in scholarship, had been critical and perilous. He was a decided favorite with the faculty and students; yet it required a great deal of hard winking and adroit management on the part of his instructors to bring him through without infringment of college laws and proprieties: not that he ever meant the least harm in his life, but that some extra generous impulse, some quixotic generosity, was always tumbling him, neck and heels, into somebody's scrapes, and making him part and parcel in every piece of mischief that was going on.

With all this premised, there is no need to say that Harry was a special favorite with ladies; in truth, it was a confessed fact among his acquaintances, that, whereas dozens of creditable, respectable, well-to-do young men might besiege female hearts with every proper formality, waiting at the gates and watching at the posts of the doors in vain, yet before him all gates and passages seemed to fly open of their own accord. Nevertheless, there was in his native village one quiet maiden who held alone in her hand the key that could unlock his heart in return, and carried silently in her own the spell that could fetter that brilliant, restless spirit; and she it was, of the thoughtful brow and downcast eyes, whom we saw in our picture, bending over the letter with his mother.

That mother Harry loved to idolatry. She was to his mind an impersonation of all that was lovely in womanhood, hallowed and sainted by age, by wisdom, by sorrow; and his love for her was a beautiful union of protective tenderness, with veneration; and to his Ellen it seemed the best and most sacred evidence of the nobleness of his nature, and of the worth of the heart which he had pledged to her.

Nevertheless, there was a danger overhanging the heads of the three — a little cloud, no bigger than a man's hand, rising in the horizon of their hopes, yet destined to burst upon them, dark and dreadful, in a future day.

In those scenes of college hilarity where Harry had been so indispensable, the bright, poetic wine cup had freely circulated, and often amid the flush of conversation, and the genial excitement of the hour, he had drank freer and deeper than was best.

He said, it is true, that he cared nothing for it, that it was nothing to him, that it never affected him, and all those things that young men always say when the cup of Circe is beginning its work with them. Friends were annoyed, became anxious, remonstrated; but he laughed at their fears, and insisted on knowing himself best. At last, with a sudden start and shiver of his moral nature, he was awakened to a dreadful perception of his danger, and resolved on decided and determinate resistance. During this period he came to Cincinnati to establish himself in business, and as at this time the temperance reformation was in full tide of success there, he found every thing to strengthen his resolution; temperance meetings and speeches were all the mode; young men of the first standing were its patrons and supporters; wine was quite in the vocative, and seemed really in danger of being voted out of society. In such a turn of affairs, to sign a temperance pledge and keep it became an easy thing; temptation was scarce presented or felt; he was offered the glass in no social circle, met its attraction nowhere, and flattered himself that he had escaped so great a danger easily and completely.

His usual fortune of social popularity followed him, and his visiting circle became full as large and importunate as a young man with any thing else to do need desire. He was diligent in his application to business, began to be mentioned with approbation by the magnates as a rising young man, and had prospects daily nearing of competence and home, and all that man desires — visions, alas! never to be realized.

For after a while the tide that had risen so high began imperceptibly to decline. Men that had made eloquent speeches on temperance had now other things to look to. Fastidious persons thought that matters had, perhaps, been carried too far, and ladies declared that it was old and threadbare, and getting to be cant and stuff; and the ever-ready wine cup was gliding back into many a circle, as if, on sober second thoughts, the community was convinced that it was a friend unjustly belied.

There is no point in the history of reform, either in communities or individuals, so dangerous as that where danger seems entirely past. As long as a man thinks his health failing, he watches, he diets, and will undergo the most heroic self-denial; but let him once set himself down as cured, and how readily does he fall back to one soft indulgent habit after another, all tending to ruin every thing that he has before done!

So in communities. Let intemperance rage, and young men go to ruin by dozens, and the very evil inspires the remedy; but when the trumpet has been sounded, and the battle set in array, and the victory only said and sung in speeches, and newspaper paragraphs, and temperance odes, and processions, then comes the return wave; people cry, Enough; the community, vastly satisfied, lies down to sleep in its laurels; and then comes the hour of danger.

But let not the man who has once been swept down the stream of intemperate excitement, almost to the verge of ruin, dream of any point of security for him. He is like one who has awakened in the rapids of Niagara, and with straining oar and wild prayers to Heaven, forced his boat upward into smoother water, where the draught of the current seems to cease, and the banks smile, and all looks beautiful, and weary from rowing, lays by his oar to rest and dream; he knows not that under that smooth water still glides a current, that while he dreams, is imperceptibly but surely hurrying him back whence there is no return.

Harry was just in this perilous point; he viewed danger as long past, his self-confidence was fully restored, and in his security he began to neglect those lighter outworks of caution which he must still guard who does not mean, at last, to surrender the citadel.

" Now, girls and boys," said Mrs. G. to her sons and daughters, who were sitting round a centre table covered with notes of invitation, and all the preliminary *et cetera* of a party, " what shall we have on Friday night? — tea, coffee, lemonade, wine? of course not."

" And why not wine, mamma?" said the young ladies; " the people are beginning to have it; they had wine at Mrs. A.'s and Mrs. B.'s."

" Well, your papa thinks it won't do, — the boys are members of the temperance society, — and *I* don't think, girls, it will *do* myself."

There are many good sort of people, by the by, who always view moral questions in this style of phraseology — not what is right, but what will " *do*."

The girls made an appropriate reply to this view of the subject, by showing that Mrs. A. and Mrs. B. had done the thing, and nobody seemed to make any talk.

The boys, who thus far in the conversation had been thoughtfully rapping their boots with their canes, now interposed, and said that they would rather not have wine if it wouldn't look shabby.

"But it *will* look shabby," said Miss Fanny. "Lemons, you know, are scarce to be got for any price, and as for lemonade made of sirup, it's positively vulgar and detestable; it tastes just like cream of tartar and spirits of turpentine."

"For my part," said Emma, "I never did see the harm of wine, even when people were making the most fuss about it; to be sure rum and brandy and all that are bad, but wine ——"

"And so convenient to get," said Fanny; "and no decent young man ever gets drunk at parties, so it can't do any harm; besides, one must have something, and, as I said, it will look shabby not to have it."

Now, there is no imputation that young men are so much afraid of, especially from the lips of ladies, as that of shabbiness; and as it happened in this case as most others that the young ladies were the most efficient talkers, the question was finally carried on their side.

Mrs. G. was a mild and a motherly woman, just the one fitted to inspire young men with confidence and that *home* feeling which all men desire to find somewhere. Her house was a free and easy ground, social for most of the young people of her acquaintance, and Harry was a favorite and domesticated visitor.

During the height of the temperance reform, fathers and brothers had given it their open and decided support, and Mrs. G. — always easily enlisted for any good movement — sympathized warmly in their endeavors. The great fault was, that too often incident to the gentleness of woman — a want of self-reliant principle. Her virtue was too much the result of mere sympathy, too little of her own conviction. Hence, when those she loved grew cold towards a good cause, they found no sustaining power in her, and those who were relying on her judgment and opinions insensibly controlled them. Notwithstanding, she was a woman that always acquired a great influence over young men, and Harry had loved and revered her with something of the same sentiment that he cherished towards his own mother.

It was the most brilliant party of the season. Every thing was got up in faultless taste, and Mrs. G. was in the very spirit of it. The girls were looking beautifully; the rooms were splendid; there was enough and not too much of light and warmth, and all were doing their best to please and be cheerful. Harry was more brilliant than usual, and in fact outdid himself. Wit and mind were the spirit of the hour.

"Just taste this tokay," said one of the sisters to him; "it has just been sent us from Europe, and is said to be a genuine article."

"You know I'm not in that line," said Harry, laughing and coloring.

"Why not?" said another young lady, taking a glass.

"O, the temperance pledge, you know! I am one of the pillars of the order, a very apostle; it will never do for me."

"Pshaw! those temperance pledges are like the proverb, 'something musty,'" said a gay girl.

"Well, but you said you had a headache the beginning of the evening, and you really look pale; you certainly need it as a medicine," said Fanny. "I'll leave it to mamma;" and she turned to Mrs. G., who stood gayly entertaining a group of young people.

"Nothing more likely," replied she, gayly; "I think, Harry, you have looked pale lately; a glass of wine might do you good."

Had Mrs. G. known all of Harry's past history and temptations, and had she not been in just the inconsiderate state that very good ladies sometimes get into at a party, she would sooner have sacrificed her right hand than to have thrown this observation into the scales; but she did, and they turned the balance for him.

"You shall be my doctor," he said, as, laughing and coloring, he drank the glass — and where was the harm? One glass of wine kills nobody; and yet if a man falls, and knows that in that glass he sacrifices principle and conscience, every drop may be poison to the soul and body.

Harry felt at that very time that a great internal barrier had given way; nor was that glass the only one that evening; another, and another, and another followed; his spirits rose with the wild and feverish gayety incident to his excitable temperament, and what had been begun in the society of ladies was completed late at night in the gentlemen's saloon.

Nobody ever knew, or thought, or recognized that that one party had forever undone this young man; and yet so it was. From that night his struggle of moral resistance was fatally impaired; not that he yielded at once and without desperate efforts and struggles, but gradually each struggle grew weaker, each reform shorter, each resolution more inefficient; yet at the close of the evening all those friends, mother, brother, and sister, flattered themselves that every thing had gone on so well that the next week Mrs. H. thought that it would do to give wine at the party because Mrs. G. had done it last week, and no harm had come of it.

In about a year after, the G.'s began to notice and lament the habits of their young friend, and all unconsciously to wonder how such a fine young man should be so led astray.

Harry was of a decided and desperate nature; his affections and his moral sense waged a fierce war with the terrible tyrant — the madness that had possessed him; and when at last all hope died out, he determined to avoid the anguish and shame of a drunkard's life by a suicide's death. Then came to the trembling, heart-stricken mother and beloved one a wild, incoherent letter of farewell, and he disappeared from among the living.

In the same quiet parlor, where the sunshine still streams through flickering leaves, it now rested on the polished sides and glittering plate of a coffin; there at last lay the weary at rest, the soft, shining gray hair was still gleaming as before, but deeper furrows on the wan cheek, and a weary, heavy languor over the pale, peaceful face, told that those gray hairs had been brought down in sorrow to the grave. Sadder still was the story on the cloudless cheek and lips of the young creature bending in quiet despair over her. Poor Ellen! her life's thread, woven with these two beloved ones, was broken.

And may all this happen? — nay, does it not happen? — just such things happen to young men among us every day. And do they not lead in a thousand ways to sorrows just like these? And is there not a responsibility on all who ought to be the guardians of the safety and purity of the other sex, to avoid setting before them the temptation to which so often and so fatally manhood has yielded? What is a paltry consideration of fashion, compared to the safety of sons, brothers, and husbands? The greatest fault of womanhood is slavery to custom; and yet who but woman makes custom?

Are not all the usages and fashions of polite society more her work than that of man? And let every mother and sister think of the mothers and sisters of those who come within the range of their influence, and say to themselves, when in thoughtlessness they discuss questions affecting their interests, "Behold thy brother!" — "Behold thy son!"

THE CORAL RING.

"There is no time of life in which young girls are so thoroughly selfish as from fifteen to twenty," said Edward Ashton, deliberately, as he laid down a book he had been reading, and leaned over the centre table.

"You insulting fellow!" replied a tall, brilliant-looking creature, who was lounging on an ottoman hard by, over one of Dickens's last works.

"Truth, coz, for all that," said the gentleman, with the air of one who means to provoke a discussion.

"Now, Edward, this is just one of your wholesale declarations, for nothing only to get me into a dispute with you, you know," replied the lady.. "On your conscience, now, (if you have one,) is it not so?"

"My conscience feels quite easy, cousin, in subscribing to that sentiment as my confession of faith," replied the gentleman, with provoking *sang froid.*

"Pshaw! it's one of your fusty old bachelor notions. See what comes, now, of your living to your time of life without a wife — disrespect for the sex, and all that. Really, cousin, your symptoms are getting alarming."

"Nay, now, Cousin Florence," said Edward, "you are a

girl of moderately good sense, with all your nonsense. Now don't you (I know you *do*) think just so too?"

"Think just so too!—do you hear the creature?" replied Florence. "No, sir; you can speak for yourself in this matter, but I beg leave to enter my protest when you speak for me too."

"Well, now, where is there, coz, among all our circle, a young girl that has any sort of purpose or object in life, to speak of, except to make herself as interesting and agreeable as possible? to be admired, and to pass her time in as amusing a way as she can? Where will you find one between fifteen and twenty that has any serious regard for the improvement and best welfare of those with whom she is connected at all, or that modifies her conduct, in the least, with reference to it? Now, cousin, in very serious earnest, you have about as much real character, as much earnestness and depth of feeling, and as much good sense, when one can get at it, as any young lady of them all; and yet, on your conscience, can you say that you live with any sort of reference to any body's good, or to any thing but your own amusement and gratification?"

"What a shocking adjuration!" replied the lady; "prefaced, too, by a three-story compliment. Well, being so adjured, I must think to the best of my ability. And now, seriously and soberly, I don't see as I am selfish. I do all that I have any occasion to do for any body. You know that we have servants to do every thing that is necessary about the house, so that there is no occasion for my making any display of housewifery excellence. And I wait on mamma if she has a headache, and hand papa his slippers and newspaper, and find Uncle John's spectacles for him twenty times a day, (no small matter, that,) and then ——"

"But, after all, what is the object and purpose of your life?"

"Why, I haven't any. I don't see how I can have any — that is, as I am made. Now, you know, I've none of the fussing, baby-tending, herb-tea-making recommendations of Aunt Sally, and divers others of the class commonly called *useful*. Indeed, to tell the truth, I think useful persons are commonly rather fussy and stupid. They are just like the boneset, and hoarhound, and catnip — very necessary to be raised in a garden, but not in the least ornamental."

"And you charming young ladies, who philosophize in kid slippers and French dresses, are the tulips and roses — very charming, and delightful, and sweet, but fit for nothing on earth but parlor ornaments."

"Well, parlor ornaments are good in their way," said the young lady, coloring, and looking a little vexed.

"So you give up the point, then," said the gentleman, "that you girls are good for — just to amuse yourselves, amuse others, look pretty, and be agreeable."

"Well, and if we behave well to our parents, and are amiable in the family — I don't know — and yet," said Florence, sighing, "I have often had a sort of vague idea of something higher that we might become; yet, really, what more than this is expected of us? what else can we do?"

"I used to read in old-fashioned novels about ladies visiting the sick and the poor," replied Edward. "You remember Cœlebs in Search of a Wife?"

"Yes, truly; that is to say, I remember the story part of it, and the love scenes; but as for all those everlasting conversations of Dr. Barlow, Mr. Stanley, and nobody knows who else, I skipped those, of course. But really, this visiting and tending the poor, and all that, seems very well in a story, where the lady goes into a picturesque cottage, half overgrown with honeysuckle, and finds an emaciated, but still beautiful woman propped up by pillows. But come to the downright matter of fact of poking about in all these vile, dirty alleys, and entering little dark rooms, amid troops of grinning children, and smelling codfish and onions, and nobody knows what — dear me, my benevolence always evaporates before I get through. I'd rather pay any body five dollars a day to do it for me than do it myself. The fact is, that I have neither fancy nor nerves for this kind of thing."

"Well, granting, then, that you can do nothing for your fellow-creatures unless you are to do it in the most genteel, comfortable, and picturesque manner possible, is there not a great field for a woman like you, Florence, in your influence over your associates? With your talents for conversation, your tact, and self-possession, and ladylike gift of saying any thing you choose, are you not responsible, in some wise, for the influence you exert over those by whom you are surrounded?"

"I never thought of that," replied Florence.

"Now, you remember the remarks that Mr. Fortesque made the other evening on the religious services at church?"

"Yes, I do; and I thought then he was too bad."

"And I do not suppose there was one of you ladies in the room that did not think so too; but yet the matter was all passed over with smiles, and with not a single insinuation that he had said any thing unpleasing or disagreeable."

"Well, what could we do? One does not want to be rude, you know."

"Do! Could you not, Florence, you who have always

taken the lead in society, and who have been noted for always being able to say and do what you please — could you not have shown him that those remarks were unpleasing to you, as decidedly as you certainly would have done if they had related to the character of your father or brother? To my mind, a woman of true moral feeling should consider herself as much insulted when her religion is treated with contempt as if the contempt were shown to herself. Do you not *know* the power which is given to you women to awe and restrain us in your presence, and to guard the sacredness of things which you treat as holy? Believe me, Florence, that Fortesque, infidel as he is, would reverence a woman with whom he dared not trifle on sacred subjects."

Florence rose from her seat with a heightened color, her dark eyes brightening through tears.

"I am sure what you say is just, cousin, and yet I have never thought of it before. I will — I am determined to begin, after this, to live with some better purpose than I have done."

"And let me tell you, Florence, in starting a new course, as in learning to walk, taking the first step is every thing. Now, I have a first step to propose to you."

"Well, cousin ——"

"Well, you know, I suppose, that among your train of adorers you number Colonel Elliot?"

Florence smiled.

"And perhaps you do not know, what is certainly true, that, among the most discerning and cool part of his friends, Elliot is considered as a lost man."

"Good Heavens! Edward, what do you mean?"

"Simply this: that with all his brilliant talents, his amiable and generous feelings, and his success in society, Elliot has not self-control enough to prevent his becoming confirmed in intemperate habits."

"I never dreamed of this," replied Florence. "I knew that he was spirited and free, fond of society, and excitable; but never suspected any thing beyond."

"Elliot has tact enough never to appear in ladies' society when he is not in a fit state for it," replied Edward; "but yet it is so."

"But is he really so bad?"

"He stands just on the verge, Florence; just where a word fitly spoken might turn him. He is a noble creature, full of all sorts of fine impulses and feelings; the only son of a mother who dotes on him, the idolized brother of sisters who love him as you love your brother, Florence; and he stands where a word, a look — so they be of the right kind — might save him."

"And why, then, do you not speak to him?" said Florence.

"Because I am not the best person, Florence. There is another who can do it better; one whom he admires, who stands in a position which would forbid his feeling angry; a person, cousin, whom I have heard in gayer moments say that she knew how to say any thing she pleased without offending any body."

"O Edward!" said Florence, coloring; "do not bring up my foolish speeches against me, and do not speak as if I ought to interfere in this matter, for indeed I cannot do it. I never could in the world, I am certain I could not."

"And so," said Edward, "you, whom I have heard say so many things which no one else could say, or dared to say — you, who have gone on with your laughing assurance in your own powers of pleasing, shrink from trying that power when a noble and generous heart might be saved by it. You have been willing to venture a great deal for the sake of amusing yourself and winning admiration; but you dare not say a word for any high or noble purpose. Do you not see how you confirm what I said of the selfishness of you women?"

"But you must remember, Edward, this is a matter of great delicacy."

"That word *delicacy* is a charming cover-all in all these cases, Florence. Now, here is a fine, noble-spirited young man, away from his mother and sisters, away from any family friend who might care for him, tempted, betrayed, almost to ruin, and a few words from you, said as a woman knows how to say them, might be his salvation. But you will coldly look on and see him go to destruction, because you have too much *delicacy* to make the effort — like the man that would not help his neighbor out of the water because he had never had the honor of an *introduction*."

"But, Edward, consider how peculiarly fastidious Elliot is — how jealous of any attempt to restrain and guide him."

"And just for that reason it is that *men* of his acquaintance cannot do any thing with him. But what are you women made with so much tact and power of charming for, if it is not to do these very things that we cannot do? It is a delicate matter — true; and has not Heaven given to you a fine touch and a fine eye for just such delicate matters? Have you not seen, a thousand times, that what might be resented as an impertinent interference on the part of a man, comes to us as a flattering expression of interest from the lips of a woman?"

"Well, but, cousin, what would you have me do? How would you have me do it?" said Florence, earnestly.

"You know that Fashion, which makes so many wrong turns, and so many absurd ones, has at last made one good one, and it is now a fashionable thing to sign the temperance pledge. Elliot himself would be glad to do it, but he foolishly committed himself against it in the outset, and now feels bound to stand to his opinion. He has, too, been rather rudely assailed by some of the apostles of the new state of things, who did not understand the peculiar points of his character; in short, I am afraid that he will feel bound to go to destruction for the sake of supporting his own opinion. Now, if I should undertake with him, he might shoot me; but I hardly think there is any thing of the sort to be apprehended in your case. Just try your enchantments; you have bewitched wise men into doing foolish things before now; try, now, if you can't bewitch a foolish man into doing a wise thing."

Florence smiled archly, but instantly grew more thoughtful.

"Well, cousin," she said, "I will try. Though you are liberal in your ascriptions of power, yet I can put the matter to the test of experiment."

Florence Elmore was, at the time we speak of, in her twentieth year. Born of one of the wealthiest families in ——, highly educated and accomplished, idolized by her parents and brothers, she had entered the world as one born to command. With much native nobleness and magnanimity of character, with warm and impulsive feelings, and a capability of every thing high or great, she had hitherto lived solely for her own amusement, and looked on the whole brilliant circle by which she was surrounded, with all its various actors, as something got up for her special diversion. The idea of influencing any one, for better or worse, by any thing she ever said or did, had never occurred to her. The crowd of admirers of the other sex, who, as a matter of course, were always about her, she regarded as so many sources of diversion; but the idea of feeling any sympathy with them as human beings, or of making use of her power over them for their improvement, was one that had never entered her head.

Edward Ashton was an old bachelor cousin of Florence's, who, having earned the title of oddity, in general society, availed himself of it to exercise a turn for telling the truth to the various young ladies of his acquaintance, especially to his fair cousin Florence. We remark, by the by, that these privileged truth tellers are quite a necessary of life to young ladies in the full tide of society, and we really think it would be worth while for every dozen of them to unite to keep a person of this kind on a salary, for the benefit of the whole. However, that is nothing to our present purpose; we must return to our fair heroine, whom we left, at the close of the last conversation, standing in deep revery, by the window.

"It's more than half true," she said to herself — "more than half. Here am I, twenty years old, and never have thought of any thing, never done any thing, except to amuse and gratify myself; no purpose, no object; nothing high, nothing dignified, nothing worth living for! Only a parlor ornament — heigh ho! Well, I really do believe I could do something with this Elliot; and yet how dare I try?"

Now, my good readers, if you are anticipating a love story, we must hasten to put in our disclaimer; you are quite mistaken in the case. Our fair, brilliant heroine was, at this time of speaking, as heart-whole as the diamond on her bosom, which reflected the light in too many sparkling rays ever to absorb it. She had, to be sure, half in earnest, half in jest, maintained a bantering, platonic sort of friendship with George Elliot. She had danced, ridden, sung, and sketched with him; but so had she with twenty other young men; and as to coming to any thing tender with such a quick, brilliant, restless creature, Elliot would as soon have undertaken to sentimentalize over a glass of soda water. No; there was decidedly no love in the case.

"What a curious ring that is!" said Elliot to her, a day or two after, as they were reading together.

"It is a knight's ring," said she, playfully, as she drew it off and pointed to a coral cross set in the gold, "a ring of the red-cross knights. Come, now, I've a great mind to bind you to my service with it."

"Do, lady fair," said Elliot, stretching out his hand for the ring.

"Know, then," said she, "if you take this pledge, that you must obey whatever commands I lay upon you in its name."

"I swear!" said Elliot, in the mock heroic, and placed the ring on his finger.

An evening or two after, Elliot attended Florence to a party at Mrs. B.'s. Every thing was gay and brilliant, and there was no lack either of wit or wine. Elliot was standing in a little alcove, spread with refreshments, with a glass of wine in his hand. "I forbid it; the cup is poisoned!" said a voice in his ear. He turned quickly, and Florence was at his side. Every one was busy, with laughing and talking, around, and nobody saw the sudden start and flush that these words produced, as Elliot looked earnestly in the lady's face. She smiled, and pointed playfully to the ring; but after all, there was in her face an expression of agitation and interest which she could not repress, and Elliot felt, however playful the manner, that she was *in earnest;* and as she glided away in the crowd, he stood with his arms folded, and his eyes fixed on the spot where she disappeared.

"Is it possible that I am suspected — that there are things said of me as if I were in danger?" were the first thoughts that flashed through his mind. How strange that a man may appear doomed, given up, and lost, to the eye of every looker on, before he begins to suspect himself! This was the first time that any defined apprehension of loss of character had occurred to Elliot, and he was startled as if from a dream.

"What the deuse is the matter with you, Elliot? You look as solemn as a hearse!" said a young man near by.

"Has Miss Elmore cut you?" said another.

"Come, man, have a glass," said a third.

"Let him alone — he's bewitched," said a fourth. "I saw the spell laid on him. None of us can say but our turn may come next."

An hour later, that evening, Florence was talking with her usual spirit to a group who were collected around her, when, suddenly looking up, she saw Elliot, standing in an abstracted manner, at one of the windows that looked out into the balcony.

"He is offended, I dare say," she thought; "but what do I care? For once in my life I have tried to do a right thing — a good thing. I have risked giving offence for less than this, many a time." Still, Florence could not but feel tremulous, when, a few moments after, Elliot approached her and offered his arm for a promenade. They walked up and down the room, she talking volubly, and he answering yes and no, till at length,

33

as if by accident, he drew her into the balcony which overhung the garden. The moon was shining brightly, and every thing without, in its placid quietness, contrasted strangely with the busy, hurrying scene within.

"Miss Elmore," said Elliot, abruptly, "may I ask you, sincerely, had you any design in a remark you made to me in the early part of the evening?"

Florence paused, and though habitually the most practised and self-possessed of women, the color actually receded from her cheek, as she answered, —

"Yes, Mr. Elliot; I must confess that I had."

"And is it possible, then, that you have heard any thing?"

"I have heard, Mr. Elliot, that which makes me tremble for you, and for those whose life, I know, is bound up in you; and, tell me, were it well or friendly in me to know that such things were said, that such danger existed, and not to warn you of it?"

Elliot stood for a few moments in silence.

"Have I offended? Have I taken too great a liberty?" said Florence, gently.

Hitherto Elliot had only seen in Florence the self-possessed, assured, light-hearted woman of fashion; but there was a reality and depth of feeling in the few words she had spoken to him, in this interview, that opened to him entirely a new view in her character.

"No, Miss Elmore," replied he, earnestly, after some pause; "I may be *pained*, offended I cannot be. To tell the truth, I have been thoughtless, excited, dazzled; my spirits, naturally buoyant, have carried me, often, too far; and lately I have painfully suspected my own powers of resistance. I have really felt that I needed help, but have been too proud to confess, even to myself, that I needed it. You, Miss Elmore, have done what, perhaps, no one else could have done. I am overwhelmed with gratitude, and I shall bless you for it to the latest day of my life. I am ready to pledge myself to any thing you may ask on this subject."

"Then," said Florence, "do not shrink from doing what is safe, and necessary, and right for you to do, because you have once said you would not do it. You understand me."

"Precisely," replied Elliot: "and you shall be obeyed."

It was not more than a week before the news was circulated that even George Elliot had signed the pledge of temperance. There was much wondering at this sudden turn among those who had known his utter repugnance to any measure of the kind, and the extent to which he had yielded to temptation; but few knew how fine and delicate had been the touch to which his pride had yielded.

ART AND NATURE.

"Now, girls," said Mrs. Ellis Grey to her daughters, "here is a letter from George Somers, and he is to be down here next week; so I give you fair warning."

"Warning?" said Fanny Grey, looking up from her embroidery; "what do you mean by that, mamma?"

"Now that's just you, Fanny," said the elder sister, laughing. "You dear little simplicity, you can never understand any thing unless it is stated as definitely as the multiplication table."

"But we need no warning in the case of Cousin George, I'm sure," said Fanny.

"Cousin George, to be sure! Do you hear the little innocent?" said Isabella, the second sister. "I suppose, Fanny, you never heard that he had been visiting all the courts of Europe, seeing all the fine women, stone, picture, and real, that are to be found. Such an *amateur* and *connoisseur!*"

"Besides having received a fortune of a million or so," said Emma. "I dare say now, Fanny, you thought he was coming home to make dandelion chains, and play with button balls, as he used to do when he was a little boy."

"Fanny will never take the world as it is," said Mrs. Grey.

"I do believe she will be a child as long as she lives." Mrs. Grey said this as if she were sighing over some radical defect in the mind of her daughter, and the delicate cheek of Fanny showed a tint somewhat deeper as she spoke, and she went on with her embroidery in silence.

Mrs. Grey had been left, by the death of her husband, sole guardian of the three girls whose names have appeared on the page. She was an active, busy, ambitious woman, one of the sort for whom nothing is ever finished enough, or perfect enough, without a few touches, and dashes, and emendations; and, as such people always make a mighty affair of education, Mrs. Grey had made it a life's enterprise to order, adjust, and settle the character of her daughters; and when we use the word *character*, as Mrs. Grey understood it, we mean it to include both face, figure, dress, accomplishments, as well as those more unessential items, mind and heart.

Mrs. Grey had determined that her daughters should be something altogether out of the common way; and accordingly she had conducted the training of the two eldest with such zeal and effect, that every trace of an original character was thoroughly educated out of them. All their opinions, feelings, words, and actions, instead of gushing naturally from their hearts, were, according to the most approved authority, diligently compared and revised. Emma, the eldest, was an imposing, showy girl, of some considerable talent, and she had been assiduously trained to make a sensation as a woman of ability and intellect. Her mind had been filled with information on all sorts of subjects, much faster than she had power to digest or employ it; and the standard which her ambitious mother had set for her being rather above the range of her abilities, there was a constant sensation of effort in her keeping up to it. In hearing her talk you were constantly reminded, "I am a woman of intellect — I am entirely above the ordinary level of woman;" and on all subjects she was so anxiously and laboriously, well and circumstantially, informed, that it was enough to make one's head ache to hear her talk.

Isabella, the second daughter, was, *par excellence*, a beauty — a tall, sparkling, Cleopatra-looking girl, whose rich color, dazzling eyes, and superb figure might have bid defiance to art to furnish an extra charm; nevertheless, each grace had been as indefatigably drilled and manœuvred as the members of an artillery company. Eyes, lips, eyelashes, all had their lesson; and every motion of her sculptured limbs, every intonation of her silvery voice, had been studied, considered, and corrected, till even her fastidious mother could discern nothing that was wanting. Then were added all the graces of *belles lettres* — all the approved rules of being delighted with music, painting, and poetry — and last of all came the tour of the continent; travelling being generally considered a sort of pumice stone, for rubbing down the varnish, and giving the very last touch to character.

During the time that all this was going on, Miss Fanny, whom we now declare our heroine, had been growing up in the quietude of her mother's country seat, and growing, as girls are apt to, much faster than her mother imagined. She was a fair, slender girl, with a purity and simplicity of appearance, which, if it be not in itself beauty, had all the best effect of beauty, in interesting and engaging the heart.

She looked not so much beautiful as lovable. Her character was in precise correspondence with her appearance; its first and chief element was feeling; and to this add fancy, fervor, taste, enthusiasm almost up to the point of genius, and just common sense enough to keep them all in order, and you will have a very good idea of the mind of Fanny Grey.

Delightfully passed the days with Fanny during the absence of her mother, while, without thought of rule or compass, she sang her own songs, painted flowers, and sketched landscapes from nature, visited sociably all over the village, where she was a great favorite, ran about through the fields, over fences, or in the woods with her little cottage bonnet, and, above all, built her own little castles in the air without any body to help pull them down, which we think about the happiest circumstance in her situation.

But affairs wore a very different aspect when Mrs. Grey with her daughters returned from Europe, as full of foreign tastes and notions as people of an artificial character generally do return.

Poor Fanny was deluged with a torrent of new ideas; she heard of styles of appearance and styles of beauty, styles of manner and styles of conversation, this, that, and the other air, a general effect and a particular effect, and of four hundred and fifty ways of producing an impression — in short, it seemed to her that people ought to be of wonderful consequence to have so many things to think and to say about the how and why of every word and action.

Mrs. Grey, who had no manner of doubt of her own ability to make over a character, undertook the point with Fanny as systematically as one would undertake to make over an old dress. Poor Fanny, who had an unconquerable aversion to trying on dresses or settling points in millinery, went through with most exemplary meekness an entire transformation as to all externals; but when Mrs. Grey set herself at work upon her mind, and tastes, and opinions, the matter became somewhat more serious; for the buoyant feeling and fanciful elements of her character were as incapable of being arranged according to rule as the sparkling water drops are of being strung into necklaces and earrings, or the gay clouds of being made into artificial flowers. Some warm natural desire or taste of her own was forever interfering with her mother's *régime;* some obstinate little "Fannyism" would always put up its head in defiance of received custom; and, as her mother and sisters pathetically remarked, do what you would with her, she would always come out herself after all.

After trying laboriously to conform to the pattern which was daily set before her, she came at last to the conclusion that some natural inferiority must forever prevent her aspiring to accomplish any thing in that way.

"If I can't be what my mother wishes, I'll at least be myself," said she one day to her sisters, "for if I try to alter I shall neither be myself nor any body else;" and on the whole her mother and sisters came to the same conclusion. And in truth they found it a very convenient thing to have one in the family who was not studying effect or aspiring to be any thing in particular.

It was very agreeable to Mrs. Grey to have a daughter to sit with her when she had the sick headache, while the other girls were entertaining company in the drawing room below. It was very convenient to her sisters to have some one whose dress took so little time that she had always a head and a pair of hands at their disposal, in case of any toilet emergency. Then she was always loving and affectionate, entirely willing to be outtalked and outshone on every occasion; and that was another advantage.

As to Isabella and Emma, the sensation that they made in

society was enough to have gratified a dozen ordinary belles. All that they said, and did, and wore, was instant and unquestionable precedent; and young gentlemen, all starch and perfume, twirled their laced pocket handkerchiefs, and declared on their honor that they knew not which was the most overcoming, the genius and wit of Miss Emma, or the bright eyes of Miss Isabella; though it was an agreed point that between them both, not a heart in the gay world remained in its owner's possession — a thing which might have a serious sound to one who did not know the character of these articles, often the most trifling item in the inventory of worldly possessions. And all this while, all that was said of our heroine was something in this way: "I believe there is another sister — is there not?"

"Yes, there is a quiet little blue-eyed lady, who never has a word to say for herself — quite amiable I'm told."

Now, it was not a fact that Miss Fanny never had a word to say for herself. If people had seen her on a visit at any one of the houses along the little green street of her native village, they might have learned that her tongue could go fast enough.

But in lighted drawing rooms, and among buzzing voices, and surrounded by people who were always saying things because such things were proper to be said, Fanny was always dizzy, and puzzled, and unready; and for fear that she would say something that she should not, she concluded to say nothing at all; nevertheless, she made good use of her eyes, and found a very quiet amusement in looking on to see how other people conducted matters.

* * * * *

Well, Mr. George Somers is actually arrived at Mrs. Grey's country seat, and there he sits with Miss Isabella in the deep recess of that window, where the white roses are peeping in so modestly.

"To be sure," thought Fanny to herself, as she quietly surveyed him looming up through the shade of a pair of magnificent whiskers, and heard him passing the shuttlecock of compliment back and forth with the most assured and practised air in the world, — "to be sure, I was a child in imagining that I should see Cousin George Somers. I'm sure this magnificent young gentleman, full of all utterance and knowledge, is not the cousin that I used to feel so easy with; no, indeed;" and Fanny gave a half sigh, and then went out into the garden to water her geraniums.

For some days Mr. Somers seemed to feel put upon his reputation to sustain the character of gallant, *savant*, *connoisseur*, &c., which every one who makes the tour of the continent is expected to bring home as a matter of course; for there is seldom a young gentleman who knows he has qualifications in this line, who can resist the temptation of showing what he can do. Accordingly he discussed tragedies, and reviews, and ancient and modern customs with Miss Emma; and with Miss Isabella retouched her drawings and exhibited his own; sported the most choice and *recherché* style of compliment at every turn, and, in short, flattered himself, perhaps justly, that he was playing the irresistible in a manner quite equal to that of his fair cousins.

Now, all this while Miss Fanny was mistaken in one point, for Mr. George Somers, though an exceedingly fine gentleman, had, after all, quite a substratum of reality about him, of real heart, real feeling, and real opinion of his own; and the consequence was, that when tired of the effort of *conversing* he really longed to find somebody to *talk* to; and in this mood he one evening strolled into the library, leaving the gay party in the drawing room to themselves. Miss Fanny was there, quite intent upon a book of selections from the old English poets.

"Really, Miss Fanny," said Mr. Somers, "you are very sparing of the favor of your company to us this evening."

"O, I presume my company is not much missed," said Fanny, with a smile.

"You must have a poor opinion of our taste, then," said Mr. Somers.

"Come, come, Mr. Somers," replied Fanny, "you forget the person you are talking to; it is not at all necessary for you to compliment me; nobody ever does — so you may feel relieved of that trouble."

"Nobody ever does, Miss Fanny; pray, how is that?"

"Because I'm not the sort of person to say such things to."

"And pray, what sort of person ought one to be, in order to have such things said?" replied Mr. Somers.

"Why, like Sister Isabella, or like Emma. You understand I am a sort of little nobody; if any one wastes fine words on me, I never know what to make of them."

"And pray, what must one say to you?" said Mr. Somers, quite amused.

"Why, what they really think and really feel; and I am always puzzled by any thing else."

Accordingly, about a half an hour afterwards, you might have seen the much admired Mr. Somers once more transformed into the Cousin George, and he and Fanny engaged in a very interesting *tête-à-tête* about old times and things.

Now, you may skip across a fortnight from this evening, and then look in at the same old library, just as the setting sun is looking in at its western window, and you will see Fanny sitting back a little in the shadow, with one straggling ray of light illuminating her pure childish face, and she is looking up at Mr. George Somers, as if in some sudden perplexity; and, dear me, if we are not mistaken, our young gentleman is blushing.

"Why, Cousin George," says the lady, "what *do* you mean?"

"I thought I spoke plainly enough, Fanny," replied Cousin George, in a tone that *might* have made the matter plain enough, to be sure.

Fanny laughed outright, and the gentleman looked terribly serious.

"Indeed, now, don't be angry," said she, as he turned away with a vexed and mortified air; "indeed, now, I can't help laughing, it seems to me so odd; what *will* they all think of you?"

"It's of no consequence to me what they think," said Mr. Somers. "I think, Fanny, if you had the heart I gave you credit for, you might have seen my feelings before now."

"Now, do sit down, my *dear* cousin," said Fanny, earnestly, drawing him into a chair, "and tell me, how could I, poor little Miss Fanny Nobody, how *could* I have thought any such thing with such sisters as I have? I did think that you *liked* me, that you knew more of my real feelings than mamma and sisters; but that you should — that you ever should — why, I am astonished that you did not fall in love with Isabella."

"That would have met your feelings, then?" said George, eagerly, and looking as if he would have looked through her, eyes, soul, and all.

"No, no, indeed," she said, turning away her head; "but," added she, quickly, "you'll lose all your credit for good taste. Now, tell me, seriously, what do you like me for?"

"Well, then, Fanny, I can give you the best reason. I like you for being a real, sincere, natural girl — for being simple in your tastes, and simple in your appearance, and simple in your manners, and for having heart enough left, as I hope, to love plain George Somers, with all his faults, and not Mr. Somers's reputation, or Mr. Somers's establishment."

"Well, this is all very reasonable to me, of course," said Fanny, "but it will be so much Greek to poor mamma."

"I dare say your mother could never understand how seeing the very acme of cultivation in all countries should have really made my eyes ache, and long for something as simple as green grass or pure water, to rest them on. I came down here to find it among my cousins, and I found in your sisters only just such women as I have seen and admired all over Europe, till I was tired of admiring. Your mother has achieved what she aimed at, perfectly; I know of no circle that could produce higher specimens; but it is all art, triumphant art, after all, and I have so strong a current of natural feeling running through my heart that I could never be happy except with a fresh, simple, impulsive character."

"Like me, you are going to say," said Fanny, laughing. "Well, *I'll* admit that you are right. It would be a pity that you should not have one vote, at least."

CHILDREN.

"A little child shall lead them."

ONE cold market morning I looked into a milliner's shop, and there I saw a hale, hearty, well-browned young fellow from the country, with his long cart whip, and lion-shag coat, holding up some little matter, and turning it about on his great fist. And what do you suppose it was? *A baby's bonnet!* A little, soft, blue satin hood, with a swan's down border, white as the new-fallen snow, with a frill of rich blonde around the edge.

By his side stood a very pretty woman, holding, with no small pride, the baby — for evidently it was *the* baby. Any one could read that fact in every glance, as they looked at each other, and then at the large, unconscious eyes, and fat, dimpled cheeks of the little one.

It was evident that neither of them had ever seen a baby like that before.

"But really, Mary," said the young man, "isn't three dollars very high?"

Mary very prudently said nothing, but taking the little bonnet, tied it on the little head, and held up the baby. The man looked, and without another word down went the three dollars — all the avails of last week's butter; and as they walked out of the shop, it is hard to say which looked the most delighted with the bargain.

"Ah," thought I, "a little child shall lead them."

Another day, as I was passing a carriage factory along one of our principal back streets, I saw a young mechanic at work on a wheel. The rough body of a carriage stood beside him, and there, wrapped up snugly, all hooded and cloaked, sat a little dark-eyed girl, about a year old, playing with a great, shaggy dog. As I stopped, the man looked up from his work, and turned admiringly towards his little companion, as much as to say, "See what I have got here!"

"Yes," thought I; "and if the little lady ever gets a glance from admiring swains as sincere as that, she will be lucky."

Ah, these children, little witches, pretty even in all their faults and absurdities. See, for example, yonder little fellow in a naughty fit. He has shaken his long curls over his deep-blue eyes; the fair brow is bent in a frown the rose leaf lip is pursed up in infinite defiance, and the white shoulder thrust angrily forward. Can any but a child look so pretty, even in its naughtiness?

Then comes the instant change; flashing smiles and tears, as the good comes back all in a rush, and you are overwhelmed with protestations, promises, and kisses! They are irresistible, too, these little ones. They pull away the scholar's pen, tumble about his paper, make somersets over his books; and what can he do? They tear up newspapers, litter the carpets, break, pull, and upset, and then jabber unheard-of English in self-defence; and what can you do for yourself?

"If I had a child," says the precise man, "you should see."

He *does* have a child, and his child tears up his papers, tumbles over his things, and pulls his nose, like all other children; and what has the precise man to say for himself? Nothing; he is like every body else; "a little child shall lead him."

The hardened heart of the worldly man is unlocked by the guileless tones and simple caresses of his son; but he repays it in time, by imparting to his boy all the crooked tricks and callous maxims which have undone himself.

Go to the jail, to the penitentiary, and find there the wretch most sullen, brutal, and hardened. Then look at your infant son. Such as he is to you, such to some mother was this man. That hard hand was soft and delicate; that rough voice was tender and lisping; fond eyes followed him as he played, and he was rocked and cradled as something holy. There was a time when his heart, soft and unworn, might have opened to questionings of God and Jesus, and been sealed with the seal of Heaven. But harsh hands seized it; fierce goblin lineaments were impressed upon it; and all is over with him forever!

So of the tender, weeping child is made the callous, heartless man; of the all-believing child, the sneering sceptic; of the beautiful and modest, the shameless and abandoned; and this is what *the world* does for the little one.

There was a time when the *divine One* stood on earth, and little children sought to draw near to him. But harsh human beings stood between him and them, forbidding their approach. Ah, has it not always been so? Do not even we, with our hard and unsubdued feelings, our worldly and unspiritual habits and maxims, stand like a dark screen between our little child and its Savior, and keep even from the choice bud of our hearts the sweet radiance which might unfold it for Paradise? "Suffer little children to come unto me, and forbid them not," is still the voice of the Son of God; but the cold world still closes around and forbids. When, of old, disciples would question their Lord of the higher mysteries of his kingdom, he took a little child and set him in the midst, as a sign of him who should be greatest in heaven. That gentle teacher remains still to us. By every hearth and fireside Jesus still *sets the little child in the midst of us.*

Wouldst thou know, O parent, what is that *faith* which unlocks heaven? Go not to wrangling polemics, or creeds and forms of theology, but draw to thy bosom thy little one, and read in that clear, trusting eye the lesson of eternal life. Be only to thy God as thy child is to thee, and all is done. Blessed shalt thou be, indeed, "*when a little child shall lead thee.*"

HOW TO MAKE FRIENDS WITH MAMMON.

It was four o'clock in the afternoon of a dull winter day that Mr. H. sat in his counting room. The sun had nearly gone down, and, in fact, it was already twilight beneath the shadows of the tall, dusky stores, and the close, crooked streets of that quarter of Boston. Hardly light enough struggled through the dusky panes of the counting house for him to read the entries in a much-thumbed memorandum book, which he held in his hand.

A small, thin boy, with a pale face and anxious expression, significant of delicacy of constitution, and a too early acquaintance with want and sorrow, was standing by him, earnestly watching his motions.

"Ah, yes, my boy," said Mr. H., as he at last shut up the memorandum book. "Yes, I've got the place now; I'm apt to be forgetful about these things; come, now, let's go. How is it? Haven't you brought the basket?"

"No, sir," said the boy, timidly. "The grocer said he'd let mother have a quarter for it, and she thought she'd sell it."

"That's bad," said Mr. H., as he went on, tying his throat with a long comforter of some yards in extent; and as he continued this operation he abstractedly repeated, "That's bad, that's bad," till the poor little boy looked quite dismayed, and began to think that somehow his mother had been dreadfully out of the way.

"She didn't want to send for help so long as she had any thing she could sell," said the little boy in a deprecating tone.

"O, yes, quite right," said Mr. H., taking from a pigeon hole in the desk a large pocket book, and beginning to turn it over; and, as before, abstractedly repeating, "Quite right, quite right?" till the little boy became reassured, and began to think, although he didn't know why, that his mother had done something quite meritorious.

"Well," said Mr. H., after he had taken several bills from the pocket book and transferred them to a wallet which he put into his pocket, "now we're ready, my boy." But first he stopped to lock up his desk, and then he said, abstractedly to himself, "I wonder if I hadn't better take a few tracts."

Now, it is to be confessed that this Mr. H., whom we have introduced to our reader, was, in his way, quite an oddity. He had a number of singular little *penchants* and peculiarities quite his own, such as a passion for poking about among dark alleys, at all sorts of seasonable and unseasonable hours; fishing out troops of dirty, neglected children, and fussing about generally in the community till he could get them into schools or otherwise provided for. He always had in his pocket book a note of some dozen poor widows who wanted tea, sugar, candles, or other things such as poor widows always will be wanting. And then he had a most extraordinary talent for finding out all the sick strangers that lay in out-of-the-way upper rooms in hotels, who, every body knows, have no business to get sick in such places, unless they have money enough to pay their expenses, which they never do.

Besides this, all Mr. H.'s kinsmen and cousins, to the third, fourth, and fortieth remove, were always writing him letters, which, among other pleasing items, generally contained the intelligence that a few hundred dollars were just then exceedingly necessary to save them from utter ruin, and they knew of nobody else to whom to look for it.

And then Mr. H. was up to his throat in subscriptions to every charitable society that ever was made or imagined; had a hand in building all the churches within a hundred miles; occasionally gave four or five thousand dollars to a college; offered to be one of six to raise ten thousand dollars for some benevolent purpose, and when four of the six backed out, quietly paid the balance himself, and said no more about it. Another of his innocent fancies was to keep always about him any quantity of tracts and good books, little and big, for children and grown-up people, which he generally diffused in a kind of gentle shower about him wherever he moved.

So great was his monomania for benevolence that it could not at all confine itself to the streets of Boston, the circle of his relatives, or even the United States of America. Mr. H. was fully posted up in the affairs of India, Burmah, China, and all those odd, out-of the-way places, which no sensible man ever thinks of with any interest, unless he can make some money there; and money, it is to be confessed, Mr. H. didn't make there, though he spent an abundance. For getting up printing presses in Ceylon for Chinese type, for boxes of clothing and what not to be sent to the Sandwich Islands, for school books for the Greeks, and all other nonsense of that sort, Mr. H. was without a parallel. No wonder his rich brother merchants sometimes thought him something of a bore, since, his heart being full of all these matters, he was rather apt to talk about them, and sometimes to endeavor to draw them into fellowship, to an extent that was not to be thought of.

So it came to pass often, that though Mr. H. was a thriving business man, with some ten thousand a year, he often wore a pretty threadbare coat, the seams whereof would be trimmed with lines of white; and he would sometimes need several pretty plain hints on the subject of a new hat before he would think he could afford one. Now, it is to be confessed the world is not always grateful to those who thus devote themselves to its interests; and Mr. H. had as much occasion to know this as any other man. People got so used to his giving, that his bounty became as common and as necessary as that of a higher Benefactor, "who maketh his sun to rise upon the evil and the good, and sendeth rain upon the just and the unjust;" and so it came to pass that people took them, as they do the sunshine and the rain, quite as matters of course, not thinking much about them when they came, but particularly apt to scold when they did not come.

But Mr. H. never cared for that. He did not give for gratitude; he did not give for thanks, nor to have his name published in the papers as one of six who had given fifty thousand to do so and so; but he gave because it was *in* him to give, and we all know that it is an old rule in medicine, as well as morals, that what is *in* a man must be brought out. Then, again, he had heard it reported that there had been One of distinguished authority who had expressed the opinion that it was "*more blessed to give than to receive*," and he very much believed it — believed it because the One who said it must have known, since for man's sake *he* once gave away ALL.

And so, when some thriftless, distant relation, whose debts he had paid a dozen times over, gave him an overhauling on the subject of liberality, and seemed inclined to take him by the throat for further charity, he calmed himself down by a chapter or two from the New Testament and half a dozen hymns, and then sent him a good, brotherly letter of admonition and counsel, with a bank note to enforce it; and when some querulous old woman, who had had a tenement of him rent free for three or four years, sent him word that if he didn't send and mend the water pipes she would move right out, he sent and mended them. People said that he was foolish, and that it didn't do any good to do for ungrateful people; but Mr. H. knew that it did *him* good. He loved to do it, and he thought also on some words that ran to this effect: "Do good and lend, *hoping for nothing again.*" He literally hoped for nothing again in the way of reward, either in this world or in heaven, beyond the present pleasure of the deed; for he had abundant occasion to see how favors are forgotten in this world; and as for another, he had in his own soul a standard of benevolence so high, so pure, so ethereal, that but One of mortal birth ever reached it. He felt that, do what he might, he fell ever so far below the life of that *spotless One* — that his crown in heaven must come to him at last, not as a reward, but as a free, eternal gift.

But all this while our friend and his little companion have been pattering along the wet streets, in the rain and sleet of a bitter cold evening, till they stopped before a grocery. Here a large cross-handled basket was first bought, and then filled with sundry packages of tea, sugar, candles, soap, starch, and various other matters; a barrel of flour was ordered to be sent after him on a dray. Mr. H. next stopped at a dry goods store and bought a pair of blankets, with which he loaded down the boy, who was happy enough to be so loaded; and then, turning gradually from the more frequented streets, the two were soon lost to view in one of the dimmest alleys of the city.

The cheerful fire was blazing in his parlor, as, returned from his long, wet walk, he was sitting by it with his feet comfortably incased in slippers. The astral was burning brightly on the centre table, and a group of children were around it, studying their lessons.

"Papa," said a little boy, "what does this verse mean? It's in my Sunday school lesson. 'Make to yourselves *friends of the mammon of unrighteousness, that when ye fail, they may receive you into everlasting habitations.*'"

"You ought to have asked your teacher, my son."

"But he said he didn't know exactly what it meant. He wanted me to look this week and see if I could find out."

Mr. H.'s standing resource in all exegetical difficulties was Dr. Scott's Family Bible. Therefore he now got up, and putting on his spectacles, walked to the glass bookcase, and took down a volume of that worthy commentator, and opening it, read aloud the whole exposition of the passage, together with the practical reflections upon it; and by the time he had done, he found his young auditor fast asleep in his chair.

"Mother," said he, "this child plays too hard. He can't keep his eyes open evenings. It's time he was in bed."

"I wasn't asleep, pa," said Master Henry, starting up with that air of injured innocence with which gentlemen of his age generally treat an imputation of this kind.

"Then can you tell me now what the passage means that I have been reading to you?"

"There's so much of it," said Henry, hopelessly, "I wish you'd just tell me in short order, father."

"O, read it for yourself," said Mr. H., as he pushed the book towards the boy, for it was to be confessed that he perceived at this moment that he had not himself received any particularly luminous impression, though of course he thought it was owing to his own want of comprehension.

Mr. H. leaned back in his rocking chair, and on his own private account began to speculate a little as to what he really should think the verse might mean, supposing he were at all competent to decide upon it. "'Make to yourselves friends of the mammon of unrighteousness,'" says he: "that's money, very clearly. How am I to make friends with it or of it? Receive me into everlasting habitations: that's a singular kind of expression. I wonder what it means. Dr. Scott makes some very good remarks about it — but somehow I'm not exactly clear." It must be remarked that this was not an uncommon result of Mr. H.'s critical investigations in this quarter.

Well, thoughts will wander; and as he lay with his head on the back of his rocking chair, and his eyes fixed on the flickering blaze of the coal, visions of his wet tramp in the city, and of the lonely garret he had been visiting, and of the poor woman with the pale, discouraged face, to whom he had carried warmth and comfort, all blended themselves together. He felt, too, a little indefinite creeping chill, and some uneasy sensations in his head like a commencing cold, for he was not a strong man, and it is probable his long, wet walk was likely to cause him some inconvenience in this way. At last he was fast asleep, nodding in his chair.

He dreamed that he was very sick in bed, that the doctor

came and went, and that he grew sicker and sicker. He was going to die. He saw his wife sitting weeping by his pillow — his children standing by with pale and frightened faces; all things in his room began to swim, and waver, and fade, and voices that called his name, and sobs and lamentations that rose around him, seemed far off and distant in his ear. "O eternity, eternity! I am going — I am going," he thought; and in that hour, strange to tell, not one of all his good deeds seemed good enough to lean on — all bore some taint or tinge, to his purified eye, of mortal selfishness, and seemed unholy before the ALL PURE. "I am going," he thought; "there is no time to stay, no time to alter, to balance accounts; and I know not what I am, but I know, O Jesus, what THOU art. I have trusted in thee, and shall never be confounded;" and with that last breath of prayer earth was past.

A soft and solemn breathing, as of music, awakened him. As an infant child not yet fully awake hears the holy warblings of his mother's hymn, and smiles half conscious, so the heaven-born became aware of sweet voices and loving faces around him ere yet he fully woke to the new immortal LIFE.

"Ah, he has come at last. How long we have waited for him! Here he is among us. Now forever welcome! welcome!" said the voices.

Who shall speak the joy of that latest birth, the birth from death to life! the sweet, calm, inbreathing consciousness of purity and rest, the certainty that all sin, all weakness and error, are at last gone forever; the deep, immortal rapture of repose — felt to be but begun — never to end!

So the eyes of the heaven-born opened on the new heaven and the new earth, and wondered at the crowd of loving faces that thronged about him. Fair, godlike forms of beauty, such as earth never knew, pressed round him with blessings, thanks, and welcome.

The man spoke not, but he wondered in his heart who they were, and whence it came that they knew him; and as soon as the inquiry formed itself in his soul, it was read at once by his heavenly friends. "I," said one bright spirit, "was a poor boy whom you found in the streets: you sought me out, you sent me to school, you watched over me, and led me to the house of God; and now here I am." "And we," said other voices, "are other neglected children whom you redeemed; we also thank you." "And I," said another, "was a lost, helpless girl: sold to sin and shame, nobody thought I could be saved; every body passed me by till you came. You built a home, a refuge for such poor wretches as I, and there I and many like me heard of Jesus; and here we are." "And I," said another, "was once a clerk in your store. I came to the city innocent, but I was betrayed by the tempter. I forgot my mother, and my mother's God. I went to the gaming table and the theatre, and at last I robbed your drawer. You might have justly cast me off; but you bore with me, you watched over me, you saved me. I am here through you this day." "And I," said another, "was a poor slave girl—doomed to be sold on the auction block to a life of infamy, and the ruin of soul and body. Had you not been willing to give so largely for my ransom, no one had thought to buy me. You stimulated others to give, and I was redeemed. I lived a Christian mother to bring my children up for Christ—they are all here with me to bless you this day, and their children on earth, and their children's children are growing up to bless you." "And I," said another, "was an unbeliever. In the pride of my intellect, I thought I could demonstrate the absurdity of Christianity. I thought I could answer the argument from miracles and prophecy; but your patient, self-denying life was an argument I never could answer. When I saw you spending all your time and all your money in efforts for your fellow-men, undiscouraged by ingratitude, and careless of praise, then I thought, 'There is something divine in that man's life,' and that thought brought me here."

The man looked around on the gathering congregation, and he saw that there was no one whom he had drawn heavenward that had not also drawn thither myriads of others. In his lifetime he had been scattering seeds of good around from hour to hour, almost unconsciously; and now he saw every seed springing up into a widening forest of immortal beauty and glory. It seemed to him that there was to be no end of the numbers that flocked to claim him as their long-expected soul friend. His heart was full, and his face became as that of an angel as he looked up to One who seemed nearer than all, and said, "This is thy love for me, unworthy, O Jesus. Of thee, and to thee, and through thee are all things. Amen."

Amen! as with chorus of many waters and mighty thunderings the sound swept onward, and died far off in chiming echoes among the distant stars, and the man awoke.

A SCENE IN JERUSALEM.

It is now nearly noon, the busiest and most bustling hour of the day; yet the streets of the Holy City seem deserted and silent as the grave. The artisan has left his bench, the merchant his merchandise; the throngs of returned wanderers which this great national festival has brought up from every land of the earth, and which have been for the last week carrying life and motion through every street, seem suddenly to have disappeared. Here and there solitary footfalls, like the last pattering rain drops after a shower, awaken the echoes of the streets; and here and there some lonely woman looks from the housetop with anxious and agitated face, as if she would discern something in the far distance.

Alone, or almost alone, the few remaining priests move like white-winged, solitary birds over the gorgeous pavements of the temple, and as they mechanically conduct the ministrations of the day, cast significant glances on each other, and pause here and there to converse in anxious whispers. Ah there is one voice which they have often heard beneath those arches — a voice which ever bore in it a mysterious and thrilling charm — which they know will be hushed to-day. Chief priest, scribe, and doctor have all gone out in the death procession after him; and these few remaining ones, far from the excitement of the crowd, and busied in calm and sacred duties, find voices of anxious questioning rising from the depths of their own souls, "What if this indeed were the Christ?"

But pass we on out of the city, and what a surging tide of life and motion meets the eye, as if all nations under heaven had dashed their waves of population on this Judean shore! A noisy, wrathful, tempestuous mob, billow on billow, waver and rally round some central object, which it conceals from view. Parthians, Medes, Elamites, dwellers in Mesopotamia and Egypt, strangers of Rome, Cretes and Arabians, Jew and Proselyte, convoked from the ends of the earth, throng in agitated concourse one on another; one theme in every face, on every tongue, one name in every variety of accent and dialect passing from lip to lip: "JESUS OF NAZARETH!"

Look on that man — the centre and cause of all this outburst! He stands there alone. The cross is ready. It lies beneath his feet. The rough hand of a brutal soldier has seized his robe to tear it from him. Another with stalwart arm is boring the holes, gazing upward the while with a face of stupid unconcern. There on the ground lie the hammer and the nails: the hour, the moment of doom is come! Look on this man, as upward, with deep, sorrowing eyes, he gazes towards heaven. Hears he the roar of the mob? Feels he the rough hand on his garment? Nay, he sees not, feels not: from all the rage and tumult of the hour he is rapt away. A sorrow deeper, more absorbing, more unearthly seems to possess him, as upward with long gaze he looks to that heaven never before closed to his prayer, to that God never before to him invisible. That mournful, heaven-searching glance, in its lonely anguish, says but one thing: "Lo, I come to do thy will, O God."

Through a life of sorrow the realized love of his Father has shone like a precious and beautiful talisman in his bosom; but now, when desolation and anguish have come upon him as a whirlwind, this last star has gone out in the darkness, and Jesus, deserted by man and God, stands there *alone.*

Alone? No; for undaunted by the cruel mob, fearless in the strength of mortal anguish, helpless, yet undismayed, stands the one blessed among women, the royal daughter of a noble line, the priestess to whose care was intrusted this spotless sacrifice. She and her son, last of a race of kings, stand there despised, rejected, and disavowed by their nation, to accomplish dread words of prophecy, which have swept down for far ages to this hour.

Strange it is, in this dark scene, to see the likeness between mother and son, deepening in every line of those faces, as they stand thus thrown out by the dark background of rage and hate, which like a storm cloud lowers around. The same rapt, absorbed, calm intensity of anguish in both mother and son, save only that while he gazes upward towards God, she, with like fervor, gazes on him. What to her is the deriding mob, the coarse taunt, the brutal abuse? Of it all she hears, she feels nothing. She sinks not, faints not, weeps not; her whole being concentrates in the will to suffer by and with him to the last. Other hearts there are that beat for him; others that press into the doomed circle, and own him amid the scorn of thousands. There may you see the clasped hands and upraised eyes of a Magdalen, the pale and steady resolve of John, the weeping company of women who bewailed and lamented him; but none dare press so near, or seem so identical with him in his sufferings, as this mother.

And as we gaze on these two in human form, surrounded by other human forms, how strange the contrast! How is it possible that human features and human lineaments essentially alike, can be wrought into such heaven-wide contrast? MAN is he who stands there, lofty and spotless, in bleeding patience! *Men* also are those brutal soldiers, alike stupidly ready, at the word of command, to drive the nail through quivering flesh or insensate wood. *Men* are those scowling priests and infuriate Pharisees. *Men*, also, the shifting figures of the careless rabble, who shout and curse without knowing why. No visible glory shines round that head; yet how, spite of every defilement cast upon him by the vulgar rabble, seems that form to be glorified! What light is that in those eyes! What mournful beauty in that face! What solemn, mysterious sacredness investing the whole form, constraining from us the exclamation, "Surely this is the Son of God." *Man's* voice is breathing vulgar taunt and jeer: "He saved others; himself he cannot save." "He trusted in God; let him deliver him if he will have him." And *man's*, also, clear, sweet, unearthly, pierces that stormy mob, saying, "Father, forgive them; they know not what they do."

But we draw the veil in reverence. It is not ours to picture what the sun refused to shine upon, and earth shook to behold.

Little thought those weeping women, that stricken disciple, that heart-broken mother, how on some future day that cross — emblem to them of deepest infamy — should blaze in the eye of all nations, symbol of triumph and hope, glittering on gorgeous fanes, embroidered on regal banners, associated with all that is revered and powerful on earth. The Roman ensign that waved on that mournful day, symbol of highest earthly power, is a thing mouldered and forgotten; and over all the high places of old Rome, herself stands that mystical cross, no longer speaking of earthly anguish and despair, but of heavenly glory, honor, and immortality.

Theologians have endlessly disputed and philosophized on this great fact of *atonement.* The Bible tells only that this tragic event was the essential point without which our salvation could never have been secured. But where lay the necessity they do not say. What was that dread strait that either the divine One must thus suffer, or man be lost, who knoweth?

To this question answer a thousand voices, with each a different solution, urged with equal confidence — each solution to its framer as certain and sacred as the dread fact it explains — yet every one, perhaps, unsatisfactory to the deep-questioning soul. The Bible, as it always does, gives on this point not definitions or distinct outlines, but images — images which lose all their glory and beauty if seized by the harsh hands of metaphysical analysis, but inexpressibly affecting to the unlettered human heart, which softens in gazing on their mournful and mysterious beauty. Christ is called our sacrifice, our passover, our atoning high priest; and he himself, while holding in his hands the emblem cup, says, "It is my blood, shed for *many,* for the *remission of sins.*" Let us reason on it as we will, this story of the cross, presented without explanation in the simple metaphor of the Bible, has produced an effect on human nature wholly unaccountable. In every age and clime, with every variety of habit, thought, and feeling, from the cannibals of New Zealand and Madagascar to the most enlightened and scientific minds in Christendom, one feeling, essentially homogeneous in its character and results, has arisen in view of this cross. There is something in it that strikes one of the great nerves of simple, unsophisticated humanity, and meets its wants as nothing else will. Ages ago, Paul declared to philosophizing Greek and scornful Roman that he was not ashamed of this gospel, and alleged for his reason this very adaptedness to humanity. *A priori*, many would have said that Paul should have told of Christ living, Christ preaching, Christ working miracles, not omitting also the pathetic history of how he sealed all with his blood; but Paul declared that he determined to know nothing else but Christ *crucified*. He said it was a stumbling block to the Jew, an absurdity to the Greek; yet he was none the less positive in his course. True, there was many then, as now, who looked on with the most philosophic and cultivated indifference. The courtly Festus, as he settled his purple tunic, declared he could make nothing of the matter, only a dispute about one Jesus, who was dead, and whom Paul affirmed to be alive; and perchance some Athenian, as he reclined on his ivory couch at dinner, after the sermon on Mars Hill, may have disposed of the matter very summarily, and passed on to criticisms on Samian wine and marble vases. Yet in spite of their disbelief, this story of Christ has outlived them, their age and nation, and is to this hour as fresh in human hearts as if it were just published. This "one Jesus which was dead, and whom Paul affirmed to be alive," is nominally, at least, the object of religious homage in all the more cultivated portions of the globe; and to hearts scattered through all regions of the earth this same Jesus is now a sacred and living name, dearer than all household sounds, all ties of blood, all sweetest and nearest affections of humanity. "I am ready not only to be bound, but also to die for the name of the Lord Jesus," are words that have found an echo in the bosoms of thousands in every age since then; that would, if need were, find no less echo in thousands now. Considering Christ as a man, and his death as a mere pathetic story, — considering him as one of the great martyrs for truth, who sealed it with his blood, — this result is wholly unaccountable. Other martyrs have died, bravely and tenderly, in their last hours "bearing witness of the godlike" that is in man; but who so remembers them? Who so loves them? To whom is any one of them a living presence, a life, an all? Yet so thousands look on Jesus at this hour.

Nay, it is because this story strikes home to every human bosom as an individual concern. A thrilling voice speaks from this scene of anguish to every human bosom: This is *thy* Savior. *Thy* sin hath done this. It is the appropriative words, *thine* and *mine*, which make this history different from any other history. This was for *me*, is the thought which has pierced the apathy of the Greenlander, and kindled the stolid clay of the Hottentot; and no human bosom has ever been found so low, so lost, so guilty, so despairing, that this truth, once received, has not had power to redeem, regenerate, and disenthrall. Christ so presented becomes to every human being a friend nearer than the mother who bore him; and the more degraded, the more hopeless and polluted, is the nature, the stronger comes on the living reaction, if this belief is really and vividly enkindled with it. But take away this appropriative, individual element, and this legend of Jesus's death has no more power than any other. He is to us no more than Washington or Socrates, or Howard. And where is there not a touchstone to try every theory of atonement?

Whatever makes a man feel that he is only a spectator, an uninterested judge in this matter, is surely astray from the idea of the Bible. Whatever makes him feel that his sins have done this deed, that he is bound, soul and body, to this Deliverer, though it may be in many points philosophically erroneous, cannot go far astray.

If we could tell the number of the stars, and call them forth by name, then, perhaps, might we solve all the mystic symbols by which the Bible has shadowed forth the far-lying necessities and reachings-forth of this event "among principalities and powers," and in "ages to come." But he who knows nothing of all this, who shall so present the atonement as to bind and affiance human souls indissolubly to their Redeemer, does all that could be done by the highest and most perfect knowledge.

The great object is accomplished, when the soul, rapt, inspired, feels the deep resolve, —

"Remember Thee!
Yea, from the table of my memory
I'll wipe away all trivial, fond records,
All saws of books, all forms, all pressures past
That youth and observation copied there,
And thy commandment all alone shall live
Within the book and volume of my brain,
Unmixed with baser matter."

THE OLD MEETING HOUSE.

SKETCH FROM THE NOTE BOOK OF AN OLD GENTLEMAN.

Never shall I forget the dignity and sense of importance which swelled my mind when I was first pronounced old enough to go to meeting. That eventful Sunday I was up long before day, and even took my Sabbath suit to the window to ascertain by the first light that it actually was there, just as it looked the night before. With what complacency did I view myself completely dressed! How did I count over the rows of yellow gilt buttons on my coat! how my good mother, grandmother, and aunts fussed, and twitched, and pulled, to make every thing set up and set down, just in the proper place! how my clean, starched white collar was turned over and smoothed again and again, and my golden curls twisted and arranged to make the most of me! and, last of all, how I was cautioned not to be thinking of my clothes! In truth, I was in those days a very handsome youngster, and it really is no more than justice to let the fact be known, as there is nothing in my present appearance from which it could ever be inferred. Every body in the house successively asked me if I should be a good boy, and sit still, and not talk, nor laugh; and my mother informed me, *in terrorem*, that there was a tithing man, who carried off naughty children, and shut them up in a dark place behind the pulpit; and that this tithing man, Mr. Zephaniah Scranton, sat just where he could see me. This fact impressed my mind with more solemnity than all the exhortations which had preceded it — a proof of the efficacy of facts above reason. Under shadow and power of this weighty truth, I demurely took hold of my mother's forefinger to walk to meeting.

The traveller in New England, as he stands on some eminence, and looks down on its rich landscape of golden grain and waving cornfield, sees no feature more beautiful than its simple churches, whose white taper fingers point upward, amid the greenness and bloom of the distant prospects, as if to remind one of the overshadowing providence whence all this luxuriant beauty flows; and year by year, as new ones are added to the number, or succeed in the place of old ones, there is discernible an evident improvement in their taste and architecture. Those modest Doric little buildings, with their white pillars, green blinds, and neat enclosures, are very different affairs from those great, uncouth mountains of windows and doors that stood in the same place years before. To my childish eye, however, our old meeting house was an awe-inspiring thing. To me it seemed fashioned very nearly on the model of Noah's ark and Solomon's temple, as set forth in the pictures in my Scripture Catechism — pictures which I did not doubt were authentic copies; and what more respectable and venerable architectural precedent could any one desire? Its double rows of windows, of which I knew the number by heart, its doors with great wooden quirls over them, its belfry projecting out at the east end, its steeple and bell, all inspired as much sense of the sublime in me as Strasbourg Cathedral itself; and the inside was not a whit less imposing.

How magnificent, to my eye, seemed the turnip-like canopy that hung over the minister's head, hooked by a long iron rod to the wall above! and how apprehensively did I consider the question, what would become of him if it should fall! How did I wonder at the panels on either side of the pulpit, in each of which was carved and painted a flaming red tulip, bolt upright, with its leaves projecting out at right angles! and then at the grape vine, bass relieved on the front, with its exactly triangular bunches of grapes, alternating at exact intervals with exactly triangular leaves. To me it was an indisputable representation of how grape vines ought to look, if they would only be straight and regular, instead of curling and scrambling, and twisting themselves into all sorts of slovenly shapes. The area of the house was divided into large square pews, boxed up with stout boards, and surmounted with a kind of baluster work, which I supposed to be provided for the special accommodation of us youngsters, being the "loopholes of retreat" through which we gazed on the "remarkabilia" of the scene. It was especially interesting to me to notice the coming in to meeting of the congregation. The doors were so contrived that on entering you stepped *down* instead of *up* — a construction that has more than once led to unlucky results in the case of strangers. I remember once when an unlucky Frenchman, entirely unsuspicious of the danger that awaited him, made entrance by pitching devoutly upon his nose in the middle of the broad aisle; that it took three bunches of my grandmother's fennel to bring my risibles into any thing like composure. Such exhibitions, fortunately for me, were very rare; but still I found great amusement in watching the distinctive and marked outlines of the various people that filled up the seats around me. A Yankee village presents a picture of the curiosities of every generation: there, from year to year, they live on, preserved by hard labor and regular habits, exhibiting every peculiarity of manner and appearance, as distinctly marked as when they first came from the mint of nature. And as every body goes punctually to meeting, the meeting house becomes a sort of museum of antiquities — a general muster ground for past and present.

I remember still with what wondering admiration I used to look around on the people that surrounded our pew. On one side there was an old Captain McLean, and Major McDill, a couple whom the mischievous wits of the village designated as Captain McLean and Captain McFat; and, in truth, they were a perfect antithesis, a living exemplification of flesh and spirit. Captain McLean was a mournful, lengthy, considerate-looking old gentleman, with a long face, digressing into a long, thin, horny nose, which, when he applied his pocket handkerchief, gave forth a melancholy, minor-keyed sound, such as a ghost might make, using a pocket handkerchief in the long gallery of some old castle.

Close at his side was the doughty, puffing Captain McDill, whose full-orbed, jolly visage was illuminated by a most valiant red nose, shaped something like an overgrown doughnut, and looking as if it had been thrown *at* his face, and happened to hit in the middle. Then there was old Israel Peters, with a wooden leg, which tramped into meeting, with undeviating regularity, ten minutes before meeting time; and there was Jedediah Stebbins, a thin, wistful, moonshiny-looking old gentleman, whose mouth appeared as if it had been gathered up with a needle and thread, and whose eyes seemed as if they had been bound with red tape; and there was old Benaiah Stephens, who used regularly to get up and stand when the minister was about half through his sermon, exhibiting his tall figure, long, single-breasted coat, with buttons nearly as large as a tea plate; his large, black, horn spectacles stretched down on the extreme end of a very long nose, and vigorously chewing, meanwhile, on the bunch of caraway which he always carried in one hand. Then there was Aunt Sally Stimpson, and old Widow Smith, and a whole bevy of little, dried old ladies, with small, straight, black bonnets, tight sleeves to the elbow, long silk gloves, and great fans, big enough for a windmill; and of a hot day it was a great amusement to me to watch the bobbing of the little black bonnets, which showed that sleep had got the better of their owners' attention, and the sputter and rustling of the fans, when a more profound nod than common would suddenly waken them, and set them to fanning and listening with redoubled devotion. There was Deacon Dundas, a great wagon load of an old gentleman, whose ample pockets looked as if they might have held half the congregation, who used to establish himself just on one side of me, and seemed to feel such entire confidence in the soundness and capacity of his pastor that he could sleep very comfortably from one end of the sermon to the other. Occasionally, to be sure, one of your officious blue flies, who, as every body knows, are amazingly particular about such matters, would buzz into his mouth, or flirt into his ears a passing admonition as to the impropriety of sleeping in meeting, when the good old gentleman would start, open his eyes very wide, and look about with a resolute air, as much as to say, "I wasn't asleep, I can tell you;" and then setting himself in an edifying posture of attention, you might perceive his head gradually settling back, his mouth slowly opening wider and wider, till the good man would go off again soundly asleep, as if nothing had happened.

It was a good orthodox custom of old times to take every part of the domestic establishment to meeting, even down to the faithful dog, who, as he had supervised the labors of the week, also came with due particularity to supervise the worship of Sunday. I think I can see now the fitting out on a Sunday morning — the one wagon, or two, as the case might be, tackled up with an "old gray" or an "old bay," with a buffalo skin over the seat by way of cushion, and all the family, in their Sunday best, packed in for meeting; while Master Bose, Watch, or Towser stood prepared to be an outguard and went meekly trotting up hill and down dale in the rear. Arrived at meeting, the canine part of the establishment generally conducted themselves with great decorum, lying down and going to sleep as decently as any body present, except when some of the business-loving bluebottles aforesaid would make a sortie upon them, when you might hear the snap of their jaws as they vainly sought to lay hold of the offender. Now and then, between some of the sixthlies, seventhlies, and eighthlies, you might hear some old patriarch giving himself a rousing shake, and pitpatting soberly up the aisles, as if to see that every thing was going on properly, after which he would lie down and compose himself to sleep again; and certainly this was as improving a way of spending Sunday as a good Christian dog could desire.

But the glory of our meeting house was its singers' seat — that empyrean of those who rejoiced in the divine, mysterious art of fa-sol-la-ing, who, by a distinguishing grace and privilege, could "raise and fall" the cabalistical eight notes, and move serene through the enchanted region of flats, sharps, thirds, fifths, and octaves.

There they sat in the gallery that lined three sides of the house, treble, counter, tenor, and bass, each with its appropriate leaders and supporters; there were generally seated the bloom of our young people; sparkling, modest, and blushing girls on one side, with their ribbons and finery, making the place where they sat as blooming and lively as a flower garden, and fiery, forward, confident young men on the other. In spite of its being a meeting house, we could not swear that glances were never given and returned, and that there was not often as much of an approach to flirtation as the distance and the sobriety of the place would admit. Certain it was, that there was no place where our village coquettes attracted half so many eyes or led astray half so many hearts.

But I have been talking of singers all this time, and neglected to mention the Magnus Apollo of the whole concern, the redoubtable chorister, who occupied the seat of honor in the midst of the middle gallery, and exactly opposite to the minister. Certain it is that the good man, if he were alive, would never believe it; for no person ever more magnified his office, or had a more thorough belief in his own greatness and supremacy, than Zedekiah Morse. Methinks I can see him now as he appeared to my eyes on that first Sunday, when he shot up from behind the gallery, as if he had been sent up by a spring. He was a little man, whose fiery-red hair, brushed straight up on the top of his head, had an appearance as vigorous and lively as real flame; and this, added to the ardor and determination of all his motions, had obtained for him the surname of the "Burning Bush." He seemed possessed with the very soul of song; and from the moment he began to sing, looked alive all over, till it seemed to me that his whole body would follow his hair upwards, fairly rapt away by the power of harmony. With what an air did he sound the important *fa-sol-la* in the ears of the waiting gallery, who stood with open mouths ready to seize their pitch, preparatory to their general *set to!* How did his ascending and descending arm astonish the zephyrs when once he laid himself out to the important work of beating time! How did his little head whisk from side to side, as now he beat and roared towards the ladies on his right, and now towards the gentlemen on his left! It used to seem to my astonished vision as if his form grew taller, his arm longer, his hair redder, and his little green eyes brighter, with every stave; and particularly when he perceived any falling off of time or discrepancy in pitch; with what redoubled vigor would he thump the gallery and roar at the delinquent quarter, till every mother's son and daughter of them skipped and scrambled into the right place again!

O, it was a fine thing to see the vigor and discipline with which he managed the business; so that if, on a hot, drowsy Sunday, any part of the choir hung back or sung sleepily on the first part of a verse, they were obliged to bestir themselves in good earnest, and sing three times as fast, in order to get through with the others. 'Kiah Morse was no advocate for your dozy, drawling singing, that one may do at leisure, between sleeping and waking, I assure you; indeed, he got entirely out of the graces of Deacon Dundas and one or two other portly, leisurely old gentlemen below, who had been used to throw back their heads, shut up their eyes, and take the comfort of the psalm, by prolonging indefinitely all the notes. The first Sunday after 'Kiah took the music in hand, the old deacon really rubbed his eyes and looked about him; for the psalm was sung off before he was ready to get his mouth opened, and he really looked upon it as a most irreverent piece of business.

But the glory of 'Kiah's art consisted in the execution of those good old billowy compositions called fuguing tunes, where the four parts that compose the choir take up the song, and go racing around one after another, each singing a different set of words, till, at length, by some inexplicable magic, they all come together again, and sail smoothly out into a rolling sea of song. I remember the wonder with which I used to look from side to side when treble, tenor, counter, and base were thus roaring and foaming,—and it verily seemed to me as if the psalm was going to pieces among the breakers,—and the delighted astonishment with which I found that each particular verse did emerge whole and uninjured from the storm.

But alas for the wonders of that old meeting house, how they are passed away! Even the venerable building itself has been pulled down, and its fragments scattered; yet still I retain enough of my childish feelings to wonder whether any little boy was gratified by the possession of those painted tulips and grape vines, which my childish eye used to covet, and about the obtaining of which, in case the house should ever be pulled down, I devised so many schemes during the long sermons and services of summer days. I have visited the spot where it stood, but the modern, fair-looking building that stands in its room bears no trace of it; and of the various familiar faces that used to be seen inside, not one remains. Verily, I must be growing old; and as old people are apt to spin long stories, I check myself, and lay down my pen.

THE NEW-YEAR'S GIFT.

THE sparkling ice and snow covered hill and valley — tree and bush were glittering with diamonds — the broad, coarse rails of the fence shone like bars of solid silver, while little fringes of icicles glittered between each bar.

In the yard of yonder dwelling the scarlet berries of the mountain ash shine through a transparent casing of crystal, and the sable spruces and white pines, powdered and glittering with the frost, have assumed an icy brilliancy. The eaves of the house, the door knocker, the pickets of the fence, the honeysuckles and seringas, once the boast of summer, are all alike polished, varnished, and resplendent with their winter trappings, now gleaming in the last rays of the early sunset.

Within that large, old-fashioned dwelling might you see an ample parlor, all whose adjustments and arrangements speak of security, warmth, and home enjoyment; of money spent not for show, but for comfort. Thick crimson curtains descend in heavy folds over the embrasures of the windows, and the ample hearth and wide fireplace speak of the customs of the good old times, ere that gloomy, unpoetic, unsocial gnome — the air-tight — had monopolized the place of the blazing fireside.

No dark air-tight, however, filled our ancient chimney; but there was a genuine old-fashioned fire of the most approved architecture, with a gallant backlog and forestick, supporting and keeping in order a crackling pile of dry wood, that was whirring and blazing warm welcome for all whom it might concern, occasionally bursting forth into most portentous and earnest snaps, which rung through the room with a genuine, hospitable emphasis, as if the fire was enjoying himself, and having a good time, and wanted all hands to draw up and make themselves at home with him.

So looked that parlor to me, when, tired with a long day's ride, I found my way into it, just at evening, and was greeted with a hearty welcome from my old friend, Colonel Winthrop.

In addition to all that I have already described, let the reader add, if he pleases, the vision of a wide and ample tea table, covered with a snowy cloth, on which the servants are depositing the evening meal.

I had not seen Winthrop for years; but we were old college friends, and I had gladly accepted an invitation to renew our ancient intimacy by passing the New Year's season in his family. I found him still the same hale, kindly, cheery fellow as in days of old, though time had taken the same liberty with his handsome head that Jack Frost had with the cedars and spruces out of doors, in giving to it a graceful and becoming sprinkle of silver.

"Here you are, my dear fellow," said he, shaking me by both hands — "just in season for the ham and chickens — coffee all smoking. My dear," he added to a motherly-looking woman who now entered, "here's John! I beg pardon, Mr. Stuart." As he spoke, two bold, handsome boys broke into the room, accompanied by a huge Newfoundland dog — all as full of hilarity and abundant animation as an afternoon of glorious skating could have generated.

"Ha, Tom and Ned! — you rogues — you don't want any supper to-night, I suppose," said the father, gayly; "come up here and be introduced to my old friend. Here they come!" said he, as one by one the opening doors admitted the various children to the summons of the evening meal. "Here," presenting a tall young girl, "is our eldest, beginning to think herself a young lady, on the strength of being fifteen years old, and wearing her hair tucked up. And here is Eliza," said he, giving a pull to a blooming, roguish girl of ten, with large, saucy black eyes. "And here is Willie!" a bashful, blushing little fellow in a checked apron. "And now, where's the little queen? — where's her majesty? — where's Ally?"

A golden head of curls was, at this instant, thrust timidly in at the door, and I caught a passing glimpse of a pair of great blue eyes; but the head, curls, eyes, and all, instantly vanished, though a little fat dimpled hand was seen holding on to the door, and swinging it back and forward. "Ally, dear, come in!" said the mother, in a tone of encouragement. "Come in, Ally! come in," was repeated in various tones, by each child; but brother Tom pushed open the door, and taking the little recusant in his arms, brought her fairly in, and deposited her on her father's knee. She took firm hold of his coat, and then turned and gazed shyly upon me — her large splendid blue eyes gleaming through her golden curls. It was evident that this was the pet lamb of the fold, and she was just at that age when babyhood is verging into childhood — an age often indefinitely prolonged in a large family, where the universal admiration that waits on every look, and motion, and word of *the baby*, and the multiplied monopolies and privileges of the baby estate, seem, by universal consent, to extend as long and as far as possible. And why not thus delay the little bark of the child among the flowery shores of its first Eden ? — defer them as we may, the hard, the real, the cold commonplace of life comes on all too soon !

"This is our New Year's gift," said Winthrop, fondly caressing the curly head. "Ally, tell the gentleman how old you are."

"I s'all be four next New 'Ear's," said the little one, while all the circle looked applause.

"Ally, tell the gentleman what you are," said brother Ned.

Ally looked coquettishly at me, as if she did not know whether she should favor me to that extent, and the young princess was further solicited.

"Tell him what Ally is," said the oldest sister, with a patronizing air.

"Papa's New 'Ear's pesent," said my little lady, at last.

"And mamma's, too !" said the mother gently, amid the applauses of the admiring circle.

Winthrop looked apologetically at me, and said, "We all spoil her — that's a fact — every one of us down to Rover, there, who let's her tie tippets round his neck, and put bonnets on his head, and hug and kiss him, to a degree that would disconcert any other dog in the world."

If ever beauty and poetic grace was an apology for spoiling, it was in this case. Every turn of the bright head, every change of the dimpled face and round and chubby limbs, was a picture; and within the little form was shrined a heart full of love, and running over with compassion and good will for every breathing thing; with feelings so sensitive, that it was papa's delight to make her laugh and cry with stories, and to watch in the blue, earnest mirror of her eye every change and turn of his narration, as he took her through long fairy tales, and old-fashioned giant and ghost legends, purely for his own amusement, and much reprimanded all the way by mamma, for filling the child's head with nonsense.

It was now, however, time to turn from the beauty to the substantial realities of the supper table. I observed that Ally's high chair was stationed close by her father's side; and ever and anon, while gayly talking, he would slip into her rosy little mouth some choice bit from his plate, these notices and attentions seeming so instinctive and habitual, that they did not for a moment interrupt the thread of the conversation. Once or twice I caught a glimpse of Rover's great rough nose, turned anxiously up to the little chair; whereat the small white hand forthwith slid something into his mouth, though by what dexterity it ever came out from the great black jaws undevoured was a mystery. When the supply of meat on the small lady's plate was exhausted, I observed the little hand slyly slipping into her father's provision grounds, and with infinite address abstracting small morsels, whereat there was much mysterious winking between the father and the other children, and considerable tittering among the younger ones, though all in marvellous silence, as it was deemed best policy not to appear to notice Ally's tricks, lest they should become too obstreperous.

In the course of the next day I found myself, to all intents and purposes, as much part and parcel of the family as if I had been born and bred among them. I found that I had come in a critical time, when secrets were plenty as blackberries. It being New Year's week, all the little hoarded resources of the children, both of money and of ingenuity, were in brisk requisition, getting up New Year's presents for each other, and for father and mother. The boys had their little tin savings banks, where all the stray pennies of the year had been carefully hoarded — all that had been got by blacking papa's boots, or by piling wood, or weeding in the garden — mingled with some fortunate additions which had come as windfalls from some liberal guest or friend. All now were poured out daily, on tables, on chairs, on stools, and counted over with wonderful earnestness.

My friend, though in easy circumstances, was somewhat old-fashioned in his notions. He never allowed his children spending money, except such as they fairly earned by some exertions of their own. "Let them do something," he would say, "to make it fairly theirs, and their generosity will then have some significance — it is very easy for children to be generous on their parents' money." Great were the comparing of resources and estimates of property at this time. Tom and Ned, who were big enough to saw wood, and hoe in the garden, had accumulated the vast sum of three dollars each, and walked about with their hands in their pockets, and talked largely of purchases, like gentlemen of substance. They thought of getting mamma a new muff, and papa a writing desk, besides trinkets innumerable for sisters, and a big doll for Ally; but after they had made one expedition to a neighboring town to inquire prices, I observed that their expectations were greatly moderated. As to little Willie, him of the checked apron, his whole earthly substance amounted to thirty-seven cents; yet there was not a member of the whole family circle, including the servants, that he could find it in his heart to leave out of his remembrance. I ingratiated myself with him immediately; and twenty times a day did I count over his money to him, and did sums innumerable to show how much would be left if he got this, that, or the other article, which he was longing to buy for father or mother. I proved to him most invaluable, by helping him to think of certain small sixpenny and fourpenny articles that would be pretty to give to sisters, making out with marbles for Tom and Ned, and a very valiant-looking sugar horse for Ally. Miss Emma had the usual resource of young ladies, flosses, worsted, and knitting, and crochet needles, and busy fingers, and she was giving private lessons daily to Eliza, to enable her to get up some napkin rings, and book marks for the all-important occasion. A gentle air of bustle and mystery pervaded the whole circle. I was intrusted with so many secrets that I could scarcely make an observation, or take a turn about the room, without being implored to "remember" — "not to tell" — not to let papa know this, or mamma that. I was not to let papa know how the boys were going to buy him a new inkstand, with a pen rack upon it, which was entirely to outshine all previous inkstands; nor tell mamma about the crochet bag that Emma was knitting for her. On all sides were mysterious whisperings, and showing of things wrapped in brown paper, glimpses of which, through some inadvertence, were always appearing to the public eye. There were close counsels held behind doors and in corners, and suddenly broken off when some particular member of the family appeared. There were flutters of vanishing book marks, which were always whisked away when a door opened; and incessant ejaculations of admiration and astonishment from one privileged looker or another on things which might not be mentioned to or beheld by others.

Papa and mamma behaved with the utmost circumspection and discretion, and though surrounded on all sides by such pitfalls and labyrinths of mystery, moved about with an air of the most unconscious simplicity possible.

But little Ally, from her privileged character, became a very spoil-sport in the proceedings. Her small fingers were always pulling open parcels prematurely, or lifting pocket handkerchiefs ingeniously thrown down over mysterious articles, and thus disconcerting the very profoundest surprises that ever were planned; and were it not that she was still within the bounds of the kingly state of babyhood, and therefore could be held to do no wrong, she would certainly have fallen into general disgrace; but then it was "Ally," and that was apology for all things, and the exploit was related in half whispers as so funny, so cunning, that Miss Curlypate was in nowise disconcerted at the head shakes and "naughty Allys" that visited her offences.

"What dis?" said she, one morning, as she was rummaging over some packages indiscreetly left on the sofa.

"O Emma! see Ally!" exclaimed Eliza, darting forward; but too late, for the flaxen curls and blue eyes of a wax doll had already appeared.

"Now she'll know all about it," said Eliza, despairingly.

Ally looked in astonishment, as dolly's visage promptly disappeared from her view, and then turned to pursue her business in another quarter of the room, where, spying something glittering under the sofa, she forthwith pulled out and held up to public view a crochet bag sparkling with innumerable steel fringes.

"O, what be dis!" she exclaimed again.

Miss Emma sprang to the rescue, while all the other children, with a burst of exclamations, turned their eyes on mamma. Mamma very prudently did not turn her head, and appeared to be lost in reflection, though she must have been quite deaf not to have heard the loud whispers — "It's mamma's bag! only think! Don't you think, Tom, Ally pulled out mamma's bag, and held it right up before her! Don't you think she'll find out?"

Master Tom valued himself greatly on the original and profound ways he had of adapting his presents to the tastes of the receiver without exciting suspicion: for example, he would come up into his mother's room, all booted and coated for a ride to town, jingling his purse gleefully, and begin, —

"Mother, mother, which do you like best, pink or blue?"

"That might depend on circumstances, my son."

"Well, but, mother, for a neck ribbon, for example; suppose somebody was going to buy you a neck ribbon."

"Why, blue would be the most suitable for me, I think."

"Well, but mother, which should you think was the best, a neck ribbon or a book?"

"What book? It would depend something on that."

"Why, as good a book as a fellow could get for thirty-seven cents," says Tom.

"Well, on the whole, I think I should prefer the ribbon."

"There, Ned," says Tom, coming down the stairs, "I've found out just what mother wants, without telling her a word about it."

But the crowning mystery of all the great family arcana, the thing that was going to astonish papa and mamma past all recovery, was certain projected book marks, that little Ally was going to be made to work for them. This bold scheme was projected by Miss Emma, and she had armed herself with a whole paper of sugar plums, to be used as adjuvants to moral influence, in case the discouragements of the undertaking should prove too much for Ally's patience.

As to Ally, she felt all the dignity of the enterprise — her whole little soul was absorbed in it. Seated on Emma's knee, with the needle between her little fat fingers, and holding the board very tight, as if she was afraid it would run away from her, she very gravely and carefully stuck the needle in every place but the right — pricked her pretty fingers — ate sugar plums — stopping now to pat Rover, and now to stroke pussy — letting fall her thimble, and bustling down to pick it up — occasionally taking an episodical race round the room with Rover, during which time Sister Emma added a stitch or two to the work.

I would not wish to have been required, on oath, to give in my undisguised opinion as to the number of stitches the little one really put into her present, but she had a most genuine and firm conviction that she worked every stitch of it herself; and when, on returning from a scamper with pussy, she found one or two letters finished, she never doubted that the whole was of her own execution, and, of course, thought that working book marks was one of the most delightful occupations in the world. It was all that her little heart could do to keep from papa and mamma the wonderful secret. Every evening she would bustle about her father with an air of such great mystery, and seek to pique his curiosity by most skilful hints, such as, —

"I know somefing! but I s'ant tell you."

"Not tell me! O Ally! Why not?"

"O, it's about — a New 'Ear's pes——"

"Ally, Ally," resounds from several voices, "don't you tell."

"No, I s'ant — but you are going to have a New 'Ear's pesant, and so is mamma, and you can't dess what it is."

"Can't I?"

"No, and I s'ant tell you."

"Now, Ally," said papa, pretending to look aggrieved.

"Well, it's going to be — somefin worked."

"Ally, be careful," said Emma.

"Yes, I'll be very tareful; it's somefin — *weall* pretty — somefin to put in a book. You'll find out about it by and by."

"I think I'm in a fair way to," said the father.

The conversation now digressed to other subjects, and the nurse came in to take Ally to bed; who, as she kissed her father, in the fulness of her heart, added a fresh burst of information. "Papa," said she, in an earnest whisper, "that *fin* is about so long" — measuring on her fat little arm.

"A *fin*, Ally? Why, you are not going to give me a fish, are you?"

"I mean that *thing*," said Ally, speaking the word with great effort, and getting quite red in the face.

"O, that *thing*; I beg pardon, my lady; that puts another face on the communication," said the father, stroking her head fondly, as he bade her good night.

"The child can talk plainer than she does," said the father, "but we are all so delighted with her little Hottentot dialect, that I don't know but she will keep it up till she is twenty."

* * * * *

It now wanted only three days of the New Year, when a sudden and deadly shadow fell on the dwelling, late so busy and joyous — a shadow from the grave; and it fell on the flower of the garden — the star — the singing bird — the loved and loving Ally.

She was stricken down at once, in the flush of her innocent enjoyment, by a fever, which from the first was ushered in with symptoms the most fearful.

All the bustle of preparation ceased — the presents were forgotten or lay about unfinished, as if no one now had a heart to put their hand to any thing; while up in her little crib lay the beloved one, tossing and burning with restless fever, and without power to recognize any of the loved faces that bent over her.

The doctor came twice a day, with a heavy step, and a face in which anxious care was too plainly written; and while he was there each member of the circle hung with anxious, imploring faces about him, as if to entreat him to save their darling; but still the deadly disease held on its relentless course, in spite of all that could be done.

"I thought myself prepared to meet God's will in any form it might come," said Winthrop to me; "but this one thing I had forgotten. It never entered into my head that my little Ally could die."

The evening before New Year's, the deadly disease seemed to be progressing more rapidly than ever; and when the doctor came for his evening call, he found all the family gathered in mournful stillness around the little crib.

"I suppose," said the father, with an effort to speak calmly, "that this may be her last night with us."

The doctor made no answer, and the whole circle of brothers and sisters broke out into bitter weeping.

"It is just possible that she may live till to-morrow," said the doctor.

"To-morrow — her birthday!" said the mother. "O Ally, Ally!"

Wearily passed the watches of that night. Each brother and sister had kissed the pale little cheek, to bid farewell, and gone to their rooms, to sob themselves to sleep; and the father and mother and doctor alone watched around the bed. O, what a watch is that which despairing love keeps, waiting for death! Poor Rover, the companion of Ally's gayer hours, resolutely refused to be excluded from the sick chamber. Stretched under the little crib, he watched with unsleeping eyes every motion of the attendants, and as often as they rose to administer medicine, or change the pillow, or bathe the head, he would rise also, and look anxiously over the side of the crib, as if he understood all that was passing.

About an hour past midnight, the child began to change; her moans became fainter and fainter, her restless movements ceased, and a deep and heavy sleep settled upon her.

The parents looked wistfully on the doctor. "It is the last change," he said; "she will probably pass away before the daybreak."

Heavier and deeper grew that sleep, and to the eye of the anxious watchers the little face grew paler and paler; yet by degrees the breathing became regular and easy, and a gentle moisture began to diffuse itself over the whole surface. A new hope began to dawn on the minds of the parents, as they pointed out these symptoms to the doctor.

"All things are possible with God," said he, in answer to the inquiring looks he met, "and it may be that she will yet live."

An hour more passed, and the rosy glow of the New Year's morning began to blush over the snowy whiteness of the landscape. Far off from the window could be seen the kindling glow of a glorious sunrise, looking all the brighter for the dark pines that half veiled it from view; and now a straight and glittering beam shot from the east into the still chamber. It fell on the golden hair and pale brow of the child, lighting it up as if an angel had smiled on it; and slowly the large blue eyes unclosed, and gazed dreamily around.

"Ally, Ally," said the father, bending over her, trembling with excitement.

"You are going to have a New 'Ear's pesent," whispered the little one, faintly smiling.

"I believe from my heart that you are, sir!" said the doctor, who stood with his fingers on her pulse; "she has passed through the crisis of the disease, and we may hope."

A few hours turned this hope to glad certainty; for with the elastic rapidity of infant life, the signs of returning vigor began to multiply, and ere evening the little one was lying in her father's arms, answering with languid smiles to the overflowing proofs of tenderness which every member of the family was showering upon her.

"See, my children," said the father gently, "*this dear one* is *our* New Year's present. What can we render to God in return?"

THE OLD OAK OF ANDOVER.

A REVERY.

SILENTLY, with dreamy languor, the fleecy snow is falling. Through the windows, flowery with blossoming geranium and heliotrope, through the downward sweep of crimson and muslin curtain, one watches it as the wind whirls and sways it in swift eddies.

Right opposite our house, on our Mount Clear, is an old oak, the apostle of the primeval forest. Once, when this place was all wildwood, the man who was seeking a spot for the location of the buildings of Phillips Academy climbed this oak, using it as a sort of green watchtower, from whence he might gain a view of the surrounding country. Age and time, since then, have dealt hardly with the stanch old fellow. His limbs have been here and there shattered; his back begins to look mossy and dilapidated; but after all, there is a piquant, decided air about him, that speaks the old age of a tree of distinction, a kingly oak. To-day I see him standing, dimly revealed through the mist of falling snows; to-morrow's sun will show the outline of his gnarled limbs — all rose color with their soft snow burden; and again a few months, and spring will breathe on him, and he will draw a long breath, and break out once more, for the three hundredth time, perhaps, into a vernal crown of leaves. I sometimes think that leaves are the thoughts of trees, and that if we only knew it, we should find their life's experience recorded in them. Our oak! what a crop of meditations and remembrances must he have thrown forth, leafing out century after century. Awhile he spake and thought only of red deer and Indians; of the trillium that opened its white triangle in his shade; of the scented arbutus, fair as the pink ocean shell, weaving her fragrant mats in the moss at his feet; of feathery ferns, casting their silent shadows on the checkerberry leaves, and all those sweet, wild, nameless, half-mossy things, that live in the gloom of forests, and are only desecrated when brought to scientific light, laid out and stretched on a botanic bier. Sweet old forest days! — when blue jay, and yellow hammer, and bobalink made his leaves merry, and summer was a long opera of such music as Mozart dimly dreamed. But then came human kind bustling beneath; wondering, fussing, exploring, measuring, treading down flowers, cutting down trees, scaring bobalinks — and Andover, as men say, began to be settled.

Stanch men were they — these Puritan fathers of Andover. The old oak must have felt them something akin to himself. Such strong, wrestling limbs had they, so gnarled and knotted were they, yet so outbursting with a green and vernal crown, yearly springing, of noble and generous thoughts, rustling with leaves which shall be for the healing of nations.

These men were content with the hard, dry crust for themselves, that they might sow seeds of abundant food for us, their children; men out of whose hardness in enduring we gain leisure to be soft and graceful, through whose poverty we have become rich. Like Moses, they had for their portion only the pain and weariness of the wilderness, leaving to us the fruition of the promised land. Let us cherish for their sake the old oak, beautiful in its age as the broken statue of some antique wrestler, brown with time, yet glorious in its suggestion of past achievement.

I think all this the more that I have recently come across the following passage in one of our religious papers. The writer expresses a kind of sentiment which one meets very often upon this subject, and leads one to wonder what glamour could have fallen on the minds of any of the descendants of the Puritans, that they should cast nettles on those hon ored graves where they should be proud to cast their laurels.

"It is hard," he says, "for a lover of the beautiful — not a mere lover, but a believer in its divinity also — to forgive the Puritans, or to think charitably of them. It is hard for him to keep Forefathers' Day, or to subscribe to the Plymouth Monument; hard to look fairly at what they did, with the memory of what they destroyed rising up to choke thankfulness; for they were as one-sided and narrow-minded a set of men as ever lived, and saw one of Truth's faces only — the hard, stern, practical face, without loveliness, without beauty, and only half dear to God. The Puritan flew in the face of facts, not because he saw them and disliked them, but because he did not see them. He saw foolishness, lying, stealing, worldliness — the very mammon of unrighteousness rioting in the world and bearing sway — and he ran full tilt against the monster, hating it with a very mortal and mundane hatred, and anxious to see it bite the dust that his own horn might be exalted. It was in truth only another horn of the old dilemma, tossing and goring grace and beauty, and all the loveliness of life, as if they were the enemies instead of the sure friends of God and man."

Now, to those who say this we must ask the question with which Socrates of old pursued the sophist: What *is* beauty? If beauty be only physical, if it appeal only to the senses, if it be only an enchantment of graceful forms, sweet sounds, then indeed there might be something of truth in this sweeping declaration that the Puritan spirit is the enemy of beauty.

The very root and foundation of all artistic inquiry lies here. *What is beauty?* And to this question God forbid that we *Christians* should give a narrower answer than Plato gave in the old times before Christ arose, for he directs the aspirant who would discover the beautiful to "consider of greater value the beauty existing *in the soul*, than that existing in the body." More gracefully he teaches the same doctrine when he tells us that "there are two kinds of Venus, (beauty;) the one, the elder, who had no mother, and was the daughter of Uranus, (heaven,) whom we name the celestial; the other, younger, daughter of Jupiter and Dione, whom we call the vulgar."

Now, if disinterestedness, faith, patience, piety, have a beauty celestial and divine, then were our fathers worshippers of the beautiful. If high-mindedness and spotless honor are beautiful things, they had those. What work of art can compare with a lofty and heroic life? Is it not better to *be* a Moses than to be a Michael Angelo making statues of Moses? Is not the *life* of Paul a sublimer work of art than Raphael's cartoons? Are not the patience, the faith, the undying love of Mary by the cross, more beautiful than all the Madonna paintings in the world. If, then, we would speak truly of our fathers, we should say that, having their minds fixed on that celestial beauty of which Plato speaks, they held in slight esteem that more common and earthly.

Should we continue the parable in Plato's manner, we might say that the earthly and visible Venus, the outward grace of art and nature, was ordained of God as a priestess, through whom men were to gain access to the divine, invisible One ; but that men, in their blindness, ever worship the priestess instead of the divinity.

Therefore it is that great reformers so often must break the shrines and temples of the physical and earthly beauty, when they seek to draw men upward to that which is high and divine.

Christ says of John the Baptist, " What went ye out for to see ? A man clothed in soft raiment ? Behold they which are clothed in soft raiment are in kings' palaces." So was it when our fathers came here. There were enough wearing soft raiment and dwelling in kings' palaces. Life in papal Rome and prelatic England was weighed down with blossoming luxury. There were abundance of people to think of pictures, and statues, and gems, and cameos, vases and marbles, and all manner of deliciousness. The world was all drunk with the enchantments of the lower Venus, and it was needful that these men should come, Baptist-like in the wilderness, in raiment of camel's hair. We need such men now. Art, they tell us, is waking in America; a love of the beautiful is beginning to unfold its wings; but what kind of art, and what kind of beauty ? Are we to fill our houses with pictures and gems, and to see that even our drinking cup and vase is wrought in graceful pattern, and to lose our reverence for self-denial, honor, and faith?

Is our Venus to be the frail, insnaring Aphrodite, or the starry, divine Urania?

OUR WOOD LOT IN WINTER.

Our wood lot! Yes, we have arrived at the dignity of owning a wood lot, and for us simple folk there is something invigorating in the thought. To OWN even a small spot of our dear old mother earth hath in it a relish of something stimulating to human nature. To own a meadow, with all its thousandfold fringes of grasses, its broidery of monthly flowers, and its outriders of birds, and bees, and gold-winged insects — this is something that establishes one's heart. To own a clover patch or a buckwheat field is like possessing a self-moving manufactory for perfumes and sweetness; but a wood lot, rustling with dignified old trees — it makes a man rise in his own esteem; he might take off his hat to himself at the moment of acquisition.

We do not marvel that the land-acquiring passion becomes a mania among our farmers, and particularly we do not wonder at a passion for wood land. That wide, deep chasm of conscious self-poverty and emptiness which lies at the bottom of every human heart, making men crave property as something to add to one's own bareness, and to ballast one's own specific levity, is sooner filled by land than any thing else.

Your hoary New England farmer walks over his acres with a grim satisfaction. He sets his foot down with a hard stamp;

here is reality. No moonshine bank stock! no swindling railroads! *Here* is *his* bank, and there is no defaulter here. All is true, solid, and satisfactory; he seems anchored to this life by it. So Pope, with fine tact, makes the old miser, making his will on his death bed, after parting with every thing, die, clinging to the possession of his *land.* He disposes with many a groan of this and that house, and this and that stock and security; but at last the *manor* is proposed to him.

> "The manor! hold!" he cried,
> "Not that; *I cannot part with that!*" — and died!

In such terms we discoursed yesterday, Herr Professor and myself, while jogging along in an old-fashioned chaise to inspect a few acres of wood lot, the acquisition of which had let us, with great freshness, into these reflections.

Does any fair lady shiver at the idea of a drive to the woods on the first of February? Let me assure her that in the coldest season Nature never wants her ornaments full worth looking at.

See here, for instance — let us stop the old chaise, and get out a minute to look at this brook — one of our last summer's pets. What is he doing this winter? Let us at least say, "How do you do?" to him. Ah, here he is! and he and Jack Frost together have been turning the little gap in the old stone wall, through which he leaped down to the road, into a little grotto of Antiparos. Some old rough rails and boards that dropped over it are sheathed in plates of transparent silver. The trunks of the black alders are mailed with crystal; and the witch-hazel, and yellow osiers fringing its sedgy borders, are likewise shining through their glossy covering. Around every stem that rises from the water is a glittering ring of ice. The tags of the alder and the red berries of last summer's wild roses glitter now like a lady's pendant. As for the brook, he is wide awake and joyful; and where the roof of sheet ice breaks away, you can see his yellow-brown waters rattling and gurgling among the stones as briskly as they did last July. Down he springs! over the glossy-coated stone wall, throwing new sparkles into the fairy grotto around him; and widening daily from melting snows, and such other godsends, he goes chattering off under yonder mossy stone bridge, and we lose sight of him. It might be fancy, but it seemed that our watery friend tipped us a cheery wink as he passed, saying, "Fine weather, sir and madam; nice times these; and in April you'll find us all right; the flowers are making up their finery for the next season; there's to be a splendid display in a month or two."

Then the cloud lights of a wintry sky have a clear purity and brilliancy that no other months can rival. The rose tints, and the shading of rose tint into gold, the flossy, filmy accumulation of illuminated vapor that drifts across the sky in a January afternoon, are beauties far exceeding those of summer.

Neither are trees, as seen in winter, destitute of their own peculiar beauty. If it be a gorgeous study in summer time to watch the play of their abundant leafage, we still may thank winter for laying bare before us the grand and beautiful anatomy of the tree, with all its interlacing network of boughs, knotted on each twig with the buds of next year's promise. The fleecy and rosy clouds look all the more beautiful through the dark lace veil of yonder magnificent elms; and the down-drooping drapery of yonder willow hath its own grace of outline as it sweeps the bare snows. And these comical old apple trees, why, in summer they look like so many plump, green cushions, one as much like another as possible; but under the revealing light of winter every characteristic twist and jerk stands disclosed.

One might moralize on this — how affliction, which strips us of all ornaments and accessories, and brings us down to the permanent and solid wood of our nature, develops such wide differences in people who before seemed not much distinct.

But here! our pony's feet are now clinking on the icy path under the shadow of the white pines of "our wood lot." The path runs in a deep hollow, and on either hand rise slopes dark and sheltered with the fragrant white pine. White pines are favorites with us for many good reasons. We love their balsamic breath, the long, slender needles of their leaves, and, above all, the constant sibylline whisperings that never cease among their branches. In summer the ground beneath them is paved with a soft and cleanly matting of their last year's leaves; and then their talking seems to be of coolness ever dwelling far up in their fringy, waving hollows. And now, in winter time, we find the same smooth floor; for the heavy curtains above shut out the snow, and the same voices above whisper of shelter and quiet. "You are welcome," they say; "the north wind is gone to sleep; we are rocking him in our cradles. Sit down and be quiet from the cold." At the feet of these slumberous old pines we find many of our last summer's friends looking as good as new. The small, round-leafed partridgeberry weaves its viny mat, and lays out its scarlet fruit; and here are blackberry vines with leaves still green, though with a bluish tint, not unlike what invades mortal noses in such weather. Here, too, are the bright, varnished leaves of the Indian pine, and the vines of feathery green of which our

Christmas garlands are made; and here, undaunted, though frozen to the very heart this cold day, is many another leafy thing which we met last summer rejoicing each in its own peculiar flower. What names they have received from scientific godfathers at the botanic fount we know not; we have always known them by fairy nicknames of our own — the pet names of endearment which lie between Nature's children and us in her domestic circle.

There is something peculiarly sweet to us about a certain mystical dreaminess and obscurity in these wild wood tribes, which we never wish to have brought out into the daylight of absolute knowledge. Every one of them was a self-discovered treasure of our childhood, as much our own as if God had made it on purpose and presented it; and it was ever a part of the joy to think we had found something that no one else knew, and so musing on them, we gave them names in our heart.

We search about amid the sere, yellow skeletons of last summer's ferns, if haply winter have forgotten one green leaf for our home vase — in vain we rake, freezing our fingers through our fur gloves — there is not one. An icicle has pierced every heart; and there are no fern leaves except those miniature ones which each plant is holding in its heart, to be sent up in next summer's hour of joy. But here are mosses — tufts of all sorts; the white, crisp and crumbling, fair as winter frostwork; and here the feathery green of which French milliners make moss rose buds; and here the cup-moss — these we gather with some care, frozen as they are to the wintry earth.

Now, stumbling up this ridge, we come to a little patch of hemlocks, spreading out their green wings, and making, in the ravine, a deep shelter, where many a fresh springing thing is standing, and where we gain much for our home vases. These pines are motherly creatures. One can think how it must rejoice the heart of a partridge or a rabbit to come from the dry, whistling sweep of a deciduous forest under the home-like shadow of their branches. "As for the stork, the fir trees are her house," says the Hebrew poet; and our fir trees, this winter, give shelter to much small game. Often, on the light-fallen snow, I meet their little footprints. They have a naive, helpless, innocent appearance, these little tracks, that softens my heart like a child's footprint. Not one of them is forgotten of our Father; and therefore I remember them kindly.

And now, with cold toes and fingers, and arms full of leafy treasures, we plod our way back to the chaise. A pleasant song is in my ears from this old wood lot — it speaks of green and cheerful patience in life's hard weather. Not a scowling, sullen endurance, not a despairing, hand-dropping resignation, but a heart cheerfulness that holds on to every leaf, and twig, and flower, and bravely smiles and keeps green when frozen to the very heart, knowing that the winter is but for a season, and that the sunshine and bird singings shall return, and the last year's dry flower stalk give place to the risen, glorified flower.

POEMS.

THE CHARMER.

"*Socrates.* — 'However, you and Simmias appear to me as if you wished to sift this subject more thoroughly, and to be afraid, like children, lest, on the soul's departure from the body, winds should blow it away.'

* * * * *

"Upon this Cebes said, 'Endeavor to teach us better, Socrates. * * * Perhaps there is a childish spirit in our breast, that has such a dread. Let us endeavor to persuade him not to be afraid of death, as of hobgoblins.'

"'But you must *charm* him every day,' said Socrates, 'until you have quieted his fears.'

"'But whence, O Socrates,' he said, 'can we procure a skilful charmer for such a case, now *you* are about to leave us.'

"'Greece is wide, Cebes,' he replied: 'and in it surely there are skilful men, and there are also many barbarous nations, all of which you should search, seeking such a charmer, sparing neither money nor toil, as there is nothing on which you can more reasonably spend your money.'" — (*Last conversation of Socrates with his disciples, as narrated by Plato in the Phædo.*)

"We need that Charmer, for our hearts are sore
　With longings for the things that may not be;
Faint for the friends that shall return no more;
　Dark with distrust, or wrung with agony.

"What is this life? and what to us is death?
  Whence came we? whither go? and where are those
Who, in a moment stricken from our side,
  Passed to that land of shadow and repose?

"And are they all dust? and dust must we become?
  Or are they living in some unknown clime?
Shall we regain them in that far-off home,
  And live anew beyond the waves of time?

"O man divine! on thee our souls have hung;
  Thou wert our teacher in these questions high;
But, ah, this day divides thee from our side,
  And veils in dust thy kindly-guiding eye.

"Where is that Charmer whom thou bidst us seek?
  On what far shores may his sweet voice be heard?
When shall these questions of our yearning souls
  Be answered by the bright Eternal Word?"

So spake the youth of Athens, weeping round,
  When Socrates lay calmly down to die;
So spake the sage, prophetic of the hour
  When earth's fair morning star should rise on high.

They found Him not, those youths of soul divine,
  Long seeking, wandering, watching on life's shore —
Reasoning, aspiring, yearning for the light,
  Death came and found them — doubting as before.

But years passed on; and lo! the Charmer came —
Pure, simple, sweet, as comes the silver dew;
And the world knew him not — he walked alone,
Encircled only by his trusting few.

Like the Athenian sage rejected, scorned,
Betrayed, condemned, his day of doom drew nigh;
He drew his faithful few more closely round,
And told them that *his* hour was come to die.

" Let not your heart be troubled," then he said;
" My Father's house hath mansions large and fair;
I go before you to prepare your place;
I will return to take you with me there."

And since that hour the awful foe is charmed,
And life and death are glorified and fair.
Whither he went we know — the way we know —
And with firm step press on to meet him there.

PILGRIM'S SONG IN THE DESERT.

'TIS morning now — upon the eastern hills
  Once more the sun lights up this cheerless scene;
But O, no morning in my Father's house
  Is dawning now, for there no night hath been.

Ten thousand thousand now, on Zion's hills,
  All robed in white, with palmy crowns, do stray,
While I, an exile, far from fatherland,
  Still wandering, faint along the desert way.

O home! dear home! my own, my native home!
O Father, friends, when shall I look on you?
When shall these weary wanderings be o'er,
And I be gathered back to stray no more?

O thou, the brightness of whose gracious face
These weary, longing eyes have never seen, —
By whose dear thought, for whose belovéd sake,
My course, through toil and tears, I daily take, —

I think of thee when the myrrh-dropping morn
  Steps forth upon the purple eastern steep;
I think of thee in the fair eventide,
  When the bright-sandalled stars their watches keep.

And trembling hope, and fainting, sorrowing love,
  On thy dear word for comfort doth rely;
And clear-eyed Faith, with strong forereaching gaze,
  Beholds thee here, unseen, but ever nigh.

Walking in white with thee, she dimly sees,
  All beautiful, these lovely ones withdrawn,
With whom my heart went upward, as they rose,
  Like morning stars, to light a coming dawn.

All sinless now, and crowned, and glorified,
  Where'er thou movest move they still with thee,
As erst, in sweet communion by thy side,
  Walked John and Mary in old Galilee.

But hush, my heart! 'Tis but a day or two
  Divides thee from that bright, immortal shore.
Rise up! rise up! and gird thee for the race!
  Fast fly the hours, and all will soon be o'er.

Thou hast the new name written in thy soul;
  Thou hast the mystic stone he gives his own.
Thy soul, made one with him, shall feel no more
  That she is walking on her path alone.

MARY AT THE CROSS.

"Now there stood by the cross of Jesus his mother."

O WONDROUS mother! Since the dawn of time
Was ever joy, was ever grief like thine?
O, highly favored in thy joy's deep flow,
And favored e'en in this, thy bitterest woe!

Poor was that home in simple Nazareth,
  Where thou, fair growing, like some silent flower,
Last of a kingly line, — unknown and lowly,
  O desert lily, — passed thy childhood's hour.

The world knew not the tender, serious maiden,
  Who, through deep loving years so silent grew,
Filled with high thoughts and holy aspirations,
  Which, save thy Father, God's, no eye might view.

And then it came, that message from the Highest,
  Such as to woman ne'er before descended;
Th' almighty shadowing wings thy soul o'erspread,
  And with thy life the Life of worlds was blended.

What visions, then, of future glory filled thee,
  Mother of King and kingdom yet unknown —
Mother, fulfiller of all prophecy,
  Which through dim ages wondering seers had shown!

Well did thy dark eye kindle, thy deep soul
  Rise into billows, and thy heart rejoice;
Then woke the poet's fire, the prophet's song
  Tuned with strange, burning words thy timid voice.

Then in dark contrast came the lowly manger,
  The outcast shed, the tramp of brutal feet;
Again, behold earth's learnéd, and her lowly,
  Sages and shepherds, prostrate at thy feet.

Then to the temple bearing, hark! again
  What strange, conflicting tones of prophecy
Breathe o'er the Child, foreshadowing words of joy,
  High triumph, and yet bitter agony.

O, highly favored thou, in many an hour
  Spent in lone musing with thy wondrous Son,
When thou didst gaze into that glorious eye,
  And hold that mighty hand within thy own.

Blessed through those thirty years, when in thy dwelling
  He lived a God disguised, with unknown power,
And thou, his sole adorer, — his best love, —
  Trusting, revering, waitedst for his hour.

Blessed in that hour, when called by opening heaven
  With cloud, and voice, and the baptizing flame,
Up from the Jordan walked th' acknowledged stranger,
  And awe-struck crowds grew silent as he came.

Blessed, when full of grace, with glory crowned,
  He from both hands almighty favors poured,
And, though he had not where to lay his head,
  Brought to his feet alike the slave and lord.

Crowds followed; thousands shouted, "Lo, our King!"
  Fast beat thy heart; now, now the hour draws nigh:
Behold the crown — the throne! the nations bend.
  Ah, no! fond mother, no! behold him die.

Now by that cross thou tak'st thy final station,
  And shar'st the last dark trial of thy Son;
Not with weak tears or woman's lamentation,
  But with high, silent anguish, like his own.

Hail, highly favored, even in this deep passion,
  Hail, in this bitter anguish — thou art blest —
Blest in the holy power with him to suffer
  Those deep death pangs that lead to higher rest.

All now is darkness; and in that deep stillness
  The God-man wrestles with that mighty woe;
Hark to that cry, the rock of ages rending —
  "'Tis finished!" Mother, all is glory now!

By sufferings mighty as his mighty soul
  Hath the Jehovah risen — forever blest;
And through all ages must his heart-beloved
  Through the same baptism enter the same rest.

CHRISTIAN PEACE.

"Thou shalt hide them in the secret of thy presence from the pride of man; thou shalt keep them secretly as in a pavilion from the strife of tongues."

WHEN winds are raging o'er the upper ocean,
  And billows wild contend with angry roar,
'Tis said, far down beneath the wild commotion,
  That peaceful *stillness* reigneth evermore.

Far, far beneath, the noise of tempest dieth,
  And silver waves chime ever peacefully,
And no rude storm, how fierce soe'er he flieth,
  Disturbs the Sabbath of that deeper sea.

So to the heart that knows thy love, O Purest,
  There is a temple, sacred evermore,
And all the babble of life's angry voices
  Die in hushed stillness at its peaceful door.

Far, far away, the roar of passion dieth,
  And loving thoughts rise calm and peacefully,
And no rude storm, how fierce soe'er he flieth,
  Disturbs the soul that dwells, O Lord, in thee.

O, rest of rests! O, peace serene, eternal!
  THOU ever livest; and thou changest never;
And in the *secret of thy presence* dwelleth
  Fulness of joy — forever and forever.

ABIDE IN ME AND I IN YOU.

THE SOUL'S ANSWER.

THAT mystic word of thine, O sovereign Lord,
  Is all too pure, too high, too deep for me;
Weary of striving, and with longing faint,
  I breathe it back again in *prayer* to thee.

Abide in me, I pray, and I in thee;
  From this good hour, O, leave me nevermore;
Then shall the discord cease, the wound be healed,
  The lifelong bleeding of the soul be o'er.

Abide in me — o'ershadow by thy love
  Each half-formed purpose and dark thought of sin;
Quench, e'er it rise, each selfish, low desire,
  And keep my soul as thine, calm and divine.

As some rare perfume in a vase of clay
  Pervades it with a fragrance not its own,
So, when thou dwellest in a mortal soul,
  All heaven's own sweetness seems around it thrown.

The soul alone, like a neglected harp,
  Grows out of tune, and needs a hand divine;
Dwell thou within it, tune, and touch the chords,
  Till every note and string shall answer thine.

Abide in me; there have been moments pure
  When I have seen thy face and felt thy power;
Then evil lost its grasp, and passion, hushed,
  Owned the divine enchantment of the hour.

These were but seasons beautiful and rare;
  "Abide in me," — and they shall *ever be;*
Fulfil at once thy precept and my prayer —
  Come and *abide* in me, and I in thee.

WHEN I AWAKE I AM STILL WITH THEE.

Still, still with thee, when purple morning breaketh,
When the bird waketh and the shadows flee ;
Fairer than morning, lovelier than the daylight,
Dawns the sweet consciousness, *I am with thee !*

Alone with thee, amid the mystic shadows,
The solemn hush of nature newly born ;
Alone with thee in breathless adoration,
In the calm dew and freshness of the morn.

As in the dawning o'er the waveless ocean
The image of the morning star doth rest,
So in this stillness thou beholdest only
Thine image in the waters of my breast.

Still, still with thee ! as to each new-born morning
A fresh and solemn splendor still is given,
So doth this blessed consciousness, awaking,
Breathe, each day, nearness unto thee and heaven.

When sinks the soul, subdued by toil, to slumber,
Its closing eye looks up to thee in prayer,

Sweet the repose beneath thy wings o'ershading,
  But sweeter still to wake and find thee there.

So shall it be at last, in that bright morning
  When the soul waketh and life's shadows flee;
O, in that hour, fairer than daylight dawning,
  Shall rise the glorious thought, *I am with thee!*

CHRIST'S VOICE IN THE SOUL.

"Come ye yourselves into a desert place and rest a while; for there were many coming and going, so that they had no time so much as to eat."

'Mid the mad whirl of life, its dim confusion,
Its jarring discords and poor vanity,
Breathing like music over troubled waters,
What gentle voice, O Christian, speaks to thee?

It is a stranger — not of earth or earthly;
By the serene, deep fulness of that eye, —
By the calm, pitying smile, the gesture lowly, —
It is thy Savior as he passeth by.

"Come, come," he saith, "into a desert place,
Thou who art weary of life's lower sphere;
Leave its low strifes, forget its babbling noise;
Come thou with me — all shall be bright and clear.

"Art thou bewildered by contesting voices,
Sick to thy soul of party noise and strife?
Come, leave it all, and seek that solitude
Where thou shalt learn of me a purer life.

"When far behind the world's great tumult dieth,
Thou shalt look back and wonder at its roar;
But its far voice shall seem to thee a dream,
Its power to vex thy holier life be o'er.

"There shalt thou learn the secret of a power,
Mine to bestow, which heals the ills of living;
To overcome by love, to live by prayer,
To conquer man's worst evils by forgiving."

THE END.

www.ingramcontent.com/pod-product-compliance
Lightning Source LLC
LaVergne TN
LVHW020931110826
845150LV00004B/830

* 9 7 8 1 4 2 5 5 5 3 0 0 5 *